INTO THE
WEST

FOUNDING OF VALDEMAR BOOK TWO

Also by Mercedes Lackey and available from Titan Books

MERCEDES LACKEY

INTO THE WEST

FOUNDING OF VALDEMAR BOOK TWO

TITAN BOOKS

Into the West
Hardback edition ISBN: 9781789099188
Paperback edition ISBN: 9781803365916
E-book edition ISBN: 9781789099195

Published by Titan Books
A division of Titan Publishing Group Ltd
144 Southwark Street, London SE1 0UP
www.titanbooks.com

First Titan hardback edition: December 2022
First Titan paperback edition: December 2023
10 9 8 7 6 5 4 3 2 1

A CIP catalogue record for this title is available from the British Library.

Printed and bound by CPI Group Ltd, Croydon CR0 4YY.

Dedication:

In memory of Ikaika and Io

I

Royal fist met commoner jaw with an impact that jolted
Kordas's right arm all the way up to the shoulder. He was
vaguely aware that his hand was going to hurt like bloody hells—
but that would be later. Right now, he had a good excuse to let his
rage take over, and a good target to vent it on. He had the surge
of adrenaline powering him, now. A little thing like pain was not
going to stop him.

Not now.

Not when pure rage misted his vision.

Not when all emotion from the pure *shit* he had gone through the
last year was piled up behind him like a tempest, and here was a
righteous target to unleash it upon.

His target staggered back. Kordas turned his footing and followed
the right cross with a left to the man's unprotected gut, driving all
the breath out of him in an explosive, guttural grunt. The man
bent over, gasping, and Kordas followed with a knuckle-splitting

right-handed uppercut that knocked his opponent right off his feet. The force of the blow sent the man flying backward. Pocketknife, kerchief, one shoe, and a spray of blood parted company with him before he even landed. Kordas would not have minded if the offender had cracked his skull on one of the tree trunks behind him, but luck was with the wretch, and he landed instead on his back, not his head. Crumpling onto the "soft" uneven ground padded by decades of fallen leaves was akin to falling on a pile of bricks covered by a few pillows.

Uppercuts always work. They're so satisfying, too.

Kordas knew better than to fight bare-knuckled, but when he saw the man's expression, drawing his sword just didn't come to mind. He could instantly read the guilt on the offender's very punchable face, and didn't even break stride throwing the first punch. *I love this rage. I want to stay inside this fury as long as I can, and just keep punching. I can kick him, I can throw him, I can snap his joints. I can punch down. And why not? I'm in power. What's anyone going to do about it? Tell me "no"? The Empire taught me early on, obedience comes from threat of harm. Anyone'll think twice about crossing me once they see me pound some criminals to paste. I have the authority. I can beat down whoever I want to.*

Kordas sucked in air between his clenched teeth.

I want that so much.

Kordas stood over the offender, instinctively stepping into a well-trained boxing stance. Kordas's vision was still fogged with rage. His hands clenched at the ready, dripping blood and starting to throb. Kordas pulled in his forearms to cover his vitals, and flexed his shoulders, just daring the fool to stand up.

They have no idea of the kinds of rage I keep hidden from them.

The fool was in no shape to stand up. He rolled partly over on his side, doubling into a semi-fetal position, wheezing. There was no other sound but that, and the tense breathing of the crowd that the fight had drawn.

They don't know how lucky they are, with me. They haven't seen what I've seen.

The downed man's face was covered in quickly purpling bruises, smears of blood, and a lacerated cheekbone. His body probably looked the same. The way he winced with each intake of breath suggested that there might be a broken rib or two, and he certainly was going to be painfully aware of his sins every time he inhaled or exhaled for at least a week.

Every single bruise and broken bone is deserved.

If his people had been harboring the notion that there was *anything* "soft" about Baron Valdemar—well, they'd just been disabused of that notion. Word would get around quickly. He hadn't exactly been looking for an excuse to burn off some of the pent-up emotions from his experiences at Court and the destruction of the Capital, but here it was.

He *wanted* the blackguard to get up and come at him—while at the same time, he didn't. The intensity of his fury just moments ago subsided slightly. His rage slammed into the full force of his conscience, and rage broke against it.

But I damned well won't be a tyrant. I want to be better than that. I want us all to be better than that.

His momentary loss of control made him just a little ashamed of himself.

But just a little.

When the fool on the ground did nothing but wheeze and moan, Kordas stepped back and motioned to the two men of his Guard—

that's what they were calling the loose policing/military group he'd put together, "Valdemar's Guard"—to come and pick the man up.

"Should we take him to a Healer, Baron?" asked the one who had once been one of his gamekeepers, a tall and weather-beaten man who frankly looked as if he'd be more than willing to add his own beating to the one Kordas had doled out if Kordas asked him to.

"Just long enough to make sure he's not dying *today*," Kordas said, his words coming out sounding harsh and angry. Well, he was still angry, and he roared the words so all present could hear him. "Splints and bandages are all he gets. No herbs. No Healing. And if he wants something to dull the pain, he'll have to forage it himself. No help allowed."

While the two of them secured the creep—and it did not escape Kordas that the gamekeeper ran his hands expertly over the fellow's ribs, before forcing his hands behind him and trussing his wrists together—Kordas turned away from the miscreant and his keepers, to address the little crowd that had gathered while he had been occupied with meting out rough justice.

And got angry all over again, because the first thing his eyes lit on was the broken Doll that the fool had been abusing and torturing for his own amusement. The torture hadn't gone on *long* before Kordas and his men had come racing up to the little secluded spot among the thickets of barberry bushes the bastard had chosen to conceal what he was doing. But it had been enough time that the Doll's arms and legs were broken in four places, and there was no telling what other damage had been done that was covered up by the padding and cloth. The sledgehammer the fool had been using lay beside the Doll where he'd dropped it after Kordas tackled him.

The Dolls *looked* like oversized children's playthings. But they had been the backbone of the Imperial Palace servant-structure, and had replaced most humans in those functions years ago. Kordas wasn't sure how long ago that had been; long after his days as a hostage, at any rate, because they hadn't been *visibly* performing those functions when he'd been held in the Palace.

Maybe Dolls were only for the elite, then. The hostages were not exactly elite. Oh, of course—an important part of having prisoners is enjoying their suffering, so there'd be humans for that suffering, not Dolls that don't display suffering. Cruelty was the Imperial Way, and I was raised Imperial. It's in me. I resent that it is, but I resent keeping it pushed down all the time, too. I can't let it out long. I can't let the Empire rule me.

I won't. I won't be like them. I can do this and not be like them.

As he lost the blinding clarity of rage, he felt his stomach churning, heard the murmurs of the crowd he had gathered, and took a moment to glance up into the tree branches overhead. His knuckles ached dully, but all the physical labor he'd done the past few moons had certainly had an effect—he wasn't in the least winded, nor did he *feel* as if he'd just pounded someone to within an inch of his life. He just felt bruised in soul and fists.

He lost his focus on everything for a moment. It may have been the sizzling pain from his hands that incited it, or the shivers—part of the comedown from adrenaline—but Kordas's mind was racing. His heart beat rapidly. His skin felt as if it was wet, and stretched thin. Pain was still just information thanks to adrenaline, but that wasn't going to last. His mind switched from subject to subject, desperate for something self-saving.

Steady now. I don't want to tremble. Everyone gets the shakes, but I don't want to look weak and undignified. Carefully, now. Don't show anything wrong.

Keep that appearance going for their confidence. He caught himself from tripping, twice, as he walked over to the helpless Doll, lying in a heap against a tree trunk. It wasn't one he recognized, but it was wearing someone's old shirt and trews, so old, patched, and threadbare that he was fairly certain they'd been taken from the common rag pile that had been established along with the other common supplies. All of the Dolls had discarded the Imperial tabards they wore as soon as they'd escaped to freedom, and the ones who had attached themselves to a particular individual or family generally wore clothing donated by that family. The rest wore whatever they could find. It hardly mattered if they wore nothing, really, but they seemed to sense that people found an unclothed ambulatory cloth creature much more unsettling than a clothed one, so the ones who weren't given clothing generally found it for themselves somewhere.

He squatted down on his heels next to the poor thing. "Are you going to be all right?"

He wondered if the Doll had a name. Or if they had even decided to call themselves something. Some of the Dolls had taken the initiative to name themselves, and had put some sort of identifier on their person. They were, as best anyone knew, multiple genders—an easy enough concept that only the most superstitious of Valdemarans took issue with, out of fear—and were natively androgynous in voice and form. He couldn't see anything on this one, but that didn't mean the creep who had tortured it hadn't torn off such a thing. This Doll also didn't have anything in the way of features other than the stitched-in eyes and mouth all of them were given at their creation. With permission, some of the children and younger folks had been clothing and decorating Dolls as a sort of hobby when their work was done, but at the moment the majority were still in the state this one was. So far, only dense Imperial ink would stick to their sailcloth "skin." Paint either didn't stick at all, or peeled off when dry. The ones with painted faces had faces painted onto canvas, which was then stitched onto their heads.

"Thanks to your intervention, Baron, this one survives to be repaired," they replied, politely, as if they weren't in agonizing pain. They were, and he knew they were, because he'd asked Rose about injuries to the Dolls, and she had told him that yes, they did feel pain when they were injured, and that the mages who had stuffed the Air-spirits called *vrondi* into these very material Dolls had said they were supposed to feel pain to keep them from mangling themselves as they went about their duties.

Kordas doubted that. He thought that the mages had been ordered to make them capable of pain so that the plethora of sadists that inhabited the Imperial Court could get pleasure from torturing something that couldn't fight back. So far as the courtiers were concerned, there was an endless supply of Dolls and no one cared about what you did to them or how you treated them. There would be more by day's end. When it came to anything in the Imperial Court, the cruelty was the point.

The Doll clearly saw his concern. "Lord Baron, these injuries are less than the torment of enslavement. You put an end to the Capital and Court, and freed us from that suffering. It is well worth this sort of inconvenience to be here with you."

And that just made Kordas feel worse.

This sort of inconvenience? Life-threatening assault, incomprehensible agony, and still they try to be positive. May I show that kind of bravery on my darkest days.

A fact of a noble's life is the inevitability of harming others. All a noble could hope to do, were they so inclined, was reduce the amount of damage. At every turn since going to the Capital, Kordas had failed far too often at reducing damage. Thinking of his people, he turned thief, and escalated his grand larceny at every turn. Spying, conspiring. Distraction ploys turned lethal. A well-intended diversion tumbled downward in untold deaths, and the destruction of a place that represented centuries of history.

There was something malevolent about that place, he'd thought many a time. *Environments change people. That deceit, madness, and cruelty seeped into me, too.* Now, the Emperor and Court were ash, the Capital a debris-strewn lava plain—and that wasn't guilt-free. *The habitat, the wildlife, people's pets, visitors. Probably a twenty-mile radius of the city was incinerated or boiled away. I only meant to trick and save. I wound up a destroyer for it. I can't deny that. I can't get away from those facts.*

But I won't let that be the sum of me.

He hadn't meant to draw the attention of a massive Earth Elemental to knock the Palace to the ground and swallow what was left. He hadn't meant to murder the Emperor—well, briefly he hadn't. He'd only meant for a diversion, so he could escape with his people so far from the Empire that the Imperials would never be able to find them.

But on the whole, he couldn't find it in himself to regret that it had *all* happened that way. The place *had* been a cesspit, fed by everything that was bad in humankind, embroiled in endless war, and led by a madman. There was no way to "reform" that place that he could conceive of, and no real way to reform the Empire. It had been that way for a very long time. Long enough that it had been his grandfather and father who started the plan to escape the Empire in the first place.

And I did give people enough warning to get out, even if all they escaped with was the clothing on their backs and their lives. Most of them didn't end up at the Lake, but some did by accident. Now they're far away by a lake and a forest, not cozy in their ancestral homes. And the same goes for my own people. No stability but what we can manage for them. Strange sounds, smells, unknown animals, even the weather is different. It's a new kind of suffering, but they are alive.

Kordas got to his feet and faced the crowd, which had grown. "Since I don't seem to have made myself clear before, *the Dolls are to be treated as fellow human beings.* Not your private servants. Not your personal set of pells when you are angry. Abusing them will get you the same sentence that abusing another person will get you. Exile!" He punctuated the word by pointing to the east with his red right hand. There were some gasps and murmurs, but as he scanned the faces around him, it didn't look as if anyone disapproved. It was more as if they had been wondering what the bastard's punishment was going to be, and "exile" surprised them a little.

Did they expect worse? I suppose I could get creative and make him take the place of the Doll he broke, but I don't think he'd learn better behavior from the punishment, and someone who'll do this to any other living thing is too dangerous to have around here. There are a lot of things we're going to have to accommodate, because some of us aren't fit twenty-year-olds with no health problems, but someone with a sick and twisted mind is not one of those things I am willing to have among us. Maybe later we'll have the leisure to take someone like that aside and make him human again. Not now.

He turned back to his guards. "Load his personal items into his boat, and give him a fortnight's worth of provisions. Make sure there is nothing on that boat that is from the common stores, only what he brought for himself when he joined us. Confiscate food and consumables like candles that are more than he needs for a fortnight. Make sure to look over his boat for anything reported missing, while you're checking the provisions. Put him on the boat with his hands tied, and leave one knife where he can reach it— eventually. Then push the boat through the Gate."

There was more murmuring. This time it sounded like people were coming around to his idea.

"Which Gate key do we use?" one of his men asked. It was a good question. The Dolls from the Palace had brought with them all the stamps for the Imperial Gate keys and a bewildering number of pre-made keys. Kordas could send him anywhere he chose.

And for one brief moment he was tempted to send the man to the Gate nearest the Southern warfront.

But he didn't know which Gate key that was, and he didn't want to bother to take the time to find out.

"None," he said.

"But where will I end up?" the bastard wailed thickly. It sounded like Kordas might have broken his jaw.

Kordas's anger flared up again, and he felt some crafty cruelty come out with it. "You'll end up somewhere random. If you're lucky, it'll be where there isn't any fighting or looting. If you're not, well, you'd better cut yourself loose pretty quickly. If you're unlucky, you'll end up in what's left of the Capital, and you'll fry in your boat. If you're *very* unlucky, you'll end up in what remains of a very fractured Imperial Army, who will certainly welcome you. They'll even give you a uniform and a shiny little hat. And a job. I think they refer to people like you as 'arrow-magnets' and 'Poomer-fodder.'" Kordas spat. "Wherever you end up, you'll be out of our lives forever, and that's all I care about."

The sign that the blackguard had lost the sympathy of the crowd came when there was a chuckle at the term "arrow-magnet."

Satisfied, he turned back to the broken Doll and saw that they had been joined by three more whole ones—ones wearing vaguely blue tabards with a white "V" and a horse's head on them, designating them as those who had assigned themselves to Kordas and his family. One was Rose, who had alerted him to what had been happening in the first place; the other two were one that had chosen the name of "Trout" and one called "Cobweb."

"Thank you for coming," he told them. "Can you three get this poor thing to the Mender?"

"Oh definitely, Baron," Rose said, nothing at all in her voice betraying if she felt any emotion at seeing her fellow Doll in such dire straits.

Then again, the Dolls rarely displayed much of anything, and that was aside from the fact that their "faces" were, at best, painted or embroidered images on the canvas of their heads. They didn't venture opinions on their own, and their voices were always even and pleasant. The perfect servants. Even the one that had been so terribly mistreated sounded as if they were prepared to have a lengthy conversation on the methods of brewing tea if he'd asked them to, regardless of how much pain they were in.

How can this moment become a memorable one? His tutors' lessons replayed in his head. *As a noble, every time you are seen is a performance of your role. Don't miss chances for weighty statements, when they present themselves. Fate can call upon you for a witty, memorable, or daring show at any time. Puissant nobles have honed the skill of recognizing such moments.*

"Thank you," he said, very aware that after his little speech people were paying very close attention to how he himself treated the Dolls. "Please tell the Mender I will be there shortly." He took a deep breath, stood, retrieved the offender's kerchief, and ripped it into bandaging strips, using his teeth and left hand. He spoke a brief spell of healing to sterilize his wounds, and let its effects be visible. He wasn't in the mood for finesse, just starting the repair.

Let them see I had magical power all along. I could have healed fully before anything else, but chose to bleed instead. They'll see me bind my own wounds, giving the impression I am utterly self-capable. And they know I don't mind being in pain. Wait. Wait. Do I actually like pain? It would explain a lot. Why do I feel like whatever it is, it's not enough work until I'm hurting from it? Why am I thinking about this right now? Concentrate.

They've seen me defend a Doll, and check on their well-being before tending to my own wounds. That should stick with them.

One thing about all of this, though. Leading by example hurts.

He gave the crowd a raking glance and a firm go-away gesture, implying wordlessly that if they were not busy, they bloody well should be. A second glance assured him that his three Dolls were taking the broken one off without any difficulty (and he hoped with as little pain as possible). Kordas walked on down the muddy path—everything about camping or deployment seemed to turn into mud—healing his hands up as he walked. The pain-blocking had been right on time, but the fractures the pain told of were still there, whether they hurt or not. His right hand seeped blood through the fray-edged bandages. What was it they said in his youth? "If the blood's fresh and clean, you'll be all right. You aren't in trouble till the blood stops flowing." His slower pace let him get the bones set and pressed. The bandages would help with that, so he left them on. Downhill to a crosspath— also mud, of course—he went where he'd been intending to go in the first place: the corral where his riding horses were.

Arial was finally in shape to ride, and the foal was in the process of being weaned, eating about half solid food and half Arial's milk, so the mare could be ridden again. She welcomed him with a whinny and a toss of her head, coming straight for him, and she even seemed to welcome the saddle, saddlebag with a pair of old trews and a shirt stuffed into it, and light bridle that he fetched from a rough thatched shelter where the tack was kept. Then again, going for a ride meant getting away from her foal, and the foal was getting to be of an age where she was a bit of a pest. Maternal instincts were wearing thin by now, and the relief of being where the foal couldn't get to her, combined with the pleasure of going out for a nice amble in relatively interesting, though unfamiliar, surroundings, must be what was accounting for her pleasure at seeing him.

Well, and she does like me, I suppose . . .

Arial whuffled at his bound-up hand, then snorted with disapproval at the smell. "It's fine, dear, it's fine. You probably just smell some sadist-face on my knuckles." Arial apparently had nothing to say, which suited him right now. He let her out of the gate—she could have easily jumped it, but there was no point in letting her know she could—and mounted up, turning her toward the lake and the path around it. Horses were creatures of habit. All the Valdemaran Gold horses had been trained to respect fences and wait for a human to open a gate, so it had happened that many of them could be stopped by a low fence that was only chest high, unless trained out of it. It made keeping all of the horses confined much easier. One thing Valdemaran Golds had in quantity was confidence, so more often than not, uncertain horses tended to follow what the Golds did.

This shore had become a city in all things but name, a long, thin city composed of barges, skiffs, and narrowboats pulled up along the shore of what they all unimaginatively called "Crescent Lake", boats docked three, four, five, even six deep. The narrowboats, where the high majority of people lived, were the nearest to the bank, with the boats storing all their goods and whatever else they had been able to get out tied prow to stern out behind them. If the tow-path was crowded, you could walk where you wanted to get from boat to boat using planks, and many people did. It had a song of its own, this arrangement. Thumps in several different tones played as slow, suffused wind chimes. When the breeze blew through, the low waves of the lake caused the whole array to bump hull to hull, so closely were they anchored. Interspersed with the thumps was the higher-pitched rubbing of hulls, something like a strange melody. *It may account for why there aren't as many predators as we expected. We've effectively beaten drums to drive them away, from the day we got here*, Kordas thought. *The insects didn't get the hint, though, and chewed us up until bugchaser lanterns were put up all along the shore. Forget what you learned from tales of quests and adventures. This is the real life of adventure: it always ends up as cold, mud, or bugs. Usually all three.*

He and his fellow leaders were trying to keep the land from being over-grazed and the woods from being plundered. That meant everyone was living in a boat, and except for those who must, such as guards and gamekeepers, residence ashore was forbidden. It was safer, too. Nobody yet knew what dangers could come out of that all-too-dark forest. The population being afloat meant they effectively had a moat around them. Kordas had his and Delia's boats tied up in the center of the lake's arc, putting them right in the middle. No one could accuse him of keeping himself out of reach of his people.

The original evacuation had been enormous, but when everything had settled and it was determined that the new Duke of Valdemar was going to be a decent man, Kordas had given people who wanted to go back home the option to do so. About two-thirds of them had queued up and returned. The Squire was not one; he was happy in his new village, and the Empress, his prize sow, was happy with her palatial new sty, so some of the Squire's children had taken two-thirds of the Squire's pigs and gone back to the Duchy, while the Squire's eldest divided the remaining third between himself and his father and was going to follow Kordas. Lots of people had done the same. Kordas reminded them that no one could guarantee their safety if they returned—but that going out into the unknown was going to be risky, probably dangerous, and at best uncomfortable, hard work.

The mages, to a man and woman, stayed. They already knew how the Empire treated magicians, and none of them were under the illusion that things would change under whatever general or Great Lord of State managed to claw his way to the Conquest Throne. And there were a lot of them, far more than Kordas had ever anticipated, far more than his little mage-enclave had hosted. Apparently mages who were not a part of the Imperial Court talked a lot to each other.

It was always a possibility that one or more of them was an agent of the Empire.

But at the moment, there wasn't any Emperor. There might not be an Empire. Whoever they had planned on reporting to probably wasn't in any position to do anything with the information anymore. Once they uprooted from this place and started on their exodus, there would be no way to get forces after them—they wouldn't exactly be burning bridges after themselves, but his plan would have the same effect.

Among the refugees there were, of course, the accidentals, the strays from the Capital who had simply flung themselves through the nearest Gate without a Gate key and randomly ended up at the

Lake. They mostly had nowhere to go until families who were leaving altogether and had no wish to go back to the Duchy had met up with the dispossessed, who found themselves going from "homeless" to "cottage and a garden, and jobs that needed hands to do them." Which might not be much, but it was more than they'd had after leaving everything behind. After witnessing the rampaging mother Earth Elemental, they were grateful to have anything at all.

Right now there were only three people who knew the truth about why that creature had torn the Palace and Capital apart— Kordas, the new Duke Merrin, and Kordas's Herald Beltran. The Duke was scarcely likely to let anyone know he'd helped murder the Emperor—*is that called a co-murder?* Kordas wondered—and kick off the carnage. Beltran could be trusted, and Kordas didn't intend for anyone else to know the whole truth, not even Isla. The Dolls knew, of course, but the Dolls were very good at keeping secrets.

To his eternal relief, the Dolls in charge of the hostages had taken their charges (and sometimes picked their charges up bodily—the Dolls, it seemed, were enormously strong), stuffed the Gate keys to the Gates nearest their homes down the fronts of their uniform tunics, and pitched them through the Palace Gates before coming here to the Lake themselves. *We know it was a merciful rescue, but technically, it was also kidnapping children. In doing good, we become someone's villains. It feels like every decision is mired in unhappy repercussions these days. Well, that's real adventure, too. Only storybooks end neatly. At least we managed to send those poor children back to their homes.*

He'd worried that he'd have to deal with almost a hundred parentless children, with no idea where their loyalties lay. He'd have had to send them home, of course, but that would mean *more* people who knew about the plans and the escape and . . . well, he was just glad things had worked out the way they had. The Dolls, it seemed, had kept their heads when everyone around them had thoroughly lost theirs—absolutely *no one* in authority had turned up at the hostages' area to evacuate them before the Dolls took matters into their own hands.

I really made a dog's dinner out of the situation, and if it hadn't been for the Dolls, things could have gone far more horribly wrong, in every possible way.

So there were about fifteen thousand people here now, mostly younger sons and daughters who would likely *never* have had the chance for a home and land of their own. So, not as many families as he had initially thought there would be, and no one with children younger than eight or nine. There were quite a few families of the Duchy who were tired of the Empire, figured that whoever eventually became Emperor was not going to be all that different from the last one, and elected to take their chances with Kordas. So they were doing better for long-term supplies than he had dared hope.

And now, everyone who wasn't going into the west with him had already left.

People were used to him riding up and down the lakeshore, and no one took much notice of him except to look up from what they were doing and wave.

He was ashamed of himself for losing his temper so badly back there—but doing so felt so damned good. It felt good to be able to take his emotions out on someone who deserved a pounding—the creep didn't even know the basics about what he hated. This wasn't mere stupid behavior, it was inept, and that only made it worse. This idiot had singled out a Doll, who told him that they already had a job to do, and made that an excuse to beat on them—unaware that what one Doll knew, they all knew.

That's what Rose had told him, when she ran to get him to save her fellow Doll. *Knowing they won't fight back. Knowing he could do anything he wanted. That's just pure evil, like torturing a puppy.*

But he was glad it happened now, and not after they got underway. *Because now people know what I won't tolerate, and what the price of lawbreaking is.* He had come to the conclusion that the best answer to most lawbreaking was going to be exile. *It's "merciful" without putting my people at any more risk.* Because risk from within was not something that they were going to be able to allow, not now, and not for a very long time.

He wished they *could* stay here. If there hadn't already been people here, people who had a prior claim to this land. And if he wasn't afraid that despite his best efforts, someone might be able to follow them here from the Empire. After all, he and his mages had managed to do it blind. What could they do if the Imperial mages got their hands on something connected to *anyone* who was in this mob of exiles? What if they had a plant here, somehow?

He looked landward, and didn't like what he saw. Already things were looking a little bit stressed—nothing that a good spring couldn't put right, but . . . over there, goats and donkeys, which would eat anything, had been nibbling on bushes and trees, and the undergrowth had been eaten down to a level where any good herdsman or shepherd would know it was urgently time to move the herds. And pigs, dear gods, what the pigs would do . . .

No, no, besides the fact that other people had rights to this land that superseded their arrival, there simply was not enough room here for his people and theirs. And the strain on the lake—

Well, other people besides him knew this. A lot of mages were Landwise, and he could tell that they were of the same mind. *I wonder how many in the Emperor's Court would have been ill at the mere thought of land management being part of a Duke's life? I say, if you want to be a Duke, well, it's vital. Work from the furthest points inward, maintain roads and safety, respond to emergencies, keep the Duchy well-defended, give respect, and always have at least three plans and escape routes.*

Right now, he didn't have three plans, but he did have two. One was to send more people back to the Duchy, if he could find any more that wanted to go. Along with that was to allow a *small* settlement here. Nothing that would compete with the locals, or make them resentful. That would reduce the strain on the environment here, and they would set up Crescent Lake as their town and hope for the best. The second was, in equal measure, desperate and daring. The scouts had already found a new river on the other side of the marshes, and four mages were setting up a Gate there. It was a lot easier getting two wooden uprights, four mages, and eight scouts across that swamp than it would have been to take fifteen thousand humans and roughly four times that many animals across—and that didn't count the chickens and waterfowl. The scouts had a Doll with them—and of course, what one Doll knew, they all knew, so as soon as Rose told him the new Gate had been activated, they could link the two and the real migration could begin.

And we'll go for as long as it takes. Rumor in the villages here says that the lands to the west are ravaged by the Mage-Wars, and no one lives there. So we find out if that is true. And we find a place of our own.

By this time, he was at the mouth of the river that trailed into the Lake, draining out of the swamp that was several leagues along. This was where most of the mages had made their own little camp of boats. Most ordinary folk liked the *idea* of mages, but didn't care for living anywhere near them. There were, after all, the occasional clouds of stinking smoke, accidental fires, and certainly odd lights and sounds at all times of the day and night. Mages, on the whole, did not much care for living around ordinary folk, either. They were, to say the least, a bit eccentric. Many of them had been bullied in their childhoods by "ordinary" folk. And when they were among other mages, they didn't have to explain behaviors like pacing for hours, muttering, or suddenly leaping up in the middle of something else to run to "try something out."

The Mender was here. He was a young protégé of Sai's who showed a remarkable aptitude for putting the Dolls to rights. A great many of them had come through the Gate injured, on fire, or both, and he had been the first to volunteer to try to fix them. He still hadn't found a way to free the animating *vrondi* from the fabric and wood shell, but he could make them as good as new when they needed repairs without putting them in pain.

The Mender had a tent on the shore, although he lived in a barge with five other mages. The tent, one of the ones that had been brought here to establish the beachhead for the migration, was for his work. The flaps were tied wide open to let in air and sun, and Kordas rode up to it and tethered Arial to a tent-peg before ducking inside.

Delia hung on Doll Ivy's every word, as the Doll described Kordas's one-sided fight with the man who had beaten and broken another Doll that Ivy had not put a name to. And when Ivy reported that Rose and other Dolls were taking the broken one to the Mender, Delia was torn—part of her wanted to go to the Baron, but the other part of her knew that although she did not have any kind of magic, the Mender found her of great use, and would probably want her. Duty won out, and she knew she would get to the Mender faster than the Dolls could bring the victim, so what she told him could give him time to prepare.

When Rose, Cobweb, and Trout arrived with the poor victim cradled among them, the tent was already prepared, with new "bones" laid out, fabric ready for patching, and a big bag of lamb's wool sifted full of sand and pre-enchanted for stuffing. This was one of the first things that the Mender had intuited, and the writings on the subject—once the Dolls had found them in the barges-full of records they had stolen—had confirmed it. One of the things that made the Dolls possible in the first place was that their "stuffing" was full of tiny crystals holding magical energy, and what was sand if not billions of tiny crystals?

The Mender had a name, but he was so nondescript, with his plain brown hair, unflappable expression, and forgettable face, that at this point everyone just called him Mender, and he seemed to like it.

With the victim laid carefully on a clean cloth, the first thing that the Mender did was place both hands over a spot in the middle of the Doll's chest where the vessel containing the bound *vrondi* was. After a moment, the Doll let out an unaccustomed sound that was very like a sigh.

"Well," the Doll said. "Not feeling anything at all is a small price to pay for not feeling pain. This is strange."

The Mender took away his hands and smiled. "Everyone says that," he replied. "Including humans. Now, let's see what damage was done. We'll start with your arms."

Between them he and Delia got the poor thing undressed—if you could call the rags the Doll had adopted "clothing"—and the first thing they both did was to hunt for the nearly-invisible knot that ended the seam holding the Doll's arms to their shoulders. Delia found hers first, teased the long ending of the thread out of where it had been buried in the stuffing, and carefully unpicked the knot.

The thread holding the Dolls together was also enchanted and the Mender didn't yet know how to make it, so when they took a Doll to pieces for any reason, they had to retain the thread and reuse it.

The Dolls had told the Mender that this was the usual case back at the Imperial Capital; the thread apparently could only be enchanted while it was being spun, and there was only one mage who could enchant *and* spin.

Fortunately the fabric of their bodies was perfectly ordinary canvas, or Delia wasn't sure what they would have done about the Dolls who had come out of the Gate on fire. *How awful that must have felt,* Delia thought, *but fortunately for everyone, repairing counts as healing up for them, and we could fix them.*

The thread seemed to resist damage to a remarkable degree, and *did* respond to spells to restore it to perfect condition.

With the arms detached from the shoulders, and a quick check showing that the clever wooden ball-joints were undamaged, the next task was to find the knot that ended the seam holding the upper arm together and unpick that seam, carefully saving every scrap of stuffing. This was where Delia was coming in very handy to the Mender; she was a deft seamstress, and her Fetching Gift gave her the equivalent of an extra hand. Plus, of course, having someone on the other side of the Doll repeating what he was doing cut his time of assembly and disassembly in half.

The Doll bones were strange things, made of wood with windings of copper strung with crystal beads. The Mender didn't know how to make those yet, either—but he did know how to transfer the spells from the broken bones to the new ones. Then he fitted the joints together—the sound of them snapping into place had been unnerving at first, but now it sounded satisfying to Delia—and they sewed the mended limbs back together, making sure that the canvas was as tight over the stuffing as skin was over muscle. By the time Kordas arrived, they were stitching up the last seams, ending each one with that special secure knot, and burying the long tail beneath the canvas skin and deep into the woolen stuffing.

It always made her giggle a little when, thanks to the sand in the wool, the needle ended up sharper and cleaner than it had been when she started.

The Mender had restored feeling to the Doll once the bones were replaced, and she was fairly certain the stitching was causing them pain, but the Doll accepted it without complaining.

"How are you feeling now?" Kordas asked the Doll, looking into their sketched-on eyes.

"This one is much improved," the Doll replied, as they slowly sat up, and gingerly moved their limbs, trying them out. "Much thanks to the Mender and Lady Delia." Kordas wordlessly handed the Doll some clothing from his saddlebags.

The Doll took it . . . with a moment of hesitation. "This one shall return these when—"

"No need," Kordas interrupted, a little gruffly. "It's the least I can do to make up for what happened to you."

"Then this one thanks you." The Doll got into the clothing—which just looked a bit uncanny, and Delia glanced away—then bowed to Kordas. "And this one thanks you, not only for coming to this one's rescue, but for exiling the human. This is not the first time he has harmed a Doll. It was only the most violent."

Kordas went a little pale at that, but quickly recovered. "If anything like that happens again, I want to know about it," he said, his voice a little harsh. "Immediately. And hereafter if someone mistreats a Doll, you Dolls are authorized to get the nearest of my Guard and come deal with the offender. I'll—actually I'll add that to my speech." He ran his hand through his hair. "I need to go work out that speech," he added with an air of distraction. "Now that I know you're all right, I should get back to that."

With that, he turned abruptly and left, with Delia's gaze upon him still.

2

"Would you mind staying here for a little longer to help me clean and organize?" the Mender asked.

She didn't sigh, but . . . those were servants' duties, and she had been doing a *lot* of servants' duties lately. Of course, that was because the servants had been doing a lot of other duties since they all got here. Well, even a young female servant was probably physically stronger than Delia was. And most of them had some acquaintance with the kind of work that needed to be done around the lake. And most of them wouldn't complain about being asked to step outside of their old duties and pick up a shovel to dig latrine trenches, or a hand-scythe to gather grasses and weeds for the grazing animals, or help with mending or cooking. She couldn't help but feeling a bit put-upon, but before the feeling had a chance to set in, something would happen, like she'd see Isla with the sleeves of her gown rolled up above her elbows, helping in their communal kitchen. And then she'd feel guilty for feeling put-upon.

Well, helping the Mender isn't nearly as bad as trying to herd those three nephews of mine. Little Jon wasn't bad, but Restil and his brother Hakkon could be like a pair of twin ferrets, into everything, and there one moment and gone the next. Freed from the duties of being pages, and because of their background, too young to really be put to any useful work, they were treating all this as the best holiday ever. She was very tired of being dragooned into "watching" them, because they treated her as a challenge to escape from, and when they disappeared, it was a given that within the mark she'd be summoned by someone who was very annoyed to "come get them out of their mischief." They'd already tried to ride every beast short of a horse that was large enough to ride, and she shuddered to think what would have happened if the sow they'd tried to turn into their pony had had her piglets with her at the time. They poked their noses into the laundry and nearly got scalded for their trouble, they'd long since been banished from *every* communal kitchen for trying to filch food, and after the ram-riding incident none of the shepherds wanted them near the sheep and goats. The cowherds had threatened to drown them if they bothered the cattle again. The goose-girls had set the ganders on them, and the roosters had defended their flocks with spurs, so they were at least keeping clear of the fowl on their own. They each seemed to have the energy of six Delias, and so far she hadn't been able to think of anything that would occupy them safely. And even if she did, chances were if they saw a bird or a butterfly they'd run to chase it.

She couldn't even hide from her sister in her own boat—because it wasn't just "her" boat anymore. Just as her three nephews had been quartered with their parents—fully filling up *that* barge—she'd had five female servants put with her. So there was absolutely no privacy, and no escaping the fact that if Isla was heard to call Delia's name, there would be at least five people who would be sure to tell Isla that "I'm sure I saw your sister in her barge."

Well, I am halfway around the lake from Isla right now, and I'd rather help the Mender than run my feet off after those boys. So she smiled. "If another pair of hands is useful to you, then I am all yours."

"Very much so when working on a Doll as badly hurt as that one was," the Mender said, coloring a little, and making her think he probably didn't have much experience being around girls. "Your Gift was exactly what was needed to hold things without obstructing my vision. A pair of *invisible* hands is extremely useful." The two of them began picking up all of the varied and somewhat odd things he needed when he was mending a Doll. She'd done this twice before, and knew where everything was now. "May this be the last time we Mend a Doll here at Crescent Lake," he said, as she carefully retrieved every thread of magical fluff and stowed it away. "I wish we could stay, but I can easily see why we can't." At her glance of puzzlement, he elaborated. "I'm Landwise. That might be why I'm good at putting the Dolls back together. I can feel the stress so many people all in one place is putting on this area. To be honest, the best thing we can do for this lake is leave it before we've started ruining it."

"Well, the local farmers like us well enough," she pointed out. And it was true. Several farmers would arrive with wagons every day to collect all the excrement of humans and their animals that would otherwise soon have overwhelmed the area.

"Well, as one of them told me, 'No farmer has ever complained of having too much manure,' though I suspect they *would* if Kordas had made the decision to stay." The Mender shrugged. "Once we're out of here, the land will rest over the winter, and everything will be fine again."

"Do you ever—" She hesitated, but the Mender seemed a kind young man, and maybe he wouldn't mind letting her talk about things. "Do you ever wish we could go back to the way it was?"

He sat back on his heels, and rolled up the leather case that held his instruments. "For myself? No. There was always the chance I'd be snatched up by the Emperor's people if anyone had ever found out about all the mages that the D—I mean, Baron, was harboring. And—" His eyes lit up. "I had no idea that the Dolls were something that was even possible! I love being able to help them. They let me study them as much as I want. And I am going to miss them dreadfully when we finally figure out how to release them."

"We will miss you too, Mender," said the Doll they had been helping. They both turned to look at the Doll with a little surprise, since most of the Dolls were not much given to spontaneous expressions of any sort. "You are a considerate and skilled man. We appreciate you."

"Well . . . thank you." The Mender blinked rapidly, as if he was trying not to cry. "I'm exceedingly touched . . ."

"Have you a need for an assistant such as this one?" the Doll continued, hesitantly. "This one would enjoy serving you."

"Uh—you mean that's possible?" the Mender replied, clearly taken aback.

"This one *is* a bit handicapped," the Doll pointed out, raising their mitten-like hands. "Fine manual dexterity is, alas, out of the question. But this one can fetch and carry, hold things, pass you instruments, and keep track of your supplies and belongings. If nothing else, this one is a pincushion."

"No, I meant, is it possible that I'd be allowed to have your services?" the Mender corrected. "I was under the impression that you Dolls were a sort of common labor pool, and no single person could—uh—require your help."

"The Baron has told us repeatedly that we may do as we please," the Doll said. "And this one would be pleased to serve you."

"Well, I guess it's settled, then." The Mender licked his lips and thought for a moment. "Do you have a name?"

"This one has not chosen a name. Would you like this one to do so?" the Doll tipped their head to the side.

"Yes. And if you don't mind, I'd like to make you look more— unique." He now looked at Delia. "I'm kind of . . . helpless with hair . . ."

"We've got wool without any sand in it," she pointed out. "That will do for hair."

It took quite a bit of time, which Delia was actually happy about, since it meant no one was looking for her to do some other unskilled chore to release someone who actually had skills for other work.

But no one sent for her (and all Isla had to do was ask the nearest Doll to tell her to come back) and no one brought in another broken Doll to be worked on, so she and the Mender and the Doll had a rather relaxed, interesting time together. The Doll settled on a name—Dern—and a look—androgynous—and they went to work. When they were done, Dern had a wig of sorts, sewn into the canvas "scalp," of short brown curls from a brown-fleeced sheep. Dern also had a face delineated with that dense Imperial ink and a feather. The Mender had a rather delicate touch for that.

"Your face looks better than the painted ones I've seen, Dern," Delia observed, as the Mender corked his bottle tightly and gave

Dern the feather, which Dern promptly stuck in their brown curls like an ornament.

"Technically the faces are painted on cloth attached to the Doll— barely anything but the most pigmented ink sticks to them. I always think that the people who had faces painted on their Dolls were going a bit too far," the Mender replied. "It's too close to real, yet not real enough. It makes me all uneasy when I look at them. This is better."

"Is it? That's good," Dern replied. "This one does not wish to be the cause of distress."

Delia sat back on her heels to study the effect of their work. "It *is* good," she agreed. "Attractive. And now that you've been decorated, I think we need one more thing that will identify you as having allied yourself with the Mender. Can you think of anything?"

Silence from both of the others, while she thought about it herself. What *would* work for that sort of thing? Kordas's Dolls all had the tabard with the Valdemar "V" and horse head on them. All of the Dolls who had assigned themselves to the Healers wore a green leaf painted on their tunics or shirts.

"Well, I suppose I am a sort of Healer," the Mender said finally. He took back the feather from Dern and inked a brown-colored leaf with oak-gall ink on the front of Dern's shirt, then handed the feather back. "Even if people don't know what that means, they'll think twice about trying to command your services."

"Which are to be used for what, right now?" Dern asked, tilting their head to the side in mimicry, Delia supposed, of the same gesture humans made.

"Organizing and packing up my tools and things, then stowing them in my barge. We'll start with things I'm not likely to need before we set out, and end with the things I'll need in an emergency."

The Mender shrugged at Delia. "Sorry, I think I won't need you now, Delia. But thanks."

"That's all right," she replied, although *all right* was not exactly what she felt. "I'll see if the other mages need help."

She quickly came to discover that the answer was "no," since each of the mages seemed to have their own Dolls, or at least, there were teams of Dolls helping them, as they, too, got ready for the migration. "I can't think of anyone that needs help except those two apprentices that are on latrine-trench duty," Sai told her, as he supervised the Dolls packing up the bricks that made his bread oven preparatory to stowing them as ballast. She sighed with regret at that. She was going to miss Sai's bread. "They don't have Dolls and they're probably sick of the work by now."

The two apprentices had been taught a spell that pulled all the water out of what it was cast on, and their job was a full-time walk of the latrine trenches, desiccating everything that was in there. Servants that were used to dealing with manure, like stablehands and gardeners, went out with the herds, collecting everything the animals dropped and bringing it to the trenches as well. From there the local farmers collected the now-dry and easier-to-handle fossilized feces and carted them away to be added to their compost piles. She'd thought this was ridiculous, and that the servants' time could be utilized much better elsewhere, until she got a look at just how much waste fifteen thousand people and exponentially more animals could produce in a day. Without things like the compost heaps and cesspits they had back home to handle it all, well, it wouldn't be pretty, and people would be getting sick faster than the Healers could help them. The farmers, meanwhile, were stockpiling what was as good as gold to them, and they were making compost piles out of it that would keep their fields well-manured for the next several years at the least. And those that didn't actually have many animals themselves were positively giddy at this unexpected bonanza.

She was pretty sure they'd have been less enthusiastic if it had been in its native state. But they probably would have taken it anyway.

She wanted to dawdle, but there was always the chance that someone would see her making her slowest possible pace back to the family boats, and people being people, someone would take great glee in telling Isla about it. Isla wouldn't *say* anything, but she'd give Delia that look that said *I am disappointed in you,* and that was worse than being scolded.

But it was hard not to drag her feet when she knew she was going back to another round of chores until well after dark. *Her* boat was in good order, and ready to be towed, but somehow the boys were managing to drag practically everything they could out of its proper place, and often out of the boat entirely. And she always seemed to be the one tasked to restore order out of chaos.

I swear, I will never, ever, ever have children.

Sure enough, as soon as she arrived back at the boats, Isla thrust a basket of clean clothing with mending materials on top of it into her hands and said, "Find a place to sit. These need to be mended before dinner," and vanished into the boat she and Kordas shared with the boys.

With a sigh, she looked around. Her boat was full of the maids stowing everything away in the most economic way possible, so she opted for a spot on the stern, where there was full sun and a nice warm spot on the decking. On top of the basket was a keeper made of felt with three precious needles in it, and a single spool of thread. At this point, no one was paying any attention to the color of thread clothing was mended with, or even the kind of thread it was. This looked like light wool, the kind you mended stockings with. And it was gray; the clothing in the basket was literally every color except gray.

But at least when I am doing this I am not trying to chase down those boys. I wish I was home . . .

Her hands stilled for a moment, and she was startled by the tight feeling in her throat and an upwelling of tears. With her back to everything and everyone, and no one to see her and ask her sharply what on *earth* she was crying about, she let the tears spill over her cheeks, mourning her past life. Mourning her home. Mourning the little room that had been hers, and hers alone. Mourning a world where "needlework" meant working beautiful images in thread, not sewing on a patch to cover a hole in the seat of someone's trews. Where every meal was carefully prepared and full of variety, not pottage for breakfast, bread and cheese for the midday meal, and the same stew, either fish or meat, served in a small round loaf you were supposed to eat when you finished. She'd helped in the communal kitchens; every possible scrap, from peel to leaves, from bones to organs, was chopped up and put in that stew, and the Healers had said to chew up the softened bones and eat them, which was . . . ugh. Nothing was wasted. Nothing.

And things will probably get worse from here. Food would run out, until they were left with nothing but grain pottage, flavored with herbs and salt or maybe some dried fruit if she was lucky. Winter was on the way, and she was sure there was no way that a boat could be made as cozy as a sturdy building. And who knew what was out there? Her imagination was quite good at populating the blank map with all manner of horrors.

Well, no one was going to know how she felt, if anyone even cared. She might as well just let the sadness and the frustration have their way. So the tears fell on her mending, and she cried in silence, as her hands worked.

———

Kordas could hardly believe his luck when he got back to the family barges and found Isla—astonishingly!—alone. Isla was working, of course; everyone worked now, often from dawn to dusk, but her ears were certainly free, and he spied her through the rearmost windows of the barge. She was all the way back in their personal barge sitting on their bed. The boys were elsewhere, and since she was making ordinary shirts into quilted shirts for winter, that was something he could actually help her with. He couldn't sew, but any fool could pick rags apart into tiny bits of thread for stuffing, so he eeled his way to their "bedroom." He sat down without a word beside her and began doing just that with the tiny rags, stuffing the resulting frizz into a rough bag she had for the purpose. She had turned a shirt inside out and, with the padding and carefully cut patches, all of identical size and shape, was doing the quilting in small squares in a neat pattern, not unlike the "checked" pattern in heraldry. The resultant quilted shirt could be worn with the original side out, or the patchwork side out, if the original got too stained to be presentable. It would be infinitely warmer than two simple shirts.

"I heard some rumors you were beating someone," she said casually, sewing a brown square down onto the padding, then carefully turning the edges under and sewing it in place next to a beige square.

"Rumor flies faster than a bird," he said ruefully. "It's quite true. Doll Rose came to get me because someone was deliberately torturing another Doll. By the time I got there, he'd broken every limb with a sledgehammer."

She stopped sewing for a moment with a swift intake of breath. "I'd have done worse than beat him," she said flatly, looking up at him. "Perhaps it's just as well Rose came for you instead of me."

He didn't ask her what she would have done, because he already had a shrewd idea of what it would have been, and besides being exiled, the idiot would probably have been singing soprano for the rest of his days. "Well, he had the bad sense to resist me with his face," was all he said. "And I took my temper out on him."

"If you are having trouble with your temper, it's best to find a target worthy of getting it in the face," she agreed.

He snorted. "In the face, and the gut, and the face again. The face a lot, actually. I broke his jaw. And I exiled him. He'll be going through the Gate on no pass before we take it down. The evilest part of me hopes he ends up in the Capital."

Isla side-glanced at Kordas's bound-up hand. "And broke your hand doing it, it appears. Healed?" Kordas nodded and held it up. She nodded slowly. "You did the right thing. Next time it could have been a child, or someone else who couldn't defend themselves. I assume there is going to be a speech?"

"I can't leave this at rumor. And I want to make sure everyone knows where they stand on this—and on some other things. That way anyone who is having second and third thoughts about staying with the migration can use what I am about to tell them as an excuse to leave without looking like a coward." He half smiled at her, and she chuckled.

He relaxed all over. Truth to be told, he liked this version of Isla rather more than "Lady Isla, Duchess Valdemar." She was a lot

closer to his old childhood friend than she had been in years. All
the fancy gowns and every bit of jewelry had been stowed in the
most inaccessible places in the storage barges or in this one, and
these days you were just as likely to find her in a heavy knitted
tunic and a pair of soft canvas trews or breeches as you were a
gown. And if it was a gown, it would be a sturdy thing, meant to
take abuse and dirt and be washed clean in the lake and dried on
a bush. She wore her hair in a single braid down her back, though
unruly dark tendrils inevitably escaped around her ears.

"I'd be lying if I said I didn't think you need to do that. In fact,
you're right to, and this is exactly the right moment for you to make
a speech about it. People here have never seen you in a fury until
now—and—" She shrugged. "You know people. There are probably
some who think you're soft, or too busy with other things to pay
attention to what's going on below you. And without a shadow of
a doubt there are quarrels brewing quietly, people looking to take
advantage of you, or what they see as your inattention, and—well—
it's like balancing all that among the manor staff, only on a vastly
larger scale. I think it's definitely time for them to learn that there
are things you won't put up with, and that the penalty for doing
those things is serious. People have already grouped together with
people they knew before, and you've already appointed leaders for
each group, and you have *those* leaders reporting to your new Guard
officers, so not only will you establish a proper code of conduct, this
will be telling those leaders what you expect them to do."

"I need to think about what I am going to say, so if you don't
mind, I'll keep making stuffing for you." He paused a moment.
"I told Rose that I was sorry we hadn't found a way to free them
yet. But the truth is, right now—we need them too much, and if

the Mender ever does figure out how to get the *vrondi* out of those shells—can we afford to let them go?"

"Have you asked them how they feel about it?" she replied sensibly, as the boat rocked ever so gently with the small movements they were making and the wavelets of the lake. It was still warm enough during the day that the shutters were open on the windows, and the hum of voices up and down the shore combined with the sound of the waves and the rising and falling of the boats' hulls was quite soothing. It made a lovely sound to go to sleep to—although he had to admit that the times there had been a storm on the lake and the barges had rocked violently and banged together had not been so pleasant. It was a good thing that the material they were made of was as tough as steel.

"Well, not in so many words," he admitted.

"Then remember what you tell me all the time. When you want to know what people are thinking, don't spin yourself into knots about it, just ask them." The sound of footsteps—the peculiar, too-even, too-precise, too-measured steps that only a Doll took—echoed off the hull from the front of the barge, and they both stopped what they were doing. Kordas felt a dim sense of apprehension. *Now what?* he thought.

But it was Rose; like the three Dolls who had assigned themselves to him, Rose wore trews of stiff canvas and a shirt of the same coarse cloth grain-sacks were made of, both of which would have been scratchy and supremely uncomfortable for a human, but which the Dolls assured him caused them no problems. Clothing was mostly to make them fit in with the humans, Rose had said; they did not feel cold or heat, and didn't actually need covering. Over the outfit, Rose wore the blue-painted canvas tabard with the Valdemar "V" and horse head that had always been associated with his family, rather than the more elaborate Ducal crest of the winged horse. Rose's once-bare head was now covered in a crop of woolen curls that had taken Isla the better part of three evenings to knot into Rose's canvas "scalp," and she had been painted with a rather sweet face by Jonaton. Rose no longer needed that little rose sketched into her forehead for him to tell her from the other Dolls. Though she did wear a rose that someone had made for her out of a scrap of red ribbon in her wooly hair.

And—he was thinking of Rose as "her," not "it."

"The Doll who was injured is fully mended, has taken the name 'Dern,' and has tied themselves to the Mender," Rose said. "Rumors are spreading about what happened. Fundamentally, people approve of your actions, Lord Baron."

"Then I should definitely make that speech tonight while they haven't had a chance to think too much about it," he said. Then took a deep breath. "Rose, I am sorry we have not been able to find a way to free you. But—I am also not sorry, not entirely. This is very selfish of me, but we *need* you. You can do things humans can't, you don't need food or sleep, and you can tolerate things and conditions humans would fold under. I—"

To his astonishment, Rose actually held up a hand to stop him from saying anything further. "We are of one mind in this, Lord Baron. Regardless of when you find a way to free us, we will serve you until you no longer *need* us. That is a promise from all of us. Hopefully, that will occur before you become too accustomed to depending upon us."

"Hopefully," he said hesitantly. *We don't dare become dependent on them, or I'll never get people to allow them to go, and they'll just be enslaved all over again.*

We can't have that. That will start us down the road to replicating the Empire.

"You freed us from a terrible slavery. Life among you has been . . ." She cocked her head to the side. "Pleasant. Very pleasant, for the most part. And there is an overwhelming likelihood that you will find a way to free us, and do so before we feel we need to remind you of your promise." She straightened her head. "So now, I will leave you to your thoughts, and go to collect some food for you from the kitchens."

She turned and left, leaving both of them to stare after her. "Well. That was unexpected," he managed. But Isla had noticed something he hadn't.

"Did Rose just call herself *'I'*?" she said incredulously.

———

Word was spreading around the encampment that Kordas was going to make a Speech, so people were getting through their evening chores as quickly as they could. Meanwhile, he set up the old family heirloom, the stately telcaster—seldom used for anything except entertainments on the estate for the last couple of generations—that allowed him to conjure up an image of himself that was twenty feet tall from the surface of the lake, and broadcast his words around the shore, and probably a lot further. It didn't seem to bother the birds and animals, at least not after the first few times they'd used it, so he didn't worry about what else was hearing him.

They'd been using the antique instrument for some time now, every night when the weather was fine, to update the entire camp on what had happened, what was scheduled, and what weather to expect. And *immediately* send telcaster-amplified warnings by bugle and shout—like the time a bear had gotten past the perimeter guards and headed for one of the kitchens.

That bear had become stew, rather than partaking of the stew. He often wondered if it was the same one that had chased Jonaton's enormous black cat Sydney back through the first Gate they had established here. If so, Sydney had probably *especially* enjoyed his dinner of bear gravy and innards.

Every night after the news and any other pressing concerns for the camp were disposed of, there was entertainment. No great Bards had made the trek here—his court hadn't been notable enough to attract even a minor Bard, and Merrin's Bard had elected to stay with the new Duke—but in fifteen thousand people, there was bound to be plenty of talent. Musicians, or at least people who could make a pleasant noise, tell a good tale, dance, or do something else that entertained others volunteered, however odd their talents may be. One family juggled goslings, one troupe did a serialized puppet comedy, and yet another couple showed ways to cook, which was an unexpected hit. They all got their chances on what was probably the biggest stage anyone could ever have imagined. And if sometimes their audience drowsed or talked through their performance, well, they'd never know, because all they could see was a group around them that was about the size of an audience in their village. Kordas smiled a moment thinking of it, because it drew a tear to his eye every time the camp joined in on an anthem or ballad, thousands of voices echoing around the lake. Whatever differences or complaints they might have, they were united in song.

The telcaster had been in his family for generations, and it wasn't an uncommon sort of object to have among the nobles of the Empire. It was considered a sort of toy, rather more backward than some of the advanced objects of its type had been back in the Capital. Among other things, when one had guests, having a telcaster ensured that no one was slighted by getting an inferior view of any entertainers. It required a mage to work it, of course, but the rulers of the Duchy of Valdemar had been mages all the way back to the first Duke, and apprentices had been taught its use.

The bigger, fancier versions went by the name of *illusionarium*.

Kordas preferred the humbler term "telcaster."

Before he could set it up, he made himself a little three-sided enclosure with a sheet pinned to the branches of one of the trees nearby, and hung a mage-light where it would give the most flattering light. He'd done this so many times he could have set up everything in his sleep, and didn't need Ivy's help, although he always accepted it. Right now, no Dolls were around him, only the black-furred bruiser watching him. Sydney's tail flicked, though the rest of him was studiously relaxed. If one knew cats, one would recognize that such a well-practiced calm meant mayhem would strike at any moment.

The last stage was setting up the object itself. It was portable, though not small. Zebrawood casing held arrays of crystals adjusted by brass rods at the front, with similar controls for sound on the other side of its "eye." Brass plates labeled what each rod did, though few laymen could have understood them. When it was time, the front cover was merely flipped back (carefully!), and its mirrored surface showed whatever was in front of it. Once the lights inside warmed up enough, it wasn't very long before the telcast would begin. Its center looked not unlike one of the black bowls used for scrying. As usual, he had to pull Sydney out of it. The bowl was always warm, and Sydney liked to sleep in it. Occasionally, since it *was* old, the thing would come on by itself for a moment using whatever residual magic was nearby, and the entire camp would get a fine view of Sydney licking his balls until someone noticed and shut the telcaster off.

In this case, Sydney had seen what Kordas was up to, and had placed himself in the eventual focus of attention. Now, removed from it, the cat realized he needed very much to be over *there* very quickly, for some reason, and darted away.

Jonaton's cats—the mage had somehow brought all of them— had made themselves citizens of the entire camp, with over half attaching themselves to families, and the rest roaming boat to boat. They avoided the shore for the most part, probably because of the smell of the livestock and trenches. Thanks to lake effect, those were seldom upwind from the boats.

While Kordas set the telcaster up and tuned it, Isla, the children, Delia, and anyone nearby who wanted to see the actual Baron making the speech rather than watching the illusion settled down on blankets in front of him.

He took a deep breath, composed himself, and began.

"Folk of the Valdemar Expedition," he said, trying to project both strength and warmth. "I'm sure by now you all have heard about today's incident. I need to speak with you about that—and so much more."

3

Delia cast her eyes over the barges nearest her. The sun had nearly set below the tree line, which signaled that the telcast was soon to begin. The temperature had already dropped, and people were bundled up, their dinner ready, their pets safely with them. They mostly sat on their barges, eyes fastened on the lake, waiting for the Baron's speech.

Nobody missed one of Kordas's addresses, and not just because they needed to know what he had to say. It was that Kordas was entertaining and reassuring, too. His speeches had revealed a highly charismatic man that most of the folk responded to as the voice of a guiding commander. Delia didn't recall him being as compelling a speaker back when they had been home, but then, she hadn't often seen him acting in the official role of Duke. She found herself hanging on his words like everyone else was, and there was none of the restlessness and muttering she often heard when news was being spread or when some of the entertainment was going on. Even the occasional breeze with ice in its teeth didn't dissuade people from sitting out here along the lake to listen to him.

Beltran adjusted the brass hoops and arms of the telcaster, twisting one to increase its brightness. Out on the water, visible to everyone on either side of the shoreline, the blue of the background came into existence, only a glowing blue ovoid right now. As Beltran altered the angle of several arms, the wrinkles in the backdrop were distinguishable in the lake image, and the white splotch in the lower quarter resolved into text. "Evening News," it read, followed by "Variety Show" and "Night Music." A few seconds' time with a pen, and a new card replaced it, reading "SUNDOWN—BARON'S ADDRESS TO ALL— HEAR AND WITNESS." It was a phrase born in Valdemar, in fact, known to everyone from schoolchild to elder. It was a polite way of saying, "Technically this is not mandatory, but you'd regret missing it."

Delia watched Kordas with more attention than her work actually called for, as he took command of everyone's attention. Whether he was telling mundane facts or describing a disaster, Kordas gave the impression that he was right *there*, to handle it personally. Maybe more importantly, that he was *supposed* to be there. *People respond to confident speakers, even if their messages are bunk,* she thought, *and he doesn't tolerate bunk.* When the Baron of Valdemar spoke, even if the news was bad, he was someone to be counted on.

Someone might fall in love with Kordas for that alone, she thought, and smiled.

The telcaster's arms were locked in place, and the glow in the bowl was matched by a glow from the lake. A flickering red light on the telcaster's face gradually became a steady one. It was time.

Herald Beltran placed a last card in the cradle, which read "BARON'S INTRODUCTION," and stepped in front of the backdrop. "Hear all, see all, Official Pronouncements of Law and Profundity will be spoken tonight. Welcome now your leader, your head of state, architect of your prosperity, Kordas, Baron of the Expedition."

The applause that followed was riddled with hull-stamping, whistling, barking, and whoops of enthusiasm. Only the cats failed to comment.

Kordas stepped into the telcaster's view on the shore, and on the Lake, a towering, brightly glowing version of him did the same. He wore his circlet, and nothing especially ornamental except for a triple-chained clasp for his mantle, bearing a gleaming enameled Valdemar family crest. It sent the subtle hint that this was not only an address by the Baron, it was something personal to him. He raised his hands, and spoke when the cheers had died down.

"Valdemarans. Friends. Allies, Guests, and Wards. We all understand that as we brave the challenges of this journey, anyone may become annoyed or angry to some degree, and that can be handled. Today, I judged a man called Donat Benin guilty of a serious crime. The crime today, however, was no simple venting of stress or armed conflict. It was a despicable act: a near-lethal assault by someone who, by my judgment, had studied the Dolls around him and, knowing they could think and feel, chose to engage one in violent torture past the point a human would have been murdered."

The implication there being that if he'd do that to Dolls, he'd do it to humans too—if he hadn't already, Delia thought. *Kordas is coming out swinging. This obviously means more to him than just a speech.* Beltran stood beside the telcaster's table. His hands moved impossibly quickly, transcribing Kordas's words onto cards, then dropping them in place on the telcaster's bookstand-turned-card-rack before the ink was anywhere near dry. Not everyone on the expedition had perfect hearing, after all, and this way anyone could read the words below the Baron's image.

"The criminal was seized, charged, and sentenced before there could be any more victims. I'll repeat now what I've declared in the past: Dolls are to be treated as you would treat your neighbor. They are not property, servants, or slaves. They are not the same as you, but their lives are equal to yours, and of equal value. That someone in our situation would willfully cause such savage harm to a Doll is reprehensible. We should be better than that—we *all* should be better than that."

Murmurs of assent, and nodding to each other, probably told Kordas what this small audience thought as he spoke, allowing him ease to work the much larger crowd facing the lake.

"What the Dolls graciously do for us now derives from *my* promise to free them, once we know how. Assault any Doll, and you assault a friend of mine. *Remember that.* One day, sooner than you might imagine, they will be gone from our lives. What they do for us now, we will entirely have to do for ourselves. In my opinion, we should all thank the Dolls, for while we rescued them, they continue to rescue us. To torture one is—unforgivable."

Kordas let the silence go on two beats too long. It was clear that he *meant* the pause to be uncomfortable, for his next words were harsh and uncompromising. The muscles of his jaw tightened, and his eyes grew hard.

"To that end, the penalty for serious lawbreaking will now be *exile*. A fortnight of provisions, a knife, and through a Gate you go, and may any god who will still claim you have pity on you. The trip is one-way. The exit is random. If you're lucky, you'll arrive where you can find shelter and live as a scavenger—briefly. If you are not lucky, you'll be conscripted into the front lines of whichever conflict you stagger in on. If you are very unlucky, your last few breaths may be in the smoldering ruins of the Capital. Further, if you are guilty of High Violation, I'll send you through bleeding, on a raft made of scrap, without a boat or goods. Those exiled will be drugged hard, and *should* you wake, you won't remember us, your crimes, or even who you are for quite some time. If ever. You will no longer be our problem."

Even from the shore, Delia could hear intakes of breath around the flotilla. *I guess that's the sound of thousands of people suddenly evaluating themselves. And in the Empire, a noble would pretend nothing bad had happened, not make a point of it.*

"I'm going to say this now, because the assault I judged today sharpened the need for it. Could any who meet us ever trust us, if they saw what Donat Benin did? No, and rightly so. This new land is only new to us. To the people already here when the first barges came through, we are likely the largest population they have ever heard of, with strange magic, fierce weapons, and incomprehensible language. We must look like an endless, invading army. We are not an army! We're not going to *conquer* anything by force of arms. We will defend ourselves from raids, wildlife, and magical attacks, and we will not act like the ruined Empire would, training and traditions be damned, by clearing our path via slaughter and annexation. Friends, it is a fool's mistake to turn away from the truth. What we do, how we actually live away from the negotiating table, is who we really are. Whatever the worst of us does, though it may be one in a thousand of us, is an undeniable part of who we are as a people. To speak of trade, peace, and discovery to the locals' faces yet commit crimes upon our own is something we *should* be damned for. We can not puff up and assume that 'if our side did it, it must be right.'

"I say that the best way to appear trustworthy, likable, and respectable is to *be* those things. Not a veneer glued over a cracked, crumbling foundation, but rather, all of us actually being as strong and adaptable as we could be. If one of us is cruel, hateful, or criminal, that one not only harms us directly, they harm us indirectly, because we never know who is watching us at the time. In military terms, there is great wisdom in the saying, *Don't provoke the natives. They already surround you.*"

The smattering of grunts and chuckles were all, no doubt, from campaign survivors.

He paused for effect, and then held his hands palm out and upward. "My people. My brave people. Many of you are still in shock over the loss of our old homes and ways. Many are anxious about our future. I understand. We were raised on tales of great deeds, and we can exemplify what we admire in songs and stories. I say that the best heroes are those who show that what they dared *can* be done. They aren't to be looked at from a distance as a novelty, they are inspirations. We can be heroes up close, in our *own* ways.

"I say to you, plainly, it is better to live with a measure of danger than a certainty of mediocrity. We have to be a band of brothers and sisters. This is an expedition with laws, but more than that, we must regulate our behavior in day-to-day life. From that, we build a reputation. Think on tolerance. Work out how to swap, buy, and bargain for peace. When you can tell that a fight is building, back off. Disengage. Take some time. Let someone negotiate for you, call a truce, or work on solving whatever upset you. Don't let it fester like a boil. Lance it, and heal up."

Delia nodded. *I bet beating and sentencing Donat Benin today felt like lancing a boil.*

"The malignancy of divisiveness, given the chance to creep deeper, would rot us. You need to truly consider that your neighbor's beliefs are as valid as yours, and not disparage or impair those beliefs. Even if your beliefs dictate that you must evangelize, or fight others—not here, and not now. The expedition comes first. The *whole* of us comes first.

"If you find in your heart that you cannot face your gods with that compromise, we will not judge you as lesser, and we will help you pack. The return Gate to Valdemar will be opened one more time so you may be faithful to your beliefs.

"About your beliefs. If you want to make a nod to a god when it occurs to you, or wear your faith's symbols and colors, or wear a sieve on your head and chant at a chicken if you feel like it, go ahead. Just support each other. I don't ask you to *like* everyone you encounter on this journey, but I *demand* that you treat them with respect. Anyone who disparages you for following this rule is going to answer to *me.*" He made a fist with his right hand, and Delia wondered if that was the same fist that he beat the criminal with. "I hope that's clear."

Kordas paused a moment, then resumed with a tone of annoyance, "And I don't want to hear some pedant whine, *'But what if they're a cannibal? Do they get to do what they want?'* or other nonsense to complicate the matter. I don't have time for hypothetical *but whatabouts,* nor do I want any of you to think this is an excuse for bad behavior. Work specifics out with your home-group, your headmen, and your adjudicators."

He let that sink in for a moment, looking around as if he was gazing over the entire lakeside. There was little feedback from that, but Delia counted that as good. *It might mean people are actually thinking about his words, rather than only listening enough to build a rebuttal. I think he's had enough of people who'd work out three arguments against him while he was still speaking, instead of listening to what he said.*

"We are not so naive as to think 'just be nice to each other' can solve all problems. In brutal honesty, this isn't even *about* friendliness at its core, but rather, this is for our *survival*. Heed this message well: *strife between any of us means more risk to all of us.* Inflexible thinking can kill, out here. We are new here—and we are renewed here. We are the ones who must change."

He gestured widely, toward the sun's remaining glow, and spoke in a lower voice. "There, further than you can yet see, the land was ravaged by our ancestors in a terrible war, fought by inconceivably powerful magicians about five hundred years ago. Proximity to that area is what shields us from being found by the remains of the Empire in the east, so obviously, we will go into the west. We will take care to find a good spot, where either the locals *ask* us to stay, or where the land is empty of any intelligent creature that claims it.

"I put much thought into this for years, and examined whether it was truly viable as a policy. I thought through how it could be exploited or twisted, as all things can be. There is a risk to living like this, without any doubt, but looked at from every angle, I found it more than possible. It is *vital*. Yet it is not something that can be made into a *law* without compromising the nature of law itself, and your freedom to live as you will. I call upon you to heed my *wish*. I call you to a *Path*.

"A *Path* is a belief embraced across all religions, toward a worthy goal. Unless we embrace this *essential* rationality, history has shown us that any population will factionalize beyond repair—split by region, by city, by coast or inland, by religion, or by who they love, or fear, or hate. Inflexible rulership over unhappy people shatters nations. The absence of this Path caused deep and deadly flaws in the Empire, leading to, well, what happened to it. Our Path, for the future of our expedition, for the well-being of those we befriend, for the land and spirits, is this.

"There is no one, true way."

The silence around the lake was so deep, and so profound, that all Delia could hear were the few late frogs that were still about, trying to catch the last insects before they buried themselves in the mud for the winter.

"There are many true ways. The unspoken truth of the Empire was that we all lived in terror of being discovered as innovative and exceptional, for that would be the end for us— either taken away to some secret fate in the Capitol, or charged and punished for audacity. We dreaded even making sense in the face of the bureaucracy, and feared the abuse that would come to everyone we loved from daring it. Even inventing a new tool could draw scrutiny for treason, for it showed too much power-threatening free thinking. We lost chances at a better life by the day there. We died of diseases we had cures for, because some noble blocked the cure's production until they could squeeze power from it. We all suffered from obeying a system that would not, and eventually, could not question itself. We all became rigid, and that became a deadly belief in there being only one 'true way' for everything—the Empire's way. I say to you, this is not the Empire.

"Embrace new ways of adapting to strange things. When you find yourself thinking the Imperial way, remember the Path. We are people with a purpose. Ours is not a flood of misery, fleeing all that we knew. This is an evacuation from an empire's collapse, which will become in time a new nation, if we stay together, yet draw the lessons of the new land into us.

"We'll make our journey, we'll support each other, and in the end, we will grow and prosper as the Empire would never allow us to do. Kindness will bring us allies. Tolerance will keep us together and make us stronger. All of us, helping all of us. I *trust* you, people of the Valdemar Expedition. I believe in this Path, I believe in our future, and I believe in you."

That closing hit home, shattering anxieties like they were cracked pottery. Thunderous applause and foot-stamping arose from all directions. He smiled, the sort of smile that could melt ice in the midst of a blizzard and make it happy that it was a liquid now. Kordas gestured and nodded his thanks to those around him, which through the telcaster looked like he was accepting approval and praise from the whole flotilla. Below him were the words, "And I believe in you."

Delia saw Kordas's eyes flick to Beltran, who returned a little smile, nodded once, and readied his pen. *That must be the cue he's done.*

Kordas called for quiet with one more gesture, and said, "Now. The locals made it quite clear that we were welcome as guests, but you all know the saying, *fish and guests stink after three days,* and we've been here rather more than three days. It's time to move on." There were chuckles from his audience, no doubt due to the break in tension that the joke provided.

"Here is Herald Beltran, with today's news and entertainment."

Kordas stepped out of the telcaster's focus and went to Isla's side, joining her and the boys. Beltran, who had made himself the daily news-teller starting with reciting his own terrifying eyewitness account of the Capital falling to the angry Earth Elemental, took his place. He beamed cheerfully around as if he could see every single person around the lake. "Good evening, friends and fellows of the Valdemar Expedition and Beyond! The first news of today is that the Gate on the other side of the marshes, on the north end of the lake, is now up and tested. That means we can begin moving at any moment, so those of you who are ready to start now are asked to unmoor your barges, requisition as many tow animals as you need, and make your way to the west horn of the lake where the exit Gate is. Some of the Guard are already in place on the other side of the marshes to protect you once you come through. Barges will be leaving in strings of eight. If you have less than that number of barges yourself, please organize with someone else to add your barges to their string. . . ."

"That went better than I expected," Kordas said, as Jon snuggled up against his father and promptly fell asleep. "At least no one declared me a tyrant and took a shot at me. I don't see torches, pitchforks, and a burning effigy approaching, either."

He spoke clearly enough that Delia figured his words had not been meant for Isla's ears alone. But she couldn't think of a proper response, so she just laughed a little nervously. "Well, my love, they haven't had time for it to properly sink in yet," Isla pointed out. "In the morning . . ."

"I fully expect we'll have some more people electing to go back," he said into her pause. "That's why I'm keeping the Gate at this end of the lake open a little longer. If anyone has been ignoring the danger this caravan is going into until now, I am pretty certain I made it clear. And if anyone has someone they can't tolerate in the group that's going, they may elect to turn back."

"There are going to be some who will decide by morning that they don't want to go back, but they don't want to go on, either," Isla said thoughtfully. "They'll want to know why we can't stay here, even though you explained it. But I have a suggestion."

Kordas made a little gesture of encouragement, as Beltran talked on in the background.

Isla continued. "I'll ride around to the headmen of the local villages, and get their agreement on how many people they are prepared to allow to make a village of their own here on the lake. When we know that, we'll be ready with an answer if a new lot of people decide they want to stay."

"That's a better solution than I had, which was none, because I haven't had time to think about it," he sighed. "That's why we're good partners. Good plan, and it will be a 'first to ask, first to allow' basis. Once the quota is filled, they must come with us or go back."

"Of course, whatever town or hold they build here, it may be populated by those who want to be hateful, but don't want to go back," Isla half-joked.

"Eternal optimist!" Kordas accused.

Beltran concluded his "town crier" function and yielded the stage to a pair with a fiddle and a gittern. They weren't expert musicians by any means, but they knew their audience and their own abilities, and were pleasant enough to listen to. He came over to join their little group, plopping himself down on a corner of a blanket, next to Delia. "I hope I didn't make a complete hash of that," Kordas said, as he always did.

"You really need to stop saying that," Delia told him. "You always do fine, and it sounds like you are fishing for compliments." That came out a bit harsher than she had intended, but he didn't seem to notice.

"I suppose you're right," he agreed. "I've certainly had enough practice by now that I *shouldn't* be making a hash of it."

Isla *tsk*ed. "Kordas, that was good. You hit all the right notes, and it was honest and sincere. People can tell. I don't think there is going to be much muttering, except from the headaches you just caused by making them think so much. And you've set important precedents— there are fifteen-thousand-something people here who now know what the level of tolerance is going to be and what the ultimate punishment is going to be. Sending scum back to an unknown Imperial destination is better than deciding what warrants an execution."

"I thought about that," Kordas admitted. "And summary execution is *not* off the table in the case of someone caught red-handed in a murder or other High Violation. I'm not at all sure that this sort of exile is more merciful than an execution," he added, sardonically. "But it does have just enough 'escape' built in that I appear merciful and keep my hands clean."

Isla grimaced. "Well, that's something else I can do: I can find out who were the village judges and the like, and pull them into the adjudicator ranks so that when we need them, we have them at hand to do all of the trying and judgments exactly as they did at home. We'll allow appeal to you, but that will mean you aren't the one handing down the verdicts. So far, thank the gods, most people have been kept too busy to get into mischief. Some of them are actually enjoying it."

"Nothing has gotten too bad yet. We've had a few deaths, accidents mainly, a few dozen fistfights and thefts. Who knows how many children have been conceived in the name of emotional comfort," Beltran put in. "That isn't an immediate problem yet. I'll collate the informants' reports an extra time each day, though, just until the dust from your address settles. Better to know where trouble is coming from early."

"Why can't people just *behave* themselves?" Delia blurted. "We have enough problems without—"

But Kordas laughed sardonically. "Because people are people and there are good ones and bad ones and mostly middling ones. Grandfather and Father and I always knew there was a chance we'd get some bad apples along with the good, and we were never able to figure out a test to apply to tell which was which before they made trouble. So we'll have to work things out as we go along, using the model of how the Duchy worked, and somehow apply it to a population that is strung out over a long distance, on the move, and probably in constant danger."

"Well," said a strange, female voice. "At least you've got a firm grasp of things. I was a little afraid that you'd be one of those well-meaning boobies who thinks everyone is good, they're just *misunderstood.*"

"No one who was raised as a hostage in the Capital would ever be under that illusion," Kordas replied, standing up to meet the person coming out of the shadows behind the stage. Two of Kordas's guards, who had been "lounging" nearby, immediately but discreetly stood up too, and casually put their hands on their weapon hilts. But the woman stopped well out of striking distance, and bowed to the Baron. She didn't seem to be one for curtsying, so, probably ex-military.

When she stood up again, she spread her hands wide to show she was unarmed, then clapped slowly. "That was an excellent speech. And with what I've learned since I got here, I think I can assume you mean every bit of it?"

Kordas eyed her. "Don't try me," he warned.

"I have absolutely no intention of doing so," she replied. "Actually I was told to come talk to you in person by your Guard Captain, and once you had finished your speech, this seemed like a good, quiet time. I rather doubt you're going to have anyone itching to speak to you about it until tomorrow at the earliest."

Kordas got to his feet. "Let's find a place to talk."

Kordas left his family to listen to whatever the rest of the evening's entertainment was going to be, and headed for the nearest common kitchen, trailed by the strange woman and flanked by his two guards, who were keeping a sharp eye on her. He noticed that Rose had also detached herself from the family group and joined them. They didn't have too far to go. As he expected, the kitchen was "dark": no one in it, and only the faint warmth from the banked ovens and the yeasty smell of rising bread to tell what the business of the place was in the daytime. He found an empty bucket, overturned it, and sat on it, inviting the woman to do the same, but she remained standing. The guards stood one on either side of her, in easy weapons-reach. Rose joined him. He conjured a small mage-light in his hand and sent it to hover higher than her head, glowing in the air between them, so that they could see each other.

What he saw was a tough-looking woman, a bit short of middle age, if he was any judge. Dark-haired, dark skinned, dark eyed. And . . . wearing an Imperial uniform. A very well-tailored Imperial uniform, so it wasn't stolen, and she was clearly no stupid recruit.

"How did you manage not to get skinned by someone, wearing that?" he asked.

She laughed. "The Valdemar badge your Guard Captain kindly gave me as soon as I was vouched for by my Valdemaran cousin. A lot of us only had the clothes on our backs when we went through, so nobody's too critical of a uniform. Story first, or what brought me to you tonight first?"

He crossed his arms over his chest, and settled into his seat. "Story first. You seem like the type to make a long story as short as possible."

"I'm from Belkenny," she said, which he immediately recognized as a town in the Duchy of Penrake, and just across from the Valdemar border. "I have kin in Briarglen in Valdemar. Name's Master Sergeant Fairweather. I was in the Penrake Guard, and when my two idiot cousins drank too much one night and got tricked into taking the Emperor's penny, with the Duke's permission I enlisted to keep an eye on them." Her generous mouth quirked in a sardonic smile. "Between demonstrations that I know what I'm doing, and a few carefully placed bribes, I managed to become and stay their officer. As I saw it, my job wasn't to be in the army to protect people—it was to protect people from the army. Now as to how I wrangled myself here, we were all on leave visiting my Valdemar kin when we found ourselves part of the biggest mass desertion I have ever heard tell of. Not being eager to get sent to the southern front, I was happy to help them load boats and skid out of there myself. The boys had no idea what was going on, bless their thick skulls, but since I was going, they just followed where I led. That's how I'm here, and that's *why* I'm here, and one of your Dolls has already run everything I just told you and quite a bit more through their truth-sensing, and passed me." She rubbed the side of her nose. "Good man, your Guard Captain. Questioned me right down to the color of my smallclothes."

He considered that a moment, as a few late-staying frogs croaked dismally that autumn was here and winter was coming. "Rose?" he said, not taking his eyes off the woman.

"Everything she has said is the truth, Baron," Rose replied.

He relaxed a trifle. There might still be Imperial agents among his people, but he was fairly certain Sergeant Fairweather wasn't one of them. "All right, then. What can I do for you, Sergeant Fairweather?"

"I'd like me and the lads to be part of your scouting party," she replied. "They've got their hair on fire to go be explorers, because aside from training camp, they've never been farther from home than Briarglen. I promised I'd ask you. What we have to offer is that we're trained soldiers, which you haven't got too many of. The boys are good, and I wouldn't say that if it wasn't true, and I'm better. Bow, crossbow, Spitter, Poomer, sling if we run out of every other sort of ammunition. I think we could probably chuck a spear or two at need. I'm a good swordswoman, the boys are good with axe and shield. We know how to form a pike line, though a pike line of three isn't going to stop much."

It was an attractive offer. The team he had planned for was to be composed of mages, a couple of his Guard, Hakkon and Jonaton (because separating them at this point was going to be impossible), Ivar and Alberdina Endicrag, and whichever of the Dolls wanted to go along, but no actual soldiers. Certainly none with experience handling Spitters and Poomers, and it would be no bad idea to send some of the Spitters and one of the Poomers and some ammunition and balls along. *A Poomer firing chain is an effective way to turn fallen trees into pocket-sized chunks, so it's practical too.*

And suddenly he had an idea. "I accept," he said. "On one condition. I'd like you to take that girl that was sitting with us along."

She gave him an odd look. "Seems a strange choice for a scouting mission."

"Well, she's got that thing they call the 'Fetching Gift.' Seems to me that might be useful if, say, you want a grappling hook set for climbing without making throws until your arm is sore, or you want something brought down from a height or across a river. If you need something from the main flotilla, she can get it for you as long as it doesn't weigh too much. If you need to send something physical to me, she can do that too."

She quirked an eyebrow. "You're leaving something important out." She held up a hand. "Just wait, let me guess. She thinks she's in love with you and you'd really rather she got her mind on anything else but you."

His eyes widened. "How did you—"

Fairweather laughed. "A couple of decades spent among a tribe of siblings and a horde of cousins. Plain as ink. I think it's a good idea. You're right, she *can* be very useful, probably more useful than here. She'll toughen up and have plenty to think about that will exclude romantic dreams, and I am pretty certain you wouldn't saddle your scouts with a spoiled brat."

"She's also good with horses, including the care of them," he pointed out. "That will free up people to do things more important than feeding and watering and rubbing down."

Fairweather snorted. "I'd expect that from your people. What is she to you?"

"My wife's sister." He sighed.

She chuckled. "Which makes things even more difficult, aye, I see it. Well, I don't see any reason to tell you no . . . but does this mean you're putting me in charge of the party?"

"You're an officer, you have experience being in charge," he pointed out. "You've been vouched for. I need someone with the patience and ability to herd cats."

"Baron Valdemar," she said after a moment, with a salute so barely Imperial that it would have enraged a superior officer. "You've got yourself a cat-herder."

Then Rose spoke up, unexpectedly. "We know Sergeant Fairweather and her cousins quite well. They have always treated the Dolls with respect. They are more skilled than she has told you, her cousins are more intelligent than she pretends, and they have a refreshingly mordant outlook on the Empire."

As he was listening to this astonishing pronouncement, the Master Sergeant shrugged. "I'm a realist, and a realist knows the Empire was rotten, so your best bet at survival was to keep your head down, your nose clean, and your ass out of sight of anyone that could send you on a suicide mission."

Rose just offered an opinion. An unsolicited opinion.

But it was an opinion he was inclined to agree with. He very much liked what he had seen and heard from Sergeant Fairweather.

"Turn up here tomorrow morning right after breakfast. We'll take the Gate with the first lot out of here to where the initial scouting party is. I'll be bringing a couple others, and Delia to complete the group."

She saluted: a brisk salute, not fancy, not with an air that she was mocking him either, but this time with only two fingers at her brow. "Will do, Lord Baron." And with that, she stepped off out of the kitchen area toward the other horn of the lake. "Wait," Kordas called, and she stepped back. "What's with the salute?"

"I'm sure not going to give you an Imperial salute. You're Baron Kordas." And she left again.

That was true. By the code, it was a salute he should *not* ever receive, in fact. *I think she just invented the new Valdemaran Salute. It'll help to remind everyone this isn't an Imperial show. I'll make it official tomorrow.*

He rejoined the others, only to find that Isla, the boys, and Delia had gone to their boats. Well, if the weather had been less chilly they might have stayed, but they could hear the music perfectly well from the comfort of the barges if they wanted to listen, and it wasn't as if there was much to see. The two musicians were concentrating so hard on their playing that they appeared to gaze at their shoes the whole time.

He stepped onto his barge and ducked his head to pass through the door.

It had been divided up into rooms in a row, and one side had windows cut into the side, with sliding glass panes and storm shutters fitted into the windows. Mage-lights hung from the ceiling of each room. Ordinary folk with no magic in them had to make do with oil lamps, or lightstones they'd brought along. The first room was all storage: a wardrobe with doors that latched shut, and cabinets, also with doors that latched shut, plus a very small table built into the deck, and a bit of seating with it, built into the bulkhead in a corner under the window, with shelves and hanging hooks above the window and the seating. Isla was positively draconian about keeping everything stored away when it was not actually in use; there was not a sign of the clutter that a person would expect of a place where three small boys were living.

The inside had been painted white, with wooden decking as the floor. There was more storage under the decking, and hatches at intervals to get into the storage.

The second room held a big bed up against the unwindowed wall, with storage under and over it in the form of cabinets and shelves. There were even hooks hanging from the ceiling to make use of every finger-length of space. Isla was waiting for him there. Past that room, he knew, was one with a stove for heat that doubled as a place to cook small things and heat water, a tiny hip-bath that currently held wood for the stove, a drain-sink barely big enough to wash your hands in, more storage, and a closet with a close-stool in it.

And past that was the boys' room, more storage and two beds. The two youngest shared one; they were small enough to fit in it feet-to-feet. Restil got the other to himself, though it was significantly narrower than the other. There was an actual sliding wooden door between that room and the rest of the barge, which was not *quite* thick enough to prevent him from hearing murmurs and giggles.

He had learned early not to fling himself on the bed as was his habit; any sudden movement rocked the barge, and since the barges were all jammed up against one another, had the potential to make it knock into the neighbors. So he slid down onto it instead.

It might have seemed more logical to put the "master's" bedroom at the rear of the barge rather than the front, because this certainly did limit privacy, but he was glad the builders had not. He knew what he had been like at the boys' age, sneaking out in the middle of the night to have adventures . . . but he had mage-locked the sliding glass in place in their room, and to get out, they'd have to get past him and Isla.

"What are they doing back there?" he asked her, a little awkwardly. This was literally the first time since the boys were born that he and Isla had actually lived with them. In order to safeguard them, they'd been passed off as Hakkon's bastards and had been living under the auspices of a nurse and tutor with the other youngsters of the manor; otherwise the Emperor would have demanded their presence at the Capital as hostages, as he had been. The children that the Emperor demanded weren't openly *called* hostages, of course, but that was what they were.

Special students.

He had been one. It had been bad then, and he had gotten the feeling conditions had only gotten worse since he'd been allowed to go home at the death of his father.

"Playing three-man marbles with that set that uses pegs in a tray, that Petrof whittled for them," she said. "I thought it would be a disaster with Jon always losing and crying, but he beats his brothers almost as often as they beat him."

Petrof was the oldest man in his Guard, and by rights he should have been enjoying his old age in a snug little cottage, perhaps with an equally snug little widow to marry and keep his bed warm.

But at least he could put Petrof on the light duty of keeping an eye on the boys and supervising their chores—everyone had chores—and letting him bed down in the second of the baronial barges with some of the other servants.

Still . . . "I hope he doesn't mind what I've assigned him to do, because I never asked him, I just ordered him," Kordas sighed.

Isla laughed. "He loves it. He's teaching them archery already, and getting them to do their letters by reading to him." He piled pillows against the wall and reclined against them. She snugged in next to him. It occurred to him that if only they could stay here, this was probably the happiest he had been in his entire life. Even with having to fight with his temper. All his life the Plan had been hanging over him, like a wave that never fell, or a black storm that moved in but never opened up with a deluge. And so had the Emperor and the Empire loomed, a maze of knives he danced through. Now both of those were gone. He'd done it. He'd saved his people, *and* foiled the Empire. He was under no illusion that the Empire was no longer a threat, it was just no longer an immediate threat.

"Do you think the Empire will forget about us?" she asked, as if she was following his thoughts.

"Well, I'd *like* them to—but the Emperor was just the *most* rotten of the barrel of bad apples," he replied frankly. "And we would be stupid to assume that once all the infighting sorts out, and a survey of all of the territories is made, whoever is in charge is going to overlook that the population of Valdemar is something significantly less than half what it should be."

"But—" she frowned. "Aren't the top men *literally* going to go to war over who sits on the throne?"

"Not if they're smart, they won't," he replied, creasing his brows as a headache started between his eyebrows. "So, they've probably begun it, right? No, the likeliest things to happen are an end to the southern war, followed by the generals down there deciding amongst themselves who to make their leader. The Princes and Grand Dukes are going to start making alliances, but the Emperor kept them short of weapons and soldiers. So what's most likely to happen, at least according to all the strategic things I learned, is that there will be one man from the blooded royals, and one general, and if they are *smart*, they will work out some way to share power between them. Then they'll go consolidate and survey everything else. That's what they've most likely been doing since we got here. Merrin Sends me regular reports, and he hasn't got much to tell me, since his information agents either died in the Capital or have been back at the Duchy with him. All he knows for sure is that things are very quiet. Quiet is not good for us. Actual fighting among the factions would be good for us."

"Actual fighting among the factions would be disaster for the people caught in the middle," she said after a while. "No one suffers in war like the common folk do."

He took her hand in both of his and kissed the back of it.

"So the sands are trickling through the hourglass," he continued. "Now, what I *hope* is, because the alliances are all so fragile, and because they are all involved in an incestuous dance of power, they'll put off looking at the borderlands like Valdemar long enough that by the time they go pay a visit to Merrin and find out that things are not what they are supposed to be, the Gates here will be long gone, and all the people who remain here at the lake will be able to pass themselves off as natives. I won't leave any Golds with them, just a couple of heavy horses, enough to start their own breeding herd, enough to put enough land under a plow that the whole village can stay fed. So there won't be anything overt to identify anyone here as Valdemaran."

"Can the mages trace us here?" she asked.

"What I said about the Mage War territories was true—we found Crescent Lake by luck. If we'd actively looked for it, the territories would have confused targeting. So that helps us. We left more than enough things behind that they could come after us using those objects as links to locate us," he reminded her. "Now . . . do they still have mages good enough to construct an entirely new Gate to here? I don't know. But I'm not willing to tell anyone that they can't. There were still plenty of competent people in the Empire, even with the Capital destroyed. If anything, the most competent ones stayed out of the Capital." He made a motion as if he was tipping an hourglass. "Time is not on our side." He thought a moment longer. "But Merrin *will* warn us if he learns anything."

"That's a comfort. I take back every evil thing I ever said about that man." She kissed his hand.

He laughed. "Oh, he's ambitious, and he's tickled to be a Duke after all, and we didn't exactly strip the countryside bare when we left. He's got the barge-makers, who all stayed. That's a reliable source of income. There were still crops in the fields, and plenty of herds that stayed there—he's in a very good position to make some shrewd alliances himself. Fundamentally he seems to be a good man, and the Dolls agree with me on this. Hellfires, for all I know, he has some plan to throw anyone who figures out we deserted off of our track. He gulled me for years, so I expect he can pull the wool over other eyes than mine."

"Oh, I don't know," she said slyly. "I've always found it quite easy to gull you."

"Wench." He took a moment to cast his ear in the direction of the end of the barge—and sadly, could still hear talking and giggles. Alas. He settled for kissing the top of her head, a private signal that said *I would really like to have some fun with you, but three large-eared imps would be certain to break out of their room wanting a snack or a drink.*

She sighed. And as if on cue, the door to the last room slid open. "Mama!" called Restil as he tumbled out, followed by the other two. "Can we have some clover tea?"

"You can have some water," she countered. "Remember what I keep telling you. We need to be careful about the things we use. Wood, food, everything. You won't want to be shivering in the cold later because we burned wood to heat the water for tea now."

"Yes, Mama," Restil said with resignation, and although Kordas could not see them from where he was lying, he could certainly hear the boys when they went to get their water. And they were surprisingly mannerly. Restil remained firmly in charge of the water jug, and insisted they use only one cup, each in turn, to keep from dirtying more that would have to be washed later.

"Who kidnapped our children and left changelings?" he asked her, although he could practically feel his heart swelling with pride and joy. The boys had accepted the information that he and Isla were their real parents, and not Hakkon, with a matter-of-fact attitude that made him think the two oldest at least had figured it out on their own and had realized that the deception was keeping them safe. And they had flung themselves into being a *family* with all the enthusiasm he could ever have dreamed of.

"It's exhaustion. They spent the entire day gathering deadfall with Petrof, and every day they have to go farther to find any. Just like everyone else." She patted his cheek. "But at least that leaves all the children run off their feet by the end of the day."

They didn't say anything else as the children put everything away, went back to their room, and slid the door shut. And when the murmurs grew sleepy, and then grew silent, with a single thought he extinguished the rest of the mage-lights and turned his attention to much more pleasurable things than worries about the Empire.

Quietly.

4

The next day, Kordas held an actual Court. He set himself up in a seat at the prow of his family barge, using a piece of stump discreetly covered with a fancy blanket, and told the Dolls to let it be known that in light of last night's speech, he would hear the petitions of anyone who had changed their mind about going "home." He was making a formal exercise of it this time; until now, anyone could leave without asking for permission. All they had to do was show up at the Gate, which was locked to the one in Valdemar near the barge-maker.

And he'd intended to have that Gate dismantled this morning, but after yesterday, he was going to give people who had gotten a sudden case of cold feet a final chance to leave. But this time, he was going to exercise his authority as Baron and make them ask him for it. And there was something more, something that as Baron, he needed to do. And for that, he needed Dolls and his Guard. As he prepared his improvised "seat of state" in the wan autumnal sunshine and ate still-warm bread and a handful of nuts and small, wild apples, he explained to Rose what he was going to do.

"We can arrange that, Baron," she said, with that uncanny calm the Dolls never lost. "I will make sure it is done."

As he expected, before he'd finished eating his breakfast, there was a queue of people waiting, arriving one at a time to line up politely just off the path that ringed the lake. Not as many as he had feared. And no one that he knew personally, which would have been very awkward indeed. He relaxed a little bit. This was a good time to hold his "court," since most people were still getting their food at the communal kitchens, and there wouldn't be a lot of gawkers around.

He took his seat, glad for the heavy knit tunic that was over his linen shirt. It wasn't Court garb by any means; in fact, it wasn't much of a step above what everyone else was wearing. Virtually all of the "good" clothing he had was packed up in one of the storage barges, and by look he couldn't have been told from one of his servants. But that "commoner's clothing" was all to the good on two counts—first, it was doing an excellent job of keeping the chill breeze at bay, and second, it brought home to everyone that he lived no better here than any of them, and he was prepared to share their hardships. Indeed, he already was.

"Well," he said, as leaves drifted down from the trees and the breeze carried the bitter scents of the ones already fallen toward him. "Let's begin." He heard the first petitioner, who stammered out his request to leave, blaming his wife's supposedly sudden "bad feelings" about the expedition. Kordas listened gravely, then nodded. "You can leave, of course. I've not stopped anyone from leaving before, and I don't intend to now. However, everything that is not part of your personal household belongings will be staying with us. This especially includes food."

The man—and everyone else in line—gaped at him.

"You know quite well that there were crops still in the fields back home that are awaiting harvest," Kordas continued blandly. "You aren't going to starve, and you're going to find plenty of seed-stock waiting for you. But we *might* starve, and we will need every grain of wheat and turnip where we are going. I certainly won't demand the tools of your trade, but if there are duplicates, we'll be having them, too. And firewood. And if you have uncut fabric, we'll be having that as well. You can take just enough of your herds, if you have any, to start again, but no surplus. I'll give you each a voucher for three barges from the makers, which you can sell to compensate for what we're taking. They can use those vouchers to pay their Ducal taxes. There will be a Doll and a Guard waiting for you back at your boats to assist you in separating your personal belongings from the food and other things that we are going to need. You will be more than compensated for the losses by the barges you have and the three new ones. And, as of today, *all* food will be held in the common store."

He had put on that face that said to anyone looking at him that "there will be no argument here."

He was quite good at reading body language, and he could tell that while the folks waiting to be given permission to go did not like this proclamation in the least, they were not going to argue about it. He'd explained exactly what he meant to Rose earlier.

"I'm not talking about that rare bottle of wine someone is saving for a special occasion, nor about someone's private hoard of sweets. I *am* talking about enough food to supply a family over the winter, and seed-stock for planting in the spring, and if it seems to you that they have more of anything than they are likely to need, you'll take it. After all, my family paid for every one of the barges here, and I am letting them keep all the ones they need to hold the things we're not taking. Plus three more when they get back. Especially we need food that will keep well or is otherwise preserved. That will go into the stocks for the common kitchens, so everyone who stays will benefit."

He was well aware that while people were supposed to be getting all their meals from the common kitchens, there were some who were cooking for themselves. Not many, because it was hard to cook on those tiny barge stoves, but enough that he knew not everyone had turned over the food they had brought with them to the common store. And he hadn't demanded that before. Now he was. There might be trouble from some of the nobles, merchants, and people of relative wealth, he was sure, but . . . they had the option to leave if they didn't like it, and they would *still* lose the food.

Food was not one of the things that his father and grandfather had thought much about when they made the Plan, probably because they expected that when the escapees took the Gate to other parts, they'd be *staying* where they'd found themselves, and that they were not going to find any other humans around. According to the original Plan, his father, grandfather, and he had all assumed they'd be Gating straight into wilderlands. Once there, the Plan assumed they would have one short growing season to get in gardens, and thanks to the preparations the Duke's family had made, they would all have plenty of grain and other long-term stores to see them through to spring.

Well, there was plenty of grain and other long-term stores, but they were not going to settle in for a long, mostly sedentary winter. They were going to be on the move. Now, in one way, that was good; forage for the animals wasn't going to run low. But in every other way, it was a problem; moving people needed more food than sedentary people, and people working out in the cold rather than huddled up in their barges would too.

Hence, the sudden edict.

It didn't go over *well*, but he hadn't expected it to. There were long faces, and a little grumbling, and some sour looks cast his way, but no one tried to argue with him.

And they all still wanted to leave anyway.

When the last of the petitioners had gone, he remained where he was, knowing that as the Doll-and-Guard pairs spread out among the barges and began making inspections for foodstuffs, he was going to get some blow-back from the nobles and wealthy.

And he did.

In fact, within a mark, they had organized themselves into a group, chosen a leader, and confronted him, still seated on his stump, as a united front.

He listened impassively while the leader made his argument, which basically consisted of "we aren't peasants and we don't intend to live like peasants," though it was couched in better language than that. All this went on in blithe indifference to the growing crowd of those "peasants" who were watching and listening, possibly expecting him to take their side. And when the leader—the middle-aged Lord Portrain—was finished, Kordas allowed silence to fill the space. Of course everyone within earshot had been paying very close attention to what was said, and there were a *lot* of people within earshot.

And most of them were . . . "peasants." Belatedly, the assembled group began to realize that they had an audience for their grievances besides Kordas, and that audience was looking stormy.

Finally Kordas spoke.

"Lord Portrain. What have I done with my horses?" he asked .

"Uh—" The man had pulled himself up and puffed up his chest, prepared to refute whatever Kordas said next. But he hadn't expected this, and he promptly deflated, caught off guard by the unexpected question.

"What have I done with my horses?" he repeated. "I'll tell you. I've put them out for common use in pulling everyone's barges, from the Tow-Beasts to my Golds. All of them except for my riding horse, my wife's, and my ward's. Two of those will be pulling *our* barges; the third isn't even a yearling yet, and is not up to work. *All* of our food is in the common store. Every bit of it. I didn't even keep sweets for my children. *All* of the manor's crops are in the common store. We are not concealing cakes and hams under the floorboards. I am not telling any of you to do anything *I haven't already done for the common good of us all."*

He let that linger for a moment. "Now, the Gate is still open. You can leave. Like the others that left today, your foodstuffs will stay, but you can leave. No one will take as much as a speck of gilding from you, just food and the *common* things that *common* people will be needing. I won't even demand that you turn your personal weapons over to the Guard, though the gods know we need them. I won't force you to leave your servants with us. But either way, stay or go, your food stays with us."

Lord Portrain opened his mouth, and closed it again.

"Now, I want you to understand, I am not only doing this for the common good, I am doing it for your protection." Portrain blinked at that, and some of the others actually looked startled, and started to glance around at the people who were listening to this conversation. The startlement turned to vague alarm at the sour looks being directed their way. "I am going to spin you a tale. It's not a wild tale. It's not an unlikely tale. It is, in fact, something that could all too easily come to pass."

He turned his gaze on all of them, catching and holding their eyes, before moving on to the next, letting his jaw set and his expression harden. "Imagine, if you will, that ice has stopped us from moving, and because of the terrain, we can't haul the barges out of the water and put them on runners to use as sleds. We are stuck where we are, like it or not, until spring. We are not running out of food—quite—but rations are short, tempers are flaring, stomachs are emptier than is comfortable—and then someone gets a whiff of frying sausages or spiced cider. They get their friends. They track the smell down. It's coming from *your boat.* Now, when everyone else is eating boiled wheat and a scrap of meat or fish at every meal, *what do you think that hungry, unhappy mob of people is going to do to you when they discover how well you've been eating while the rest are doing without?*"

He paused again to let them think hard about that. And look at the faces around them. There were murmurs now, but not from the delegation of the privileged. From the commoners who were muttering to each other, things like "damn right," and "what he said."

"*Of course* the Guard will come to your rescue. You weren't guilty of a crime, just a bit of selfishness. But that rescue won't be immediate, now, will it? Because the Guard will be strung out all up and down the line of barges. It will take time before enough of them can assemble to help you." He nodded at their stricken expressions. "On the other hand, if you go back to your barges, and start piling up foodstuffs on the bank to be taken to the common store, well, people will only recall when times do get hard that you were generous with what you had, when times were easier. Have I made myself clear?"

Portrain swallowed visibly and audibly. "Perfectly, my Lord Baron," he managed, after a glance at the others drew slight nods of agreement.

"Again, if you want to go back to the Duchy, Merrin will welcome you. And I truly, sincerely hope you all prosper, and the Empire remains a distant cloud on the horizon, and nothing worse than an annoyance at tax time. But remember what I have told you before this. The likeliest outcome of what happened when the Capital was flattened by that monster is that the infighting over the Imperial Crown has already taken place, and the victor is consolidating his position. He will eventually be looking to the outer reaches of the Empire to supply his needs. And those needs are likely to include men for his army. You have servants and sons you would rather not give up, most of you. And I have no doubt you have plenty of other things you'd rather not have seized. But the old Emperor didn't ask, he took, and I doubt that the new one is going to change that policy. If you are prepared to dance the same gigue I did to preserve your wealth and your families, good luck. If you'd rather take your chances with us, then you are as welcome as you were when you first got here." He gave a final nod, signaling that the audience was at an end, and stood up. They took the hint, and left.

He turned back to the barges to see that Isla and Delia had both been listening. Delia looked stricken. "Do you think that would really happen?" she asked in a small voice. "I mean, that's nothing we ever talked about before."

"We never talked about having to move on, once we got to what we presumed would be a sanctuary, either," he pointed out. "Father and grandfather never envisioned that. So I am forced to revise the plan."

At just that point, Ivy turned up with Arial, already saddled and bridled, as he had asked her to do through Rose this morning. "Going off to talk to the village headmen?" Isla asked.

He mounted, and nodded once he was seated, with Ivy pulled up to perch on the pillion behind him. *What one Doll knows, we all know* had turned out to be a godsend. Ivy would relay anything he needed Isla to know back to the camp, and Isla could tell that to the families that didn't want to move on. "Hopefully the number of people they are willing to accept for a new lake village will not be fewer than the number of people who want to stay. If it is?" He shrugged. "I'll think of something."

Without a doubt, some of the more thorny souls will stay back solely so they don't have to give up their hate and prejudices, he thought grimly. *I'm optimistic, but I'd be a damned fool to think anyone was above human nature because they're "mine." Nor should I think their bravery is without limit. This might be as far as they will go.* A great mistake that any leader could fall prey to was thinking that because anyone under their charge has done one thing successfully, they will always do it again the same way. Every effort made would lose people, due to their individual lives and crises, so efforts must be maintained with morale as much as any other resource. *The nearest anyone can get with followers is to improve their likelihood of excellence, and accept when they fall short, without scolding them. Scolding them only makes followers remember the scolding—it doesn't change their hearts enough. Only the follower can do that, and for a smart leader, that is best done by ensuring that your way is clearly an actual better way. That means anticipating problems and having solutions ready. A wise leader plans for failures—an inspired leader turns failures into new forms of success.*

The Empire had made even thinking of Imperial failure a seditious act. When leaders were discouraged from even planning for accidents, then ongoing consequences from accidents were inevitable. *It hurts every day, thinking of what I did. It is so hard to push back what happened, but I know, as consolation, that something else would have happened with the same results—and with far fewer people escaping. What scares me now is, did I bring everyone here to die in a new place, rather than give them the comfort of living their last days in their old homes?*

Kordas had never given so many life-altering commands in such a short time, and it was already an undeniable strain upon him. As tiring as it was, he knew he had to give the mental cost its due, or he'd break unexpectedly.

Plan on exhaustion? That's my plan?

———

Kordas got a consensus from the villages around the lake pretty quickly. "Forty families, at most," was the verdict; they reckoned any more than that would mean there would not be enough fish to go around without depleting the breeding stock. In a way, that rather cheered him. These people were careful stewards of their land, and he made clear to them that they were the ones in charge—and that they had the authority to make certain any people he left here would do the same.

He was also mindful of a frank exchange with the town's warrior-leader. "We see what you are," he had stated bluntly. "We know that you could remove every trace of us, if you wished to. You could take our homes, animals, crops, children, and sacred places. We would curse you and die fighting you. Even others of our kind would do so, given the chance and your forces. That you would consider our wishes honors us, and it saves many lives. You are a fact in our world now, and our future has been forever altered by your choices. May we see your face again some day, still as wise as now."

To Kordas's great relief, Ivy was able to report on the way back that thirty-seven families wanted to settle at the lake, seventy-two families were leaving, and everyone was pulling out personal food stores and other goods and leaving them to be collected with, if not good will, at least the understanding of his reasoning.

"Everyone," Ivy said insistently, with an emphasis that sounded like Rose.

"Huh. I suppose word must have traveled fast, and people took that little story of mine to heart," he said out loud over the clopping of Arial's hooves.

"That is what your lady says. She also says that those barges that have been emptied of food while we have stayed here at the lake are now going to be full again." Ivy's breathy voice in his ear could not have uttered more welcome words.

Well, that's one crisis averted. Now to go on to the next. I wonder just what kind of a tempest I am going to cause by ordering Delia to go with the scouts?

Delia stared at Kordas, her mouth falling open. "I'm—what?" Delia said, feeling stunned, even as her sister said at the same time, "She's *what?*"

Kordas had gathered them both up and brought them into the barge's tiny sitting area while Ivy took Arial back to be penned with the other horses. Now she knew why he had done that. This was not something he wanted to have an audience of strangers for.

Slowly and carefully, as little wavelets made tiny slapping sounds against the hull of the barge, Kordas laid out his reasoning, point by point.

But she couldn't help but wonder—had he noticed her attraction to him? They'd been living practically on top of each other ever since they got here, and surely her control must have slipped now and again.

If he had—well, this didn't hurt as much as an outright rejection would have, but it certainly made *his* feelings clear.

Kordas caught her eye. "Delia, you managed just fine in the mage's camp when we were setting up the Gate," he said. "In fact, everyone says that you were welcome, and did your share and more. You're actually going to be with the one group that is going to find food—wild food, at least—plentiful, so you'll eat better than we do. Hakkon says you do very well with a hand-crossbow, but you could probably knock ducks and geese out of the sky and tree-hares out of the branches with your Gift, and that will certainly be welcome." He turned back to Isla. "There are going to be three trained soldiers from the Imperial Army with the group, as well as Hakkon and Ivar. I'm going to send Spitters and at least one Poomer with them. Delia has Fetching Gift, which means that if something needs to be brought from the main group, or sent to me, as long as it isn't something heavy, she can do it. And that Gift can be used in a dozen other different ways that Sergeant Fairweather thought of when I suggested it. She's good at tending the horses, and that will free up someone who is bigger and stronger for guard duty and other jobs that need more strength and muscle." Kordas paused. "Delia, if you really loathe this idea, I won't make you go. But you can do all of us a lot of good if you take the task on. And I am completely confident not only in your abilities, but that the group will be better off with you than without you."

So . . . she thought about it. Really thought about it for a moment. *I won't have to watch the boys anymore. I won't be mending, or patching, or anything* nearly *as tedious, except for my own things. I like Hakkon, and Jonaton is very, very funny. Ivar and Alberdina are nice, and I can learn more about healing—herbs and things—from Alberdina, and I'd like that.*

Maybe it wouldn't be all bad to be away from Kordas. When he'd been in the Capital, the constant ache of seeing him with her sister had vanished. There was still the ache of not being with him *herself,* but at least it had only been one source of pain rather than two. Now—oh, it was hard, so hard, when they were all living and eating together without the formality they'd had before. It gave her stabs of actual pain when they would look at each other and there was clearly much more going on between them than there had been before he'd gone to the Capital. Isla was not her rival for Kordas—she was Isla's rival. But she was completely outclassed, and unless something awful happened to the Lady Baron—

I don't have a chance. And I don't want anything awful to happen to my sister!

And one more strange little thought occurred. *And if it did . . . I would be completely responsible for those boys. I'm—I'm not sure having Kordas to myself would be worth that.*

"Ivar has traveled all alone in the wilderness in the deep winter several times already," Kordas was continuing, this time to Delia. "He knows what it takes to stay comfortable and healthy, and he's making all the arrangements." His tone turned coaxing. "I know you've been bored here. I can promise you absolutely will not be bored out there."

That clinched it. "Why not?" she said, raising her chin. "Your decisions have held as good as your luck, so far. It sounds like a fine plan to me."

"Excellent!" He beamed at her, and she felt her heart clench, though she did her best to smile brightly. "Most of the scouting group is back; we only needed to leave a couple of guards and one mage to watch the receiving Gate. So let's go tell them the news and see what they have to say."

Isla looked from her husband to Delia and back again, then shrugged. "Well, at your age I'd have leapt to have an adventure, and you're surely going to have that. I'd trust Hakkon and Ivar with my life, and they will certainly take care of yours. Don't worry, love, I'll make sure you are properly packed up for this." Her face grew thoughtful. "In fact, there's that ridiculous fur-lined cape-of-state I think I've worn twice packed in the storage barges. I'll ask one of the girls where it is and we'll cut it up and sew it into two over-tunics, one for you and one for me."

Delia felt a pang of guilt to think that Isla was going to sacrifice that magnificent ermine-lined cape for someone who—well, never mind. That "someone" was going to be going away shortly, and would no longer be any kind of temptation to the Baron. Kordas rose, and so did she. "Let's ride," she said, knowing that by riding they would be cutting any time they might have for talking severely short. Right now, the last thing she wanted to hear from Kordas was more praise about how much good she was going to do, and how pleased he was that she was leaving him—no, sorry, going along with this plan.

I can't deny that this hurts. Other side of the world for all I know, and still infatuation is hard to let go of. I imagined so many things with him. He . . . thought about my feelings, at least, so I made a good impression on him.

This is the right thing to do.

Doing the right thing doesn't always feel good, though.

———

The mage camp was almost identical to the one that had been at the center of the lake-crescent when she had first come through, with the exception that there didn't seem to be any ruins at this end. The river that ran into the point of the crescent here drained right out of the swamp they were going to have to bypass, and so was bursting with fish, crawfish, and frogs even now.

Bursting rather less with frogs than it had been when the camp was set up. Sai's new apprentice, a young, balding man called Venidel, had turned out to be quite the expert frog-"gigger"—that was what he called himself, anyway—and absolutely no one in the camp ever turned down a dish of Sai's frog legs. Nothing went to waste, of course, because the rest of the frog became bait for crawfish and fish. Even the frog skin was dressed to make condoms, as were animal intestines, turtle membranes, and eel skins. They were in demand, considering at this point most of the expedition had little else to do, and babies were definitely *not* wanted at this point.

As they rode up into the camp, Sai hailed them cheerfully from the camp kitchen. "Crawfish stew over boiled wheat?"

"Yes, please!" Kordas replied, before Delia could say anything. "Breakfast seems to be three days ago."

Sai waved them over to the area in the middle of the camp where the common kitchen had been set up. Before it had gotten so cold, flat-topped ovens with curious chimneys at one end had been created using rocks, mortar, mud, and magic to bind it all together, in order to maximize the amount of heat they could get out of their fuel. The local villagers had been intrigued by the unique design of their bread ovens, because they used so little fuel—and in fact, they were doing quite well, still, just using windfall. Even the tiniest little scrap of a twig was useful. Delia didn't understand it at all, but something about the way that the stoves were built made them use very little wood and store heat for a very long time. Sai had told them how to make the ovens without using magic, and now there was at least one in every village, and because of how well they radiated steady heat, the villagers were making plans to put them in every house. In kind, the villagers had taught the expedition which creatures, fungi, and vegetation were edible, as well as recipes for them.

Pots and pans were always on those flat tops, heating water for washing and tea, and cooking things that were best done "low and slow," while bread went in when the ovens were hottest following their morning firing, and meats got roasted slowly in their own juices and Sai's bone broth once the day's bread was out. Nobody fried anything anymore, and no one cooked over open flames, at least not in the encampment. And certainly no one wasted *anything*, not just fuel. Even turnip and carrot tops went into stew, chopped fine. Vegetables were scrubbed, not peeled, as Delia knew very well, having scrubbed more than she cared to count.

Well, even if I still have to do that, there won't be nearly as many of them.

Sai and his brother Ceri were dishing up the crawfish stew onto the herbed boiled wheat in the bread bowls. They were both stern-looking, usually silent, with massive white eyebrows and long, straight white hair. Ceri wore his in a tail on the top of his head. Sai used to wear his unbound and combed until it looked like a fall of ice. Not since they came here, though. Now he had it braided down his back. *I guess it was too much trouble to keep loose when we're all crammed into little boats and running around outdoors all day,* she thought; she'd felt the same, but her reaction had been to have her sister chop it all off at about chin length, and keep it trimmed that way.

She and Kordas took their bread bowls and got their spoons off their belts. And that was another change: now, everyone kept a spoon and a small all-purpose knife with them at all times, and cleaned it for themselves after eating. No one ate off plates, or even bowls. The fewer things that needed cleaning—or could be lost or broken—the better.

"So," said Sai, motioning to his brother to stir the pot. "Dole is on magic duty on the other side of the new Gate today, along with a handful of your Guard, but I assume you'll be putting together a permanent scouting party now that we are leaving for good?"

Kordas nodded. "You assume correctly."

There was a cluster of cut-off sections of tree trunk along the back side of the ovens, so that people could sit and put their backs to the warm—was it clay?—of the sides of the ovens while they ate. They all sat there, Sai in the middle. All of the Six Old Men (as Kordas called them) tended to dress similarly, in practical, hardwearing trews and loose tunics in muted browns and grays. Now that it was colder, those tunics were heavily quilted, and she suspected the trews were layered over lighter trews. Sai's tunic had something special: the outline of a dragonfly quilted into the back.

Delia dug into her food without hesitation. The cooks at the common kitchens varied from adequate to competent, but Sai and Ceri were something extraordinary when it came to cookery. She was always glad to eat here. Even the boiled wheat was delicious.

"I assume you want me along?" Sai continued. "We ought to have at least three mages; my apprentice and I can be two of those, but do you want one of us Six Old Farts besides me?"

"Didn't Endars train in things that would be useful for a scout?" Kordas asked. *As if he didn't already know. I think he knows what every single mage in the camp can do.*

"He can mind-ride on birds, yes, yes, yes. And he's good at fires. Putting them out, starting them, throwing fireballs. He can light up a pine cone and toss it. If the party gets stuck somewhere with the wettest of fuel, he can make it burn." Sai wrinkled his nose. "He's a terrible cook, though. He thinks meat should be charred on the outside and raw on the inside."

Kordas chuckled. "That would be why we'd have you along."

Sai preened a little. "Well, of course! And I assume Jonaton; that will be four experienced mages, and Jonaton is very good at Gates. That will make up for the rest of his shenanigans."

"He won't be 'borrowing' from you any more, Sai, at least on the scouting party. You won't have anything with you that he won't have himself," Kordas pointed out.

"Hmm, true, true, true. And Jonaton means Hakkon, and I like to have a good slab of beef between me and trouble." He cackled. "So who else?"

"Alberdina and Ivar, and three people you don't know. Former Imperial fighters, a Sergeant Fairweather and her two cousins. At least one Doll, maybe two." Kordas paused. "And Delia."

"Oh! *You're* going!" Sai exclaimed, turning toward her. "Oh, I can think of a lot of ways you can be useful! You were a great help when we put the Gate down here, and who knows? There might be some actual talent for magic in you! We can find out!"

Delia was relieved to hear that out of Sai; he didn't suffer fools *at all,* and he never gave out compliments if he didn't truly mean them.

"I wish we could take cats," Sai continued, a little wistfully. "Aside from the fact that I'll miss them, there is nothing like a cat blanket on a cold night." He shrugged. "Oh well. Ceri will take care of them, just like the last time. Even Jonaton's Black Terror."

"I would *almost* say to take Sydney-You-Asshole, except that he probably is under the impression he can take on a bear, and

Jonaton would be heartbroken if anything happened to him," Kordas responded.

"Too risky." Sai shook his head. "What if we have to abandon the boats? The anti-wandering charm is centered on the boats."

Delia knew—because she'd helped—that one of the first things that had been done whenever any animals came through the Gate to arrive at the lake was to put on them what Sai called an "anti-wandering charm." Pets literally could not go more than six furlongs from their home boat. The same went for ducks, geese, and chickens, although *their* "home boat" was the one that served as their roost at night. Those charms also impelled them to go into their home boat at sunset and remain there until sunrise. The larger animals had charms that their herders carried so they could not wander further than six furlongs from their handler by day, and would follow the handler into a corral for safety at night. Delia had helped by marking every animal that got the charm on it with a splotch of white or green paint on the top of its head, so they knew that all of them had been taken care of.

"You saw my speech?" Kordas was asking.

"It was a good one! Well done! So how many more did we lose?" Sai said this as if he expected it. Which he probably did. He was very old, one of the oldest people Delia knew, and people seldom did anything that surprised him.

"Not that many. Seventy-odd families. And there are thirty-seven families that asked for and got permission from the locals to make a new village out of the ruins we found when we got here."

"Good, good, good." Sai's head bobbed. "Well, I am sorry that poor Doll was hurt, but I am glad this happened. The more weak and wavering parties we can shed before we leave, the better. And

I am certain we have a few more brutes amongst us, but this will make them think twice about throwing their weight around, or bullying anyone."

"That was more or less my thought." Kordas glanced over at Delia. "Do you mind if Delia joins you up here with her things? It will be easier for her to leave from here."

She hoped she managed to control the pang those words gave her. *He's trying to get rid of me already?* But—if he had guessed how she felt, *her* presence was probably making *him* feel uncomfortable.

"Not at all, not at all! She can stay in the boat Alberdina and this Sergeant of yours are going to use! It's empty right now, but there's four beds and the rest of it's fitted up for an infirmary for Alberdina." He cackled again. "It'll be the most privacy she's had since we got here, I venture to say!"

Well . . . that's true. She brightened a little.

"How long do you think it will be before we move out?" Sai continued.

"Not less than three days, not more than six," Kordas said, pulling thoughtfully on his mustache for a moment. "We need to be Weatherwise about it. I want to get the advance guard through the Gate first, and the scouts on the other side back. You'll go right after the guards have done a thorough sweep of the area."

"Good! Delia, you can help me in the kitchen until we move. Ceri will be happy to be off chopping duty." He made a shooing motion. "Go, get your personal gear. Ivar was very particular about how he wanted the scouting gear set up, and he and a half dozen Dolls have been working at it since we knew Kordas was going to be all right, so you won't need to concern yourself about preparing for cold weather."

Oh—she knew about that! At least some of it, because Kordas and Isla had discussed the plans over dinner many times. On reflection, Ivar had decided that the advance party needed to sleep in boats at night. The barge shells were incredibly tough, and they could probably take being frozen solid into the ice if the river froze over. And it would not be hard to fit the runners he'd had made to the hulls so that they could be hauled over land like sledges if the river they were following had a patch a barge couldn't traverse, or dwindled down to nothing.

But as for the people—Ivar had had sleeping "sacks" made of a patchwork of every sort of fur that came off of an animal they killed for food, from a tree-hare to the couple of bears and wild boars they had taken down. They were made with the fur inside, and additionally, there was a second quilted sack that fit over the fur one. Between the boats keeping them from the wind, their own bedding, and these sleeping sacks, Delia was fairly confident they'd be comfortable enough at night, even without a fire in the wood stove.

As for day, he'd had similar oversized "tunics" with hoods made. Those would go over your clothing and coat if the weather was too bad for the coat alone.

"No one is bringing a cloak," he had said firmly. "All that flapping around in the wind! Cloaks are only for people who want to look impressive."

"So expect Jonaton in one," Kordas laughed. By now Ivar not only had more than enough of both for the number of people going, he had enough to start distributing them around the encampment. All the mages had them, for instance, and after them, the Healers all had the sleep sacks for any patients and the hooded tunics for themselves. If anyone was grumbling about the mages and Healers getting preferential treatment, Delia hadn't heard about it.

Then again . . .

You don't want a Healer annoyed with you. They don't have to be nice *when they treat you, just competent.* And it wasn't as if by now people didn't know how to make these things for themselves. There would be more skins to tan and turn into warm bedding and clothing as they moved along, too, because Kordas was surely planning on hunting as they moved.

"I'll go get my things," she said, standing up.

"All your cold-weather clothing, the bedding you really want, and bring a couple of sets of warm-weather clothing." At Kordas's raised eyebrow, Sai just shrugged. "We don't know what's out there. We might go through a valley of summer, and then wouldn't we wish we weren't wearing wool and fur!"

"Yes, Sai," she said, and got her horse for the ride back to pack.

5

Kordas personally saw the last of the returnees off—at least partly to reassure them that there were no hard feelings, and that no one blamed them for deciding that an uncertain trek into a likely dangerous wilderness, on short rations, in an unknown winter, was not for them. The Gate had been moved slightly after they had all arrived. In the beginning it had been planted at the edge of the water, and every craft in the flotilla splashed down, bringing Imperial water with them. *May the gods of water and reeds forgive us for what we brought here.* Kordas knew from the ways of farms that any kind of new bug, fish, or waterscum introduced to someplace would have cascading effects. *Another part of the Plan that wasn't thought out enough.*

Now the Gate was actually *in* the water, so that people could have their barges shoved straight through. He was making them pole their way, however. The boat- and barge-strings were forming up for the next part of the journey, and the expedition needed every horse they had. That was fine. Merrin knew they were coming, as evidenced by the canal-people he could see on the distant shore.

A breeze blew around him from the Gate. It bore Valdemar's scents.

Realization struck him, with a clutch in his chest, that the landscape he saw through the opened Gate could be his last glimpse of his homeland. It was sobering, enough that he had to step away for a while. *That is my birth home. That will always be my home. Not just "mine" in the sense that it's a personal home, but as its Duke. Well—Baron. My rulership.*

Kordas absently made a hand gesture derived from blowing dandelion seeds. *Whatever I am now, in a land with no standings or titles for comparison. I think I'll choose "King" when we're successfully established. If you ever get to name your rank, don't stop at "Baron."*

He laughed to himself at that, but only briefly. *My responsibility will always be based upon what I was there, I think. I can't imagine myself not putting the people of Valdemar first, but I have to be realistic. Nothing stings later like a hesitant action. I've already felt it here at the Lake—as dire as things could be, part of me still feels like I'm taking thousands of my people on a camping trip, and that Valdemar is just—behind a tree. Over there. I haven't cut myself off from thinking like I'm still based there and I'm missing the place that I just—abandoned. No, wait.*

No.

Believed in.

Even if three-quarters of the expedition were here solely for evil deeds, the remaining quarter's belief in what Valdemar means would overcome anything dire. As much as I frame my thinking in terms of a nation, what we are is a tribe. A resourceful tribe that has brought its bravery and faith as tools more powerful than swords or shovels. I've said it many times, but at this moment, I intensely know what is right—that Valdemar is a people, not a place. I believe these people can make our future incredible. I know they'll tackle any obstacle.

Valdemar's passion, its potential, and its past lives in me, and it's as much a part of me as the grain of my muscles and the strain of my brow. I will be Valdemaran, wherever I go.

I hope. Oh gods, how I hope.

He took a few more breaths before turning back to face the sweet smell of the Valdemar he'd known, and the breeze went with him as he rode away, quickly enough that nobody would see his face was wet.

Furlongs later, Kordas decided that he was satisfied with the proto-village he was going to leave to the thirty-seven families who had elected to stay. Those shells of ruined buildings had been improved considerably, although if *he* had been planning on remaining here, he'd have just spent the winter in his barge. He'd already given orders about what provisions from the common stores he was going to leave with them, and between that and the lake full of fish, they would be fine. There were a good two-dozen stone houses standing here at the center of the crescent that now had proper roofs and half-finished floors, thanks to the efforts of anyone who had a moment or two to spare, and that pleased him immeasurably. For fifteen thousand people, this spot was inadequate. But for a few hundred, it would make a fine place to build a new life.

"All right. Clean break," he called to the four mages waiting for his command, and dropped his arm. "Take it down now."

Deactivating the Gate wasn't nearly as impressive-looking as putting it up had been. It did require physical contact, though; two of the mages rowed out there in two small coracles, and put their hands to the curved wooden "horns" of the Gate. Between the horns, fog formed vertically and boiled upward like steam, hissing as the space between the uprights went from transparent to translucent.

That air's increasingly turbulent rippled-water effect wobbled, and then vanished with the sound of a tiny thunderclap. If anyone thought establishing a Gate could be dangerous, they hadn't seen what dismantling one was like. Handle it poorly, and the survivors would testify to more than a tiny thunderclap. Before the echoes even returned, there was nothing between the two uprights but clear air.

That was the signal for the rest of the crew to come out with a long, empty barge, ropes, and grapples. One of the four mages was Dole, one of the "Six Old Men," a cheerful fellow with an impressive head of iron-gray curls down to his shoulders, and a nose that could have doubled for a boat-prow. He was the one who would be doing the hardest work. He stood on top of the barge that would soon be holding the Gate-pillars, and held a piece of wood about as long as his forearm between his hands. It began to glow, a gentle golden color.

And so did the upright nearest him.

As the other three mages detached the pillar from its little stone island, it continued to stand upright, even past the point when it should have started toppling over sideways. When the pillar was entirely free, Dole carefully, and slowly, moved the stick in his hands until it was parallel to the water, and the gently curving pylon slowly rotated in midair until it had taken the same position above the anchor point.

Moving as slowly as a sleepwalker, Dole pivoted, and the great pillar of wood pivoted with him, then began serenely floating just above the water to the barge. As Dole stepped aside and lowered his hands, the pylon sank down onto the roof of the barge, and the barge itself dropped a couple of thumblengths into the water as it took on the whole weight of the pylon. The golden glow faded, and Dole clutched his piece of wood in one hand and doubled over, sweating.

"Are you all right?" Kordas called. "Do you need my help?"

Wordlessly Dole waved him off, taking slow, deep breaths as he steadied himself. Finally he straightened. "I'm fine. But I am going to want to lie down after the second one."

Satisfied that the dismantling of the Gate was well in hand, Kordas mounted his horse and headed back to the corral.

With Arial turned loose in the corral after a good rubdown, Kordas headed for the family barge, knowing he was already late for supper and had missed the boys eating. Isla and Restil were watching for him, and the other two boys burst out of the barge at Restil's call of "Father!"

Being pounced on by three enthusiastic little boys was not a new experience at this point, but it definitely never got tiresome, no matter how exhausted he himself might be. He scooped up Jon to ride on his shoulder while the other two romped alongside him in the loping gait that children everywhere adopt when they are pretending to be horsemen. With a sudden shriek of "I'm a gryphon!" Hakkon put up fingers like they were fearsome talons, and gave chase with them raised high. "I'll eat you! Rarrh!"

"Gryphons don't eat people!" came the running retort, and the now-a-gryphon yelled back, "Not you! I'm after your horse!" Their chase escalated, but was suddenly dropped because of an important question.

"Papa! Papa! Are you going to tell us a story? Your stories are better than anyone else's!" Hakkon clamored—although, truth to tell, his "clamoring" was neither loud nor unwelcome.

"If you go to your beds and let your father eat his supper in peace, he'll come and tell you a story when he is finished," Isla said firmly.

All three of them cheered, and the two older boys sped ahead, vanishing into the barge like a couple of young otters diving into their den. Kordas followed, stooping a little to get through the door without hitting his head. The warmth of the barge was welcome after the damp chill of the breeze outside. He set Jon down just inside, and let him follow the other two back to their room. But Jon paused just long enough to throw himself at his father's legs for an enthusiastic hug before retreating.

"I still can't believe that they just accepted us as their real parents so easily," he marveled, as he sat down to a decidedly cold and congealed mess of stew and a soggy bread bowl. But that was no matter, not for a magician. A little concentration, and the brief sensation that energy was draining from him—because it was—and the food looked exactly as it had when Isla had gotten it from the common kitchen.

It was a simple, easy spell for magicians to use, and had a lot of practical applications, even if it couldn't be used on anything still alive. Most mages just saved it to reheat a hot drink or renew their food, though he had used it several times to put a thrown shoe temporarily back on a horse, or mend a girth strap for long enough to get back home.

"We weren't exactly absent from their lives," Isla pointed out. "Where Hakkon mostly *was*. Every time we saw them, we were kind, with gentle authority, and we didn't ignore them or act as if they were a bother. I'm not gifted with Mind-magic, but I can imagine it's possible that they used to fantasize that we actually *were* their parents, which would make the revelation more like a dream come true than a shock."

"Have they ever said anything to you about it?" he asked, spooning up hot stew before the bread bowl turned soggy for a second time. It wasn't as good as Sai's stew, but it was quite palatable, and hunger made it taste even better.

"Not yet," Isla said, pouring him a second cup of clover tea after he had quickly downed the first. "I must say that Delia is taking to being sent on with the scouts better than I feared." She frowned a little. "This is harder on her than it is on us. We've spent our entire lives in the service of the Plan, and we knew what we were getting into. She—didn't." Isla sighed. "The life of a young woman of noble birth doesn't prepare you for *this* kind of life."

"True. And she hasn't complained at all, even though I very much doubt she had any idea at all what she was getting herself into." Stew gone, he took a big bite of the chewy, gravy-soaked bread. "I was prepared to send her back to Merrin and bribe him with horses to set her up in his household, perhaps as lady-in-waiting to his wife. I'd have done it if she looked in the least unhappy, but she seems to be doing just fine."

"Oh, she would have been traumatized by your stinging rejection, no doubt. She certainly seemed cheerful enough to me when she turned up this afternoon asking for advice on what to take with her. Do you think she might have an interest in Ivar now?" Isla asked, as he finished his meal.

He laughed. "No, nothing like that. But I do think she's been bored. The only things she's had to do around here are menial tasks anyone could manage, and I think she sees this as a chance to make her own adventure, maybe even make her own mark on our landless Barony."

"Hmm. Well, why not?" Isla put everything away, wiped off the table with a rag and a drop of vinegar, cleaned his spoon and handed it back to him, and waved him toward the back of the boat. "Your audience awaits, Lord Baron."

He chuckled, rose, and went all the way to the stern of the barge, where all three boys were crowded onto one bed, leaving a conspicuous place for him to sit. He took the hint and sat down, putting his arms around all of them.

"Well now, what kind of story would you like to hear?" he asked.

"Tell us 'bout de Empwess," Jon said, sticking a finger in his mouth. "I wike de Empwess. I want a pig like her when I grows up."

He knew very well they did *not* mean the late Emperor's wife.

"I can do that," he agreed. "So, let me tell you about the time that the Squire's rival in piggery decided that he was going to turn the Empress loose. Have I told you that one yet?"

All three shaggy little heads shook vehemently, and all three boys leaned forward to catch every word. *It's a good thing no one from the Emperor ever got a good look at them, because there would have been no doubt at all who their father was. They look just like me.*

"Now, this is actually about the current Empress's grandmother," he began. "And I had not yet been sent to the Capital. I was staying with the Squire because my father had Imperial visitors, and he thought it best to give the impression that I was so unimportant to him that he'd shoo me off to stay with a pig farmer."

"The Squire's not just a pig farmer!" Hakkon said with emphatic indignation.

"Well, *we* know that, but the Emperor's spies and flunkies didn't," Kordas told them, and went on with the story, doing his best to make it funny and light, through the moment when they saw the Squire's rival running for his life with the angry Empress in surprisingly hot pursuit, right up to the conclusion where they finally found the Empress sedately making her way back to her luxurious sty with one trews-leg dangling from her mouth. This, of course, made the boys squeal with laughter. When they calmed down, he asked them about their day, listening attentively as they each took turns narrating what they had done in great detail.

He probably would not have believed it if someone had told him *before* all this happened that he would not only listen to little boys natter on about every single stick they had picked up, and every single errand they had run, he would welcome listening to it.

But he did. And he loved every minute of it.

Father used to do this, he remembered. *As long as he was sure there was no one spying on us.* The memory made him feel warm inside, and not for the first time, he wished that his father had lived to see this day. Not just because the people of the Duchy had finally escaped the claws of the Empire, but because he would have been able to smother his grandchildren in unfettered and open love as he had not been able to do for Kordas.

Not that he doubted how much his father had loved him, and he had certainly loved the old Duke right back. But it had all been choked by the need to make it look as if the Duke thought nothing of his heir . . . and in fact, there had been deceptive ploys on everyone's part to make it seem as if the old Duke just *might* cut his own son out in favor of Hakkon.

Heh. I just realized that Hakkon is a better actor than I ever considered. He pulled that off—and then he pulled off the ruse that he and Isla were having a torrid affair when I was in the Capital.

When the boys had finished telling him about their archery lessons, their words had started to slur, and it was clear their eyes were getting heavy. He kissed all three of them and said, "I am going to go help your Mama with making lists. But do you know you can practice things like archery just by thinking about them?"

All three of them perked up. "You *can?*" replied Restil.

"Absolutely. You need to lie quietly, and think, very carefully, and very slowly, about every action you need to take to shoot an arrow. Picture yourself putting the arrow to the string. Picture yourself drawing the arrow back to your ear. Remember how it feels to hold that bow firm, and the arrow loose in your fingers—not holding it, remember. You pull the string, not the arrow. The arrow should just float between your forefinger and middle finger. Picture the target. Then picture yourself loosing the bowstring, and *see* it hitting the center ring." That would keep them quiet and busy until they fell asleep.

And it had the added benefit of being true. The more you practiced something mentally, the better you got at it. From practice, to second nature, to first nature.

They all scrambled into their nightclothes and then into bed. There was no evening entertainment tonight, nor would there be—well, for a while. Tonight everyone was considering what they were going to need close at hand for a journey through the winter, and trying to remember where those things were all packed. And tomorrow the scouts would go through, getting a head start on the rest of the migration.

He slid the door between their roomlet and the rest of the barge closed, and, with a sigh, joined Isla on their bed. He felt absolutely exhausted, but then, he felt that way every day. There was just too much to do, and not enough time to pack it all into, especially as the days got shorter and shorter. He knew that he was going to lie in bed staring into the darkness, trying to think of what he might have missed, rather than getting the sleep he needed.

Isla was already in her nightgear—not the lovely, delicate shifts she used to wear to bed, but soft lambswool tunic and leggings—and was already in bed, though not asleep. Thinking longingly of the hot baths he used to enjoy regularly, he did his evening "spot-wash" and pulled on an identical set of nightclothes, as she pulled the blankets aside for him to crawl into. With a flick of a finger, he extinguished the mage-light in the ceiling, but alas, he could still hear the boys talking sleepily to each other.

"You're going to lie there staring at the ceiling trying to figure out how you can be three people at the same time, aren't you?" Isla asked in a low murmur. She put her arms around his shoulders and pulled his head down to her chest, like he was a child. That actually made him relax a little.

"You know me too well," he replied into the darkness.

"It's not all on your back, you know," she said, with just a touch of remonstrance. Then he felt her shrug. "But you wouldn't be the man your father raised, the good man I married, if you didn't carry on as if it was."

"It will get better," he told her, though that, of course, was much more of a wish than a promise. "I have to do a lot now, but once everything is in order and we are on the move, I can take time to rest."

"So—never, you mean," she snorted. He loved that about her. She never held back with him. "I could almost be grateful for that bastard who hurt the Doll. He made things come to a head to the point that we were able to shed the bad apples, the uncertain, and the wavering before it was too late and they became a drag on us."

"Most of them, anyway," he agreed. "I'm sure there are enough people in the group that there are a few bad apples left."

"I'll have a long talk with Rose," she said, as she rested her head atop his. "I think the Dolls can help there. First, they can always tell when someone is lying, and second, they are far more observant than anyone but the mages and you and I give them credit for. I mean, I hate to say I am going to set them to spy on everyone, but in essence, I think we have to. When we know there are problems brewing, we might be able to do something about them before they are more than a faint irritation."

"I should think most of them would have gotten quite clever about spotting trouble and avoiding it," he said after a moment. "Given the courtiers, I'd be more surprised to discover that some of them *weren't* abusing helpless creatures than that some of them were."

"I think the part I like best about your speech was telling people that we were not some kind of conquering army," she continued. "Hopefully that will make them all think twice before antagonizing anyone."

"We'd be stupid to act like a conquering army," he pointed out. "Oh, I suppose if we find ourselves going through lands with a population like this one, we could take over a village, maybe two—which would leave us surrounded by enemies who know the land better than we do and can take the time to pick us off a few at a time at very little risk to themselves. All they'd have to do would be to concentrate on the few fighters we have, and after that, it'd be us that would be in danger. But it's the right thing to do anyway. We're not the Empire, and we're not conquerors. Our passage has to be light on the land, and we need to find a *vacant* place and make it ours."

"It would be nice if someone invited us to stay," she sighed wistfully.

"It would be nice, and we'll certainly do that if it happens, but I am not counting on it. It's probably wise if we assume people we encounter are going to be hostile when they see this many people on their river. Nevertheless, we are not going to take anything that is not offered freely, and we are not going to places where we are not invited." He forced himself to relax; after all, Isla was not in disagreement with him, though he was sure she wished, and strongly, that he'd made the decision to remain here.

"I think we need to add one thing more," she said thoughtfully. "I think we need to look for ways to help those we encounter, even if they are hostile or wary. Kindness is never wasted, and it might come back to us."

"And this is why I married you, wise woman," he said, and then cocked an ear toward the rear of the barge. "Is that silence I hear?"

"I believe it is," she responded, her lips against his neck.

———

In the barge Delia would share with Alberdina and the former Imperial officer, there was no space for sitting and eating, just lots of storage, the kitchen in the first room, the chamber-pot closet and a basin and ewer, and four beds in the rear. There were much smaller windows in the rear than in the usual living-barges, little round things with hinges that allowed them to be opened to let in air and clamped down tight to keep the cold out. The glass was particularly thick and bubbly; it was hard to see through it. And the beds were stacked, one atop the other, in a frame with a rope ladder attached to reach the top ones. There was little space between the beds, nor between the top one and the roof, but at least each bed had two of those round windows. The lower bunk on the right already had blankets, pillows, and a fur sleeping sack in it; she guessed that one would be Alberdina's. The other three had just the sleeping sacks.

Delia considered grabbing the other bottom bed, but—*At least I know Alberdina, and I don't fancy sleeping above or below anyone I don't know.* This was silly, and in her heart she knew it, but nevertheless she threw her blankets and pillow up onto that top bed, pulled open the little cupboards that were everywhere a cupboard could be until she found empty ones, and stored her clothing and personal items in a couple. It appeared that the bottom-bed sleepers were expected to use the cupboards beneath their beds, and the top-bed sleepers were expected to use the cupboards built into the rear of the barge in such a way that they covered parts of the beds.

In fact it's . . . not so bad, she thought after some reflection. It would give the illusion of privacy if you put your pillow behind that cupboard. And one of the windows was right there, so you could have wind on your face in summer. *In fact, if I can figure out how to rig a curtain, I'll have actual privacy.*

With her belongings put away, she went looking for someone to tell her what to do.

The first person she found as she poked her head out of the door to the barge was Jonaton. It normally wasn't hard to spot Jonaton; he didn't wear mere robes, he wore Robes of Splendor—silk, velvet, wool plush, embroidered, beaded, and so flamboyant that a male firebird might have thought them "a bit too much." Today, however, it was only his lantern jaw and tousled, mousy-brown hair that let her pick him out from the clot of mages bent over a crude table, gesturing at something. Today, he looked like—well, everyone else. Baggy brown wool breeches it would be easy to layer more things under, tough leather boots to the knee, a knitted woolen tunic that was a little lighter in color than the breeches, and a long scarf wrapped around his neck knitted out of bits and scraps of yarn of every color, though mostly white, black, gray, and brown.

As she closed the door to the barge behind her, he straightened, looking satisfied, and turned away from the group, who continued their animated conversation. She waved at him, and he spotted her, and came strolling insouciantly over to the barge.

"Jonaton, I hardly recognized you," she teased. He raised an elegantly groomed eyebrow.

"I wear what's needed for the job," he said. "I just wear it better than anyone *else* here. So, petal, I understand you are coming with us?"

"The Baron and Sai seemed to think it was a good idea, so I said yes," she admitted. Obviously, she didn't want to let it slip that the main reason she was coming was so that she didn't have to mind the three boys.

"It's not a bad idea," he agreed, pulling on his chin. "But you need to remember, once we are on the other side of the Gate, there's no changing your mind and wanting to go back."

She glowered at him. "When have I ever acted like that?"

He shrugged. "Alberdina can use the help. And I can think of a lot of ways that your Gift would be useful." Just then a flock of wild ducks came into view, flying from the marsh to the lake. They had to be wild, because all the domestic ducks had one wing with the flight feathers clipped to keep them from joining the wild ones. This didn't stop the wild ones from trying to join them, and bully them away from their rations of grain. Jonaton narrowed his eyes, grabbed her shoulders, and pointed at the ducks. "Quick! Pull one down!"

Startled, she didn't think, she just did it.

The duck vanished from the sky. It reappeared with a strangled *quack* at her feet. Jonaton pounced on it before it could recover and snapped its neck. Then, with the duck under one arm and his free hand on her elbow, he hauled her along to another group—she recognized Hakkon, Ivar, and Sai, but didn't know the woman or the two young men with her.

"Look at this!" he crowed as soon as he was within earshot, holding the limp duck aloft by its neck.

Everyone turned to look. "It's a duck," said Sai. "Not that it's not welcome to go in the stew, but it's a duck."

"It's a duck that Delia pulled out of the sky!" Jonaton corrected.

Well, that got everyone's interest, and she suddenly found herself the focus of all eyes.

"That . . . is going to be incredibly useful," Hakkon mused. *"Incredibly* useful. Hunting without wasting arrows? I have—" He stopped himself before he said anything more. "Incredibly useful."

I wonder if he was going to say he changed his mind about having me on the trip? Well, it didn't matter what he had thought before. It was clear he was quite happy about her being among the scouts now. "I can probably get fish too if I can see them," she pointed out, feeling rather more enthusiastic because of the way the rest of them were reacting. She felt a little sorry for the poor duck, but moons out here making the most of every bit of food that came to hand had made her a lot less sentimental and very much less squeamish about such things.

And it wasn't as if it hadn't been a quick death.

Sai pulled himself up. "You are now our designated hunter and fisher," he declared. "We'll have you ride the barge so you can see fish, if there are any."

"How many barges in the string?" she asked.

"Five. Yours, a second sleeping barge, a supply barge, and two flat-tops for the Gate uprights and the skids if we have to turn the barges into sleds. The Baron gave us a Tow-Beast, and even with the Gate uprights, it'll be like pulling bags of feathers for him. If we have to turn the barges into sledges, Hakkon and Ivar will hitch their horses to a barge apiece. But I hope we won't have to do that," said Sai. "There's twelve plus a Doll in our party, which is not too many, and not so few that dividing up night watches is going to be awkward."

"I can tend the horses too," she reminded him. "How many of them are we going to have, including the Tow-Beast?"

She was hoping he would say "twelve," and he did. "We'll need a mount apiece if for some reason we have to cut the barges loose and run back to the main body of the caravan," Hakkon said with authority. "If we have to make speed, I want everyone on their own horse. Did anyone explain how this is going to go?"

She shook her head, and he gestured to her to come over to the table. The object they had all been bending over turned out to be a map.

"Here's the lake. Here's the river that drains into the lake," he said, tapping the left-hand "horn" of the crescent. "This is all swamp; there's no way that we'd get our herds through there even if it was frozen—a frozen swamp is a nightmare to try and traverse. But Ivar and the other scouts he's training have been to the other side, found a new river draining *out of* the swamp here." He pointed to a short stretch of river newly drawn on the map. "So this is what we do. We've got a Gate set up here—" He put a stone on either side of the river flowing into the "horn." "We have another Gate set up here—" He put two stones on the new river. "And first we go through with four more Gate uprights, and we keep going, and the rest of the caravan follows. They'll be much slower than we are, so we'll start getting further and further ahead of them with every day. The Doll we'll have with us will keep us abreast of their progress. If we get too far ahead, we'll stop for a little bit and take a rest. Meanwhile, once the last of the caravan is through *this* Gate, Ceri and Dole will make a temporary Gate, take this one down, and go through the temporary one with the Gate uprights, so we leave nothing behind us that the Empire mages can use to find us, much less send people after us. And if we find, say, a stretch of bad water, or the river peters out to nothing, most of the scouts will stop and set up a new Gate, while Ivar and I and maybe one of the Fairweather lads will go on ahead and find smoother water or another river. As long as it takes us in some combination of west and north, it'll do. When we find a good place to resume our travel, we'll come back and get Jonaton and Sai and set up the destination Gate. Meanwhile, there will be two flat-top barges following us with nothing but Gate uprights on them. When they catch up to where we're stopped, we'll take their uprights and load them on our empty barges, and they'll return."

It was an incredibly well-thought-out plan, at least as far as she could see. "But what if the river starts to freeze over?" she asked.

"Well, we have two options. One is, if we find a place with enough stuff for the herds to live on, we just stop until spring. The other is to put runners on the barges and continue that way."

"I'd rather not do that unless we have to," said Ivar behind Delia. She jumped; she hadn't heard him come up. "It's risky. It'll be hard hauling the barges up on the bank fully loaded. It'll be hard levering them up onto the runners. And the footing along the riverbank is going to be treacherous if the river has frozen over. We could lose horses if they stumble and fall into the river and break the ice."

Hakkon nodded. "But we'll hope that doesn't happen. The river we're heading for has a pretty brisk flow. We can put a metal blade from the lumber-finishers onto the front of the first barge to break any ice for the others, and we can dedicate one Tow-Beast just for that barge."

"But staying has its risks too," Ivar pointed out. "The barges will have to be hauled out on the bank if the ice starts to threaten the hulls, and they're not the best shelter in a bad winter. But—" He shrugged. "They're not the worst either. I've wintered in snow huts. The barges are better than that."

He gave her a sharp look, as if gauging whether or not his blunt words were putting her off.

But now that she had committed to this . . . she was looking forward to it.

"Now, you go find Alberdina and Sergeant Fairweather and see which Doll is coming with us, and the three of you figure out what they're going to need for their comfort, because I haven't a clue," Ivar added, laughing. "Then we'll all meet up for duck stew and any last-minute planning, and we'll leave in the morning."

So soon? But . . . there was really no reason to wait. She had everything she needed. And her sister was right. This *was* going to be an adventure.

Instead of feeling unsettled, suddenly she could not wait until morning.

6

"Excuse me, Baron," Rose said, as Kordas stood on the bank and watched the first lot of barges jockeying around to get their strings in place. Although they were, indeed, going through in strings of eight, there was other positioning he was insisting on. That every eighth barge be a supply barge, for instance, because if the convoy got separated, or if there was truly hideous weather, he didn't want all the food at the rear, or the middle, and out of reach. It wasn't merely grain that was on those barges, although the bulk of the cargo was barley, oats, wheat, and rye. They'd weighed the advantages of having meat that was transporting itself on its own four feet against the disadvantage of possibly having to feed all those animals if forage ran out, and the disadvantage won out, so after a careful culling of everything that would have been slaughtered for winter back home, there was a lot of dried, salted, pounded, potted, smoked, and otherwise cured meats or preserved meats and bones as well as foraged and preserved or dried fruits, vegetables, mushrooms, herbs, and—anything remotely edible was on those barges as well.

He was interspersing all those barges full of weapons and ammunition among the rest as well, for the same reason. And also because, as his tactical lessons in the Games when he was a hostage had taught him, if some portion of the convoy elected to have a revolt, he didn't want all the weapons to fall into their hands. And every fourth string of eight had with them a common kitchen barge, with ovens made from the fire-bricks potters had been carefully crafting all the time they had been here, then covered with clay mixed with fibers as a binder. He had given permission for these barges to be used as sleeping spaces overnight. But the only things to be stored in them were cooking implements, pots and pans, fire-handling equipment, and just enough food for that day. That way if there was a kitchen-barge fire, no one would be trying to save *anything* rather than give the priority to getting out safely, and no more food would be lost than a single day's worth.

"What can I do for you, Rose?" he asked, not taking his eyes off the clumsy shuttling of barges around.

"It seems that now that we are leaving there are some individuals, not families, who wish to depart from their families and remain, and some from the local villages wish to join the convoy." Rose's matter-of-fact tone confused him for a moment, as did the statement. *Why would—oh!*

There had been quite a bit of mingling of the Valdemarans and the people from the surrounding villages in the moons since they had been there. Trade, for one thing; the villagers had been very willing to trade dried vegetables for meat during the cullings. And with a population of fifteen thousand—quite a heavy percentage of them marriageable age—there was bound to be mingling of another kind.

So now that the time has come to part, there are wails and sulking and "Father, I can't bear to be parted—" I should have seen this coming. Do I make an official edict about this too?

No . . . he rather thought not. "There is no one true way" meant people should be allowed to make up their own minds about themselves and their families. Even if he personally didn't like the decisions they made, it was strain that tested resolve. Begin as he meant to go on.

"Rose, let it be known that I will not interfere in parents' decisions about children that are not adults. Nor will I interfere in the decision of a child that *is* an adult. And if they are old enough to make this kind of life-changing decision, they are certainly old enough to find a way to get on a barge. If someone wants to give space on their barges for a couple, fine. If someone wants to barter space on their barges for a couple, also fine."

He thought about adding, *Adults will be allowed to join or leave us now, but in the future, they are stuck with the path they chose.* But . . . who was to say that they wouldn't have another situation with a friendly village, and a lad or lass who wanted to stay, or persuaded a new lover to go? "That's the condition, Rose. They have to find a barge of their own, somewhere, one that is not already earmarked as storage, or find room on someone else's barge *on their own.* I can't be spending my time going from one end of this lake to the other trying to organize a ride." There were a lot of creative ways this could be done, but if the couple in question couldn't figure this out for themselves, well . . . too bad. This was part of growing up.

"I will pass this on, Baron. It is a sound decision."

He smiled a little to himself. *Talking about herself as "I" and freely saying what she thinks.* Rose must have taken the fact that he encouraged her to have opinions and think of herself as more of an individual to heart.

Of course, he had given the order that today was the day for people to start getting their strings in order and moving through the Gate, and as evidenced by the lines of people on both sides of the river, there were plenty who had been ready long before that order went out. This gave the laggards who waited until the last minute plenty of time to get themselves and their belongings to rights. And meanwhile, down at the very middle of the crescent where the ruins of that ancient town were, barges had already been hauled up out of the water, and their owners were pondering various ways of winterizing them. Those stone houses would be wonderful— next year. But winter was coming, and between a barge and a half-finished stone house, there simply was no comparison.

Some people had laid claim to a house anyway, by widening the doorway and having the barge hauled inside. And when some of the people remaining had come to him, indignant about the "theft," he pointed out that they were not under his jurisdiction anymore, and they should talk to their own headman.

"But we don't have one!" someone had protested. At his stern no-nonsense glare, they had amended, meekly, "So we'll go pick one."

Not my millpond. Not my otters.

He could have made it his business, of course, but that would have set a bad precedent for everyone.

Not being a complete monster, aside from whatever flocks and herds and seed-stock they had, he actually *had* ordered a couple of the grain barges to be hauled out for them as well. One of the older mages, not one of the Six Old Men, but a mage named Siman, and Siman's apprentice, were staying with the new village. Kordas more

than half expected that the news of this was what had changed
the other villages' opinion of the new one from "grudging" to
"welcoming." He didn't blame them at all. A mage was a force-
multiplier if anything nasty came after you. And if nothing nasty
came after you, they were useful in so very many ways that it wasn't
often people in tiny villages like these got within seeing distance
of one. But Siman reckoned that he could live out a comfortable
old age here, with his apprentice handling the bulk of any work
they were asked to do, and unlike the Six, who seemed to thrive
on adventure and uncertainty, poor old Siman had not greeted the
advent of their escape with any pleasure. But to remain behind
meant the certainty of being scooped up by whatever power broker
ended up on the Imperial Throne, and he'd liked that idea even
less. This had turned out to be a happy compromise for everyone.

Well, watching people bumble barges around was getting a
trifle irritating. The thwacking and thumping of vessels colliding
sounded like a band of drummers dropping their instruments
down an infinite staircase. Yelling—most of it unnecessary,
which only made it more annoying *(this shouting could have been
a note!)* seemed to run in waves up and down the staging area.
Still, best not to have runners in action now, so, shouting it was.
And yes, of course he could have called all the mages here and
gotten them to do it magically—but magic was a manageable
resource and one he intended to preserve until needed, and
most of the people here had no idea just how many mages he'd
collected under his roof. He had no intention of letting them
find out. Firstly, he was certain there was at least one person out
there who would be willing to sell them all out to the Empire
if they thought they could get away with it and the pay would

be enough, and he especially did not want the Empire knowing how many mages he had. People would be people. *They will do what seems best for them at the time. It's not that anybody would "turn evil" in an instant, it's usually that someone ran out of good solutions at the same time an opportunity to do harm comes along. That can happen to anyone, and there is fear here, so let-downs and betrayals are inevitable. You don't have to utterly trust them to love them.* Secondly, if they knew how many mages there were, people would be coming to him all the time to try to get the mages to do with magic what they could very well do, albeit with difficulty, with their own hands and those of their neighbors. That was a bad habit to get into. Mages were people too, and people got annoyed, even angry, when plagued with too many petty requests. People got testy when overworked.

And the mages were of different specialties and all levels of strength and skill, starting with Jonaton and the old men at the top, down to Sai's new apprentice Venidel. But Kordas had noticed more than once in the past that to most people a mage was a mage was a mage and they were all interchangeable.

Not unlike Dolls. Or servants. Or Dukes or Barons. People think of each other as what they can do for them first, and as individuals second. It's not evil, it's expedient. We don't have a lot of time to be cozy.

So rather than find himself or his mages enmired in countless exercises in futility, Kordas and his staff just simply did not let people know how many magic wielders they had, nor who they were. The mages appreciated that; many of the ones he'd sheltered had suffered from fools, the thoughtless, and those who thought magic was "effortless"—even to their faces.

Even while trying to keep the idiots alive despite themselves.

"Well, this is going about as well as I'd expected, and not worse, which is a relief," he told Rose. "So let's get back to our own strings and see that we set an example about being organized."

I almost wish there had been a way to siphon off some of that young Elemental's magic and store it for later, he thought, as he and Rose got well away from the busy footpath around the lake and walked back to their section. It would have been more than useful. It would have made setting up the new Gates they were inevitably going to have to put up a lot easier.

But that would have been wrong, he decided. *The poor thing was being tormented, and making use of what it produced in response to the torment would have made me no better than the Emperor. Maybe worse, because I, at least, know better, and I'd have taken it anyway. I could have justified it, too. Then again, thanks to the Dolls, we saved who we could, or so I tell myself.*

He exhaled strongly, pulling himself off of *that* well-trodden path of thought. For now, if he had followed his own wishes, he would have been with the scouts, as one of the mages there to protect them. All anyone knew, including the people who lived around Crescent Lake, was that the further north and west you went, the more magic and danger you were likely to encounter.

But—I can't do that. He couldn't take Isla and the boys with him, and he didn't want to leave them. For the first time, ever, they were allowed to be a family, and he was enjoying that. In fact, except for the danger and uncertainty facing them, this was the happiest he had ever been in his life. Now that his family's plan was in motion—

Well, Isla had put it best. Good leaders know how to let go and let competent people do their jobs. Leave petty grievances and squabbles among neighbors to their own headmen. Leave cooking and figuring out rations to the quartermasters, former housekeepers, former Seneschals, and cooks.

Leave scouting to the scouts. Leave leadership to those who can't escape it.

And with that in mind, he stepped up his pace.

———

From where Delia stood on the stern of the first barge in their string of five, the land on this side of the Gate didn't look much different from Crescent Lake. Wooded, almost up to the riverbank, but at least there was enough open space on either bank to act as a towpath. Some of the trees she recognized, most she didn't, and she didn't know the names of *any* of the bushes, but that was mostly because she didn't know much about plants that weren't growing in a garden. The chief difference was that this part of the country must have been hit with a hard frost at some point in the very near past, because the evergreens stood out like doleful sentinels against the flaming reds, oranges, and yellows on either side of the river. It was breathtaking; back home the trees didn't burst out into colors nearly this bright.

I need to stop thinking of it as "back home."

Grass on this verge was up to a horse's knees, but the horses weren't being allowed to snatch mouthfuls on the way. They'd all had a nice grain meal this morning, they'd get a chance for some green stuff when they stopped for a rest and water at noon, and they'd be allowed to graze all night. Letting them mosey along, snatching up grass as the mood dictated, did two bad things, at least according to Stafngrimr: the horses would slow down to nothing to stuff themselves, and they'd get the bad habit of expecting you to cater to their whims when they wanted to eat. *"Snacks on your terms, not theirs,"* he'd said. *"Or they are the leader, not you. And you don't want a horse thinking he's the one in charge."*

And besides, letting them eat with a bit in their mouths meant you'd be spending hours cleaning mucky, nasty bits and bridles.

A couple of the mages' mounts had objected to not being able to do as they pleased, but the former Imperial Sergeant, Briada Fairweather, had stopped the entire group for a moment, gone and cut some willow switches in full view of all the animals, and then—making sure each mount knew she was handing a switch to its rider—dealt them out.

"If you beat these nags, I'll beat you," she said flatly, as she got back on her horse. "But now they know that if they disobey you, there'll be consequences, and if Stafngrimr is half the horseman I think he is, they all know about those consequences. Put your heels to them if they won't stay with the group, and just give their rumps a little flick with the switch if they don't keep up after that." She smiled at Delia. "Don't need to hurt them, just get their attention."

Since the mounts all immediately behaved themselves, it appeared that Briada was right.

The Sergeant's two cousins were in the lead, both with hand-crossbows and a Spitter, as well as an eye-opening number of knives, and axes that looked well used. Ivar's huge black mastiff Bay ranged on ahead, but not that far; if his master called him back it would take him two breaths to be at their side. The dog worked his way in a zigzag from one side of the path to the other. Once in a while he stopped long enough to sniff in the air or the ground, but evidently he didn't find anything to alarm him, because he went right back to his own version of scouting.

Ivar brought up the rear, also with hand-crossbow and Spitter, also with an axe instead of a sword, and two knives almost as long as Delia's forearm instead of a lot of smaller ones. Next to him was the Sergeant, armed with a sword instead of an axe as her cousins were. Delia guessed that when they had deserted the Imperial Army, they had taken their arms with them. They had armor, but it wasn't obvious. It was underneath the enormous knitted wool tunics they all wore. That had been Briada's idea.

"Baron said we aren't an invading army, so don't look like one," she'd explained to Delia. "Man makes sense. We want to get through territories peacefully. If we've got weapons, that's only good planning. If we've got armor, well, you don't armor up against boars and bears, and that makes it look like we're looking for trouble."

Delia could easily pick out some of the Valdemar horse lines by eye. Manta, Ivar's horse, was a Charger out of the Bearheart line. The three Fairweathers all had Chargers too, but out of a slightly smaller line, the Grimjack line. Chargers were specifically bred and trained for war; you could brandish a sword around their ears and they wouldn't turn a hair. They were also trained in harness, so the big chestnut Tow-Beast, Tight Squeeze, could get some rest if he ran into terrain that made him labor. Hakkon had his very own Valdemar Gold, Skydancer. Jonaton was mounted on a mule, since speed was not going to be needful, but steadiness was. He and his mule Carrot knew each other very well, and she wouldn't blink if he started performing magic on her back.

Sai and his apprentice also rode mules and so did a mage Delia didn't know well, named Endars; apparently mules were the mount of choice for a mage when fast travel was not required.

Alberdina and Delia's mounts were not what Delia had expected; they were False Golds. At two years old, they were not their full size yet, but they were up to bearing the weight of the smaller women. The important part was that they had been trained to follow where Hakkon and Manta went, and they were gentle and strong. They could also haul the boats at a pinch, and Delia's Buttercup was doing just that alongside Tight Squeeze.

The last member of their party did not actually have a mount, because she didn't know how to ride: the Doll Amethyst. Someone had done a beautiful job with this doll, embroidering a lovely, stylistic face with beadwork surrounding an amethyst cabochon in the middle of her forehead. She hadn't spoken much to Delia, and she didn't seem to speak much in general.

Just look at us. It's easy to dwell on danger and homesickness, but just look at us! Each of us strong, competent, and ready for whatever lies ahead. She wondered if anyone but her took a minute to simply take in how they looked. She, for one, felt reassured by it in ways she couldn't put words to.

Delia found her spirits rising—despite the fact that the distance between her and Kordas increased with every passing moment—and couldn't help but take in deep breaths of the crisp, clean air, slightly bitter with the scents of leaves dying. She hadn't quite realized how much *smell* there was around the lake, what with cooking and sweating animals, sweating people, and the very occasional whiff of a latrine trench the mages hadn't gotten to yet. The sun shone over the trees to the east, thanks to her warm clothing she wasn't in the least cold, and if only the rest of their trip could be like this—

Well, it won't be, she thought, resigned. *So I had better enjoy the good part.*

"Delia!" called Hakkon. "How much can you pick up with that Gift of yours?"

She hadn't been spending the last several moons practicing for nothing. "As much as I can lift myself," she said, a little proudly. "About fifty pounds."

"Can you skip back to the fourth barge, look for deadfall at the edge of the trees, and drop it onto the deck and the roof? That'll save us a lot of time we won't have to spend looking for firewood when we camp."

"Oh! What a good idea!" It pleased her on several levels. She was going to be *obviously* useful from the start. She'd be able to save camping time, and Hakkon thought enough of her ability to just ask her to do something to begin with, rather than ignoring her as a supposed burden or a card to be played.

"And if you see ducks or geese or pheasants, bring them down. Three please," said Sai. "That will give each of us a quarter bird for supper, and the bones and extra quarter can go in the pease-porridge to cook overnight for breakfast in the morning."

Pleased enough to feel a little giddy, she began looking for deadfall, not just in the grass at the feet of the trees, but for dead branches still in the trees that she could snap off. It was just about as tiring as it would have been to go to where the branch was, pick it up, and carry it herself to the boat, but she was prepared for that. When she began to feel winded, she stopped Fetching wood and began breaking it up with a hand axe and arranging it in neat stacks on the deck between the railing around the edge of the barge and the oblong bulk of the upper half.

It was very nearly noon by the sun when Bay suddenly alerted, stopped, and looked back at his master. Ivar stood up in his stirrups, shaded his eyes with his hand, and peered ahead. "Flush!" he ordered the dog, who bounded ahead, barking. A moment later there was an explosion of geese from the water upstream.

Most of them flew in their opposite direction, but a smaller part of the flock came toward them.

Delia "grabbed" one out of the air; it appeared at her feet, dazed and disoriented. And before she could feel guilty about what she was about to do, she took a full swing at its head with the back of her little hand axe.

To her relief—relief that almost brought tears to her eyes—she killed it instantly. She looked back at the geese in the air rapidly moving away from them, honking as they flew, and made a second grab for one. It was a strain, but it appeared at her feet and she killed it the same way she'd killed the first one. Delia didn't like to think of herself as a killer. She didn't like killing. But all those heroes in stories had to eat something, and in matters of survival, the mathematics of it made sense—meat comes from somewhere, and everything alive more often than not consumed something else alive. She was as thoughtful about it as one could be—quick deaths and usage of everything taken from the target's life and body. She knew she'd better get used to this. One day she'd pass her thousandth kill without even knowing it, and every time, she would give the game a pause of respect before dressing it out. It was that it was an involuntary sacrifice to her needs that made her squeamish, she decided. That made her feel dirty, that she'd ended a life so abruptly and now their story was done, by her hands. She could only sigh about it and carry on.

"Pluck and clean them now or later?" she called to Ivar, who was in charge of their group—at least unless or until they encountered an armed threat, in which case Briada was in command.

"Now," he said. He didn't have to tell her to save everything. That was a given. She exerted herself and Fetched an empty sack from the storage barge under her, a ceramic pot with a lid from the barge where she was sleeping, and finally a cooking pot from where Sai had stored the cooking things. Of all things tedious, plucking a goose had to be the worst, but by the time Ivar signaled the Fairweathers to halt for lunch, the birds were bald, beheaded and gutted and in the big pot, the liver, gizzard, and heart in there under them, the heads, feet, guts, and lungs in the ceramic pot with the lid on, and the feathers in the sack. All but the wing feathers; those were saved out separately.

And she had put back the pot full of geese in the pantry in Sai's boat, the wing feathers with the archery repair gear, and only the pot full of entrails was still in her hands. Which fact she proudly announced as her barge got moored up to the bank and she hopped off.

"Well, that's quite a budget of work for one morning," Sai said, pleased.

"I thought Bay should have the guts," she said to Ivar, who grinned at her.

"So he should. We can give him the heads and feet for his supper," Ivar agreed. "Of course, if he catches himself a rabbit, we can just save them for his breakfast. Oh! That reminds me. If you spot a rabbit, or he does, and you can drop it at his feet, he's trained to do a quick, clean kill, then bring it to me."

Another relief. It was hard enough killing those poor geese and ducks, and they didn't have big, soft eyes, adorable twitchy ears, and a plush coat. She could eat cooked rabbit without a qualm, and had on innumerable occasions, but nothing could make her kill one. At least not right now. *Maybe if I am starving.*

Venidel made a fire. Sai brewed everyone tea, and passed around small loaves of bread stuffed with sausages. "Enjoy these while you can," he said. "Once these are gone there won't be any proper bread. Grain doesn't spoil like flour does, so I won't even be making flatbread unless we have time enough for me to grind some up in my hand mill, or we find a village with a mill and we can somehow trade for some."

Delia sighed, but didn't complain. It was unlikely that anyone else in the entire convoy was going to be making bread either; all they had were hand mills, and the barge kitchens were not set up to do anything but make stews and porridges.

They slipped the bits on all the horses—Jonaton "shortened their tethers," as he put it, altering the charm on them so they would not wander more than thirty arm-lengths from the barges, not even if they were startled. That allowed the horses to happily tear up huge mouthfuls of the grass they had been eyeing all morning.

Amethyst simply stood quietly to one side of the fire, and Delia admired the beautiful needlework on her face, the careful way in which what were usually mitten-like hands had been sculpted with separate, and apparently working, fingers, and the clothing she had been dressed in. She was clearly still wearing what she had fled the Imperial Palace wearing: soft, sueded deerskin tunic, boots, and trews that had been embroidered with black and gold thread in an abstract pattern. In addition, she had been wigged with what looked like horsehair, braided into thousands of tiny braids, each one ending in an amethyst bead. Amethyst seemed to sense her regard, and turned to face her.

"May this one serve you in any way, Lady Delia?" she said in a soft, breathy voice much like Rose's.

Delia flushed with embarrassment. "It's just Delia, Amethyst, and no, I was just admiring your face, your hair, and your clothing."

"This one was a rare gift to Lady Meriposa from the Emperor," said the Doll. "She found it amusing to dress this one as she had her childhood toys. It is fortunate that on the day the Capital fell, this one was garbed in one of the more practical outfits. Trains six feet long and sleeves that swept the floor would not have fared well during the escape, or later."

"Was she—kind?" Delia asked. Somehow, the answer seemed important. Maybe because she didn't want to think that someone who could create something of beauty was in her heart cold and cruel.

"Very. She knew that the Emperor had his eye on her and intended to add her to his kept women as soon as he had rid himself of some of the older ones. In fact, her parents had sent her to Court as a hostage with that intent. She was very brave about it, and confided much to this one." Amethyst raised her head ever so slightly, as if with pride and defiance. "So when the Dolls were included in Baron Kordas's plan of escape, this one obtained a Gate pass to the Temple of Diony the Tale-Weaver, and set aside a casket of the Lady's most valuable jewelry where this one could snatch it up quickly. When the alarm was sounded, the Lady froze. That enabled this one to seize the casket and the Lady, press the pass into her hand until she grasped it, run to the nearest Gate, and thrust both her and the casket through it. Then this one followed the rest of the Dolls to Crescent Lake."

By this point everyone around the fire was staring at the Doll with mouths agape. Amethyst had not said five words in total since she had been assigned to them—and now this extraordinary story!

Slowly, Briada began to clap. Her cousins followed. Then Hakkon and Ivar and all the rest joined in. Amethyst straightened a little more, obviously pleased with their response.

"Now I see why Kordas picked you out. You are very good at quick thinking, Amethyst, and at planning." Briada smiled. It wasn't a grin, but it seemed genuine. "Why do you say 'this one' instead of 'I'?" Briada asked.

"'This one' refers to the habitation of this body by my self. We were not willingly placed into these forms, so we do not refer to them as 'ourselves.' This one is Amethyst, to all of you, which is simpler and accurate enough."

Suddenly Amethyst froze. "There has been a development," she said. "It seems we are not alone."

It took longer than Kordas had hoped to get the first strings organized and lined up properly, make sure the load wasn't too much for the horse, and get them through the Gate. *At least once we get them all on the move we won't have to do all this all over again,* he thought with a touch of exasperation. *But really . . . they've known for moons this day was coming. Couldn't they have at least practiced a little?*

The scouts should have been an example to them all, but of course, no one was paying attention when barges were colliding, people were shouting and swearing at each other, and the horses waiting to be hitched up watched all this with—he could have sworn—looks of impatient disdain.

By the time the first of the strings was actually through the Gate, the sun was much higher in the sky, and he was fairly certain that the scouts were several leagues away and completely out of sight. Well . . . that really didn't matter, now, did it? They were *supposed* to be well ahead of the rest.

"Rose, how far are the scouts from the Gate?" he asked anyway.

"Amethyst tells me they are quite out of sight, and that she is not very good at judging distances." Well, that confirmed that he was right. At least it meant the scouts were making good time. "But we have a more immediate problem," she continued. "It seems we are not alone on this river, and the first barges are being detained. Your—"

"Never mind, I'm on my way!" He vaulted into Arial's saddle

and urged her into a canter, very conscious of the hand-crossbow and Spitter at his side and hoping he would not have to use them.

After the timeless point of disorientation that Gate-passage always subjected him to, he found himself about to run full-tilt into the haunches of a Tow-Beast, and pulled Arial up short.

His heart dropped, and he went cold all over, as he saw what Rose had meant.

The couple of guards he had, and the clearly rattled Valdemarans, faced off against what looked like a group of armed farmers and hunters. There were bows in plenty, all of them at the ready, some nasty-looking pitchforks and mattocks, and even a couple of wicked pruning hooks and boar spears.

He drew himself up as tall as he could, knowing that at least he had the advantage of height on them, being as he was on a horse, and walked Arial up to the front line of the mob.

"Might I inquire what the matter seems to be?" he asked, in the local dialect—or at least the one that was local to Crescent Lake.

One big man in a blacksmith apron—those seemed to be universal—stepped up to the front, eyed Kordas while hefting one of his hammers, and replied.

Well, it was similar to what the people at Crescent Lake spoke, but the accent was so thick it was hard to understand. Oh, not the alarm masked with anger, that was easy enough to read. But the words were almost unintelligible.

Quickly, because he didn't want anyone to have time to react to what he was about to do, he looked straight at the man, gathered his magic, readied his spells, and uttered the trigger words for the first.

"Be still."

The blacksmith froze. Kordas nudged Arial up to him before

the others could realize what he'd done, and touched the man's forehead, triggering the second spell.

There was a moment of dizziness. His eyes glazed, then cleared, and he backed Arial up. *"Awake!"* he said, breaking the spell.

The blacksmith swayed a little, came back to himself, and paled. "What didja do to me, warlock?" he roared in anger and alarm.

Anyone with weapons on them reached for them.

"Peace!" he shouted before anyone could move. "I was just making sure we could understand each other!"

"You—" The blacksmith froze. "Wait—!" he shouted to the others, then turned toward Kordas, looking distinctly shaken. "A moment ago ye was speakin' jibber-jabber!"

"I know, I know," Kordas said soothingly. "I just needed to touch you to use magic to learn your tongue. The last thing I want is for us to start hacking at each other over nothing!"

That just made the blacksmith angry. *"Nothing?"* Ye set up yon uncanny door, ye start bringin' people into *our* lands, and then ye start bringin' boates full of gods only *know* what, and ye say that's *nothing?* Nothing to *you* maybe, but it's *us* that's got the opinion that matters!" The mob behind him growled.

"It's a misunderstanding," Kordas replied, keeping his tone quiet, and not matching the blacksmith's anger with his own. "We're just passing through, following the river. We're looking for a land to live in *that doesn't already have people in it.* Now that we know you're here, we aren't going to leave the river. Truly."

He had to say this quite a few times, paraphrasing it each time so he wouldn't sound like he was mocking them. In between he added little things like "Our land wracked with war," and "Evil men were pursuing us, but we got away," being very, very careful to phrase these things so that they were, at least, technically true, just in case one of them had a power like the Dolls did to tell what was true or false. Each time he repeated what he wanted them to hear, they did calm down a little more, and the anger slowly turned to suspicion and something he suspected was plain old *dislike of the stranger.* He couldn't blame them, especially if they had never seen a Gate before. It was obviously powerful magic, and the people who could do things like that were rightly to be feared.

It took a lot longer than he wanted to, and the entire time he couldn't help but think of all those Poomers and Spitters back there on the other side of the Gate, and how much easier it would be to just bring them through and clear these people out—

Well, he wouldn't actually use them on anyone. All he'd need to do was to scare the living hell out of them, and a barrage of Poomers turning the trees behind them to splinters would certainly do that.

But it wouldn't be right. It wouldn't be ethical. We'd be acting just like the Empire had: coming in, displaying force, and intimidating everyone we encountered. And if a display of force failed to get the desired results, how tempting, how easy it would be, to just use that force on whoever was there. The Empire was always assured of having "more," no matter what. Resist the army once, and five times more respond, and if they met opposition, twenty times more would come next. Records weren't kept of what cultures were in an area before the Empire expanded. Soldiers returned from "defending the territory," meaning, the territory just conquered. When no natives were left, after all, the land was protected from them. *Besides, "defense" sounds so much nicer around the homelands than "invasion force," a term that could scare people. "Defense" implies there were omnipresent, powerful enemies to defend against, and everyone likes thinking of themselves as the victim when they have defenders.*

So Kordas coaxed, and cajoled, and promised, and eventually, grudgingly, the natives consulted with each other and the blacksmith turned to give him their verdict.

"Tha' can pass through. But no stoppin' and no stayin'—"

"I can't promise that," Kordas countered. "There are a great many of us, and we're going to have to stop for the night. The horses can't safely tow the boats if they can't see. But I promise we won't go more than a few lengths away from the river, and we'll move as quickly as we can."

They looked sullen.

"Look," he finally said, as some children decided that they didn't want to stay inside the barges when there were exciting things happening on the riverbank. "We've got children with us! Would anyone sane risk their children by fighting?"

It might not have been the best answer he could come up with, but the sight of those curious faces must have caused some thawing, because finally the blacksmith nodded. "Aight," he said. "Stoppin' for the night. But no longer."

With that assurance, Kordas waved to the front group, which started off—slow as a snail at first, as the horses strained against the weight they were being asked to haul, but speeding up as the barges got momentum.

There was a Doll standing next to the Gate to relay messages back through it to Rose and the rest. He looked at the Doll and nodded. As the first barges cleared the Gate area, a pair of mule heads poked through the shimmer of the Gate and slowly their barges emerged.

Great. Part one of the negotiations. And as soon as they get some idea that there are a lot more of us than they thought, and that begins to rile them up all over again, I'll begin the part of the negotiations where they actually get something out of this.

7

F ood forgotten, all of the scouting party sat with hands clenched and eyes fastened on Amethyst, who relayed the encounter with the suspicious locals. Fortunately, it appeared that Amethyst was not one of those Dolls who never said a word unless they were asked a direct question. Maybe all of them listening with interest to her story emboldened her. For whatever reason, she literally recited everything that happened, every word Kordas and the strangers said, and even narrated the strangers' reactions. And when she finally said, "And so they agree, and now the barges are moving again," they all sighed with relief simultaneously.

"What are they going to do when they finally realize we outnumber them a thousand to one?" Briada Fairweather asked aloud, making Delia tense up all over again.

But her cousin Bart barked with laughter. "*They* won't be doin' a thing. But they'll likely get a-feared, and Kordas will have to soothe 'em all over again."

Of course he was right. And of course Kordas *would*, because Kordas, she was increasingly certain, could fix anything that had to do with managing people.

"Well, this isn't getting us moving," Ivar pointed out, and set the example for the rest of them by heading for his horse Manta. In a moment he had put the bit back in her mouth and mounted up. Sai cleaned up what little there was to pick up, tossing the bits of bread left to Bay, and the rest went to their horses—or, in the case of Delia, to the last barge.

Amethyst came with her. "This one can chop the wood that you Fetch, Delia," the Doll offered. "And this one can carry it to be stacked on the next barge if we run out of room."

Ahead of them, Tight Squeeze strained in his harness, and Buttercup did her best behind him; the first barge moved, then the second and third, and with a little lurch, the one they were on crept up the river, gradually gaining speed.

"That would be very kind of you, Amethyst," Delia said gratefully. "Extraordinarily kind, in fact. Thank you. Are you going to be sleeping in the women's barge?" she added, with a pause to Fetch a dead branch about as thick as her wrist from the top of a tree; it broke with an audible *snap* and landed at her feet. Amethyst took the hand axe out of her hand and began breaking the branch into neat sections about the length of her forearm.

"This one does not sleep," Amethyst reminded her. "And this one sees very well in the dark. This one will be taking the night watch all night, alongside some of you."

"Oh." She blushed at her own forgetfulness. "I—hope that won't be tedious."

"Before the Dolls escaped, this one rarely saw anything outside the Palace," Amethyst pointed out. "And when this one was a free Elemental, this one rarely paid much attention to the world." She paused. "A mistake. If we had spent more time studying humans and less time in play with each other, we might not have been caught in that trap."

Delia took care with her reply. This river was rather sluggish, which was just as well, but at least the horses weren't having to pull against the current at the moment. Somehow, the water smelled cold and green; at least, that was how she would have described it. There must have been a hard frost along here last night, since on this section, the trees were every color between yellow and a dark purple-red she'd never seen in an autumn leaf before.

"Well, now you know," Delia replied, after an uncomfortably long pause punctuated only by the *thuds* of branches hitting the barge and the *thwack* of the hand axe.

"Now we know," Amethyst agreed. "But also, the senses these material bodies have are much different from our native senses. Everything is endlessly interesting to this one. And since the Baron has pledged to set us free, our time in using them is limited, so this one, at least, is observing all that is to be observed, and saving the memories."

Delia was going to say something, but she was interrupted by Ivar shouting *"Flush!"* and looked up to see ducks coming her way.

Most of the irate locals had gone back to their village, but the blacksmith and two more burly fellows remained. And as the sun climbed higher in the sky and then headed into the west, and the barges didn't stop coming, Kordas was paying careful attention to their faces.

When at last they displayed what he considered to be the correct degree of alarm—which was about at the point where the blacksmith probably figured that the adult Valdemarans outnumbered his villagers by at least ten to one—he slid down off Arial's back, ground-tied her, and walked over to them.

"*Now* we can begin the real negotiations," he said genially, while they eyed him with distrust. "Now, you take a look down that path—" he continued, pointing at the line of horses. "And pay close attention to all that nice, useful horse dung. That'll be yours for the taking."

At least one of the three men must have been a farmer, because his face lit up with understanding and a little greed.

"And we'll have herds and flocks coming through here to add to that dung. And it's all yours. Now, do you see what my people are doing up there? Raking it to the side so it doesn't get trampled and made useless, then one of my mages will come along and make it as dry as if it had been baking in the hot summer sun for a seven-day. Easy for you to gather, easy to move, light as cured hay, and easier to stack." The farmer nodded. He got the idea, and fast. "Dried out like that, you can break it up quick, manure your fields with it now without burning them, and plow it under to mellow over the winter."

Now the other two got it. The blacksmith stroked his chin thoughtfully. "Aye, but—how many on ye are there? Ye'll be a-breakin' down yon bank, be ye ever so careful, yer flocks will be eatin' the verge bare, an' how ye gonna make up for that?"

"That's what you and I are here to decide, without every man of your village wanting to put in his own opinion," Kordas replied, which got a snort from the farmer and a dry laugh from the blacksmith. "We have cattle, sheep, goats, and pigs. We're prepared to part with some. So, what do you reckon that damage is worth? Remember, these are all stock of breeding lines you've never seen before. You're going to get a great bargain out of this. It'll renew your herds with one breeding season."

The blacksmith looked to the farmer. "Well," the farmer said, grounding his pitchfork. "As to that—you'll know that every family in the village is going to want a bit of that new blood—"

The price they settled on was perfectly reasonable by Kordas's opinion, and he had the Doll relay the numbers, the kinds, and whose herds they were to come from. Mostly his, which seemed fair, from the herds of his manor farms. The time would probably come when they'd have to bargain like this again, and when it did, he wanted people to remember that he had been the one to part with *his* stock before anyone else did.

The important items in this trade were, as he had expected, males. One female could only produce so much in a season, but one male could and would happily service every female of his kind in the village, producing a new crop of beasts with half new blood in them. The third man ran back to the village to bring herders. And when the first boar, ram, billy, bull, and stallion came through the Gate, they were greeted, for the first time, with the admiration and approval of the native villagers who came to accept them. It was literally the first time Kordas had seen any of them smile. There was a pause while Dole took the spell off that kept them tied to the boats, and then Kordas turned them over with a flourish.

All of the animals except the stallion were young. The boar was out of one of the Empress's litters, and was two years old. Like all of the Squire's male shoats that didn't get castrated with an eventual end as bacon, he had been raised not unlike a dog. So, like a dog, he obeyed the instructions of his handlers, including "Stay." At some point in his family's history, the Squire's pig-raising forbears had gotten tired of charging, rage-filled boars and decided to try training them. And it had worked.

Kordas could not help but wonder how much of this lesson the villagers would take in.

The natives looked at the boar and his handler as if they were both mages. This was a greater wonder to them than Rose the Doll was.

The ram and goat were not so amenable, which troubled the shepherds not at all; they had brought their dogs. The stallion was a five-year-old cobby bay fellow that had been one of the "failed" False Golds—not gold, and not the size of a Tow-Beast. But he was a beefy lad, with broad feet and broader shoulders, perfect size for plowing. Of course *he* was mannerly, but that was not the marvel a boar that obeyed directions was.

There was some time while the handler mastered words in the speech of the Empire that he'd need to make the boar obey. But plenty of directions were just a sound and a gesture, including "Follow," so Kordas was pretty certain they'd get the pig to the village and into a sty without issue. Especially since the villager evidently knew his pigs, and had brought a sugar beet with him. The boar probably had not seen one of those since he'd left the Duchy, and it was very clear from his body language he would have learned to sit up and beg if that was what it took to get that beet.

It took most of the daylight for all this to be agreed on (and meanwhile, the barges kept coming through), and through all of it, Kordas could not keep himself from thinking of those Poomers and Spitters in their barges at the end of the tail, and how much easier it all would have been if he settled things "Imperial fashion." And he allowed himself those indulgent and dangerous thoughts, just to purge them out of his head. All he needed to do to make them fade away was to remind himself that "Imperial fashion" always ended in people dying. Always. Force never bred anything but force, and bullying never bred anything but resentment. And he'd had more than enough of all of that.

Now, let's hope I don't back us away from fights we should take on.

Finally the last of the locals left, the last of the sunlight left, and that was an end to the expedition movement for the day. Everyone up the line stopped, moored their strings to the bank, unharnessed the towing animals, and staked them to graze. Flocks of chickens and geese were bribed into the "coops" with grain, flocks and herds settled to eat and sleep. And Kordas went back through the Gate, leaving Rose to keep track of what was going on. Amethyst was with the scouts, Rose would stay at the Gate, there was Pansy on the first barge through the Gate, and other Dolls with other barges on either side of the Gate, either as night watchers or night herders. Ivy would keep him informed of what any of them observed.

Kordas was tired, chilled, and hungry, and if he got back soon enough, his dinner would be warm. He reached the middle of the lake just as the last light faded in the west.

Isla was watching for him from the prow of the barge, and offered her hand up to the deck. "What happened out there?" she asked. "I got bits of it from Ivy, but she was doing most of her talking to Dagger, the Doll with your guards on this side. They wanted to raid the armaments barges, and Dagger had to keep talking them down."

He squeezed his eyes shut and pinched the bridge of his nose. "What we would do without the Dolls, I do not know. That could have been a disaster. They'd have had good intentions, but they probably would have come through ready to attack, just as I was making the passage deal. Which went well, really." He followed her into the barge, where a plate of sausage-stuffed rolls and a hot cup of tea waited for him. Ivy was just shutting the door to the boys' room.

"Good work, Ivy!" he said, as he sat wearily and reached for a roll. "I was just telling Isla that I don't know what we'd do without you. But—" he added hastily, lest she think that meant he was thinking better of his pledge to free them, "—we'll have to learn to do without you eventually. Maybe I should start a concerted effort to find the folk with Mindspeech. There have to be *some* of those among our folk . . ."

"That is a brilliant idea!" Isla exclaimed. "I'll get to work on that. We'll pair them with Dolls for redundancy, and practice on their part."

He took a bite from the still-warm sausage roll and sighed. *One potential problem derailed. Millions more to go.* There would probably be no more than a handful of people with useful Mindspeech, but as long as they were spaced out along the convoy, the problem of getting messages around without the Dolls was solved. He was already dissatisfied with the necessity of the tow animals working along an unprepared bank. In old Valdemar, the towline courses were well prepared, with paved ground or hard clay pack. Now, their beasts were putting themselves at risk with every step into the mud, or foothold of a root. Only the guidance of their handlers gave them an advantage.

"You may do that, Lord Baron," Ivy said placidly. "But we will not leave you until you have a home, regardless of when you learn how to free us."

He had absolutely no doubt that Ivy spoke for all of the Dolls. *Bless them.* "Then thank you, Ivy," he said. "It'll be a good idea to have two ways to send word up and down the line; what if something comes along and—I don't know—drains you of magic?"

His temple throbbed. "The Healers will be able to tell who has Mind-magic; they probably already know."

"And Doll Panacea is asking them about it now," Ivy replied. "She says to tell you that your Healers will have the names by morning, and we'll have some of us talk to the people in question to explain it all to them. We assume—" and by her body language, "we assume" meant "we expect or you'll regret it," "—that those with the Gift you require will be kept secret to avoid exploitation, and will be compensated well."

Did Ivy just get—crafty? Was I just intimidated? I suppose if anyone would be conscientious about exploitation, it would be the Dolls.

"You see?" Isla said to Kordas while retrieving their butter jar. "It's not all on your back." She patted his hand. "Remember back on the estate; you were never the sort to try to manage every little thing in the Duchy. You knew who to trust to do their jobs, you told them what we needed, and you left them to it. Just do the things no one else among us can do. Like negotiating with potentially hostile people. That was a very shrewd move of yours, to wait to offer livestock until just before they might have turned on you."

Well, that wasn't *quite* how things had gone, but—near enough, he supposed.

"Meanwhile I've enlisted the boys into what they are calling the 'Page Army.' I don't suppose you remember a retired Imperial Army lieutenant named Sol Adrescu? He's organizing all the children into groups to run errands and forage, with a fifteen- or sixteen-year-old in charge of each group, and a Doll to keep track of what they are doing. He recruited our lot. He's running them off their feet, in a good way. It means they are tired and happy and willing to go straight to bed once supper is over." Isla gave him a sharp glance. "Speaking of which, please eat."

"Oh. Right." He finished the now-not-quite-so-warm rolls, and his tea. "I have concerns about them being too easily accessible as hostages for somebody desperate, but I should trust you all to be watchful. As for the river, I'm just glad I thought to put the Poomers and Spitters and their ammunition at the end of the convoy. That way, they won't be the first thing anyone thinks of when we run into trouble. And hopefully, most people will forget they exist. And if we end up losing a few boats at the tail, it will be something we don't *need*, and hopefully, something no one else knows how to use. I'd sink all of them right now, but . . ."

"But we might encounter something that nothing else will work on." She picked up his cup and plate, wiped them off and put them away, and took his wrist. "Tomorrow will be another long day."

"It's all going to be long days, for quite a while," he agreed, and followed her to their bed, while Ivy went out to take a watchful position on the roof of the barge, serenely gazing up at the stars from time to time.

The next day ended with both him *and* Isla in the saddle. Isla, to go interview all of the people with Mindspeech that the Healers had identified, and him to ride up and down the lakeside, making sure that things were going as smoothly as possible.

When much of your command is because of personal charisma and trust, a wise leader makes himself seen and has personal visits whenever possible. It reminds followers that they are important for more than their tasks, and it replenishes their morale. Nobody wants to dare the wild following someone fifty leagues away, but they'll follow the leader they saw last week. When appealing to the heart, make it personal and keep it personal, and apologize for when you can't. Those were the words of his father, and wise ones. Certainly nothing he learned in the Imperial hostage school.

The impression wasn't hurt when an elderly couple gifted Kordas with a basket of warm, morning-baked twisted breadsticks, explaining they were their grandparents' recipe from home. Kordas shared the bread with minders, headmen, and guards along his route, passing the story along. Being seen giving food personally was good, but being talked about doing so was even better.

His quick check to the other side of the Gate told him that the flotilla was on the move again. Or at least the front part of it was. There was no sign of the native villagers, although, of course, they could have had one of their number up a tree keeping watch from afar. Rose assured him that all was well with the scouts, that the leading barges of the convoy had matters well in hand and had picked up speed, and that she would make sure he heard about it if any of that changed. So he took Arial back through the Gate to fret his way along the lakeshore, imagining all the things that could go wrong, and trying to think of solutions before they did. Passing through the Gate was a matter of timing, when boats were in motion. They came through at a steady pace, but returning to Crescent Lake meant jumping Arial onto a moving barge, rushing to the end before it came through, and leaping off on the other side of the Gate's shimmer to the waiting jetty. Fortunately, head-on collisions were very unlikely; the laws everyone knew about Gate travel were good ones, and directional travel safely went through from opposite sides of the uprights. Similarly, the vessels came through with the same protocols they'd left old Valdemar's canals by—straight through the Gate, then immediately break starboard to clear the way for following traffic, siding outward by half beam. If that hadn't been ingrained in everyone who brought a boat through, they'd never have gotten a dozen barges to Crescent Lake.

The remaining mages had set up a camp just out of the way of the convoy, and before he could look for any of the Six Old Men, Ceri strolled up to his side. "We've each got our personal barges ready to attach to a string, and we've already calculated how many barges need to pass before one of us joins the string," he said, without waiting for Kordas to ask him anything. "Kordas, you've spent every minute since we got to Crescent Lake organizing things so that each section of the caravan can pretty much manage itself. You want some advice?"

Kordas had pulled himself up a little when Ceri had said that—because it was absolutely true. Every village was in its own section of the group. People who didn't have a village—like the Squire's offspring—had organized with neighbors. Every group had a designated cook and a portable kitchen, and a common supply barge. Every group had a leader. Every group had more than one Doll. Even if some disaster separated the groups, they all had the means to communicate, get help, and survive until they met up with, or were rescued by, others.

"Yes, please," he said.

"Let them. Tell your subordinates to think of all the ways things could realistically go wrong, and to work out solutions." Ceri grinned, showing a set of surprisingly white and strong teeth for someone his age. "That way, we narrow down the number of ways we can be unpleasantly surprised, and you don't exhaust yourself."

"But—" he began.

"Yes, yes, I know," Ceri said dismissively, sounding, in that moment, exactly like Sai. "We will still be unpleasantly surprised at some point. But you will have narrowed down the number of times that can happen by anticipating it and having solutions on hand.

What you're needed for are emergent situations, and leadership. Not spinning yourself up with anxiety solving every possible problem, which you probably won't be there for anyway. Now go away."

Kordas knew better than to argue, and sent Arial back to the family barge. When he wasn't riding her, she would be giving a hand—or a hoof, as it were—to Dasha, the enormous False Gold mare he'd selected to pull his string of barges. A filly foal—Delia's personal horse—was with Dasha as well, but she was much too young to do anything other than amuse the boys and be made much of. Each barge-string was going to be responsible for its own towing beasts, whether they were horse, mule, set of ponies or donkeys, or the infinitely patient oxen. Their little homing talismans were now attached to the first barge in their string, as opposed to a herdsman or corral. As far as he was aware, pretty much every animal that could be put into harness was towing a vessel of some sort.

And for as long as grass could still grow this late in the year, the Six had solved the problem of forage. Each mage had been taught the spell that made the grass grow unnaturally fast. When the column stopped for the night, the first thing each mage was supposed to do was hop out and start growing the grass. Even gorging themselves, the herds wouldn't be able to eat it all—with this spell going, you could quite literally watch the grass grow.

Even if the spell drains the ground with the growth, the herds should replenish it as they digest. At least partly. It would not do to render the soil useless after promising we would do no harm. We're doing more than enough harm just by being here.

When he got to the family barge, the whole family except for Delia was there, with Isla directing servants, children, and a couple of his Guard as if she was an Imperial Officer. Dasha was waiting patiently in harness, tethered to the family barge, and Isla greeted his arrival with the command, "Get Arial out of her tack and in harness. Our supply barges just arrived and we're not that long from moving."

"Yes ma'am!" he said, laughing so it wouldn't sting. "I'll be right back."

It was kind of a relief to be in a position to be ordered around, instead of the one doing the ordering.

Funny how affection can take the edge off of anything. Anyone else and I'd frown over that. It must be love.

With the long caravan of barges now coming through the Gate, the scouts were on the move. According to everything that Amethyst had relayed, Kordas had the situation with the rightful dwellers of this land well in hand, so there was nothing stopping or delaying that ever-growing snake behind them. *Of course he does,* Delia thought, without any irony. *I really think there is nothing that Kordas cannot handle, and he's just letting us do things so we feel special and wanted.*

There could be something to that, actually. *Finding this river must have been a huge relief for Kordas.*

For her part, she was getting into the rhythm of exploration. And making sure to enjoy what she could about this part of the journey, because things could and probably would get a great deal more difficult. Certainly it was already colder, and none of them knew anything about the climate of this part of the world. *So expect the worst, and prepare for it.*

She'd done the little *she* could by catching extra birds every day, stockpiling the firewood, and taking on the chores that anyone could do, as opposed to the more specialized things only a mage or Ivar or Briada could do.

That let her concentrate on traveling for literally the first time in her life, knowing that decent, if plain, meals were right at hand, and a comfortable bed awaited her at the end of the day. She didn't even need to take a turn at night watch! Consultation between Briada Fairweather and Ivar had led to the conclusion that, since Doll Amethyst could, and had indicated she would, spend the entire night on watch, Amethyst would stand watch on the lead supply barge where the horses were going to be left to graze and sleep in the night. Meanwhile, the two Fairweather cousins, Ivar, Hakkon, and Briada would divide up watches on the rear barge carrying the Gate uprights, which was where anyone trying to sneak up on them would probably come from. For now, Ivar's dog was sleeping on the roof of the women's barge in the middle, and that was a third set of senses all night. From Delia's experience, it was impossible to sneak up on Bay. Even when he looked like he was sound asleep, if you moved, an ear would point right at you. And his bark could wake the dead.

That is something I will miss about Crescent Lake. The noises. All the wildlife, stock, pets, and children sounding off, bits of music, the occasional whoop or howl from storytelling, or chants during chores. I may never hear that again. It might never happen again. This is the real here-and-now, but it's also history. I heard that with my own ears, and I couldn't even have imagined it as a concept a year ago. The idea of so many of us, who were spread across hill, dale, and meadow, put all together in one place? Incredible. This is scary, but it's amazing, too.

Meanwhile, she was cheerily getting on with the two jobs she had been assigned: wood gathering, and hunting for dinner.

Or, in this case, fishing for dinner. She had discovered just by trying it that what worked in the air also worked as long as she could see through the water to her target object. She had no idea what *kind* of fish she was catching, she only knew that they looked nice and fat, and Sai had approved of the first one. She was belly-down in the stern, watching the wake, where it seemed fish liked to gather and snap at things jumping into the water from the bank. There were five fish in the basket hung in the water at the prow of the boat, and Delia was hoping to add a sixth, so everyone would get half a fish for dinner tonight. As she narrowed her eyes against the light on the water, she heard footsteps on the walkway behind her.

"If you can catch a sixth fish, everyone will get half a fish for dinner tonight," said Sai, in an echo of her thoughts. "Fish and flatbread with that watercress I found where we camped last night. I'm shocked the geese hadn't been at it."

She didn't ask him if he had tested it to make sure it actually was watercress; he'd already lectured everyone about how they could not count on plants that *looked* like something they knew was edible actually *being* that thing. She sighed, but quietly; she didn't want Sai to ask her why she was sighing, because it was . . . pretty trivial. She missed the battered, fried fish the cook had made back home, when there was always plenty of everything and no need to worry about using up the last bits, and there were so many kinds of fat, from lard to butter, that one could waste it frying battered fish.

"And I'll use a little of that goose fat you got us to fry up the dried mushrooms that are soaking in the kitchen," Sai continued. "Now, there's something even the late unlamented Emperor wouldn't have turned up his nose at."

A dim form slowly rose up through the green river water. Delia tensed, waiting to make sure it looked like the rest of her catch. It rolled up to the surface, and she identified the little telltale arrowhead in dark gray on the top of its head that all the other fish had. She reached, imagining she was snatching for the fish with two invisible hands—

And the fat silver fish lay flapping on the walkway just at Sai's feet. Before she could move, he seized it in both skinny arms and trotted to the front of the barge where the netted fish-basket was, cackling with anticipation.

She rolled over and looked at the sky, waiting for the pain behind her eyes to ease, and grateful that it was cold and the chill could soothe the ache. She had used her Gift more since she had joined the Scouts than she had in all the time she'd lived with Kordas and Isla. Thankfully, when she had explained that using her Gift too much made her head ache and she sometimes needed to lie down and rest, everyone had understood.

Am I that desperate not to be thought to be slacking?

She stared at a puffy little cloud.

Well, yes. She was that desperate. Because she wanted everyone here to actually *want* her here. She wanted to be thought well of for herself, to be thought of as a valuable part of this expedition. She wanted them to think of her first as herself, and not as the Baroness's sister.

And if Kordas sent me along to get me out from underfoot . . . I want them to think that if they'd had a choice, they would have asked me along themselves.

Because as they had all been camped around the lake, practically in each other's pockets day and night, it had become increasingly obvious, at least to her, that something had changed between Kordas and Isla. They weren't acting as they had at home. In fact, if she'd been forced to put a name to things, she'd have said they were in love with each other. They weren't just friends and partners anymore.

And surely one of them had noticed *her* feelings about the Baron. She probably wasn't any good at hiding her feelings . . .

A face interposed itself between Delia and the sky. "Rested up, yet?" Briada asked, with a half smile.

"More or less. Do we need more wood?" She clambered to her feet. Briada stepped back to give her room.

"Good gods, no. I was just curious about something. That thing you do—can it push as well as pull?" Briada tucked her thumbs in her belt and stood in a deceptively relaxed stance as she waited for Delia to reply. Delia knew it was a "deceptively relaxed stance" because Delia had seen the woman go from this exact pose to ready to take someone apart in barely the time it took to blink.

But Delia had to take a minute to work out what Briada meant. "Um . . . I've thrown stones with it?" she finally said.

Briada considered that, as wavelets lapped against the hulls of the barges, and the steady, dull clopping of hooves on the bank marked their continuous passage. There was an actual path here, which suggested that people used the riverbank as a sort of road, but so far none of those people had put in an appearance.

"Well," Briada said, finally. "What I had in mind was . . ." Her face screwed up as she sought for words. "Could you *magic* an arrow into a target? Guide it, or shove it there or something."

Delia did not correct Briada to say that what she did was not precisely magic, at least not as the mages practiced it. Over the last few days she had at least learned not to over-explain things. The Fairweather cousins made no attempts at concealing their thoughts or feelings, and their exaggerated expressions of boredom when she started to explain something had soon cured her of doing so. Instead she shrugged. "I've never tried," she admitted. "It's called 'Fetching Gift,' not 'Arrow-Guiding Gift,' after all." She eyed Briada with speculation. "You want me to try it, don't you?"

"Well, hell, if we ran into trouble, you could do us all a hell of a lot of good if you could send an arrow into a target no matter how much it dodged," Briada pointed out—inadvertently adding another layer of difficulty to what Delia had proposed. But what could she do? She didn't actually *know* what her capabilities in that regard were, and saying she couldn't do it without first trying would be—

—well, it would probably sink her in Briada's eyes.

"When would you like me to try?" she temporized. "And where?"

"You could move back to the rearmost barge, I can give you a hand-crossbow, and you can plink at trees. I'll retrieve your arrows—"

"No need," she said, with a slight smirk. "I can Fetch them back myself, remember?" And the more she thought about this idea, the more she wanted to try. It was one thing to contribute to the scouts in a sort of passive way; it was quite another if she could actually be of use in a fight.

"Well then, I'll just get you a hand-crossbow." Briada chuckled, and hopped barges until she got to the supply barge. She was remarkably agile, and the bobbing and swaying didn't seem to trouble her even a little bit.

For the remainder of the afternoon, Delia perched on the four Gate uprights strapped to the top of the barge and experimented with the lightest of the hand-crossbows. She didn't want the bolts to stick too deeply into the trees she was shooting at; just as there was a limit to how much she could Fetch, there was a limit to how hard she could pull.

At first her results were no better than just aiming, but she had a kind of . . . pulling or reaching sort of feeling, the kind she got whenever she tried something new that actually was going to work. Like when she had first tried assisting at the difficult birth of an animal on the manor farms. In that case it had been a lamb, and eventually, after a lot of sweating on the parts of both her and the shepherd, she'd gotten the little creature out before something dire happened.

So she persisted, sending the same crossbow bolt into trunk after trunk, while the horses clopped along up ahead, Hakkon and Jonaton brought up the rear, and the three Fairweathers perched on the middle barges with heavy mankiller crossbows in hand.

About the time that Ivar and Bay came back from scouting ahead to let them know he'd found a good spot to tie up for the night—

Something in her just felt like a tile falling into place. And in the next moment, she planted the bolt exactly where she wanted it to, in a barely visible canker in the bark of what looked like a walnut tree. She yanked it back into her hand, riding on a surge of elation, and picked a new target.

She'd managed to repeat her shot a little less than a dozen times when she felt the pressure-bordering-on-pain that meant she needed to stop if she didn't want to regret it for the rest of the night.

At that point, Alberdina was slowing the horses so as to bring the barge-string to a gradual stop, and Delia hung the crossbow beside its quiver on her belt and ran to help set up the land side of the camp for the night.

It was only when they were all enjoying Sai's fish around the cookfire that Briada cocked her head and said, "I asked Delia to see if she could use that magic of hers to think an arrow into the target this afternoon."

"But that's not m—" began Venidel, when Sai elbowed him.

"Don't go off on a meaningless tangent," Sai scolded him, then looked to Delia across the fire. The last light was just leaving the sky and the temperature had dropped down to the point where Delia's nose was definitely getting unpleasantly cold, so she answered the question before Sai could answer it.

"It actually worked!" she said. "I wasn't sure it would, but it did!"

Ivar perked up at that. "That's good news!" he exclaimed. "When it gets colder, you can come up ahead with me, and we can guarantee we'll bring back a deer or something like one!"

"Why wait until it's colder?" Delia asked, at the same time that Briada put in, "Well, that wasn't what I was thinking of—"

"We haven't encountered any hostiles yet, Sergeant," Ivar replied to Briada first. "The most useful thing she can do is bag us a deer." Then he turned to Delia. "Because right now we're doing fine with the geese, ducks, and fish you're catching, but when it gets colder, the geese and ducks will be gone, the fish will sink to the bottom of the river to sleep because there are no insects to eat, and we'll need to find game that is active. Rabbits, yes, but a man can starve eating rabbit, even if he stuffs himself."

She looked at him dubiously. Surely he was joking. . . . Briada had the same expression on her face.

"It's true," Alberdina verified. "There's not enough fat. In about a week living only on rabbit, or on rabbit and grains, you'll get sick, and if you don't get some fat, you'll die."

"Huh." Bret and Bart looked as stunned as if Alberdina had declared that she was the Emperor returned. Briada didn't looked stunned, but she did look surprised.

"That's why I am hoarding all the goose and duck fat," Sai said.

"It's your job to think about that," Briada finally replied, as the flickering light illuminated all their faces. "It's my job to think about defense. And now, in Delia, we have something better than all the Poomers in the world." She grinned.

And Delia said nothing, but her heart swelled.

8

The convoy was *almost*—not quite—past the village they had first encountered when they crossed the Gate, and Kordas was about ready to put that potential source of problems out of his mind.

I am putting more furlongs on poor Arial than I ever did at home, Kordas thought, as he neared the midpoint of the convoy, after having ridden all the way to the end and back, making sure that everything was going according to plan. The only complaints that the people at the end had were that the herds in front of them had decimated the available browse by the time they reached a spot. But they admitted that their beasts were not suffering. The mages always made enough grass to grow to feed the herds overnight, and Kordas could see for himself that the horses and herds were still in good condition, so he just chalked the comments up to "people need something to complain about," and was glad it was nothing worse than that.

If worse came to worst, so he had been told, some of the mages would be able to make grass grow even in the dead of winter. *He* didn't know how to do that, but Sai had assured him that for the "green mages," of which there were several, it was not only possible but trivial. At least, as long as they themselves had adequate rest and food. This was how the Imperial gardens at the Palace had been able to produce fruits, vegetables, and flowers all year around.

"Rose," he said to the Doll riding behind him. "Ask the Dolls with the green mages to say I want them to do something about the grass all along the riverbank please. More of it, please, not less of it. People at the rear are complaining the ground has been eaten bare."

"Certainly, Lord Baron," the Doll replied pleasantly.

Kordas wanted the expedition's pace to be brisk, not least because the faster they were, the less of a shock they would be on the ecosystems they passed through. One of Jonatan's crude but true remarks was that most environmental-theater spellwork was like building a wagon, but good luck, you weren't allowed to move from where you were standing. The act of building a spell kept the mage from observing all of its possible effects, because its structure as a spell *at all* was in the way of their senses. That, factored with the scale of some undertakings they had in mind—yes, a thing could be attempted with magic, but minor effects on a smaller scale became major ones that tipped over into entirely *new* dangers once they crested certain thresholds. "Inconvenient" side effects at room-scale, like glass breakage, became "the ground split open, and we're losing cows" at village scale.

Non-mages don't think of it much, but if a mage is there to talk with you, it means they've survived their own work, and you should be impressed. A universal truth of magic-casting was that if energy was being altered, formed, repurposed, or modulated, that meant heat would be a byproduct of the alteration, as much as a millstone made heat while doing its work.

Small wonder that magic is most practiced in the winter, when the heat is needed anyway.

The mark of mastery was if the mage was crafty with where to dump the heat. Snap spellcasting, like combat tactical spells, began with the mage stabbing a unseen "spear" of anchoring magic into the earth, and an instant later, the spell was castable without igniting one's own clothes. Or fellow casters.

The expedition's mages were being as safe as they could, and the spellcasting standards they'd agreed upon built firm anchors, like lances stabbed into hay bales, and sent the thermal recoil from magic manipulation deep into the ground, to simply warm up stone. Now, scale that up a hundred times, and that's a lot of heated earth, which could be devastating to the life cycles within a land. Bugs, fish, and worms don't take well to being boiled in their bathwater while some mage makes plants grow furlongs away. Kordas had placed the natives' and the expedition's survival into the mages' hands, and muttered a short prayer of thanks for the cadre of mages with them—and that so far, they all liked and backed him.

I wouldn't take kindly to boiling in my bathwater, either.

The convoy wasn't moving any faster than a leisurely stroll, but that was to be expected. They were moving through a broad shallow, and boat piloting was all about dodging sandbars against the current—a sluggish current, but it was definitely still a factor—and the ratio of barges to horses was definitely a big factor. Some of the narrower barges were simply used as floating piers, and wagon ferries were employed to get livestock through past unsympathetic terrain, and were shuffled to wherever they were needed. This slow pace meant that the barnyard fowl could forage and still keep up with their shelter-barges, and the swine, sheep, and goats easily could do the same. It also meant that people stuck as "passengers" could do some frog hunting and fishing, and for the time being, the management of the kitchen barges wouldn't need to think about slaughtering more animals than they needed for a single communal meal. It was all part of Isla's carefully calculated organizational plan. There were so many barges and people per kitchen; so many supply barges for each kitchen; and methods for splitting or filling rosters when a boat got stuck, or some accident disrupted progress. Each kitchen got a set amount of fresh meat for the morning meal, depending on whether people in that group had hunted or fished for it, or if they'd drawn lots over who was going to supply it from their herds. Breakfast was usually the biggest meal, and the one that featured things that could be baked or stewed overnight in the coals of a small fire. Dinner was flatbread, cheese, and pickled or raw vegetables; as part of the stockpiling, Kordas and his people had been storing waxed wheels of cheese for two generations, and there was a lot of cheese on those supply barges. Supper was flatbread, and soup or pottage. For a treat, there was flatbread and jam, jelly, or honey. Anything that turned up besides that, well, the people who found it got to decide what was done with it. They'd waited until the weather had turned cold to start their journey, so the bees were all sleeping in their hives and the hives could be closed up and packed together on their own special barges.

At this point, if anyone was hoarding treats, the amounts were insignificant, and wouldn't matter to anyone's survival in a crisis. The only exception to the "each kitchen gets meat from the barges assigned to it" was when Kordas, who had more farm beasts than anyone else, allotted one of his to some part of the convoy that was animal-poor. And so far, no one was complaining about the food, or the way the food had been allotted. *Isla is an unsung genius at this.*

Just as Ceri had advised he get others to do, Kordas had been spending every bit of free time thinking of every possible disaster he could, and trying to work out a way to prevent it or at least soften the effects.

"Kordas," said Rose into his ear, making him jump. The Doll was so quiet that even though she was riding pillion behind him on Arial, he often forgot she was there. "Villagers have come running to the rear of the convoy, begging for help."

At first, what she said didn't quite register. The villagers? Begging for help? But—

Idiot. There was only one reason they would come running to the convoy for help. *Oh gods. They're being attacked by something they can't fend off by themselves.* Or worse. Something, maybe, that farm implements couldn't drive off.

Or we attracted it with our noise. None of what we do has been quiet, and for good reason—we don't know what kinds of creatures are ahead, so making a commotion should scare away predators that might otherwise have a go at them. But, there are no guarantees out here—we could attract things too.

He considered not helping only for a fraction of a moment. There really was no choice; if nothing else, he had to set an example to the rest of his people that standing aside and doing nothing when others were in trouble was not going to be looked on with favor. His actions, fortunately, spoke louder than his inner monologue.

Oh gods. I've never actually fought anything deadly but the Emperor.

His heart clenched, then raced, and he blessed the foresight that had led him to strap on his crossbows and quiver this morning along with his sword and dagger. "I am responding! Tell the guards in the back third to arm up, and form on me at the tail," he said, turning Arial on her heels and sending her back in the direction he'd come from at a canter. "If they have horses, use them. If they don't, get running. Brief Isla and Hakkon, set reserves, get some Mage-gazes on the situation and advise. Sound horns in the tail quarter, and get me more information!"

His heart pounded in his ears, keeping time with the drumming of Arial's hooves. She had entered the particular intensity that made her so prized by Kordas. She wasn't just "running," she was running *selectively*, actively planning steps yet to be taken. She wasn't compliant, she was *determined* to get wherever she was pointed. Kordas felt Arial switch up to her "spark" by the rapid, subtle swings of their center of gravity as horse-and-rider, as her hips and withers moved to their fastest route for each stride. Kordas and Arial were a single unit made of man and mare, surging ever faster. To Kordas, his lower back felt like he was rowing while also being the waves; all the momentum flowed, and the wind bowed before them.

His "Guard," for the most part, consisted of his own personal guardsmen and farmers and hunters who were at least on conversational terms with weaponry. They didn't really have uniforms at this point, but they at least knew each other. It wasn't an impressive force by Imperial standards, but it probably passed for an army here.

And if they were lucky, sheer numbers would overwhelm whatever had alarmed the villagers so badly.

A group of about forty guards, mixed between mounted and foot, had gathered for him when he arrived at the end of the convoy, and Arial reared upward when she rounded to stop. Pacing and punching his fist in his palm, with them was the agitated blacksmith and a young lad, who looked ready to promise the moon for some kind of aid. As soon as the blacksmith spied Kordas, he bellowed "You! Come on! We need ye!" and pelted off in the direction of the village.

"You heard him!" Kordas shouted to the hearteningly responsive would-be fighters, about half of whom were mounted. "Move out! Foot, follow him at speed!" Barely slowing by half, Kordas held his crossbow high and shouted, "Engage by heart!" a phrase known by educated soldiers that meant, "Use your best judgment and compassion." It was a command guiding how soldiers should react to what they were about to see, as well as a reminder that they were going to be seen doing so. At this moment, too little of the situation ahead was known for him to give any more specific orders. The cry bolstered morale immediately. It told soldiers and guards that their senior commander trusted them, and that led by him, theirs was a righteous cause. The sound of senior soldiers repeating "Engage by heart!" fell away behind Kordas, and his heart surged. It was the first time he'd ever given that command outside of games, and it felt right.

Kordas and the mounted guards overtook the reluctant blacksmith and passed him, leaving him to serve as a guide for those on foot. By horse, the distance was trivial, yet Arial already outdistanced the escorting riders. Bad form, for several reasons, and Kordas noted, hopefully not as a last thought, that a field commander being the first upon a battlefield was never likely to end well. The village was just over a hill, and Arial answered his urging with her best speed again. He'd be there in a heartbeat.

Screams met his ears as the village of rock-built cottages came into sight, and he drew the compact, deadly light crossbow and cocked it by the lever of the pommel. He had a bolt nocked and locked before he saw the cause of those screams.

With a belly-twist of revulsion and horror, what he saw, he instantly knew, were no natural creatures. His first impression was that they were voids, an absence of light, not just "black," but like light wasn't allowed to be near them. When they moved, the things didn't hold a definite outline. Their edges stuttered in and out randomly, as if they were sun-shimmers tearing the air itself. Mages like Kordas were more used to otherworldly and horrific things than nearly anyone except, maybe, the rare Summoner, and these things were *unnerving* to Kordas. The stone in his stomach told Kordas that these had never even *been* natural creatures.

Oh no, no, tell me we didn't open up a demon pit. Tell me it's not an overrun. Tell me we didn't cause this.

These unnatural foes they faced were a pack of . . . leaping, dodging, vanishing *things*. Things that looked like the bastard children of a snake and a greyhound, by way of a demonic midwife, with enough of a mastiff to make them enormous. They didn't so much run as *flow through each other's paths* with those shuddery, waving silhouettes only adding to their menace. In color they were a smoky black, with skin that gave an impression of smooth scales rather than hair when it gave up some light. Reactant to their movements, strobes of colored light in vaguely geometric designs lit up and moved down their bodies. The skin displayed afterimages of the creature's background or others of their kind every second, or darkened to make fake shadows. Sometimes the lights flared and dazzled, but added up, the main effect was to make these things *horrifically* hard to keep track of. The things had long, long necks, too long by far, and arrowhead-shaped heads that were an uncanny mingling of viper and canid, with yellow, pupilless eyes that actually glowed. The teeth in those narrow muzzles were needle-sharp, too numerous, and as long as a man's thumb. They had bodies like greyhounds as well, but the legs and tails seemed unhealthily stretched, and the bodies unnaturally flexible.

They swarmed along what passed for a lane among the cottages, attacking, nipping at, and attempting to drag off anything they saw. Three of them had faced off against the prize bull, two more challenged the young stallion, and one had seized a screaming, half-grown pig by the hind leg, and the pig was swiftly losing the battle to get away. The villagers attempted to fend the creatures off with anything they had at hand, but the things merely ignored adult humans in favor of livestock. Some of which—no, most of which—were the animals from the passage deal.

Kordas made arm gestures and his guards set themselves in short lines and made ready for archery, and the horseborne fanned out behind them, bringing up assault bows. In rushes of releases, arrows and crossbow bolts filled the air between them and the pack of those unholy things. All the shots were carefully aimed. He *saw* them aim.

He saw the shots fly true. He expected shrieks or howls when the arrows found their targets; instead, there was nothing. No sound of reaction. The shafts that outright missed the creatures made normal *thwap* noises when they hit, but the few that struck the creatures made no noise at all—nor did the creatures. It dawned on Kordas what this would mean if the creatures weren't out in the light like this. *You couldn't see them coming, or count them once they were in your presence . . . and you couldn't hear them close in. Not even running around do they make noise, and they should still have made some kind of yelp when they were struck. Wait, maybe they did, but we couldn't hear it. Yes! I bet that is it! When they trip or crush something and knock things over, we don't hear that either. It's not just that they are silent, it's that they're stopping sound.*

Arial froze stock-still, refusing to come any nearer to these creatures than she was now. Kordas saw that of the scores of shots taken, only the few heart-shots had been effective. The other wounded creatures paused just long enough to chew off the shafts before looking for the source of their pain.

"Heart-shots!" he shouted, and he nocked another bolt, firing it as soon as he got the crossbow cocked. "Center of the chest! Heart-shots!"

Disturbingly, the monsters' worrying at the livestock all stopped in the same instant, and they wholesale ignored the villagers. They fixated on Kordas and the soldiers, and to Kordas's dread—they multiplied.

The creatures oozed and slunk around buildings, climbing over carts and under fences to gather into a roiling mass of shadows, half-bodies, and shimmers. Each of the creatures appeared to split and expand, though it was almost unfollowable how quickly or how many they might be by the moment. Scores of pairs of yellow eyes turned in unison upon the archers as the creatures massed together. The exact size of this mass of darkness wasn't even clear, because groups of the things would dodge and leap in and out in knots of movement, making the eye follow them. Then there were hundreds of yellow eyes, all moving in pairs, with more joining into the deepening darkness all the time. They were all ignoring their previous prey. All getting closer.

How many are there? Were there hundreds that have been invisible? Were they there all this time, or waiting to arrive? What is this? We can't fight this many—anythings.

The hypnotic, fear-provoking gathering of creatures split into two slow flows. One mass fixated on Kordas. The others closed in on the ground troops, and the tension finally broke. With a slithery sort of sigh, what looked like thirty or more masses of the things came at the defending guards, closing ground as a pack, and moving faster than any canid Kordas had ever seen before. And still eerily quiet. *It could make you think they weren't even really there.*

Like they were illusions.

Kordas didn't actually *think*; a decade and a half of Imperial training in war games dictated his change in tactics. His gut knew, before his mind said a thing.

He gathered his power within himself, reached for the nearest ley-line, stabbed his anchor into it, and just as the pack leaders got within two barge-lengths of the front lines, he threw up a curtain of fire right at their noses, between them and his guards.

The weirdling beasts ran straight into it, and despite being entirely hairless, somehow caught fire. Kordas sent the flames roaring upward, and pushed the conflagration against the rush of the creatures. Harm spells could be "mixed," and his fire wave had been mixed both to cause physical burns and to dispel the cohesion of any illusions.

That should have broken their illusions, so now we can pick off the real ones.

And still, the creatures made no sound as they broke and ran in all directions, biting at their burning flanks, shaking their heads and pawing at their eyes. They rolled on the ground, trying to put themselves out, or thrashed around, felling hedges and stacked-rail fencing. The fire only made discerning their shapes more difficult, and hundreds of pairs of eyes looked out from the darkness while they regrouped.

They—weren't illusions. Oh, what have I done? All those eyes—they're still there. They weren't illusions. My best shot was maybe two-thirds wasted breaking illusions that weren't there. I was so sure. Now they're closing, and I used the wrong spell.

By this point the blacksmith and the guards afoot had largely switched to hand weapons, and the blacksmith screamed at the top of his lungs, *"Ware the bite! Ware the bite!"* as he charged toward one of the things and swung his sledgehammer at what appeared to be its head. The blow connected well enough that the thing's head was forcibly deformed two handsbreadths to the left from the rest of its body. There was no sound except for the huff of exertion the blacksmith had put into it.

Ware the bite? What about the bite? Biting, attack . . .

"Poison fangs!" Kordas shouted—even if that wasn't the actual truth, it was close enough to make his people watch themselves. Horse troops maneuvered themselves into hit-and-run attrition on the creatures, succeeding in kettling many of the things, then chopping them down in waves of weaving ride-by attacks. The foot troops and the villagers formed into back-to-back defensive lines, with crossbow reloaders in the middle, and edged toward Kordas. They were soon enveloped, but held their own. These creatures preferred to nip at their targets, presumably to make use of their toxic bites. Amidst the expanding, shifting battlefield around him, Kordas saw the unfortunate creature the blacksmith had clocked in the skull stagger away from its pack. Toward Kordas. It ultimately dropped a horselength away from Arial, and still afire, it expired on its side right before him. Some of its skin had charred to ash. To Kordas's momentary shock, he saw that the whole surface of its body that wasn't burned had eyes. Pairs of glowing eyes looking outward, squinting, and peering around, while the body that bore their images died.

They weren't illusions. The creature's undamaged skin was murky-dark, with hundreds of convincing eyes glowing in it. *They suddenly made themselves seem like hundreds—which would cause complete panic in their prey, and to anyone who could sling a spell, it undoubtedly had to be an illusion, right? It was a trick. To make someone . . . think it was an illusion . . . be impressed by themselves . . . get cocky for figuring it out . . . and waste a spell. Which I did. I fell for it. And now they're breaking off, just . . . retreating*

The beasts—the ones that still could—fled into stands of trees as far from the village as they could find. The ones that couldn't run met their ends from axes and scythes, arrows, crossbow bolts, and one Spitter in the hands of Beltran, when he was charged at. Unexpectedly, Beltran dropped his Spitter as soon as he'd fired it, covering his hand up and screaming amidst a sudden cloud of frost. He shook the damaged hand and Kordas could see it seemed intact, though frosted over. *Spitters shouldn't do that. Permanent enchantments in the metal safely hold the cold inside. Without that magic, as often as not they'd explode and take a hand with them.* With a second thought, Kordas realized that the weapon had fired before Beltran even had a finger on its trigger. *It was going to go off anyway. Beltran happened to be aiming when it did.*

It wasn't long until everyone entered the dazed "What just happened?" phase of combat. Monster bodies twitched, dogs barked, people yelled for their children. A quarter of the combatants were at the stage of after-action shock in which staring was the maximum they could offer anyone. Another quarter rotated among each other, repeatedly asking if everyone was okay. Kordas couldn't blame them. Nobody could have been ready for that.

Kordas dismounted and extinguished the flame curtain with a gesture, and the poor blacksmith sat down heavily right where he was. His gore-pasted hands were shaking. Kordas went to him, leading Arial, who was getting over her own experience. Kordas was still filled with the lightning of his first actual battle, and felt as if, if he could win against that, he could conquer anything. *Right up until that end. If the reinforcements hadn't run to the rescue, those creatures could have strung defenders out and picked them all off over the course of hours. I am never going to tell anyone how close that was. Everyone but me saw a successful fire attack come out of me, and I won't bring up the details.*

But his brain was back in control now, and not his training and instincts. His instincts wanted him to pursue those things; his mind warned him that was a bad idea. Still, this was a win, and while there were injuries, there had been no deaths he knew of yet, and a win felt—

Euphoric. He hadn't felt a crippling moment of doubt or fear once he'd spotted those beasts, and now that they were dead or fled, the feeling coursing through his veins right now was as heady as distilled spirits.

The blacksmith looked up at the Baron with tears in his eyes. He was obviously no stranger to fighting, and even more obviously, this village was his life. He'd have died today if that was what it took to make his people safe. "Y's good a fighter as diplomat. Y'came. I'se desp'rate, an' ye came t'help. Arter how we met ye—ye helped us anyroad."

Calm down. Think. Choose your words carefully. Kordas went to one knee, and offered his kerchief to the blacksmith to clear up the—substances—caked on his hands from the battle. The big man accepted gratefully, and offered the disgusting remains of the cloth back to Kordas. He declined. "You didn't treat us any differently than we might have treated you, if our positions had been reversed," he said, hanging his crossbow back on his belt. "What in the names of all the gods *are* those things?"

He looked down at one with a bashed-in spine—the "eyes" on its skin had faded away, and its death twitches fired off broken patterns of lights on its skin. A dozen or more dots of light came up through the intact skin and clustered as bright strobes. *Do they do that to attract attention when they fall, to draw off attackers from the others? Are they sneaky even when they're dead?* His mind was still processing what all had even *happened*, and he did take notice of something. He knew what coursing-hounds should look like, lean, but with good muscles. He could see every bone on this thing's body; the strange, hairless, smoky-gray hide was stretched as tight as a drumhead over its bones.

"And why are they starving?" he added, wondering out loud.

The blacksmith got to his feet. "Dunno what they's called elsewhere," he said, slowly gaining back his composure. "We calls 'em hell-dogs. They got poison fangs. They stay 'way. Ne'er see'm like this."

"Was anyone bitten?" he called over his shoulder, but no one answered, so he took that as a negative.

"Dunno why they's starving," the blacksmith continued. "There be plenty game hereabouts—"

But Kordas was now going from body to body, and he noticed that there were differences in each of them. All of the beasts looked to be starving, but some had twisted limbs, some had swellings of the hips or shoulders, and some had bloated bellies, incongruous on those bony frames. "They've either got some sort of disease," he said aloud, "or they're far, *far* too inbred. Maybe both; maybe they are so inbred that they've all got the same crippling diseases." He looked back at the blacksmith. "I don't think more than four or five escaped. They were all wounded, and I don't think they are going to last the next moon, much less last the winter."

"From yer mouth to the ears of the gods," the blacksmith said fervently. "They ain't never come into the village; we only ever had run-ins with them out huntin'. An' then it was on'y two or three. That whole pack come down on us like a thunderstorm." The blacksmith picked at his ear with a twig, freeing up some wet who-knew-what from the side of his head. "They fought wit'all they had. S'like if they didn't, they coulda dun nothin' more. An' us, best day, we couldn't'a done what ye did. How'll we ever thenk ye?"

"If someone comes through here after we take down that door in the air, pretend we were never here," Kordas told him promptly. "I don't *think* anyone will, but if they do——"

"What? Travelers?" the blacksmith said, his face a study in abject stupidity. "Nah, we ain't seen nonelike, the bank allus looks like thet. The wild pigs tear it up somethin' cruel, this side of the river."

Kordas clapped him on the back, and went to check on his guards.

Despite the shudders and nightmare-inducing sights, they were utterly unscathed, and though they lamented the loss of the arrows and crossbow bolts, no one wanted to touch the carcasses to dig what was left of the heads out. The villagers were emerging from their cottages and the blacksmith directed them to haul the bodies into a single pile——and Kordas noticed that none of them touched the bodies directly. They used shovels, or strips of rag tied around the feet. The men building the pile of bodies used pitchforks to manipulate them.

When they were piled up, the blacksmith returned to Kordas, hands clasped on the shaft of his hammer. "I don't s'pose ye'd bring down the magic fire agin to set them things t'ash?"

Kordas chuckled shakily. "As long as I'm not likely to need it because another pack of those things is on the way——"

"Nay, no, don't think so," the blacksmith replied, but looked warily over his shoulder as he said so. "They went after th' beasts ye traded, an' hit'em an'like, but didn't kill'em. S'like takin' th'milk, y'ken? Like they meant t'come back, but, when battle started, 'twas for their lives then, an' they was gonna fight ye."

"They could have all escaped unharmed if they'd run, but they attacked us. So what was so special about those trade animals?" Kordas murmured. He thought on it. They were all fine beasts, they'd made the journey without harm so far, and they'd stuck with their barges until they'd been traded. Ordinary. Ordinary for where he was from, maybe, but ordinary for here? To be honest, probably, since the species of animals were close enough to the natives' that they should have interbred just fine. There was some part of this that would have made sense to *them*, that *he* was missing. Something wasn't *wrong*. He scratched at his left ear. No, something was *unclear*. The things were uncanny, but apparently acting in their "normal." Kordas squinted and scanned around the aftermath with his mage-sight. He made himself receptive to minor, background magic within a quarter mile, from the villagers gathering up livestock that had bolted, to all the soldiers and guard here, and the residual magic from his spellcasting, which wasn't there.

Wait, what?

The area was "clean." More accurately, it was *scrubbed* wherever the creatures had moved. Not even the tiniest pockets where magic was usually held in seedpods, or bees, bugs, or birds flying through the village held magic right now. He gave an "I'm thinking" gesture to Beltran, who carried over his Spitter wrapped in a kerchief, while he paced and pieced it out.

Unnatural creatures attack new livestock but don't kill, they all look starved and miserable, and now there's no leftover magic, because . . . because they took it with them. The traded animals would have had the remains of the tethering spell on them. That's what was new about them. Kordas took three steps and pulled the Spitter from Beltran's hand. Its magic, too, was gone. *All but a trace in the metal. Its enchantment remains, it's simply—unpowered.* The structure of its enchantment was there, but the energy was only now beginning to recover. He told Beltran, "Sink it in the river when we return. You shouldn't trust a Spitter once they've endured cold-firing. They look fine to us, but they crack up inside and can burst right apart." Beltran frowned without any pretense; he was not happy about losing his weapon. At least it wasn't one of the pair he had stolen from the Emperor. "We'll issue you another one," Kordas murmured as he looked away.

The things knew I was a spellcaster, yet they went after the troops. It was obvious to anyone that I was in charge, so it made sense for them to go after me as their biggest threat, but they didn't. They went after those protecting me, leaving me free for more spellcasting. Kordas did not care at all for where this was going. *Because? Because they needed the magic. The mortally wounded one tried to reach me. It could have fled or hidden—but I must have smelled of magic to it. Magic it needed . . .*

The one that was struck by Beltran's shot was only a horselength away, and the Spitter was closest to it at that moment. So the things had to be close by to take magical energy in.

Kordas looked Beltran in the eyes and said, "Those things . . . by their emaciated look, even though food was around aplenty, they needed magic to—eat anything. To digest. Food all around them, but—I think this was something to do with their diseases and stunted shapes. Their bodies didn't work right. This was all they could do, Beltran. It was their last chance to live."

Beltran asked, "Then how many more are around us? Around the expedition?"

There was a very cold silence between them for a while.

If the Spitter misfired without Beltran, it wasn't because the spike ruptured the pellet, it was because the pellet ruptured on its own. Contained by the chamber, the pellet decompressed and launched the bolt. If it hadn't been in that chamber, the pellet could have detonated in every direction. Beltran would have been blown apart. And he was carrying reloads. One of the creatures nearly reached me, too, Kordas thought, and with that came a mental image of everything enchanted he had on him either igniting or exploding. Both of them had come a horselength away from a terrible end.

None of the villagers looked happy about being near enough to the things to stack the bodies. Ultimately, they didn't pile them as much as pull them near each other and back off. Kordas pulled on the ley-line until he was full of power, then released it with a gesture at the pile of loathsome bodies. Fire erupted from them with a *whoom*, and a wavefront of heat that made everyone stand back.

The villagers all stared at him with expressions of awe that were very gratifying to him. Even more gratifying was when their expressions changed, first to faint surprise suggesting that something had occurred to them, to a mixture of gratitude and something else, which he suspected meant they had just now put two and two together and come up with a very unsettling "four."

That he'd had this power all along.

That he could have used it on *them* to drive them out of their homes and resettle his people in *their* village.

That he hadn't. That he'd instead bargained for passage like a peaceable and reasonable fellow.

The expressions turned again, to bewilderment. Because since he *did* have all this power, why hadn't he used it on them?

To be honest, he really didn't want to get into an explanation. Just let them keep wondering and counting their blessings.

"Now," Kordas said, "I think we'll be getting on. We may have a very long way to go before we find our new home. But I suggest," he added, prompted by his training, "that you make some plans, and perhaps some channeling-walls and pit-traps, in case those creatures *do* return. Where did they come from?"

The blacksmith answered gravely, "North an' west. We thought y'was mad to take the river. Everything bad in the world is up there."

Of course it is.

A guard and a villager briskly approached, and offered up sacks of— he didn't want to go into that right now, but they were undoubtedly body parts from the things. "We was pickin' up, an' we thought the mages would want parts of 'em. An' we was policin' bolts an' arrows, an' we—we thought you oughta see this." The villager handed over a fistful of arrows she'd tied together. Their tips were spotless, serrated steel backswept barbs, designed to bite deep and stay there, and they bore helical fletching to induce silence and accuracy. None of the arrows were fully intact, but two things were crystal clear about them.

They all had fresh monster blood drying on them, and they were neither of villager nor Valdemaran make.

———

The silence around the scouts' campfire was absolute, and it was so cold now that the sun had set that the only sounds to punctuate that silence were the lapping of water against the bank and the barges, and the crackling of the fire in the middle of their circle of tired and hungry faces. The downriver scouting hadn't been obviously dangerous but it had been painstaking for them, and stopping for rest and reporting over a warm meal was welcome all around. Delia and the scouts listed off the things they'd made note of, and then Amethyst spoke up.

When Amethyst stopped her calm recitation of the encounter Kordas and his Guard had had with the monstrous hound-things, the expressions of weariness, at least on the faces that Delia could see, had been banished. Though they all had food in their hands, no one was taking another bite, and no one was chewing.

For her part, Delia stared at Amethyst in mingled shock and outrage. "*Why* did you wait until we stopped for supper and sleep to tell us all this?" she demanded, before any of the others could speak.

"Because nothing bad happened," Amethyst said placidly. Delia continued to stare at her in disbelief. Anger started to rise in her. *How dared* the Doll not tell them—or at least her!—that Kordas had been in danger? Amethyst had *no right* to keep such things from her!

But before she could have another outburst, Sai tossed a pebble at her, hitting her cheek and distracting her.

"Amethyst is right," he said. "There was no point in stopping to hear what was going on. We were all busy with the task the Baron set us, which was to scout ahead for dangers and for potential places to build a settlement. It doesn't affect us—"

"I'd dispute that," Ivar replied mildly. "We need to watch out for packs of monster snake-dogs. Or were they dog-lizards? With poison fangs, apparently."

"All right, point taken," Sai replied, a little crossly. "But aside from that, we are much too far ahead of the front of the migration to have gotten back in time to help, and Kordas is a perfectly capable mage on his own, besides having had some of his Guard with him. He had Rose. He could easily have had her summon more guards, or more mages from parts of the convoy that actually *were* close enough to be of some help. No matter what happened, Amethyst knew it would all be over before anyone here could say 'We must ride to the rescue!' which would have been stupid, anyway." He turned back to Amethyst. "Is there anything else we need to know?"

Amethyst shook her head.

"All right, then." Sai went back to setting up the big pot full of hearty stew they'd be eating in the morning after it spent the night buried in the coals and ash of the cookfire. "Now we know there are strange and dangerous creatures out here, and we need to be more vigilant. There are things that Jonaton, Venidel, and Endars and I can do that will give us some protection."

"Shield shells," said Jonaton, rubbing his hands together with anticipation of something more interesting to do than keeping a bored eye on the forest bordering the river. "We aren't going to need shields all the time, and it would be a waste of energy to keep them up that way, but we should have spell keys and break triggers made up so we can deploy shields in an instant. Big ones for the boats and camp, small ones for each of you."

"I've got good night sight," offered Endars. "I don't mind sleeping days to keep watch at night. We won't be moving in the dark, so the shield won't have to be as large to cover us and the horses. Might be a time saver, over protecting a whole boat."

Venidel, Sai's apprentice, added, "Our first ones should probably make spherical shields, to save time. They can't stop everything, but they're strong for their size. I guess we should just go for fast and simple." Venidel was an earnest, gangly, ginger-haired lad near enough to Delia's age not to matter, who looked useless, and was anything but. A farmer by birth, affable Venidel had come into his power fairly late by mage standards, but he took it seriously. "Hotseeds could hold the spellcharge, since none of it's meant to be permanent. I think we have hotseed pod shells in the provisions, though I hate to use them up."

"We can live with bland soup, as long as we're living." Jonaton chuckled. "Straight twigs, cleaned mud, seedpods, what else will we need—"

The four mages dove into a conversation that left the rest of them out in the cold, but Delia didn't mind; she was too busy trying to sort out her galloping feelings. On top, and dominant, was that Kordas had been in danger and she was angry she had not been there to help him.

Because surely, went her runaway fantasy, *he would have seen that I had run to help him, rather than running away to hide. And maybe one of the creatures would have attacked him at a moment when he was unaware, and I could have saved him, and he would have taken me into his arms and . . .*

And she found herself blushing so hotly that the fire on her cheeks felt cool, and she was mortally glad there was no one about with Mind-magic to "read" this preposterous faradiddle and laugh at her.

It had been one thing to entertain such fabulous notions before Kordas had been summoned to the Capital, when they had all been safe in the manor and the worst danger any of them faced was a late supper. It was quite another when they were here in a strange land, and when practically within *days* of the first party crossing the gate, these hellish monsters appeared.

Instead of making up fancies, I should be listening to Sai and the others discuss what magic tricks they can use to ward off danger, and to fight. And I should be trying to figure out how my Fetching Gift can help if some weirdling creature lurches out of the forest with a belly full of hunger and the certainty that we look tasty!

So for once, she listened to her more sensible side and accepted the flatbread-and-jam slice that was passed to her, occupied her mouth with *that*, and listened while the mages all speculated.

"I think," Sai said at last, "there was a book in your library, Jonaton, that talked about Change-Circles and what sometimes happens inside them?"

"Oh good gods, I haven't cracked that book in a dog's age. And now it's—" He waved vaguely to their rear. "Well, *if* I am remembering correctly, if you got two or more creatures caught inside one, there was about an even chance each that they'd die, get weakened in some way, get enhanced in some way, or fuse together in some hellish monstrosity that might or might not die. Something about life itself makes them fuse—there are no accounts of nonliving things joining."

"That sounds like those snake-dogs, doesn't it?" Hakkon asked.

"Well yes, except that you never got the same thing twice out of a Change-Circle, and there was an entire pack of those things." Jonaton pulled on his lower lip thoughtfully. "Amethyst, what did Kordas tell you about them again? Besides the description and the poison fangs."

"That he believed they were either diseased, heavily inbred, or both," Amethyst replied. The firelight made the amethyst cabochon embroidered into her forehead glow as if it was a third eye. "Rose saw them, and attests that they did have various obvious deformities."

"So they probably aren't the product of a Change-Circle," Endars opined.

"But . . ." Everyone looked at Venidel. He gulped, but bravely continued. "But there are creatures like worms and slugs, snails, and some fish that don't need male and female because they are both."

Delia stopped chewing, because that sounded too mad to be true. But it was clear that the mages, at least, had either known that already, or were prepared to believe it coming from Venidel.

He is an expert on animals and how they react to magic. He was the one who had concocted the idea of the charms put on their animals that kept them "tethered" to their home barge.

The elder mages looked at each other, then back to Venidel, then at each other again. "I suppose it's possible," Sai conceded. "We knew that we could encounter anything, and we are officially in Undiscovered Country."

"The people who live in it certainly discovered it!" Bart Fairweather laughed. "Well, expect the worst, hope for the best, I suppose. It's too bad none of us can fly. It would be awfully nice to have something or someone scouting overhead."

Sai and Jonaton both broke up in laughter. "Sadly, flying is a dream," Sai informed him, as Jonaton wiped his eyes over the change of subject. "Oh, every baby mage *dreams* of the day he can fly, but . . . well, you can do it, but it's not very practical. You run out of your own power to control the magic, and when that happens—" He picked up a pebble, held it high, and dropped it. "Splat."

"The few mages I ever knew who could do it just used it to impress women," Endars said sourly. "And all they did, really, was rise up to about head-high, spread their arms, and smirk and look important. Or at least they were under the impression they looked important."

"Did it work?" Venidel asked, now clearly intrigued. "On women, I mean."

"Yes." The tone of Endars's voice, and the way he bit off the word, suggested to Delia that there was a story there.

Probably a sad story about Endars wanting to impress a particular woman—or girl—only to see one of the show-offs win the "contest" before it could start.

"You never see *female* mages pulling that particularly obnoxious piece of asshattery," snickered Jonaton. "It's always the boys with no brains who make up for their lack of wit by strutting and flashing their feathers." He smacked Endars on the shoulder. "Trust me, anyone who falls for that trick isn't worth impressing."

Endars's mouth squinched over to the side as if he didn't quite believe it, but he nodded after a moment.

"So you fell for it?" Sai poked back.

"Only twice," Jonaton replied, and the laugh was welcome all around.

"Besides, it takes a special sort of crazy person to have a relationship with a mage, especially if they themselves aren't mages," Hakkon said lazily, as he held up a bit of bread and jam to Jonaton, who opened his mouth like a baby bird wanting to be fed. Hakkon feinted the bite away, then popped it into Jonaton's mouth. "And would you really *want* to be with someone as crazy as me?"

"Of course I do!" said Jonaton, and made silly puppy eyes at his partner. "And I am known far and wide for my excellent taste."

Delia rolled her eyes, recalling a few of Jonaton's outfits that . . . well, they looked like bags. Colored in hues not found in nature, and with some impressive ornamentation, but bags nevertheless. *Not* something she would have said was in "good taste."

"I'll pass, thank you," Endars replied, but he didn't look nearly as sour.

Delia was the first to head for bed, and not just because she was still trying to sort through some very uncomfortable feelings. The barges used for the scouts had been modified. The one the women were using was one of the "kitchen" barges, the kind that would accompany workers to remote sites. It had been modified for Alberdina's use as an apothecary and infirmary as well as for Sai's special cooking. The front two-thirds was the kitchen, which was how these were normally set up, but instead of stored food, the back third held the close-stool and the women's beds and personal storage. And since Alberdina was not young, and one of the bottom beds needed to be reserved for someone injured or ill, that meant that Delia and Briada were on the top bunks. Delia was above Alberdina, and it was just less awkward all around if she was *in* the bunk when Alberdina came to bed. No chance of accidentally stepping on Alberdina, or flailing and kicking her.

Besides Sai's food, there was another thing that the scouts had that most of the rest of the convoy didn't. Apparently a good long while ago, when he first started venturing out past the borders of the Empire, Ivar had come to Sai with a request. He'd wanted some way to remove his scent—and maybe to clean himself up at the same time—that he could use at least daily.

Sai had presented him with a towel that could be used morning and night that did just that. And once they'd arrived at Crescent Lake, he'd been making more such things—even a scrub with a rag and warm water was going to be less than pleasant come winter. The towels were made, he claimed, of mushrooms. They were supposed to be living sheets of fungus that would absorb and thrive on whatever filth was rubbed into them. He'd given two to each of the scouts when they were putting their personal things away. *"One to clean yourself, the other to roll your smallclothes in when you go to bed,"* he'd said. *"In the morning, your smalls will be cleaner than if they'd come from the Baron's laundry."*

It wasn't anywhere near as nice as a good long soak in a proper bathtub with proper hot water, but it did clean you really well, including your hair. And Sai hadn't exaggerated about what the second one did for underthings, either. They came out of the rolled-up towel better than the laundresses had ever cleaned them.

And that was another thing: it was also less awkward if she got her "wash-up" before the others bedded down. She still felt uncomfortable being naked in front of two people she didn't know very well. It wasn't that she was particularly bodyshy, but rather that Valdemarans tended to associate nudity with privacy. Healers often made private examinations when the patient was nude, but bathing was done alone, and unless one was extremely wealthy and could afford a handmaid, clothing changes were done in private as well. Therefore, being bare made her feel like she *should* be alone.

The little stove was going, but it was still cold enough that she hurried through her cleanup and back into a particularly warm, loose shirt and trews and clambered into her bunk. There was just enough soft light from the little lantern at the front door to aid her into place. Outside she could hear voices; it sounded like the mages were bidding everyone goodnight. Then Alberdina apparently said the same. A moment later she heard and felt Alberdina board the barge.

She pretended to be asleep, on her side with her face to the wall. After an interval of soft sounds and the slight rocking of the barge, she heard and felt Alberdina settle into the bottom bunk.

She carefully eased over onto her back and pulled the covers up tight under her chin. There were so many thoughts buzzing in her head, like a hive full of annoyed bees, that it was just too hard to sort them out. And her emotions were tangled up in all of it. Finally one thing rose to the top. *Kordas sent me away on purpose. And it wasn't because of my Gift.* Really, there was no other conclusion that anyone with the sense the gods gave a goose could come to.

A part of her was angry, and part of her was jealous of her sister, and another part of her was determined to do so well out here that her name would be in every single report that Rose gave to Kordas on their progress. That part of her was a whole different little tangle all on its own. *Send me away, will he? I'll show him!* And *Think you can send me off and forget me? You'll hear about me more often than if I was still back there!* And *Will you be sorry you sent me away?*

Part of her wanted to be *vital* to the group. She did like them, she liked all of them, and Hakkon and Jonaton she loved like brothers, and Sai was practically her grandfather. She honestly wanted to make them proud of her and happy that she was there, so happy that they'd fight to keep her with them.

Delia had listened to Amethyst's calm recital of the attack on the village with horror. Even more so that Ivar and Sai had seemed unsurprised to hear about it. As they had lived at Crescent Lake, her early fears of being in a wilderness had faded—with that many people all in one place, it wasn't really a "wilderness" so much as a temporary city, and the things she had feared, like bears and wolves and pards, if they'd had any sense, wouldn't come within sniffing distance of Crescent Lake.

The convoy was nothing more nor less than the moving version of that temporary city. Animals, probably even weird magical animals, would hear it coming for a league, and avoid the river while they passed.

But not us. And now it wasn't just bears, wolves, and pards she needed to think about.

So part of her was afraid.

And part of her didn't want to disappoint anyone.

And part of her thought, basely, *To all the hells with them! Isn't it my right to choose to keep safe?*

And yet another part scolded her for being so selfish.

With that war going on inside her, like a circle of debaters interrupting each other, she somehow fell asleep.

9

There was more than enough wood, fish, and game aboard this afternoon, so Briada asked Delia to take a turn on the first barge to watch for Ivar. He had ranged far ahead on Manta with Bay ahead of him to sniff out danger. He usually did this right after luncheon, in part to hunt out a good spot to anchor the barges for the night, but there was a special urgency the last three days. The river was definitely running narrower and faster now, and there was concern from Ivar that this could mean they were about to find at least part of the river impassable by barge. And so far they had not found whatever it was that Kordas and his informal council of farmers and the Landwise considered to be a good place to call their new home.

Delia had no idea what they were looking for—but then, she hadn't asked, either. Maybe it was just "somewhere with enough farmland for all our people where no one is living at the moment," because Ivar mentioned nearly every day that he'd seen signs of settlement—several columns of rising smoke in thin streams, for instance—that told *him* there was a village, or at least a building or two, not that far from the river. Which only made perfect sense; with no roads to speak of, the only way to travel to other people would be by the river, and the most reliable source of water without a well would be the river. Endars, who was Landwise along with his other powers, would generally say something like, "We wouldn't want to try and settle here anyway," so that more or less settled anyone suggesting something like sending for Kordas and seeing if they couldn't negotiate with the potential neighbors.

The wind had flinty teeth today, but at least the sunlight warmed her a little. The beautiful leaves were gone; carpeting the riverbank, floating along the river. Here and there evergreens stood out starkly among the bare branches. She spotted Ivar in the distance, long before the others did. "Ivar's coming!" she called, but in a spirit of resignation. *He didn't leave all that long ago. So it's not a good night-anchor site he's found.*

"Hakkon!" Sai called. "Time to pull in again."

With the same resignation she felt, they tied the barges up to the shore, and by the time they were done, Ivar had dismounted. "Luck's run out!" he called, sounding far more cheerful than he had any right to, in Delia's estimation. "Rapids ahead. This stretch of river is better than anything I passed, so it might as well be here we make base camp. I'll walk perimeter now, an' around sunup we can scout out a place to put a Gate to get past it all."

And with that, Sai began unloading camping materials, while some of the others went to their barges to pack their own rough-camping gear.

A "base camp" turned out not to be any more elaborate than the usual night camp, but with one exception. Six horses had their charms muted; as long as their riders directed otherwise, they wouldn't automatically try to get back to their barges. But if something happened, where the rider was not with the horse, or was incapacitated, the charm would bring them back as long as they could move.

This was because, in the morning, three pairs of riders were going to go scouting in different directions; one pair would travel along the current riverbank to see if things smoothed out ahead, one would go to the northwest, and one would go to the north-northeast. *Nobody* really wanted to go so much as a furlong back in the direction of the Empire, but if that was what it would take to find another navigable river . . . then that was where they would go, and hope that the river either bent westward again, or they could find a third river that *was* going the direction they wanted.

The first team, following the course of the river they were currently on, would be Briada Fairweather and Jonaton. They wouldn't need to be Woodswise and able to map as Ivar and Hakkon were; they just needed to follow the river—for two days, or however long it would take to get past the bad stretch, whichever came first. It was Jonaton going, because if they found smooth water straight ahead, Jonaton would be able to prepare the site for the exit Gate. The second team, going into the deep unknown to the west, was Ivar and Bart Fairweather. The third team was Hakkon and Bret Fairweather.

That left all the mages (except Jonaton), and Delia and Alberdina, to mind the base camp. Four days, perhaps five. That was how long they would be here, with all of the people with experience in fighting gone. But they knew there was no choice in the matter; better send those who were adept with weapons out. If those left behind had to, they could barricade themselves in the barges. And if they lost all the horses at the base camp, they could still go on with the six the others were riding, and get more when the convoy caught up with them.

The last several nights, the mages had been working out how to create devices called "shield pods," which, when armed and broken, would put up a barrier against most things—for a time. They were fortunate to have two mages who were extremely good with shields (which only spoke of tragic pasts, in Delia's romantic mind) to take the lead in inventing these improvised versions, using mainly local found materials. Delia admitted to being a bit in awe of what she was a part of. She knew the mages were smart, but seeing them in motion was remarkable. Apparently, this inventing task was something they'd expect to have a salon or laboratory for, and yet, they were going to create it from twigs and mud? On a boat? Surrounded by weird animals and unknown danger? There they were, not only working the problems, but laughing and enjoying the process. It helped with Delia's anxiety, if all was said honestly. One couldn't help but be uneasy out here where anything might try to digest or poison you. Hearing the mages fearlessly making things, and loving it, made her feel safer.

So far, they hadn't had much luck in keeping the shield pods up for very long; it was as grueling for them to craft the prototypes as if they were doing hard labor, so they were pretty seriously immersed in the work.

But she certainly wished they'd been more successful as she eyed the rocky shore where they were now anchored. "Is there anything I can do to help prepare the camp?" she asked, as they all unharnessed and unsaddled the horses and rubbed them down before turning them loose to browse.

"Take your crossbow and Venidel, and the two of you do some scouting for browse you can cut and haul back here," Ivar said, patting his horse on the neck as a sign that she was free to meander to a patch of still-green grass she'd been eyeing. "They're going to eat this spot clean by noon tomorrow, and I want them kept right by the barges while we're gone. Hells, if there was an easy way, I'd put them *on* the barges."

Delia glanced up and down the bank again, and suddenly, as if a candle had been lit in her mind, she realized why Endars kept saying, "We wouldn't want to settle here." When her attention had been on hunting or target-shooting, she truly hadn't paid a lot of attention to the land beyond the bank; that was just the backdrop to what she was doing. But *now* she got a good look at the land, and what she saw was not promising for farming. The soil seemed to be sandy clay. The trees were some sort of oak, but not as tall as the trees back "home," as if they were stunted from lack of nourishment. The underbrush was weeds mixed with some kind of leathery-leafed evergreen, and the horses showed no interest in sampling it. The only thing that the horses showed any interest in were the tall grasses that grew where the forest ended and the riverbank began. Stones peeked through the soil . . . a lot. You could certainly raise goats here, and maybe sheep, but cattle would starve, and horses wouldn't prosper.

And as for actual farming? Well, she was anything but an expert, but she didn't think much of the seed the expedition carried with them would grow well here.

Endars let his eyes wander over the bank, though they had an unfocused look to them. He shook his head. "This area floods every spring when the snow melts. Not a good place to stop when that happens, much less a place to settle."

"Good thing it's not spring yet, then. Not waiting to see if he's right," Ivar replied agreeably, and jerked his head at Delia. "Don't go out of sight. This kind of forest all looks alike once you get inside it, even to me."

Delia went back to the barge for her weapons, and collected Venidel. He had a great many skills in a great many areas that had nothing to do with magic. Sadly, Venidel's many skills didn't include anything to do with combat, fighting, or hunting, but Delia sensed that Ivar intended for Venidel to be the one looking for suitable browse, while Delia watched for trouble.

Venidel had a pocketful of bits of colored yarn—imperial stringettes, often used by the Army for marking where a path was— and whenever he found something he was sure would be good for the horses, he marked it with a bit of yarn. "Let's start here," he said, stopping a couple of furlongs past the last barge. "I'll go beat my way into the forest. You shout when you can't see me."

She nodded, and they worked their way downriver until the barges looked like toy boats, and the horses no taller than the first joint of her finger. By this time Venidel was covered in some kind of tiny burrs or seeds, there were twigs in his hair, and he'd ripped the right knee of his trews. And yet, he was uncommonly cheerful as they walked back along the riverbank, which here was just about wide enough for two horses side by side in harness. "How are you going to get those sticky seeds off?" she asked.

"Oh, I know a spell," he replied, and stopped for a moment.

He crossed his arms, furrowed his brow with concentration, and barked six unintelligible words.

The seeds all flared up, hundreds of tiny, instant flames, and disappeared. She gaped at him. He brushed the ash off, nonchalantly, and winked at her.

"Now, if I was to go home and look for a wife, *that's* a trick that would impress the kind of girl I like, way more than hovering in midair would," he grinned, in a reference to what Endars had said about "flying." He motioned to her to come on.

She thought about saying something like "Well, it impressed me," but that would imply she was Venidel's kind of girl . . .

I don't know how to act around a boy my age who isn't a servant. Or a girl my age, for that matter. She suddenly felt awkward and tongue-tied. Not because she wanted to impress Venidel, but because she simply didn't know what was the safe thing to reply.

So much of her life had been spent solely in the company of adults, usually ones old enough to be her father. And even when Kordas and Isla took her in, that really hadn't changed. There weren't any families of rank near enough to make casual visits, and Kordas hadn't encouraged anyone to visit the manor except at Midwinter. Given how many mages he had been hosting and all the other secrets he had been hiding, that probably had been a good idea. She could handle herself in conversations with older people, even really elderly ones. But it left her feeling very awkward around someone like Venidel.

Would he take such an answer as flirting? Wary now, she just asked, "I take it that lady-mages are unimpressed by floating in midair?"

"The ones I know would laugh at the idiot who thought it would impress them," he told her with a snort. They both were silent for a moment, navigating a patch of slippery stones with the potential to dump them in the cold, cold river. "I'll be glad when we're in one place at last again and have a home. We can even have a proper Mage Circle, and maybe a school where I can get formal lessons. We couldn't have that back in the Duchy. The Emperor's mages would have noticed that big a concentration of power."

"How many of you are there in the convoy?" she asked curiously. "All I ever knew about were all the ones living at the manor."

"Mages and apprentices together? Dozens. *Way* more than anyplace else in the Empire except the front lines of the wars, and the Imperial Palace." He nodded at her start of surprise. "For three generations now, the Valdemarans have been hiding mages who were pacifists, just didn't like the way the Empire works in general, or managed to get on the bad side of an Imperial mage and were hoping to find a place to disappear into."

"I always thought most of them were living at the manor . . ." She faltered.

"No. Oh, no. Most of them were scattered in nice, comfortable little cottages around the Duchy, acting as hedge-wizards and herbalists. Now they're scattered all through the convoy, with people they already knew." He glanced over at her. "Once we're settled, with this many mages? If we can find a nexus of ley-lines, we're going to be able to do amazing things. We're going to have a real city much faster than you'd ever believe is possible."

She wrinkled her brow with a sudden thought. "Is that why you are all having such a hard time keeping up those shield-things? No nexus of ley-lines?"

"Not only no nexus—that's where two or more ley-lines meet and cross—but no ley-line at all right now. This river meandered right off the ley-line that was where we planted the Gate, and none of us have been able to find one within easy reach." He shrugged again. "Power is everywhere, but it's like water. Back in Valdemar we were on a strong source, like a river, that bisected the Duchy, with a small nexus where three lines met under the manor itself. There was a big nexus of seven lines back at Crescent Lake, or we never would have been able to link Gates so far apart. Right now . . . the Power is there, it's always all around us, but it's like a misting rain. It's hard to gather enough to get a good drink out of it, much less do anything that requires a lot of energy."

Those words sent a chill down her back, and she glanced at him sharply. Because so much depended on being able to use Gates—

"But what if there's no ley-line where we need to go?" she blurted, her voice tight with anxiety.

"We can store power in things, and we have, for just that reason," he said reassuringly. "In the Gate uprights themselves, just for a start."

Oh, idiot. This Plan has been decades in the making. If Kordas's grandfather didn't think of that, his father would have, and if he hadn't, Kordas or one of the Six would have.

Venidel suddenly raised his head and sniffed. "Oh my word. I think I smell roast goose."

So did she, and her mouth watered. No matter how many times she had it, she never got tired of goose. And if the footing had been any better she might have challenged him to a race.

But that would have been an exceptionally bad idea on these rocks. Best to save the bad ideas for when they really needed them.

"What do you like about all this the best?" she asked instead, which seemed a safe topic with no potential flirting traps embedded in it. And it proved to be, since he was still rattling off all the reasons he *loved* doing the scouting when they arrived back at the camp.

———

Delia deeply appreciated the presence of Bay on the roof of their barge. The soft sounds of him alerting and looking around, perhaps getting to his feet and lying down again when whatever had alerted him proved to be nothing, was one of the most comforting things she could think of. It reminded her that there were two beings, Bey and Amethyst, who could be relied on to call an alarm if *anything* approached that wasn't a rat or an owl.

She just knew she wasn't going to be able to sleep when the three teams left. She felt as if, even if Sai told her to go to bed, she'd need to stay wakeful, as if by not sleeping she could somehow detect danger outside the barge.

Which was utterly ridiculous, of course, but she was having no luck convincing her nerves of that.

There was a wind tonight, and it whipped up waves on the river that made the barge rock. *The men's barge is going to be half empty. I wonder if that is going to bother anyone.* Not Sai, surely, but perhaps Venidel?

She tried to think of pleasant things. Sai had put bread dough to rise in the warmth of the barge, something he had not bothered to do until now because there would not have been time to bake it in the mornings before they needed to be on their way. She had thought of a clever way to gather fodder tomorrow, if Venidel agreed and had a way to help. It would even be possible that the convoy would catch up with them while they waited for the scouts to return, and she could astonish everyone with her prowess with Gift and crossbow.

But as she stared into the darkness, aware that the ceiling was within a hand-length of her nose even though she couldn't see it, all she could think about was that the wind would make it hard to hear anything creeping up on them from the forest. All that was between them and danger were the senses of an air spirit trapped in a magical rag doll, and no one had any real idea how good or bad those senses were.

And as far as she knew, she was going to be the only one left here with any sort of skill at arms when the three teams went out. Maybe the mages had something offensive—but when, in their entire lives in the peaceful Duchy of Valdemar, would there ever have been an occasion to *use* such spells? Had they ever even practiced such things? And would they have the power to do so in the first place?

So the barge rocked, and she fretted, and she didn't actually remember falling asleep, but the next thing she knew, gray dawn light glowed through the little window of her bunk.

She beat everyone to the morning chores. Not even Alberdina stirred as Delia wiped herself down, got her clean underthings from her towel, and dressed in double layers of knitted wool, followed by a sheepskin coat. It was *cold* this early in the morning, and there was a skin of ice on the buckets of water Sai had left to settle last night. She made it her business to rake the last of the coals and the ashes away from the cookpot where the morning stew was, and start a cookfire so that there would be nice hot coals for Sai to bake his bread in.

The morning fog wasn't so thick as to be a danger, but it did limit visibility to a couple of barge-lengths. There was a quality to sound, when air was cold, that made every splash, thump, and clank very discrete. Sounds were more defined in morning cold; they started sharply, and ended abruptly without followup. Birdcalls pierced the fog's thick silence, and echoes were absent. As far away from all she'd known as Delia was today, she had to admit there was such a stark beauty to this morning that she should take a few minutes' time just to experience it. The earliest birdcalls were answered by more from another direction. Today's avian audio war had begun.

We think they sound beautiful, but those songs are declarations and dares, warnings and challenges.

Ivar and Sai emerged from the men's barge together, talking about something in voices too low to make out the words. Sai carried his precious risen dough in a covered bowl, and greeted her effort with a nod of approval. He didn't have to tell her what he wanted; with her Gift, she raked a bed of hot coals a little apart from the fire, and placed a three-legged iron pot in the middle of them. Sai carefully rolled his lump of dough into it, and clapped the lid on it. Then she used her Gift to pile more hot coals on the lid.

I have to admit, I get smug about my Gift. Fortunate enough to have a Gift, and with it I can Fetch an object from one place to another instantly, and move it around once I have? It's the best.

"You make a fine shovel!" Sai teased, then sobered. "This is much safer than mucking about with the fire the ordinary way. Heavy clothing makes us move clumsily, and I am afraid we are very flammable under these things." He held up his arm; rather than a coat, he had a sort of cape, like a circle of very heavy wool with a hole in the middle and a hood sewn to the hole. Unlike a cape, this had no armholes.

"You stay away from poking the fire in that thing," Alberdina scolded from the barge. "You let us play with the coals, or else find a sensible coat."

"I have one, somewhere," he replied vaguely, as he pulled the second pot out of the ashes and embers of last night's fire. "Now, this should be good with fresh bread." He took up a stout stick, threaded it through the two rings welded to the lid, and lifted the lid off. Apparently the savory aroma of goose-and-spiced-lentil stew penetrated the hulls of the barges, because shortly after that, everyone had gathered around the fire with their plates and spoons and looks of anticipation.

Alberdina always made the tea. Delia wasn't sure what was in it, or if it had any purpose other than tasting good, but Alberdina *had* said that it was safer to drink the river water boiled, and that if she was going to boil water regardless, she was damned if she wasn't going to make tea with it.

Those who were riding out ate quickly, then fetched their traveling kits from the barges. Delia didn't envy them. Unless they got lucky and shot game, they'd be eating trail biscuits and tea for every meal they had out there. And sleeping on the ground, and hoping for clear weather. They had canvas shelters, but those were little more than rectangles of waxed canvas that would cover two people in a no-more-than-moderate rainstorm. She couldn't imagine being in a thunderstorm and trying to keep dry under that scrap of fabric. For a moment, she had the mental image of someone sleeping under their horse while that tent barely draped over the horse's back.

Breakfast was excellent with real bread, but no one talked about anything but their plans for the ride. No one lingered over breakfast or farewells. The three teams were in the process of mounting up when Sai handed Delia and Venidel a pair of hand-scythes, and made a shooing motion.

"Ah, fodder duty," Venidel said, hanging the scythe on his belt. "Have you a plan? Because I don't."

"I do, actually." She felt a little warm glow that he had deferred to her. "If you have some magic way of gathering what we cut into a kind of ball or bale, I can mark a spot among the horses to drop it with my Gift."

"Oh!" He brightened. "So we needn't carry the bulk of it at all! I should have thought of that. Well, it'll surely take effort on both our parts, but I'd rather put in the effort with magic than manual labor in this case."

"I feel the same," she agreed. "I could do the gathering-up too, but I think it'd exhaust me to do both. So that's on you. And I thought that we'd start parallel to yesterday's trail, at the farthest place we marked, and work our way back. So instead of my having to move things farther and farther with each grass ball, I'll be doing it shorter and shorter. Plus, we might find something good along the way." She walked over to the horses, who greeted her with a glance and whicker. After some toeing about, she found a stone shaped a little like a rabbit. That would do. Just to be sure, Delia defined the rabbit's appearance with pocket chalk, and set it upright against a larger stone.

Venidel made a fancy bow and waved her on. Together they scrambled over the rocky shoreline until they were both sure there were no more bits of yarn to be seen in the forest underbrush. Venidel sighed as he regarded the tangle of vines immediately in front of them. "Well," he said with resignation, the wind whistling through the branches of the trees, and brown leaves flying, "this will still be work. We'll still have to cut the damned stuff."

"You mean this isn't the glamor of magic?" Delia teased Venidel.

"It is exactly that! A 'glamor' is an illusion! All of us have learned these past few weeks that the daily utility of magic is what's valuable. But it isn't pretty! No, the great tales never speak of drying sewage or raising grass. Or razing grass. It's always some monsters, or invasions, or demons. So many demons."

What the horses would eat as fodder tended to be concentrated in lopsided circles, tiny meadows where the tree cover was interrupted. There was generally not too much for her to lift when Venidel muttered under his breath and twirled his finger in the palm of his hand, and the cut grasses and weeds swirled as if there was a whirlwind animating them, compacting in no time into a ball that weighed just about as much as a toddler, and was about the same size. As soon as the whirling stopped, Delia "grasped" the grass ball, pictured the rabbit-shaped stone she'd found among the horses, built up her power, took a deep, grass-scented breath, and *pushed* the volume of space the grass ball filled, and blinked.

The ball vanished. Venidel nodded approval, and even the rattling of branches above them sounded a bit like applause.

"And that is why we will never be employed as babysitters. Much better plan than mine," he said. "Which involved my making grass balls, but then called for us to borrow one of the horses, hitch it to a basic sledge, and haul it that way. It seemed a better plan than carrying the damned things two at a time."

"Do we *have* a basic sledge?" she asked in surprise, because surely something like that would have been hard to hide—

"Well, no," he admitted, "we'd have had to build one."

"Still not a *bad* plan." She stopped to rub her forehead. "When we go back to camp for luncheon, we can make a better guess how much more fodder we'll need to cut today, because we'll see how much the horses ate."

"Hopefully they'll still eat it, since the sky threw it at them," he giggled. Delia trudged toward the next bit of yarn, a bright spot in the brown and muddy-green foliage. She had discovered those little sticky seeds he had been covered in yesterday, clinging to the sleeves of her coat even though she didn't remember encountering anything that had seeds like that. There didn't seem to be any way of avoiding them.

"I hope it's not an issue," Delia offered. He trudged behind her, having the good sense to follow a trail someone *else* was breaking. Well, she didn't mind breaking the trail for him. "I'd forgotten how hand-cutting grass uses muscles you generally forget you have. I have the feeling that by luncheon I'm going to be as sore as the first day I ever rode a horse."

"Hyah, I'm already there. We should stop a while a'fore Amethyst has to relay, 'Two overconfident idiots are dead, after a tragic grass-cutting mission. Their bodies were found nowhere near their camp, obviously worn down to the bones. They worked too hard to keep the horses fed, and didn't even stop for tea when they should have'," Ivar confirmed. "'When interviewed, the horses were indifferent to their demise, and then asked for more food.'"

———

With the last of the boats through, and the Gate uprights from Crescent Lake and the Gate on this river both taken down, the folk at the tail end of the convoy were treated to a—well—literally magical sight. The uprights got strapped to a pair of basic hulls, a Tow-Beast was harnessed to each, and a mage who was also clearly an experienced rider mounted up. Then the horses *trotted across the river to the other bank*, barges bobbing behind them. Spontaneous cheers and applause erupted once the spectacle was in clear view of everyone below.

The mages had created a surface that the horses could walk on, of course, because there was a good strong ley-line to draw on here, and these two horses had been trained to trust that the surface would be there when their riders urged them to cross the river. But this was necessary if the Gate uprights were going to catch up with the scouts; there was no other way to pass the convoy, except through tedious shuffling of transfer barges.

This was important. The scouts had two sets of Gate uprights with them already, but those would eventually be set up when the convoy needed to get past a difficult stretch. Once the new Gates that the scouts put in place to get around bad patches of water or jump to new rivers were up, they'd need to replace the two sets they'd carried with them.

This was probably the most dangerous task that any two people in the convoy could do right now. And the most uncomfortable. They would be moving at the best speed they could, and the Tow-Beasts were formidable enough to make an entire wolf pack decide to look for easier prey, but they would just be two people, all alone out there. Which was why Kordas had chosen two mages who had been combat mages before they sickened of slaughter and sought asylum with him.

It looked like a miracle, the two horses at a brisk trot in the bright sunlight, seemingly walking on water, a barge behind each of them. They clambered ashore, and were off at remarkable pace. The size of the Tow-Beasts meant long legs, and long legs ate up distance even when the horse was pulling a barge against the current. Moving with the current as they were, the barges were scarcely a burden to the strength of the massive horses.

"The river moves away from the ley-line today, Baron," Rose reminded him as he mounted Arial.

I hope we can find another. Or better still, a nexus. A nexus would be ideal, of course; any reserves of power that had been depleted could be recharged. If anything, the available supply of magic would be as critical for them as any other supply. With magic and food, they could survive almost anything that nature, or the unnatural, could throw at them. At least, he thought so. In fact, if the dangers out here were no worse than that pack of snake-dogs, things would be fine.

The blacksmith and his two apparently constant companions showed up as the last of the barges with the Poomers in it lurched into motion. He said nothing to Kordas, nor did it appear that he was doing anything other than making sure they all left. Or perhaps that was ungenerous thinking; the man gave Kordas a grave salute. Kordas responded with a bow from the saddle, and urged Arial up through the ambling herds.

Ambling was the right term; it was a slow walk, allowing everyone but the horses to snatch whatever bites of anything edible they could see. Geese and ducks swam alongside the barges, mostly snatching at stuff along the bank where the footing was too uncertain for even the goats to venture. Chickens sat grumpily on every available surface of their coop-barges. Like the geese and ducks, they were fed in the morning when they were let out, and in the evening when they went back in, but they were not allowed to forage on the way, and *their* charms kept them right on their barges. It was clear they were tolerating this situation, but were not in the least happy about it.

The guards were in the forest, forming a living fence to ensure no sheep, goat, or pig went too far inland, working in concert with the herders. They also formed a barrier against wild things, weirdling or not, that might be tempted to risk an encounter with humans for a chance at all the tasty stock.

He couldn't help but think of those *things* that had attacked the village. Whatever they were, he was certain of one thing that they were *not*, and that was natural. *Unlikely they're from a Change-Circle.*

They are mage-made, I'm certain of it, he thought, and the consensus among all the mages was the same. The question was, if they were made-things, then who had made them? And when? Recently? If not, how far in the past? And why? Such things were *possible*, although he did not personally know anyone who was capable of it. There was only one way to answer those questions, but he was not inclined to waste power they might not have to spare on it. Past-scrying. It would be easier to do with some bits of one of those things, and his curiosity had been aroused to the point that it was like an itch he wanted badly to scratch. But no. Not unless they met up with more of them. Indulging his own curiosity was no excuse for wasting magic. Two days ago, Kordas couldn't have imagined such things existing. Two days later, and they not only existed, but outsmarted him, too. And they were met far away from where they should be, if the blacksmith's information was true, which was also where the flotilla was now headed.

Morale was good, all things considered—and there was a lot to consider. They had lost three dozen barges to fire since massing at Crescent Lake. Twice as many as that had outright sunk once they'd reached the lake, though most slowly enough to unload in time. Collisions, bad landings, or simple breakage of equipment put sixty more out of commission, to be dismantled for spares or used as roofs for buildings. There had been over two hundred deaths—not an abnormal amount given the timespan, but since it was on this side of a Gate, it was taken as more ominous than if they'd just died on the other side. The number of fights and thefts had gone up steadily while the whole expedition was at Crescent Lake.

And that's the hidden truth of why we're on the move now, and I'm keeping it hidden. Putting everyone on barges in motion means each vessel is a container.

People aren't mixing at close quarters, they're divided into little packets that aren't meandering off or looking for fights. It makes census quicker, which makes rationing immensely easier. It keeps groups from forming factions against other groups, which prevents more confrontation. And, while on the boats, people are crafting, and learning new skills that will be useful when we do settle. Just . . .

Well, that only accounts for known issues, Kordas thought while riding for the front of the expedition. They were sailing into the unknown.

———

The end of the first day left Delia absolutely wrung out, and the muscles of her arms lamented that there would be more scything tomorrow. *I thought I was in good shape!* She was no stranger to hard work—not since the evacuation to Crescent Lake, at any rate—but Venidel had been right; this had used muscles she didn't remember ever needing to use before.

Why? I seriously mean it, why? Why do I have muscles to pull my palms sideways or pull my shoulderblades down? Why are they so loud about being unhappy?

She gritted her teeth and fought through it during supper, comforted a little by more fresh bread, but was about to beg Alberdina for help when Venidel broke down first. Even in the flickering firelight, his expression was equal parts pained and begging. "My arms wish to part company with my body on the grounds of abuse," he said firmly, as they all drank the last of the tea, and Sai buried tomorrow's breakfast in the coals and ash—having found his coat, after all. "Please tell me, kind Healer, that there is something you can do, or I'll be tempted to dis-arm myself."

"Me too," Delia spoke up quickly.

Alberdina had the grace not to laugh at them. Instead she went to the barge and back, and gave them pots of something that smelled suspiciously like the stuff Stablemaster Grim used on horses suffering from strained muscles.

It wasn't an unpleasant smell, although it did make her *and* Alberdina sneeze when she smoothed it on in the shelter of their barge. But it was worth it! Whatever was in the stuff soothed the aches and numbed them. Although she had expected to spend a wakeful night, listening for any sort of suspicious sound, she dropped off immediately.

She woke to hear Alberdina stirring, and stifled a groan as her arms protested stiffly. Today was going to be hard . . . and she was not in the least looking forward to it.

But when she emerged for breakfast into a brighter, lighter fog than yesterday's, she discovered that Endars was waiting for them with a hand-scythe at his belt. He shrugged when Delia looked at him quizzically, but said nothing, and when she and Venidel headed downstream, he came with them, leaving Alberdina and Sai to take care of camp chores.

"Thanks for coming with us," Venidel said, though with a faint hint of a question, as if he wasn't sure why Endars was with them either.

Endars shrugged again. "Might as well," he said, and nothing else.

Frost coated every stem and twig with a thick, white fuzz, and although there was no wind, the air warned that there was no chance of warmer weather until spring.

Endars bent and worked with a will, cutting the time needed to clear the tiny meadow in half. When Venidel did his little grass-ball spell, Endars didn't stop the young mage, but he *did* ask for Venidel to speak more clearly the next time, and every time after that, he stared so intently that his gaze seemed likely to burn a hole in Venidel's hands. Endars was not someone that Delia knew at all, but Sai had picked the mages to scout, and Delia would have trusted Sai even if he'd told her to set her hair on fire. Endars didn't speak much, and on the surface he seemed a little grumpy, so until this moment she had been hesitant to say much of anything at all to him.

"That's a damned clever thing you've invented," Endars finally said, after the eighth ball went off to the horses.

"Oh, I didn't invent it," Venidel corrected hastily.

And that was when Delia saw it. A tiny, approving little smile. *Endars was testing him!*

"No, it's just some hedge-witchery I learned, and Sai helped me turn it into something useful while we were at the Lake," Venidel continued. "I figured it would be a good way to compact fleeces when we needed to shear and slaughter sheep on the way. But Delia said something yesterday that made me realize I could make grass bales that way too."

Endar's smile broadened. "Well, boy, you're smart, to study every bit of mage-craft you come across, be it ever so lowly."

Venidel showed just a flash of temper, but damped it down. "I *am* a farmer," he just said.

"And my pa was the miller of Goverton," Endars countered. "Not every mage is a Kordas Valdemar."

"Ah!" was all that Venidel said, but he managed to pack a lot of meaning into that single syllable.

But things seemed a lot more companionable between them after that.

She was quickly coming to the end of her strength, though, at least physically. Her arms felt as if they were on fire, and her cutting got slower and slower as she forced herself on. *Bend, gather, cut, drop,* she told herself, wishing she could stop. *Bend, gather, cut, drop.* She was glad she was wearing gloves, as were the other two, because the leather of the palms was definitely getting scored by the sharp-edged grasses, and she hated to think what her hands would have looked like without protection.

Then she felt a hand on her shoulder. "Save yourself for what only you can do," Endars said, as she started and looked up. "No point in cutting the damn grass if we have to walk it to the horses because you're too tired to Fetch it there."

Anger rose, but she quelled it, because he was right. It smarted, though, and she felt as if she was somehow letting Kordas down.

It made no sense to feel that way, but as she leaned against a tree, aching on the inside as well as the outside, she decided that "sense" really didn't matter.

Feelings did not answer to any logic but their own.

If only they did . . .

10

The afternoon of the third day found Delia, Endars, and Venidel back at camp; with three of them cutting, they were able to gather enough forage for the rest of the day and into the night between breakfast and luncheon. Her arms still ached. Not as badly as the first day, but between that and her feet hurting from walking on those rocks, what she *wanted* to do was lie on her bunk and doze. But Sai was baking more trail biscuits and needed help. So just after luncheon she was kneeling next to the fire, moving coals onto the top of the baking pot, when Amethyst gave the warning call of a blue-crested shrike, something they had all agreed was a good alarm call. It carried far better than a shout. Delia looked up sharply and followed the Doll's gaze.

Amethyst's sight was certainly sharper than hers was, because she didn't spot their uninvited visitor until it pushed through the underbrush and moved to the rocks at the river's edge, about as far away from their fire as the average village street was long.

It was a bear. There was no mistaking that shape, or that rolling gait. Its shaggy brown coat had blended perfectly with the weeds at the forest edge until it moved into the open. But it was not "just" a bear.

Amethyst should have done more than whistle. This thing was a monster.

Delia had been up and down this stretch of the river enough times to know just how tall everything on it was, and this bear's back brushed the branches that overhung the path, which meant it was the size of the Tow-Beast.

And it was looking right at them.

She froze. Sai froze. Alberdina was in the barge, but with a "danger" signal, she knew to stay inside it and arm up with whatever was handy. Endars was behind Delia, so she couldn't see what he was doing, but Venidel whispered a curse.

"Don't move," Sai whispered back. "Bears have good eyesight, but we're downwind of him, and if we don't move he might not know what we are."

The horses, of course, scented the creature, because they all brought their heads up at once, and the Tow-Beast snorted. Another breath of icy breeze brought the scent to them, and not only was it strong enough for a human to smell, it was a strange, bitter musk, nothing she'd ever smelled before.

The bear reared up on its hind legs, and Delia's mouth dried and her stomach clenched when she realized it was well twice as tall as a man that way. Its stance conveyed the sheer weight of the thing.

The horses, sensible for once, froze.

The bear stuck his nose up into the air, sniffing so loudly they could hear him.

But now that it was on its hind legs, Delia saw something else that was even more alarming about it. Instead of fur, its belly was covered in leathery scales, like a lizard. So were its paws and its muzzle. It opened its mouth and wrinkled up its lips, like a cat does when it wants to get a better scent, and the yellowed, stained teeth looked from here to be as long as her hand. Every row of them.

Her skin crawled, and she had to fight the urge to get up and run. "What do we do?" she hissed at Sai.

"That's not a natural beast," Sai replied obliquely, still not moving as much as a hair. "I don't know about those things Kordas saw, but I'll bet ten cakes that thing came out of a Change-Circle. We can't assume magic will work on it."

Once again, she had to fight down the urge to run. Running would be the *worst* thing she could do. Even normal bears could easily outrun a human, and could sometimes, over short distances, outrun a horse. This thing would probably have her before she'd gone twenty paces.

But Sai continued, as if he was thinking out loud. "We don't want to get it angry, and I don't think your crossbow bolts would do anything more than *make* it angry. We don't want to chuck fire at it, or put an actual fire curtain between us and it—the brush is tinder-dry, and finding ourselves trapped between the river and a forest fire would be as bad as having that thing charge us. We need to chase it away somehow—"

"Would it believe an illusion of fire?" Endars asked.

"Let's try," Sai agreed.

In the next moment, a curtain of fire stretched between the forest and the bank between them and the bear.

The bear made a grumbling growl, but did not drop down to all fours.

The illusory flames leapt higher, as tall as the bear.

Now the bear dropped down to the ground, but it did not move away. Instead, it stood swaying in place, moaning. Clearly it didn't care for the fire—but it wanted to investigate what it thought it had seen.

This time of year bears are fattening up for sleep. I know they kill deer. Does it think the horses are some kind of deer?

It wasn't interested enough *yet* to charge them through the flames. But it still wasn't going away either. She felt cold and hot all at the same time. But somehow the terror made her mind sharper. She felt a dozen ideas pass through her mind, and rejected them, since they didn't fit what Sai had asked for.

What can I do that won't make it angry—that will drive it away because it's something it doesn't understand, rather than something it thinks is attacking it? What is quick, what is nearby?

The water!

The river water was just about freezing cold. Armored skin or not, the bear wasn't going to like getting a face full of it. But it wouldn't associate getting dowsed with a cascade of freezing water with *them*.

She'd played around with water and her Gift back at Crescent Lake, in no small part because she didn't much like using the water right at the edge for cooking or washing. Water from the middle of the lake just seemed cleaner. But this was going to take a lot more than a bucketful. She didn't want merely to startle it. She wanted to make it decide to flee. *Gods, gods, what to do—*

"I'm going to give him something else to think about," she said, and before she could lose her nerve, she steeled herself—

—because water was heavy, and this was going to be hard. And she knew from previous experience of trying to lift too much of it that this was going to hurt. *I think I was on to something yesterday, though, when I grabbed the shape around the target, not the target itself. So, a sphere of water then, I'll Fetch a sphere with water in it.*

She gritted her teeth, stared at the bear through the leaping "flames," and *pulled*.

Shit shit shit shit shit. Her whine of pain as her gut spasmed and every muscle in her body locked up was drowned out by the sound of four or five barrels-worth of icy water hitting the bear right on his head.

The bear let out a startled bellow and hopped up and down on its front feet, head swiveling in every direction to see what had just happened to it.

"Oh gods," she whispered, because she didn't want to have to do this again. But she did it again anyway. A second splash struck it hard on the skull.

That was all the bear could take.

It was all she could take, too. As she bent over double in pain, falling over onto her side, the bear bellowed again and fled.

She curled up involuntarily, as Alberdina came clambering out of the barge bearing cleavers, and Sai bent over her. "It's . . . all right," she said through clenched teeth, even though all her muscles were knotting up in terrible cramps. *Is this normal?* "But I don't think . . . I'm going . . . to be moving grass . . . for a while."

"Don't worry, child," Alberdina said gruffly. "*This* warrants something stronger than tea or liniment. And before you ask, I've never treated anyone with Fetching Gift before, but I think this is normal." She placed her hands on Delia's head and shoulder, and suddenly Delia felt a wave of warmth flooding through her from those hands, driving the pain in front of it, until it was gone. So *this* was what it felt like for a Healer to actually use their powers on you!

Oh, that was good. I admit it, that may be better than Fetching.

She had just that single moment to enjoy the feeling, and then she dropped unceremoniously into absolute unconsciousness.

She woke up in the bottom bunk—the "patient" bunk—in her barge, feeling as if she could have eaten that entire bear if they'd caught it, and she didn't think she'd even need to wait for it to be cooked.

She was still in her clothing, so she got up—dizzy for a moment as she stood—and made her way back out to the fire. It was dark, and even colder, and she huddled inside her sheepskin coat as she headed for her friends. The sound of her footsteps made everyone at the fire look up.

"We saved you supper," said Alberdina, reaching for the ladle to dish her share out of the pot.

"I made you a little jam pie," said Sai.

Endars just got up and gestured to a spot at the fire where someone had placed some cushions on the ground and against a piece of log that could be used as a backrest. She wobbled her way over to it and sat down. A moment later, she had a bowl of duck-and-barley soup in her hands, and was balancing a pocket-pie on her knee.

Conversation resumed where she must have interrupted it. The bowl was about twice as much as she usually ate, but she not only downed it like a greedy little pig, she felt as if she could have done with another serving. But there was that pocket-pie, so she began eating that with slow bites. Normally something like this would have been so sweet it would have made her teeth ache, but tonight it just tasted delicious.

When she had finished, Alberdina handed her a cup of tea. "Well," the Healer said. "That was an impressive move."

"I never want to have to do that again," she replied. "I wouldn't have been able to hit him with a third deluge."

Sai nodded, and waggled his thick white eyebrows. "Well, that served three purposes. Now you know you *can*, now you know how many times in a row you can, and you did a very good job of scaring off the bear."

"He's probably swearing at you in bear, still," joked Venidel.

That made her smile. "I'm sorry I couldn't think of a way to kill him for you, Sai," she added apologetically. "I know the fat would have come in handy."

He waved his hand in the air. "Not sure I would have trusted it was fit to eat. And now that you have filled your empty belly, you should probably get back to bed."

"Use the patient's bunk," ordered Alberdina as Delia got shakily to her feet. "No point in you risking a fall trying to get into your own."

"You're right. Thank you," she replied, and somehow staggered back into the barge, got undressed, voided, cleaned, and crawled into the lower berth. At least, she thought that was what she'd done, because she didn't actually remember doing any of it when she woke the next morning with the savory smell of breakfast stew and fresh bread in her nose.

———

"A *lizard-bear?*" Kordas asked Rose incredulously. She tilted her head to the side.

"I merely say what Amethyst saw," she replied.

Kordas had been wolfing down a late luncheon of trail bread up at the head of the convoy, sitting just off the path on a boulder as a flock of mixed sheep and goats flowed slowly past him, heads down, snatching at weeds and grasses as they walked. Then Rose had interrupted that brief respite with the announcement that the scouts remaining at the base camp were in danger.

As he leapt to his feet—futile, of course, since there wasn't anything he could have done—Rose continued to describe the crisis in clinical detail. And it was over much more quickly than he would have dreamed possible.

And, to his intense relief, without anything more than Delia getting cramps from over-using her Gift.

"Oh, I don't doubt you, but . . ." He shook his head. "This is nothing we were prepared for. Bears yes, but it sounds like this thing could have *thrown* a Tow-Beast." He suppressed the urge to mount up anyway, and send Arial off after his scouting party at a gallop. He'd never get there in time to help with anything. In fact, he could probably gallop for two days before he reached them. So the only thing he'd do would be to take himself *away* from his duties and the bulk of his people who looked to him for leadership. *Doesn't exactly show good leadership to leave them, does it?*

Oh, but Delia rose to the challenge. Sending her off had been exactly the right thing to do. He had decided that she needed to have something to concentrate on besides her infatuation with him, and it certainly seemed that not only had his plan worked, she'd discovered a lot of ways that he hadn't even considered to make herself a full member of the scouts.

I can't make the excuse that I didn't know what we were getting into, because the further you go into the west, the more remains of that ancient war you find. It makes sense that if Change-Circles can cut sections out of trees, anything that blunders into one is in danger of being affected by the magic that made them. Whatever that was. No one knew much about that war, distant in time and space alike. Only that the mages who had waged it had been far more powerful than any in the Empire, now or ever.

"Have you Dolls passed this on to anyone else?" he asked Rose, who shook her head. "Keep it to the Five Old Men, then. I'd better tell Isla about this myself." *I only hope she won't skin me for letting Delia go off into a dangerous situation.*

There was a gap in the herds, enough to allow him and Rose to get to his horse and mount into the saddle. Once atop Arial, it was a lot easier to push their own way against the flow of sheep, goats, and swine than it would have been afoot.

But easier didn't mean fast. It was nearly supper, and vessels slowed and bunched tighter. People were stopping for the night, anchoring their barges to the bank, unharnessing and rubbing their beasts of burden, and setting up the group kitchen barges to make their nightly food. It was a touch surprising to him that he never picked up quite the same scents as he moved past those barges. No two barges in a row seemed to be making the same things. Honestly, he loved it. Regional dishes normally not found near each other blended their scents with each other in ways that ranged from shocking to seductive.

Some were better than others . . . but at this point in the migration, the really bad cooks had been weeded out and replaced—sometimes at cleaver-point!—with people who were at least competent at more than boiling water.

He was late for his own supper, but that was all right. It wasn't the first time, and it wouldn't be the last. In fact, by the time Arial had picked her way through the herds, all the animals were bedding down in the vicinity of the barges they were "tied" to, and they complained when they were disturbed. And even though his particular string of barges didn't have any herds immediately associated with it, there were just so blasted many animals associated with this convoy that they filled up all the available space and were happily munching away as far into the woods as their "tethers" would let them go. And with most of them settling down close to their "comfort zone," that meant his household barges, which contained his family and all the families and individuals associated with the manor, were knee-deep in sheep.

Well, this keeps the boys from slipping out at night. Not that the sheep would have stopped them, but they'd object to being disturbed, and all three of the boys were distinctly averse to stepping in manure. Sheep and goat wasn't bad, but cattle and equines produced shit you could lose a shoe in, and pig was uniquely unpleasant. Not to mention, it was hard enough for a grown man like himself to wade through the livestock, so the boys would have been unable to see far and would have wound up lost not a barge-length away.

He did his duty to Arial, left her with a grain bag on her nose, and turned her loose. One of the grooms would take it off in a candlemark or so. Only then did he finally set foot on his own barge. The boys hurled themselves at his legs, and told him all the exciting things that their "Captain of the Page Army" was having them do. Mostly collecting wood and bringing it to the barge strings, where older boys who could be trusted with a hand-axe chopped it up into pieces small enough to feed the stoves. But they were learning all manner of things about the herds around them, and Kordas reckoned that was, at this point in time, more useful than any lessons they could get from books. He sat down at the tiny table while they bounced and babbled around him, and ate the leftover soup and flatbread, using a touch of his own magic to warm it up again. Isla let them babble away, because he got a lot of pleasure out of listening to them, sorting out their tiny problems, and answering their questions, although he was privately thanking his gods that they didn't seem interested in the scouts or Delia tonight.

Isla's prediction that the "Page Army" was going to run them out of energy had proven to be true. Every time he got back to the home barge, they fell on him like a pack of otters, but they soon wore out, and by the time he and Isla were using another touch of magic to clean everything up and store it for tomorrow, they were yawning between sentences, and the littlest had actually sat himself down on the floor, knuckling his eyes.

"Do you want a story from Mama, or me?" he asked them, looking into three pairs of big brown eyes fighting to keep from closing.

"Mama," said Jon. "It's my turn to pick and I want Mama."

Which meant he wanted a soothing story without anything bad in it. He and Isla had set up this pattern—he told adventure stories and funny stories. She told soothing stories and things that weren't actually "stories," but more family history. That way if something had happened, and they wanted reassurance at bedtime, they could get it by asking for "Mama" instead of saying "nothing scary," and possibly incurring teasing from a sibling.

"All right then, off you go." But first, each of them got a good, solid hug and a kiss. When there was no chance of an Imperial spy catching wind of such "softness" toward their children, that was how all Valdemars had been raised. Not everyone in the Empire did that. Child-rearing among the nobly born and wealthy of the Empire ranged from "turn them over to servants and tutors until they are nearly adult," through what Kordas's father had done, with side passages for those who treated their boys like tiny army recruits and schooled their girls from the time they were old enough to reach a tabletop in how to run a household and how to make the utmost of their looks. There might be plenty of contact with parents, but it was all in the role of "parent as pedagogue" rather than Mama and Papa.

Well, my lads are getting a mix, like I got. Mama and Papa in the morning and night, and off for instructions and useful work by day. I don't think they'll come to harm with that.

"Come on, my little ferrets," Isla said, and ushered them into the rear of the barge and their room.

He got a notebook he'd made out of a spare account book down out of the overhead cupboard where it had been wedged in among other books he and Isla felt needed to be kept close at hand. With it was his precious graphite marker encased in three layers of waxed string. Graphite was fragile, but using a pen and ink in a barge was perilous, and lead didn't leave a strong enough mark. He started as he always did, going back over yesterday's notes to make sure things that he'd noted would need handling had been dealt with— or at least a start had been made. Then, using the tiniest writing he could manage, he carefully added to his notes. Mostly it had to do with keeping supplies balanced along the convoy—he had underlings all along the migration to keep eyes on their particular sections, so he reckoned that as long as they were being honest with him, no one was going to come crying favoritism.

The only reason we have food as good as we do is because of the cook, not the supplies.

Their cook from the manor, who had elected to come with them rather than returning to serve the new master, could wring the least little bit of flavor out of anything he was given, and his two under-cooks were just as good.

"Food is about the most important thing for morale on this escape." He could still hear his father saying that, for what must have been the

fiftieth time. And the old man had been right. As long as people were out of the weather and warm enough—

Ha. He paused to make a note. *Collect all the fleeces, and distribute them to be used as mattresses for people too poor to have one.* It wasn't as if anyone was going to be doing any spinning and weaving on this trip. Knitting, yes, but not weaving, and you needed a clean fleece for spinning anyway, which these were not. Fleeces they'd shaved from sheep about to be slaughtered for food would make a big difference in warmth and comfort the colder it got.

He made a few more notes while Isla's voice murmured at the back of the boat. The lads must have been extra tired today, because he felt the barge move as she rose, and heard her quiet footsteps as she came forward. He looked up at smiled at her. "What do you think about distributing fleeces as mattresses?" he asked.

"Well, actually, that would empty out quite a few storage barges," she said. "And if someone wanted to take the effort to sandwich a fleece between two pieces of fabric, they'd have a very nice wool-stuffed comforter." She tilted her head to the side. "Are you getting any pushback about all the common-sharing we've been doing?"

"Me personally? No. And my subordinates in their 'villages' have a standard answer: You knew this was going to happen when we left Crescent Lake. If you don't like it, we'll get a horse and a mage to take you and all your people and beasts and supplies to the other side of the river and you can settle there and won't have to share anything." He thought that had been a rather elegant solution. People *could* live for several years just in the barges. It wouldn't be elegant or comfortable, but they could do it while they were building proper houses. And this wasn't the best land for farming or herding, but it wasn't barren, and people should be able to hack out a nice little village not unlike the one they had disturbed when they first crossed. Of course, that would largely depend on how many *other* people in their respective strings they could convince to stay as well. Anyone who wasn't strictly beholden to the complainer . . . well . . . they weren't farming rented land anymore, and for some, that was the only thing tying them to a less-than-pleasant landlord.

The social order had got turned right around. It didn't matter how rich you *had* been now. Money was useless for the moment. What mattered was whether you were generous with the things your money had bought for this trip, and whether you yourself were demonstrating useful skills to the betterment of those around you. Kindness was currency.

That was why the Squire's children had been so welcome in their respective part of the convoy. And why certain other people had seen which way the wind was blowing and elected to go back to the lives they'd known in Valdemar.

"Empty storage barges can hold frozen fish and meat as soon as the weather gets cold enough," he observed. "And firewood now. And maybe fodder, if the ravenous herds leave anything behind."

Isla tilted her head at Rose, who was standing like an abandoned scarecrow in the corner. "Rose? Can you please relay that to the Dolls at the supply barges holding the fleeces, and to the supply masters and the Captain of the Page Army? And tell the "mayors" to identify people who will need the fleeces. Then the lads can run fleeces to the right folks."

"Already done, Lady Isla," Rose said calmly.

"Are we going to put some noses out of joint here?" Kordas asked her, as she sat down at the tiny table with him.

She laughed. "Not if we don't clean the fleeces first. They are loaded with lanolin, which does not have a particularly nice smell. They're full of twigs and bits of leaves, and probably some sheep shit."

That last startled an involuntary chuckle out of him, and she smiled.

"Anyway, no one used to a prosperous life is going to want to sleep on something like that, and neither they nor their servants are going to know how to clean a fleece or want to. So no, the poor will be grateful and the prosperous will feel sorry for the poor who have to sleep on smelly fleeces." She paused. "They'll smell like sheep, of course, but I don't think they'll mind. And of course, they always have the option to clean the things. No?"

"Yes," he agreed. And after all, if the better off saw the worse off laboring away cleaning their "free" fleeces, they'd be far less inclined to think that the "free" fleeces were actually worth anything.

I swear, leading this expedition takes more diplomacy and maneuvering than living in the Imperial Court. Then he smiled to himself. *But it's a lot more pleasant. These are mostly people who are trying to live together and become a community, not that den of infighting and throat-cutting that the Court was.*

Well, this was as good a time as any to tell her he'd put her baby sister in deadly danger. "The base camp scouts had an . . . incident," he began.

"Well, since you are not telling me that Delia is dead, in pieces, in need of seven Healers, insane, ran off with scary forest-people, or is deserting the scouts to run back here, I assume everything worked out," she replied, much calmer than he'd *ever* expected she'd be. "So, since I am not going to scream at you, or tear your scalp off for putting her in danger, what are the details?" she continued, cocking her head to the side not unlike Rose did. *Has she always done that? Or did she pick it up from Rose? Or did Rose get it from her?*

As briefly and lightly as he could, he gave her the basic details. She nodded with what appeared to be satisfaction at Delia's solution for the monster lizard-bear, and actually smiled—another reaction he had not expected—at the fact that Delia had exerted herself until she passed out cold.

"You're taking this well," he said tentatively.

"Having her remain with us was not an option." She rested her elbow on the table and her chin in her hand. "I *know* you know that, just as I know you recognized her infatuation with you, and that was why you sent her off with the scouts. An infatuation that runs deep enough can render somebody useless, and make everyone around them miserable. I am not sure you realized that with you there to think about, she wasn't thinking about much of anything else. She was going to remain a lovesick girl as long as she was here. Out there—" Isla waved vaguely with her free hand in the direction of "upstream," "—she has been forced to turn outward instead of inward. And that's going to make her grow up. I don't know if it's going to cure her infatuation, but that's not on either of us. I do know she becomes less of a girl with everything she has to handle out there. And that's as it should be."

"She couldn't stay here," he agreed flatly. "If we were still back home, maybe it wouldn't have mattered, but—"

She held up her hand. "You don't need to tell *me* that. Oh, I think we are going to have to deal with Lord Hayworth's household sooner rather than later."

Kordas sighed. Not that he wasn't expecting this, but it was going to be an annoyance. But not a disaster, thanks to Isla. "Lord Hayworth is not going to know what to do when you turn up with your accounts and lists," he said, with a bit of grim satisfaction.

"Lady Hayworth does not have the training to run a Duchy that your mother gave me," she said serenely. "Frankly, I'll be glad to see him gone. I wish he'd stayed back at Crescent Lake."

"I'm glad he didn't," Kordas replied. "I actually *like* the people who stayed. No, I wish that he had stayed back in Valdemar. He'd be fine there. He might actually have been persuaded to be of some help to Merrin." At her incredulous look he grimaced. "I actually understand him. When he was faced with 'flee or lose everything' it was an easy choice. But then things changed, and he's been second-guessing his decisions ever since. He's used to being an autocrat in his own little domain and he does not understand and does not like being 'one among many.' And I don't have the time, the patience, or the inclination to cosset and coax him until he comes around."

"Nor should you," she agreed. "If he's lucky, most of his household will either be of like mind, or be convinced that money will still be of worth out here. And if he's not—"

"Then he's not our problem anymore." He reached across the table and gently caressed her hand. "And I want to think of other things, now that I know you aren't going to emasculate me for putting your sister in danger."

I *did not expect Isla's prediction to come true so soon,* Kordas thought
with utter resignation, seeing a stone-faced fellow wearing a
tabard with Lord Hayworth's device elaborately appliquéd on
the front and back approaching on pony-back. At least Hayworth
hadn't had the unmitigated gall to pull one of his horses off barge
duty to mount his herald "properly," but had assigned him what
looked like one of his household's aging ponies. The pony was so
short that you could not see its legs for the wooly backs of the sheep
it was pushing its way through.

Did Hayworth have any idea how ridiculous this looks? That's going to
reflect on his standing in the mind of anyone who sees this. Probably not.
In fact, Hayworth was probably laboring under the delusion
that his herald was properly mounted, and the mere presence of
such a functionary, resplendent in the trappings of the Imperial
Court, was going to impress Kordas and make him uncertain.

When what had probably happened was that the herald got his

orders, trotted off to the horsemaster and demanded a mount, and the horsemaster had given him one of the only beasts that wasn't sick or towing. And no matter how the herald would have protested, it would have been in vain. Horses couldn't be taken off towing without slowing everything behind them down, so it was a pony or walk.

He would have been laughable, with his knees up to his chin thanks to the short stirrups, but Kordas did not have the enthusiasm needed to muster a laugh right now. "Rose, please have Ivy tell Isla that I am going to need her and her books at the barge, because Hayworth is about to air his grievances. And then tell the other Dolls with my Councilors that I am going to need them there too for the same reason."

His nose was uncomfortably cold, and he sniffled a little, and caught the herald surreptitiously doing the same while trying to scrape together a few shreds of dignity. Then he rode forward to meet the poor man—it wasn't *his* fault that his master was about to pull a temper tantrum—and saluted him gravely. "It beats walking," he sympathetically offered to the fellow. The herald sighed, as if hearing an unwelcome truth.

"My master, Lord Hayworth, lately Baronet of Hayworth, begs the favor of your attention, *Baron* Valdemar," the herald said, putting just enough emphasis on Kordas's new title to convey an entire world of meaning. To begin with, *how the mighty have fallen,* through *you're only one very short step above my master, you know, and I know it, and you know I know it,* to end with *you got us into this, and we're not happy about it.*

Well, there went any sympathy I was going to feel for him. He's about to become a fireside joke. "Remember how Hayworth's herald showed up with his knees at his chin mounted on a pony that was practically swimming through sheep?" Now, as he'd pointed out to Isla, most of the people who felt that way had gone straight back to the Duchy—was it still a Duchy? He supposed it must be, since Merrin was a Duke now. He had the sneaking suspicion, however, that Hayworth had seen this not as an escape or an exile, but as an opportunity. Hayworth had always had ambition, but had been unable to satisfy that ambition, either through advantageous marriage or through trade alliances. Hayworth had his own little private army, and he had been extremely put out that Kordas had not leapt to arm them with Spitters, but had, in fact, forbade them to carry anything that was lethal at a distance. This was in no small part because Hayworth had refused to relinquish them to help form the new Guard. Now, a charitable man would have assumed that this was because Hayworth was planning to take over guarding his entire section of the convoy.

And Kordas, being charitable, had assumed precisely that, until the Dolls informed him otherwise.

Nor were Hayworth's servants joining everyone else in hunting, foraging, fishing, and wood-gathering for the common stores. Granted, Kordas had not specifically *said* this was supposed to happen, but most of the wealthy and nobly born were sharing out their excess with those whose luck was not so good, or who were busy with dawn-to-dark work.

Not Hayworth. The Doll Peridot had reported that any excess food was preserved by an increasingly irritated chief cook, and stowed away in unlikely places, as if Hayworth feared someone would come looking for it—and any excess wood mysteriously vanished into the "bilge storage" under the floorboards of the barges.

And Hayworth had made things very, very clear to his underlings that if *he* had been in charge, the whole convoy would have stopped right after they crossed the Gate, taken over that village by force of arms, and settled down right there with the former villagers reduced to serfdom.

Yes, Hayworth had somehow gotten infected with the "Imperial Disease." He had realized that his ambitions would no longer be constrained by boundaries he dared not trespass as they had been back in Valdemar. In this wilderness, he could take over as much land as he and his household could hold. He could style himself whatever he wanted. Viscount? Earl? Duke?

Prince?

King?

None of these titles were out of reach. And he thought, because he was rich and accustomed to thinking that way, that the silver and gold he surely had stored away (given the steady guard on one particular barge) was actually *valuable* out here. And very likely, because they had not missed so much as a single meal yet, his men thought the same. It didn't occur to any of them that in the situation in which they all found themselves, you couldn't eat or burn money, and the good will of your fellow travelers was going to be the coin you traded in.

Well, don't let him see he's irritated you.

"By all means," Kordas said, genially. "I will be happy to see him on my barge immediately. I will meet him there."

And then he rode away before the herald could counter with a demand for Kordas to come to Hayworth.

Hayworth's strings were near the tail of the convoy, which gave Kordas plenty of time to assemble mage Dole, Isla, and the rest of his Councilors, and have some of his own tail-riding guards discreetly move in on Hayworth's people as soon as he and his escort were out of sight. And Dolls. Lots of Dolls. And Ponu, Wis, and Koto. They were all going to be carrying out orders Hayworth did not anticipate. Hayworth might even think there was going to be a coup. And if so, he would be right—but not about who he thought was going to come out on top.

Lord Hayworth arrived wearing *completely* inappropriate Court garb of the sort that Kordas had been forced into wearing at the Capital. Not as rich or as elaborate, but it was ill suited to the cold of this late-autumn day, and his Lordship arrived shivering in his saddle, sniffling just as Kordas had been a moment ago, and looking thoroughly miserable. He was riding a rather delicate palfrey, as were the men of his entourage. At least he'd had the sense not to take towing horses off the barges. He and his entourage started to dismount. From the deck of the barge, Kordas interrupted them.

"Just you, your Lordship," he said politely. "I was just having a meeting with my Councilors and there simply isn't room for your people."

Hayworth, a strongly built man of late middle age whose personality inclined him to the sort of extremely "masculine" activities, like daily fighting practice, that kept him fit—mostly so that he could boast about how fit he was—looked as if he was about to object, then shrugged, rode a little ahead of the moving barge, had his herald hold his horse while he dismounted, waited for the barge to get to him, and climbed aboard, disdaining Kordas's outstretched hand.

He looked a bit taken aback when he saw how many people had squeezed into the first two rooms of the barge, but the welcome warmth of the place took him off guard, and he made the mistake of allowing the heat to relax him. Kordas read it in the slight slump of his shoulders, and knew at that moment that the battle was over and in his favor.

About half of his Councilors were seated, either on the bed or on folding stools in the walkway. The rest stood. Kordas took the second seat at the tiny table—Isla had the first one—and did not offer Hayworth a seat.

Hayworth puffed out his chest a little and smoothed down his dark hair, and the tone of his voice when he began to speak was that of someone admonishing a child. "Now see here, Baron," he began. "What the hell are you doing, dragging us past perfectly good land into gods only know what kind of forsaken wilderness is ahead of us?" His cold gray eyes narrowed a little, perhaps in anticipation of a fight he was certain he would win.

He surely expected Kordas to counter with all the reasons he'd given for leaving Crescent Lake—that the Empire was eventually going to come looking, that they needed to put enough distance between them and the Duchy of Valdemar—and enough Gate-crossings—to throw them completely off the scent. That there was no such thing as "too far from the Empire."

He might have suspected that Kordas would add that all the Landwise thought this was a poor place to settle. Surely *someone* who was Landwise would have told him this . . .

Well, maybe not. If they already knew he either doesn't believe in the Landsense, or thinks they're all in my pocket, or if they just don't like him, they might not have bothered.

So instead, he simply smiled and cut straight to the chase. "Well, Hayworth, I have made it clear all along that anyone who cares to leave us is absolutely free to do so. So if that is what you want to do, I am not going to lift a finger to stop you."

Hayworth, who had his mouth open for whatever demands he was planning to make, looked as if Kordas had actually struck him.

His hard mouth worked as his brain tried to reconcile what it had expected to hear with what Kordas had actually said. And his eyes glazed over for a moment in sheer shock.

Kordas continued, concealing his glee. "Now, of course, if this means any of your people wish to stay with us rather than going with you, you are not going to be allowed to coerce them. I have explained this to all of you. While we are on the move, and until we have established something like a stable settlement, we are all equal. You cannot make life decisions for them. Only they can do that." He looked over at Rose, who took the cue.

"Indeed, Lord Baron, and even as we speak, we are asking every member of the good Lord Hayworth's household if they choose to remain with him or go with the convoy."

Hayworth's thick eyebrows furrowed, but beneath them, his usually hard gray eyes just looked dumbstruck. He'd barely gotten a sentence out and found himself outmaneuvered.

"Now, Lord Hayworth," Isla said, with a charming smile on her face as she opened up the first of the ledgers she had piled up beside her. "Since you will be departing, we'll need to go over the inventory of what belongs to you and what belongs to the convoy. Specifically, supplies."

By the time it was all over, half of Hayworth's entourage had "mysteriously" disappeared with their horses. The personal barges in Hayworth's strings had all been detached from the convoy, reorganized, and ferried over to the *other* side of the river, because Kordas had no intention of making it easy for him to just trot his people back to that village and do what he'd intended to do. Given the chance, at the moment he had even more impetus to do so, since about half of his household of a thousand had elected to stay with the convoy. That village was a nice stand of already-built houses and already-worked fields. Very tempting.

So Kordas elected to put temptation out of reach. He was fairly certain that there was no way Hayworth would be able to cross the river as it was, and he had no way to build a bridge. It was too deep to ford, too cold to swim the horses across, and while the current wasn't excessive, it was too dangerous to try in this weather.

And if he tried, he'd only find himself faced with rebellion. The freezing, wet riders would be disinclined to do anything but build a fire to try to warm themselves, not march on a village to conquer it.

Following which, they would probably curse him under their breath and ride back up the bank to catch up with the convoy.

Meanwhile, thanks to Isla's bookkeeping, all he'd be granted besides a reasonable portion of grain and seeds was what was in his personal barge. She knew exactly how much of the common supplies he had been entrusted with, and as soon as she knew how many people were going to "leave his service" on the spot, she also knew exactly how much of those supplies she was going to order the Dolls and guards to take back.

"For your convenience, your loyalists are being moved to the western bank, where you all should be safer from the harshest weather on the way. You can keep the barges I've loaned you, of course; I'm not a monster," Kordas finished, trying not to relish how Hayworth looked as if he'd just been run over by a farm cart. "That way you'll have nice, cozy shelters to spend the winter in, and, as a gentleman farmer, I advise you to put off building anything but barns and stockpens until you've got enough land under plow to support all your people. Food on the table is going to be far more important than a replica of Hayworth House." He stood up and clasped Hayworth's hand. "No hard feelings. I perfectly understand not wanting to go any further. And who knows! We might still protect you by being a diversion. Any Imperials that come looking for us are likely to roll right past your little settlement without even noticing it."

He worked very hard not to put emphasis on the word "little." *Call yourself whatever you like, Lord Hayworth. It still won't change the fact that you are "King" of just over five hundred people.*

Hayworth shook his hand, limply.

"Off you go, then!" Kordas continued, turning him and gently moving him toward the door with a not-at-all-subtle hand on the small of his back. "You'll have a lot of organizing to do and not a lot of time to do it in!"

If his mind was working at all, he'd take that as the urgent need to get back to his barges and figure out how to keep from losing roughly half the common supplies that had been entrusted to him.

But from the way he looked . . . Kordas figured that he was still trying to make sense of the fact that Isla had been coolly ticking off things in her ledgers with "Yes, you can keep half that," and "these Tow-Beasts and Chargers here, here, and here, are actually Valdemar property," and "Now, we'll be having *that* back; it came out of the Imperial Armory, as you can see noted right here . . ."

Not Poomers and Spitters, but he does have a lot of crossbow bolts and quarrels from the supplies that never made it to the front lines, and he doesn't get to keep them all. It's purely "coincidental" that Ilsa's number came in at enough to hunt with, but not to take on a defended town.

If Hayworth noticed that he was far short of the number of guards and underlings he'd had when he arrived, he didn't show it. "His people" were deserting him already. Probably the smart ones, who had figured out that his money was worth nothing now.

Well, good. If they joined Kordas's Guard, they'd be treated decently. If they had betrayal in mind, they'd be further every day from Hayworth's place to run *to*, and it would be on the opposite bank of the river.

Meanwhile, Hayworth might be too stunned by the way he'd been outmaneuvered to notice much of anything for a while. If luck was with Kordas, his lordship wouldn't realize how badly he had screwed himself until they were long out of reach. Oh, he *could* hitch his own, personal horses, only a few of which were as heavy as the Tow-Beasts, and any of his tenant farmers' oxen (if there were any left) to the barges and try to catch up. But Kordas had confiscated at least half of his towing power, so the going would be very slow, even if he decoupled some of the lighter barges and managed to get saddle horses and ponies to submit to harness and pulling.

And if he did catch up?

He'll have to get the vote of at least sixty percent of the people here to be allowed to stay. That seemed . . . unlikely.

Not my henhouse. Not my chickens. I'll worry about it if it happens. If he has any brains, what he will do is sit put for a few days, see what he has, organize what he has, then go back and negotiate with that village to join them. He can make a bridge out of barges for his animals if he just takes the time to work it out.

Just as Kordas pressed Hayworth out of the door, Hayworth hissed, close enough for Kordas to feel his breath, "This is trickery! I'll get you for doing this, you—"

"Hush, Hayworth. I don't think you're a good enough swimmer to afford finishing that sentence," Kordas murmured back, and pushed him through.

Things pretty much fell out with the separation of Lord Hayworth from the convoy as Kordas had expected. Kordas made sure his people were absolutely scrupulous about what they took to common stores. He even left Hayworth's household a supply of chopped wood, because his people had a surplus. He made sure their barges were anchored firmly to the riverbank and that the charms on their herds were working properly, and even got a couple of volunteers from the mages to make a ramp into the river so they could easily pull their boats ashore if they decided to make a settlement where they were, and didn't want to winter in barges amid the cold water and ice. Kordas didn't actually know what would happen if the barges were completely encased in ice. Would the hulls be strong enough to survive? They did all right with simple collisions, although absolutely nobody wanted to make a test of that in rough water full of rocks and rapids. Would the pressure on the hulls by the ice just serve to pop them up out of the water to balance on the ice itself?

Well, that was one question the entire convoy was going to face eventually.

All of that sorting, reclaiming, and rearranging was accomplished while the main convoy continued to move forward at an unaltered pace.

He himself did not oversee this, but he had his proxies in the form of the Dolls, who were doing a lot of the work of culling out the things going back to the main group. The Dolls, of course, did not respond to begging, threatening, cajoling, or any other attempts at interference, and they were much stronger than humans. Now, they had never used this strength *against* humans, and it was possible that the spells locking the *vrondi* into those wood and cloth bodies prevented them from doing so. But Hayworth didn't know that. Fortunately, as it turned out, Hayworth's people were wary of them, and the Dolls didn't have to display their strength—just their complete indifference to anything the humans said to them.

Kordas did briefly wonder about the people who remained with Hayworth as he settled in next to Isla the next morning to go over her notes, having enjoyed a very different breakfast meal than *his* household cook usually prepared, courtesy of Hayworth's *former* chief cook. Kordas would have been suspicious of poisoning were it not for the cook's near-endless, truthful vitriol about Hayworth's whims. "He wouldn't let me *cook*," the man growled. "Not *really* cook. Can you imagine being able to do magic, and then being told, 'No, you'll only use magic to make little pies, because no one but *me* gets little pies'? That's what he was like." The cook had made a savory boiled pudding with oatmeal and meat scraps. A good thick slice of it, along with a sort of "bread" made of mashed tuber, mixed with flour and a little butter then fried, sat in front of Kordas now.

This was new to him, but absolutely delicious.

It was now far too cold in the mornings to eat outside, so he'd had their shares brought to them in the barge. He didn't often exploit his rank, but since he was also conferring with Isla at the same time they were eating, he felt it justified.

And he was really not looking forward to leaving the warmth of the barge for the raw wind and a trip on Arial's back. She and the other smooth-coated horses in his herds had all been growing very furry coats over the last few sennights, and he sincerely hoped this wasn't a portent of a terrible winter to come.

"I hope you aren't having second thoughts about Lord Hayworth," Isla said, when he had been quiet for a while.

"Not really." But his tone was as uncertain as his feelings. Not that he thought he'd done the wrong thing; he was just concerned that he'd punished the innocent along with the troublemaker.

She reached out and took the ledger away from him. "They're upstream from that village, which will make it a lot easier for people who decide they've made the wrong choice to get away from the group and see if they can't talk the villagers into taking them in. And right now, if all my information from the Dolls is correct, he's lost most of his little army. They are currently figuring out which households will take them. I made it clear we'd take any that weren't otherwise claimed. They all figured out the obvious: winter is soon, and even if we find a place to settle before then, it will be years, even decades, before money in the form of gold, silver, and copper has any value to us. So any ideas he had about squashing the villagers in Imperial fashion are not going to happen. So if he does the humble but smart thing, and travels back upstream to *ask them nicely* if he can move in, he and his people will be fine. They can haul their barges out of the water and into the village and live in them quite comfortably."

What sounded like a riot broke out right outside their windows.

Shouts of anger, the squeals of pigs hurt or terrified, and a strange cry, like someone tearing canvas.

He leapt to his feet, grabbing his crossbows and the quiver, and ran outside without a coat, just in time to see a strange, black, winged shape struggling into the air just off the bow of his barge with a young pig in its claws.

The pig screamed in agony; blood ran down from the wounds where the creature's claws pierced its fuzzy hide. He fumbled a bolt in place, aiming and firing.

And *he* screamed, in frustration, as something about the thing's feathers made the bolt bounce harmlessly off it. It craned its head around on its long, snake-like neck and hissed at him, then sadistically bit the pig, making it squeal, all the while pumping its huge black wings in a labored effort to get away.

There were more strange creatures in the sky, swooping and feinting down on young pigs and young sheep, although so far only *this* bastard had gotten prey. The animals on the bank milled around in a panic, all sense lost under the attacks of these *things* they had never seen before, blundering against the barge, making it rock and throwing his aim off.

A toddler is the size of a pig—

"*Pelias!*" someone shouted, and threw a fishing net to someone on the next barge, someone he recognized as one of the Valdemar mages, a gangly young teenager. *What*—he thought, and then instantly understood, as if by alchemy, as the same person yelled "*Kordas!*" and threw one at him.

He caught it, wadded it up like a ball, and flung it as hard as he could at the creature making off with the struggling pig. It was all instinct at this level—a whirl of mage energy to keep it in ball shape, a tailwind of more energy to send it farther than he himself could possibly throw. And at the very last moment, as it sailed just over the creature's head and into its flight path, an *explosion* of energy to splay the net out to its fullest.

With a surprised wheeze that sounded like a whistle, the thing flew right into the net. The net obliged without Kordas's help to foul and entrap the creature's wings.

And with a croak and a horrible squeal, creature, pig, and net plummeted to the ground. Men with spears swarmed it. Enemy dispatched, Kordas turned to see how Pelias was doing.

Pelias had already imitated his master, and a second, unlucky monster landed among the pigs, which set on it with squeals of rage, trampling it and snapping at it. In no time at all it was as dead as the one Kordas had taken down.

All up and down the line nets flew into the air. Anywhere there was a mage nearby, the creatures were knocked out of the sky and set upon with spear, axe, sword, and hoof.

And before he could get his breath and look for another net, it was over.

Another of those tearing-canvas screams came from somewhere above, and the creatures abruptly cut off their attacks and headed for the low-hanging, gray clouds filling the sky from horizon to horizon. In a moment, except for the panicked animals and the last, futile struggles of the ones that had been brought down, it was as if there had never been an attack at all.

"Rose, please relay my orders to bring every carcass of those things to the mage's barge," he croaked, suddenly aware that his heart pounded hard enough to break a rib, and he was wet with fear-sweat, and very, very cold. "Tell the Five Old Men I want them there too." He turned back to the door of the barge, intending only to get his coat and leave.

But Isla stopped him. "Finish your breakfast," she said firmly. "We do not *ever* waste food on this journey. Every mother with picky children is making that a commandment, and I am commanding you."

His gorge rose. A natural reaction after terror, of course, but—

"I can't eat," he said, wondering if he looked as green as he felt.

"Sit down. Drink your tea. Tell me afterward if you can't. It's going to take people some time to collect those bodies and deliver them to the Old Farts, and you know it. You can take the time."

Obediently, because he had the feeling her head was a lot clearer than his was right now, he did as he was told. The spicy, minty tea somehow settled his stomach, the breakfast still smelled amazing, and before he quite realized it, he had scraped the plate clean.

By that time the rest of him had settled down as well. His head cleared, his hands stopped shaking, and the sweat dried. He stood up, she passed him his sheepskin coat, and he went out. "Rose, please stay here," he said, then collected his saddle and bridle from their box on the prow of the barge and hopped off into the still-upset herds to whistle up Arial.

Getting through the jumpy herds of animals proved to be quite the challenge. Normally he'd have been able to just have Arial shove her way through them, but with them agitated, he had to be careful and move without any impression of threat. The hens, apparently, refused to come out of their coop-barges at all, and the geese and ducks had taken to theirs as well, and not even corn tempted them out.

By the time he actually got to the mages' barge, the most intact of the bodies had already been draped over the roof and there was quite a gaggle of interested parties examining them. He stood in the stern of the barge and watched as they poked, prodded, picked up, put down, and whispered to each other. And the patient Tow-Beasts, first to calm down from the attack, kept right on towing the barge along.

Now that the creatures were dead, if anything, they looked even more terrifying than when they had been in the sky. Long, narrow heads with both teeth and a hooked thing like a beak at the end of their snouts sat atop necks like a heron's. And the *size* of them! That was a lot harder to estimate when they were in the air. The wingspan was enormous; wings trailed over the side of the barge and into the water on both sides. They were covered in metallic, black feathers.

"*Six* limbs?" he said incredulously. It hadn't registered with him during the fight that the creatures had had forelegs, hindlegs, *and* wings.

"Made creatures," Dole said definitively. "There is no living thing that isn't mage-made that has four legs *and* wings. Of course, if you just look at them with mage-sight, you'll know that anyway."

He could have smacked himself in the forehead for not thinking of that. Maybe he was more shaken up than he thought. Cautiously, he did just that, and the creatures lit up with rapidly fading magical energies that were draining away as the bodies cooled.

"Feathers will be useful," Dole said dispassionately, as if he wasn't talking about winged monstrosities that could have hurt or killed not just animals, but some of their children, had things turned out differently. "Feathers retain magic for quite a long time, and we can make use of that." Now he turned to face Kordas directly. "I assume you brought the carcasses here because they're ours, now? The carcasses belong to the mages, I mean."

"I can't think of a better use for them," he said. "Oh, and Pelias was outstanding. I think you can elevate him out of his apprenticeship now."

"I'll tell his master. Timon will probably agree with you." There was a gap in the crowd. Dole took Kordas by the elbow and eased him to where he could handle one of the things himself. And it was then that he saw in these creatures what he had seen in the snake-dogs.

"Look at this, Dole!" he exclaimed, holding up the creature's head nose on to Dole's gaze. From that position it was obvious that one eye was very much higher than the other in *this* monster, but not the next one. "And this!" He dropped the head to pick up the two foreclaws. Both of them showed evidence of malformed toes. In one, the claw pointed up instead of down.

"Inbred?" Dole ventured, stroking his bare chin thoughtfully.

"Inbred," he said decisively. "Just like those snake-dogs. You think there's someone around here who made these things, scryed and saw us, and is setting their pets on us?"

"Not bloody likely," snorted Ceri, tossing his head so that the tail of white hair on the top of it lashed the air like the tail of a restless horse. "First thing is, the snake-dogs attacked that village, not us. Second thing, these ugly birds aren't big enough to cause us much trouble, just inconvenience. Although . . ." He paused and stroked his chin, in an unconscious imitation of Dole. ". . . both raids could have had the purpose of filling someone's winter larder."

"Huh." Dole raised his voice. "What do you lot think? Are the snake-dogs and these things connected? Could their master have been looking to steal food animals?"

Well, that set off a virtual avalanche in which each of the mages had to have their say. This wasn't *all* of the mages with the convoy, but it was all of the most senior ones, and they represented a pretty even cross-section of the varied nations in the Empire. Unlike the native Valdemarans who, like virtually everyone in their part of the Empire, were dark of eye and hair and definitely brown-skinned, the mages—the ones whose hair hadn't turned entirely gray or silver, that is—had every possible shade of hair and eyes and skin. It made them a bit of a startling group when you saw them all together like this.

Normally they were scattered through the convoy, doing the things only mages could do, or assisting with things that magic made easier. Bringing down dead wood from the tops of trees, for instance—there were spells to do that. Or something that Kordas had not even *thought* of when he'd implemented the Plan, because he hadn't known there was a spell for it: *making the grass grow*. Not just grow, but grow fast enough that it was knee-high in a single mark, so that there was always something to browse on for all their herds, no matter how far back in the convoy they were. It couldn't have been done at all if the animals hadn't been liberally crapping everywhere they went, because there simply wouldn't have been enough nourishment available to sustain such an insane rate of growth. But they were leaving trails of poop, and there was plenty of nutrient to feed the grass, and that had alleviated Kordas's biggest concern about the animals.

It wasn't going to work when the grass died, which it was likely to do any day because of the cold and frost, but as long as it was alive, the mages could literally work their magic on it.

Kordas had offered to learn the spell himself, and all five of the remaining Six Old Men had turned on him and scolded him for even thinking of it.

"This isn't a spell for just anyone!" Dole actually yelled, his curly hair seeming to double in size with his exasperation.

"Have you *any* idea what that takes out of a mage?" Ceri demanded, as if he was a particularly stupid schoolboy.

Koto placed a fatherly hand on his arm, which was somehow worse than being yelled at. "There is only one Baron Kordas," he pointed out, as if Kordas himself was not aware of that fact. "We have dozens of mages, but only one of you. Do what you do best and leave us to fill in what's needed."

It would have stung less if that hadn't been exactly what Isla had been telling him, almost every other night. And he was *trying*! But just as he had in the Capital, when he saw a need it was very hard not to jump in and personally fill it.

I suppose I should be grateful they aren't shoving me toward Arial and telling me to get back to doing my duty.

Finally the ruckus among the mages stopped. One middle-aged woman—so enveloped in an enormous shawl over a bulky knit tunic and loose, thick trews that it was impossible even to guess at what she looked like under all that wool—raised her hand.

"The consensus is that yes, it is entirely possible, in fact likely, that the wave of terror-birds was sent to harvest meat from our convoy. Some of those snake-dogs did get away, and they would have had no difficulty in following your trail back to the river. If the master of the pack controls the pack from afar as would have to be the case if he expected the dogs to bring home meat instead of eating it, he too would have seen the convoy and our herds."

And that's why you don't try to do everything yourself, Kordas. He sighed. *You are only one brain, and one set of eyes and ears. They are dozens, and most of them have entirely different experiences than you.*

Not that long ago, he might have rushed back to the barge that held his magic books to try to find out what the damned things were, and maybe how they could fend them off better next time, or—

But he stopped himself right there. "As you know, you have every resource I can dig up to figure out what to do about these things and their master, or masters." *Meanwhile, I need to track down those men who were formerly in Lord Hayworth's personal train, find out what they can do, and assign each of them to a guardsman. I've wanted to have the guards going about in pairs. This is a good time and reason to start.* "For now, revise the herd-minding for better defense. Double up the Guards into pairs, armed for range. Set a walking line of donkeys on the landward side of the herds, if they aren't towing. They can smash anything smaller than a pony, and we may as well use them as walking guards."

"We'll take it from here, Baron," the woman said, with a quirk of her eyebrow that said, wordlessly, *It's about time you stopped mother-henning everything.*

He flipped the long rein tethering Arial lightly to the barge over to the land and jumped off the barge. Arial had already moved off the path for the towing animals, and waited patiently for him to mount.

Was I that obvious? he thought ruefully. But of course, he already knew the answer to that question.

12

It was the third afternoon since the three river-hunting groups went out that Jonaton and Briada came riding back downriver to the base camp.

Delia could not have been happier to see them.

It had been bad enough that immediately after their encounter with the lizard-bear, Amethyst reported the attack of the terror-birds on the main convoy. At that point Delia had been as nervous as a cat surrounded by hunting dogs. It seemed far too much of a coincidence to her—first the snake-dogs, then the lizard-bear, then the terror-birds. Either this wilderness was crawling with hungry monstrosities, or something or someone was stalking them. Maybe even testing them.

She perched on the roof of the barge beside Amethyst, because otherwise she'd just have been lying in bed with her eyes wide open, jumping at every sound. She went to sleep only after she kept nodding off, and was up at the first light, long before anyone else, and again sat on the roof of the barge, scanning the sky. She knew what she was going to do, of course, if those *things* came after their group. Just what she did with the geese. Of course . . . they were much bigger than geese, and she planned to slam them into the ground at a distance and fill them full of arrows while they were still stunned. It was a strategy that should work for birds or dogs. She tried not to think about the fact that Kordas had tried shooting the birds to no effect—after all, she could put some extra force into her arrow strikes. *It should work. Right?*

She stayed up there until after breakfast, then Sai sent her and Venidel out as usual. She hadn't wanted to go cut fodder, but there really hadn't been a choice; the horses needed it, and there were two mages awake and ready to respond if anything attacked. Right? But at least they were cutting fairly close to the camp, so she could keep one eye on the sky and one on the short, but sharp, scythe in her hands.

And as soon as luncheon was over she took her position on the top of the barge again, even though her eyes burned with fatigue, and she would have given up Daystar at that moment if it meant she could take a nap.

So when two moving specks appeared on the horizon, she stood and pointed and croaked "Something's coming!" and felt her gut knot up with fear as Sai and Endars dropped what they had been doing, peered in the direction she was pointing, and took a "ready" stance.

And a moment later, when those moving dots resolved into Briada and Jonaton instead of a pair of lizard-bears or some other horror, she felt ready to weep with relief. Of all the people she wanted right now, those two were at the top of the list. What Briada couldn't eliminate by brute force, Jonaton could probably set on fire or turn inside out, or just make it explode. Sai had admitted in Delia's hearing that the only reason the Six Old Men hadn't decided to become the Seven Old Men was that Jonaton wasn't old. In every other way, he was the equal or superior of one of the Six.

"Hey!" She waved down at Sai and Endars, in case her eyes were sharper than theirs. Their heads turned. "It's Briada and Jonaton! They're back!"

The camp erupted. Sai hastened to stir up something quick for them to eat, Venidel hauled two of the more choice fodder bundles to the upriver side of the camp for their horses, and everyone else gathered to greet them. Not shouting and making noise—not a good idea to attract the attention of anything that might be out there in the woods. But waving was quiet.

They didn't even bother to dismount before speaking. "Rapids end at a forest and there's a strong ley-line there," Jonaton said as he was swinging a leg over his horse's rump. "I planted an anchor and I connected it to the ley-line. As we figured, just like we did downstream, we're going to have to set the Gates half on land and half in the water, because the river is so wide."

"What else is on the other end of the rapids?" Endars asked, helping Jonaton with his saddlebags and the saddle.

"Weird forest," Briada added, shaking her head as she unbuckled her horse's saddle and eased it off its back. "Very, very weird forest."

"How weird is weird?" Sai asked, while Venidel took over rubbing down her horse, then leading it to the fodder, and Endars did the same with Jonaton's horse.

Jonaton made a gesture of helplessness. "You'll just have to see it for yourself," he said, after a long pause during which he seemed to be groping for words. "Well, anyway, the good news is that once the Gates are up and linked, we'll be able to feed both of them off that ley-line. So, how bored have you been?"

Delia burst into laughter that was only a *little* bit hysterical.

Jonaton gave her a side-eye, but sobered when Sai described the lizard-bear and how Delia had driven it away. He didn't *say* anything, but she saw something in his eyes she had never seen before when he was looking at her.

Respect.

He'd been mildly annoyed when she'd been dropped on the crew by Kordas. He'd covered it well, and he hadn't treated her unkindly, but it was clear he had a good idea why Kordas had sent her to the group. Then, once she proved herself useful, he approved of *her*, but she got the feeling he still wanted "the child" back at the convoy.

But now she had his respect. And despite being ready to drop, she felt a sort of energizing glow.

Then Sai brought Amethyst into the conversation to have her retell what had happened back with the main convoy—both Lord Hayworth's defection and the attack by the terror-birds—and Jonaton's eyes narrowed, as did Briada's.

But before he could say anything, Sai held up a hand. "Let's discuss further when Delia isn't falling over. She's been bravely watching the skies just in case for far too long, and I think she needs a nap. Tonight, over dinner. I'll make something good."

Despite the fact that her legs felt completely boneless, Delia was already halfway to the door of the barge by the time Sai finished that sentence, and she bundled herself up in her sheepskin coat, pulling her legs up to her chest, without bothering with blankets.

Briada came and woke her for supper at sunset, which was, as Sai had promised, good. The soup was as thick as gravy, and very spicy. With the soup was flatbread with some of their precious cheese rolled up in it and melted. Sai had been managing to grind grain into flour for flatbread almost every day, with the aid of an ingenious rig that Hakkon contrived, using the river- current to power the hand mill. She nibbled her share to make it last while the rest discussed these new attacks. Overhead the stars were out, but in the west there was a rapidly fading line of umber-to-red light, showing the sun hadn't quite sunk.

"I don't think the bear was an attack," she put in, between nibbles. "It acted surprised to find us." The water lapping against the hulls of the barges only made her feel colder, but her feet were toasty, and she wanted to be part of the discussion instead of shunted off to the side.

"It acted as if it had poor eyesight as well," Sai agreed. "Which is odd, because bears have vision as good as we do." He toyed with the ends of his long hair. "Lizards don't have good distance vision, though. Perhaps that's the answer."

"It also didn't act as if something was urging it on beyond its own idea we might be good to eat," Endars observed dispassionately.

"Well," Jonaton said after a moment, taking a flatbread and rolling some jam into it, "looking at the few facts as we know them, I think we are probably talking about two different origins for the three sorts of beasts. Sai, you said you were very sure the lizard-bear was the product of a Change-Circle. The mages back with the convoy seem pretty certain what attacked them and the village were mage-made creatures."

"The flying ones have to be," Sai said flatly. "You don't get six limbs on an animal or bird unless it's mage-made or one of a handful of kinds of skink. And on top of that, you don't get a lot of creatures that all look alike out of a Change-Circle. Even if, say, a den of snakes and a pack of mastiffs got caught in a Change-Circle, every single one of them would look completely different, because every one of them gets random changes."

"What's a skink?" Delia whispered to Venidel.

"Kind of lizard," he whispered back.

"So we have a singleton that seems to match all the earmarks of a Change-beast, and we have two packs of creatures of two different kinds that have the earmarks of being mage-made." Jonaton did not seem to feel the cold as night closed down, but Delia couldn't help but shiver when stray gusts of wind managed to get down her neck despite her collar being up. Or maybe it was fear.

Probably it's both.

Endars pulled on his lower lip, which meant he was thinking. But Briada spoke up before he could say anything.

"If that weird forest is what Change-Circles look like, there's good odds the bear came from there, rather than back downstream," she said. "I can't imagine having parts of you exchanged with lizard parts is anything but painful. A bear would have run a pretty long way after being hurt like that, and it would certainly have followed the river. They can run leagues without stopping if they've got a mind to or something terrifies them. And the bear doesn't match the descriptions you gave of the terror-birds and the snake-dogs, where you can't say, 'Oh, that's a snake head, and that part is a black eagle.' It looked pretty much like patchwork: 'Here's a lizard belly, here's lizard claws.'"

"According to what Rose saw of the birds and the dogs," Amethyst spoke up, "that's very much the case. The birds look like entire creatures, not bits of two or three thrown together. The dogs were the same, only more so. It wasn't a patchwork where mismatched things are fitted together. It was, I would say, seamless."

"Planned and designed, you mean?" Alberdina asked.

"I would say so, yes," Amethyst confirmed.

"So the long and the short of it is that we have come into a land where—even if we can't *find* much at the moment—magic energies must be readily available," Endars said. "Available enough that mages can actually create living creatures—"

"Maybe, maybe not," Sai replied, the flickering firelight making his face look slightly sinister. "We're getting closer to where those wars five hundred years ago were fought. These things could be left over from that. The terror-birds and the snake-dogs, that is." He brushed his long, straight hair behind his ear, a habit he had when he was thinking aloud. "If there weren't a lot of them to begin with, they'd be inbred pretty quickly." He poked at the fire with a stick. "The impetus for why they showed up to us or to the convoy, though, seems to be quite different as well. The bear probably found us completely by accident. But I just don't like it that the birds attacked after Kordas drove off the dogs. What are the odds of that?"

Jonaton sighed. "I don't like that either. It's too much of a coincidence, don't you think?" He looked at Endars, who shrugged, sending writhing shadows all over his torso.

"Or there are more packs of both of those creatures than we know of, and it was just a matter of time before they found us," Endars pointed out. "If we don't assign causality. True randomness includes clusters. And at any rate, the Gate will take us far away from this part of the river. That just might answer the question as to whether this was a targeted, deliberate attack or a mere coincidence. If they come after us when we are on the other side of the new Gates, then clearly, we should adopt the posture that they're sent to attack us."

Sai nodded, and the conversation turned to how quickly they could get Gates up and get moving, because winter was not "coming" anymore, it was here. Sooner or later they were going to have to stop and wait it out, and they were going to need a pretty large expanse of safe, not-flooding-in-spring land to hold all of them. *But are the Gates taking us to where the lizard-bear came from?* Delia wondered. *And are there more monstrous things there that we haven't any idea about? And what about that forest has Jonaton so perturbed?*

The other two teams came back on the morning of the fifth day, and the work erecting the Gates began. By this point the third and fourth set of Gate uprights had arrived on their own barges, towed by a pair of mages, each riding a Charger. They weren't mages Delia knew well, so she just greeted them and stood back.

The first and second sets of uprights had already been unloaded—not by magic, nor Fetching, but by the simple expedient of putting planks under each end and sliding them down to the riverbank. They didn't roll, because they were curved, but they slid just fine. The new uprights came off their barges the same way, and went back on the scouts' barges while the mages worked on the first Gate.

The meeting and greeting didn't take long. The two mages turned the empty barges to point downstream, hitched up the horses, and were away before anything but a few courteous words, some warning about the terror-birds, and a quick meal in the form of flatbread wrapped around steamed fish filets and herbs.

Delia couldn't help but notice the two mages kept one eye on the sky as they rode off. She didn't blame them. According to Amethyst, the birds hadn't gone after human adults in the convoy, but they were huge, and they might consider a massed attack on two humans with two horses to be worth the risk.

The uprights for the temporary Gate were spaced so closely together on the narrow shoreline that there was just enough room for the Tow-Beast to get through, dragging two of the uprights behind him. If Delia understood correctly, they'd have had to make the opening that small no matter what; the amount of power coming via the anchor right now just wasn't enough for anything larger. They could make a temporary Gate on that side, but not only did it have to be small, they couldn't keep it open for long. Once the proper Gate had been set up, there would be enough power for both Gates to operate all day and all night.

Now they split the party in half. Jonaton went through the Gate to the other side accompanied by Ivar and Hakkon; obviously, being the expert, he'd be able to get the receptive Gate up in the course of the morning, and that new ley-line would be feeding magical energy to the entire arcane construct in no time. As soon as his crew was through, Sai set about the work of creating a mooring point for the water-side upright. Jonaton would be doing the same, of course; in fact, that would be his team's first task.

Delia had no idea what Sai was doing, and he didn't bother to explain any of it to her. It was obvious that he was doing something; he kept staring at a point in the river that was about a cart-length from the bank. Far enough that the barges would be able to move smoothly through it even if their roofs were laden with things that stuck out over the sides. He made odd little movements in the air with his fingers, and his furrowed brow had little sweat beads on it.

Then she spotted something dark just under the surface of the river, right where he was staring. It wasn't long before it rose slowly to the surface and broke it, like a fish coming up for a fly: a perfectly square pillar of what looked like rock. Gray rock. A bit darker than the water today. *Is it rock? Or is it made of magic, somehow?* It looked a lot like the rocks here on the shoreline, but what did she know? The Emperor had mages that could build entire manors with magic, after all.

When the top of the pillar was just about exactly even with the shore, Sai straightened and dropped his hands to his sides. "Well, that's the hard part done," he said to Delia. "The hard part on our side, at least. All of the uprights are tuned to each other, so they all resonate at—" Delia must have looked baffled, because he barked a short laugh. "I've spent too much of my life with other mages. Doesn't matter. Endars, Venidel, and I will move the upright and make it one with the pillar, do some other things you won't be able to see, and invoke a full Gate spell with the power for it coming from Jonaton's ley-line. Jonaton will be doing *all* the work on his side, and everything will be controlled from his side. Then Endars, Venidel, and I will need to fall into our beds for a while, Jonaton will need to do the same, and the Fairweathers will be in charge of bringing the barges through to Jonaton's side."

"Is there anything I can do to help?" she asked anxiously.

He pinched the bridge of his nose and closed his eyes. "Police the campfire, make sure no one's left anything that should be in the barges, load whatever's been left onto a barge—it doesn't matter which one—and make sure the fire is out, the embers soaked and scattered. Oh! And if there are any fodder balls left, or wood bundles, load them on a barge. No point in wasting them." He then turned to Venidel and Endars, who had waited until he was done talking to her to approach, and the three of them went into a conference. They were stopped by Sai for a moment, and he said, half-turned her way,

"You're adapting to the life of a scout pretty well."

Delia felt a blush, and beamed.

Bret and Bart were already harnessing up the horses and either putting them in place to tow, or tethering them on very long leads to the other barges. Amethyst, Alberdina, and Briada vanished inside barges to make sure everything was stowed and secured. That left her with the camp—which was not a great deal of work. Sai hadn't left so much as a cucumber seed behind, it was the work of a moment to Fetch the last four bales of fodder and secure them to the already-secured wood on the top of the supply barge, she Fetched about four bucketfuls of water right down on top of the fire with a *sploosh*, and after that, there was nothing left to do but make certain the embers were stone cold and scatter them.

And meanwhile, all three mages were practically staring holes in the Gate upright, as it drifted smoothly and serenely toward its stone pillar, eased softly down to its proper place—

And then there was a brief flash of light that blinded her for a moment. When she could see again, the Gate upright was in place, looking as if it had always been there, standing tall and slightly curved against the background of water and riverbank. And between this upright and the one still on the bank stretched the peculiar reflective-water effect of a Gate that was ready to use.

"Has Jonaton gotten his Gate up already?" she asked Sai in open astonishment.

The old man sighed and sagged a little. "Very likely. Of course, this just might be a sign that the power from the ley-line on the other side is coming to this Gate through the anchor, but I doubt that very much. The boy is good, and he's younger than we are, curse him. He can do alone what it takes two or three of us Old Men."

"And he's handsome, too! This is how we know all the gods hate us," Venidel chimed in.

"Every last one," Endars agreed.

At just that moment, there was a plop and a splash—and a crude little boat made of bits of wood held together with a bit of string with a leaf for a sail swirled away from the Gate on the sluggish current.

"Well, there's the answer. The other Gate is up. Jonaton did all the heavy work at his end, and we might as well get moving," Sai said.

"*You* are going to lie down in your bunk," Briada Fairweather said, with a jerk of her head toward the barges. "Leave the moving to us."

Since there really wasn't anything else to be done at the camp, Sai allowed his fatigue to show, and plodded over to the men's barge, followed by Endars and Venidel. Delia ran back and jumped onto the middle barge to keep a lookout next to Amethyst. She was pleased to see that the Fairweather lads took up similar positions on the first and last barges bearing full-sized crossbows and deadly war bolts meant for piercing armor.

As for Briada, she had a war bow of her own, and was mounted on the Charger that Kordas had given her. Anything that the arrows or Delia brought down, the horse would turn into broken bones, blood, and feathers. Briada chirruped to the Tow-Beast to tell him to move on.

The Tow-Beast knew his business and did not need a leader or someone to guide him; he responded completely to voice commands. And now he strained in his harness, and Delia braced herself for the little jolt as the barge ahead of hers started to move, the ties strained, and her barge jerked into motion.

She braced herself again for the Gate transition, but this one must have covered a shorter distance than any other transition she'd experienced, because it was just a momentary sensation of cold and falling.

And then . . . they were on a whole new section of the river. And the noise! She looked behind her, and since the Gate didn't even cover a quarter of the river, she had a clear view of the rapids that they had just bypassed. But she would have known they were there without looking; the water roared and thundered, and the barges actually vibrated with the sound. There was so much spray in the air that it smelled like rain, and thanks to all that moisture, the air felt like ice.

She'd never actually seen rapids before—there hadn't been anything like rough water at Crescent Lake, and all the waterways around the Valdemar manor were man-made canals. One look at the churning river and enormous boulders sticking up everywhere made her knees feel a little wobbly. On this side of the river was what was left of a cliff; it looked as if at some point in the past the entire thing had collapsed into the river, narrowing the channel and forming the rapids.

We'd never have survived trying to tow the barges through that.

And . . . the collapsed cliff went back as far as she could see—and a lot farther beyond that, since it must have taken Jonaton and Briada at least a day to ride past the rapids to this point. *What brought that much rock down all at once?* It looked as if it had happened a long, long time ago. *Was it that war of mages they keep talking about?*

The Gate had been set up at a point where the river resembled the stretch they had just left behind, and immediately after that the banks narrowed dramatically and the water, now forced to go through a smaller channel, sped up to the point that it surged over the rocks in its path and leapt into the air in standing waves.

She had expected Jonaton to have set up a camp here, but he just added his horse to the Tow-Beast so they were now pulling double in harness, waited for the men's barge to come even with him, and with assistance from Ivar, managed to roll himself over the railing and onto the barge, where he lay on the narrow deck for a moment. Then Venidel helped him up and into the barge itself.

. . . *if something comes along that only magic can defeat . . . we are in big trouble.* With *all* of the mages needing rest, was this really the time to be moving forward?

On the other hand, you couldn't hear much of anything here, and the damp and cold couldn't be good for them. Maybe it was better to move. *Ow. This mist coating everything we have in ice would be dangerous, and there would be more every day, if we stayed here. We'd be found in the spring melt, glazed like a bad candy.*

Ivar mounted his horse, which was tied up beside the Gate, and sent it trotting up to Hakkon. She couldn't hear anything they said over the roar of the water, but he came back to her barge, loose-tied Manta to it, and he and Bay leapt aboard.

He and Bay clambered up on the roof to sit there beside her and Amethyst. The Doll began petting Bay's enormous head without prompting, and the dog put his head in her lap, overcome with doggy bliss. *Strange how all the animals seem to like the Dolls,* she thought. *Maybe they understand that the Dolls would never hurt them.*

"We've got a campsite marked out ahead, away from the rapids but *before* the weird forest," Ivar told her in a half-bellow. "We have to get away from the rapids, no matter what. Otherwise we aren't going to be able to hear conversations, much less hear things coming through the brush at us. And I don't fancy trying to sleep in damp blankets even once. Jonaton and Briada said they didn't have any trouble passing through that uncanny forest, but I got a look at it, and I don't want to take any chances." He paused a moment. "When we reach it, don't leave the barge. And don't kill anything. I . . . just have a feeling. Keep to supplies aboard. Even if you think we are desperate for firewood, don't snap off what look like dead branches; don't Fetch anything that isn't lying on the ground. The further north we go, the weirder the animals get. This time out, we spotted vanishing herons. Turn to the side and they disappear; just their legs show. Anything hidden by feathers? Invisible. We only saw them when we were two horselengths from them. Find that on a predator, or on razorvine, well. Bad day. We may not be able to trust what we see."

It wasn't just because of the damp cold that she shivered. "Can we get through it in a day?" she asked.

At this point, Briada noticed they were talking, added her horse to the string, and dismounted with *impossible* agility and skill right onto the barge. "Please tell me we are stopping short of the forest," she shouted.

"We're stopping short of the forest," Ivar told her. "Delia is concerned about whether we can get through it in a day."

"That won't be a problem. My horse couldn't get out of it fast enough. If we start early-early-early, feed the horses and mules well overnight, and hitch every animal to the barges, we should get out of it well before sunset. The beasts are going to need a good rest afterward, but that's a small price to pay for not being in that place when the sun goes down."

"I am relaying all this information to Rose," Amethyst said, pitching her voice high to carry over the noise of the water.

There was no forest right here by the rapids, only rocky banks in the bottom of a narrow valley covered in scrub brush and tall grass.

Now Delia was very glad that she'd loaded down the last barge with wood, although it didn't look as if they were going to be in any need of fodder for the horses.

She glanced up ahead; it looked as if the river made a big curve to the west, following the valley. Perhaps that would cut off some of the sound from the rapids.

Briada and Ivar were talking, but she couldn't hear them. It didn't really matter; neither of them looked at her for a reaction or an answer to anything, so they were probably discussing the camp and what provisions to make for guarding it. She went back to watching the sky. Bay would certainly alert if something came over the hill, and his senses were far superior to hers. But he probably would not pay attention to the sky; dogs were seldom attacked by anything overhead. Really, what *could* successfully attack a mastiff the size of Bay that could also fly?

Those terror-birds, and that's about it, I think. Can you call them "birds" if they have four legs? But they also have beaks.

Whatever they were, she sincerely did not want to actually see any with her own eyes. Adventures were all very well when they were safely confined within the pages of a book. You could close a book and keep all the danger inside it.

But even in books, the heroes make mistakes, and there isn't always a happy ending.

That thought would never even have occurred to her before. *My life has turned into "before" and "now," hasn't it? It's good. This is good. This pace, this intensity. I think I like it, I really do. Not out of pretense or rebellion, but out of simple satisfaction. Gathering, helping, investigating things from beetles to balms, and every step is a genuine adventure. This is living what we've imagined heroes in stories doing, standing majestically against a new vista in warm orange light, their amazing clothes whipping in the wind. This actually makes more sense to me as a way of life than being in a castle. It's doing things, it's being with people who are there to be with you, and feeling good to do so, big task or small. And there's genuine danger, don't ever forget that there is danger. Forget danger for a moment, and it's the moment you die. Ah! I think I like that. But still, even if I didn't really feel or quite believe it, we were in as much danger before as we are now. Not heighten-the-tension danger like in a book, but tensing-you-up, react-to-every-sound-and-shadow fear. It's like sharpening the edges of your thinking and whirling it around your heart a while.* But of course, there was one other consequence of all this tension and excitement. *It's tiring.*

All she had to do was look at her own life to understand that. When her father had died, the Emperor had ruled that neither she nor Isla could inherit, and had given away her home and lands to a stranger. And she was lucky, in a way, that the stranger had come with a wife, or she might have found herself married to that stranger, with no one to protect her.

A different kind of danger perhaps, but the difference, in the end, between being murdered by your husband for your lands and being murdered by a terror-bird is rather moot. Dead is still dead.

They rounded the curve of the river, and indeed, to her relief, the roar faded to a murmur echoing off the sides of the valley. And there on the river she spotted a goose.

She didn't even think about it; out of pure habit, she Fetched it; Bay leapt up, seized its neck and broke it, and dropped the whole goose in his master's lap, waiting for praise. Ivar made much of him, and Delia slid down the front of the barge and went inside to stow it in the kitchen. With no fire in the stove, the inside of the barge was as cold as the outside, and the goose would keep.

When she came back out again, it was to discover that Ivar and

Briada had each shot more geese on the shore, which Bay had gone to fetch. "There's dinner sorted," Ivar said with satisfaction as she took one goose from Bay's mouth and the other from the deck of the barge.

"And the mages will need it. I'll cook it if you'll clean it. Just gut it, don't take the feathers off," Delia offered, just as she spotted a little red bit of ribbon tied to a branch ahead. "Bay can have the innards and the head and feet. I'll cook them separately for him. And there's our camp." She pointed to the ribbon.

As the mages slept off their exertions, the rest set up the camp, starting the cookfire inside a crescent of boulders with plenty of room for people to sit between the rocks and the fire. Once the fire was ready, Delia took the heads, innards, and feet of the goose while Bay watched with interest and put them in a pot to simmer together beside, but not in, the fire. She needed the bones to soften so they weren't dangerous for a dog to eat, and that meant long, slow cooking. She had noticed that there was clay between the rocks of the riverbank, and she scooped out enough clay to cover all three birds about a thumb-width thick. She wet the birds down, stuffed them with herbs, salt, and some onion, dripped in a bit of wine that was going off, then coated the geese in clay. She made sure the clay worked down into the feathers and smoothed the clay over the encased birds until they looked like large stones. Then she put them on a bed of coals, and raked more coals over them. Then she found a nice flat rock, cleaned it well, and put it at the fire to heat up to make flatbreads.

Normally she wouldn't have rendered the feathers useless by coating them in clay, and normally she would have cooked the geese on a spit with a tray to catch the fat, but this was the most foolproof way of cooking them that she knew. There was very little chance of them burning or drying out this way. They already had more goose quills for arrows than they would ever use, anyway, and the feathers from three geese weren't going to fill more than a quarter of a pillow.

Venidel emerged as the sun neared the horizon. Endars followed shortly after. But Jonaton and Sai did not appear until she had broken open the hard clay and pulled the pieces away from the birds. The feathers came off with the clay, the skin broke, and the air filled with an aroma that was virtually identical to the geese Sai cooked. And *that* brought everyone to the fire.

She gave Bay his cooked heads, feet, and innards, and he slurped the entire concoction up in no time.

The four mages were still looking a bit shaky, so she scolded them into sitting down and fixed plates for them: flatbread, goose breast, and pickled carrots. Sai tasted the goose gingerly, then with more enthusiasm.

"Who taught you how to cook goose in clay, rich girl?" he teased.

"You did," she reminded him. "All that magic must have erased your memory."

He looked as if he was trying to think of a good retort, but shrugged, gave her half a grin, and just dug out another sliver of goose from the breast and ate, slowly, chewing carefully.

Jonaton looked even more exhausted than Sai, but then, he'd been doing the work of three mages. He would stare at the food in his lap, slowly pick out a bit that was about bite-sized, slowly put in his mouth, and slowly chew. Alberdina set aside her own dinner and moved over to where he was sitting. He slowly raised his head and looked at her.

"Headache?" she asked.

He nodded and winced.

She left for the barge and returned with a bottle. She took his cup of water and poured some of it in. "Drink," she ordered, and he did, the whole thing, down all at once.

Alberdina snatched a hot flatbread off the stone and spread a thick layer of jam on it, rolled it up, and handed it to him. "Eat that," she ordered.

He did, chewing slowly, as the sun sank and the wind got colder. Ivar raked the fire closer together now that she didn't need the coals to cook the birds anymore, and they all slid down the boulders to use them as shelter against the wind.

Jonaton went back to his goose, but he was looking much better. It was hard to tell in the flickering firelight, but she thought he was getting his color back.

"Next time take me or Endars," Venidel said sternly. Or at least, he tried to say it sternly. It was a little hard to believe him being stern when he had just the barest fuzz of beard coming in and everyone else, except for her, was at least a decade older than he was.

"The better idea would be to ask Sai's brother to join us from the convoy," Amethyst observed. "Two very senior mages on one end and three mages on the other should even out the strain."

Jonaton sighed and the last of the pain lines eased away from his eyes. "I was fine—well, almost fine—until I lay down. As soon as I relaxed, it felt like someone had hit me with a bag of hammers."

Sai stopped chewing long enough to shake his head and say, "You know, youngster, the fact that you *only* feel like someone hit you with a bag of hammers is a tribute to how strong and skilled you are."

Jonaton raised his head, his eyes wide with shock, and stared at Sai in disbelief.

"And now you can forget I ever said that," Sai added, and cackled.

13

Alberdina swore under her breath in a language Delia didn't understand, and then shouted, "Hakkon! *Stop the horses right this moment!*"

Delia did not blame her in the least, because rising up before them on both sides of the river was a thing that could not, by any standard she knew, be called a *forest*.

Oh, there were tree-like objects, and lots of them. It was just that under no circumstances would she have called them *trees*.

There were no variations in them other than height. There were no conifers or evergreens. They were as uniform as a planted orchard, and spaced just as neatly apart: about the length of a horse and farm wagon, to be precise. Not only were they leafless— which was to be expected, since most of the leaves at this point were on the ground, and those that weren't belonged to things like holly—their limbs were contorted and twisted like no tree she had ever seen before. Once, before Isla had married Kordas and she and her sister had both shared a tutor, the tutor had taken them out on a bright summer day with glass bowls and a sieve and a dipper and a little, but very strong, pocket magnifying lens to examine the tiny animals in the estate's ornamental pond. These things looked something like one of the creatures they had seen that day. Except they were big. Big as the oldest apple trees in the Valdemar orchard.

The trunks, covered with a heavy, dark gray bark, sprouted branches that contorted and spiraled in ways that could not possibly have been due to wind and made very little sense in terms of growing things. The only time she had ever seen branches that looked like this was on climbing vines. In fact, they gave the impression of movement that had nothing to do with a breeze. As Hakkon tried to slow the string of barges and they got nearer to this forest, she noticed something else. The trees on both sides of the river were the strange ones, although there were normal trees just at the edge of the forest on the other side. But the closer they got to this "weird forest," the stranger and more sinister the place looked. Patchy with green moss and sporting odd, transparent fungi, there were places on the trunks that looked less like boles or cankers than open mouths with teeth in them.

And as Hakkon managed to bring the string to a complete halt, she noticed, with a sensation of great unease, that there was something else about the branches of those trees. The underside of each and every twisty, contorted branch sported odd symmetrical round marks. Or were they another kind of fungus? But what fungus grew in regulated, evenly spaced rows, one or two rows per branch, from the base of the branch to the pointed tip?

"What in all the dark hells . . ." Alberdina said aloud, as Jonaton poked his head out of the barge and looked from the forest to her and back again.

The ground *seemed* to be covered with a reddish-brown matter of some sort. Fallen leaves? Maybe . . .

Flitting among the trees were reddish-brown winged insects that looked like dragonflies. Which should have been impossible. It was more than cold enough for insects to be dead. Were they some sort of bird? But what bird had *four* wings?

Jonaton hopped over to their boat as Alberdina stared. "I don't want to go in there," she said flatly. "Those . . . I won't call them *trees* . . . there's something very wrong with them."

"Well, the horses agree with you," Jonaton replied. "But Briada and I went all the way to the end of this forest and back, and took no harm. Can you be a little more specific about what you think is wrong with them?"

Alberdina shook her head. "Lad, I'm a Healer, not a mage, but . . . this is a place that doesn't much like things with warm blood in their veins. That's my impression, anyway. It's as if this entire forest is one single creature. And it's dormant . . . at least I think it is. But I wouldn't want to wake it."

"Are those . . . mouths with *teeth*?" Delia stammered.

"To be honest, we didn't go close enough to it to find out. It could just be imagination. Or an illusion, a trick of coloration and texture that *looks* like teeth to keep animals and birds from making holes in the trunks." That was what Jonaton said, but it was in a tone of voice that made her think he actually did not believe what he was saying. "Look, there's no choice here, we have to go through. But that's why we're going to go as fast as we can without exhausting the horses. We'll be in the clear before sunset."

"That's all very well for us, but what about the convoy?" Alberdina demanded. "We are stopping here, right now, and we're going to ask Amethyst to contact Kordas." She turned to the Doll. "Is there *any* way that you can show him what we see?"

Jonaton sighed. "No need," he replied, and turned to Amethyst himself. "Amethyst, please get in contact with Kordas, and ask him to scry where we are. He can see for himself."

Kordas stared into the depths of the scrying pool that Ponu had conjured up. All the rest of the Old Men, and some of the other mages, had gathered around it as well.

Alberdina's insistence, through the Dolls, that he see what they were about to traverse for himself had been so vehement that he had decided to get some of the best of his mages to join his "look ahead." And now he was glad that he had.

"Can we, dare we, move the point of view closer?" he asked Ceri. "Alberdina is pretty adamant that she feels as if those things are hostile. Would they react to being scryed?"

"If they would, they're too dangerous to pass through," Ceri opined. "And it's better to find that out now than later."

Kordas grimaced, but Ceri had a point. And if the trees—and whatever depended on them, maybe—reacted with hostility, there was the option to get the scouts to collect the Gate uprights, speed through the forest, and establish that second Gate somewhere else if they had to. Granted, it wouldn't be on that powerful ley-line, but maybe Jonaton could find another.

"Moving in closer," said Ponu, and the point of view moved past the scouts and closer to the strange forest, although Ponu did *not* take it any nearer than the horses and barges would be on the river.

"Are those mouths in the trunks?" asked Koto, rubbing his bald head nervously. "And *teeth*?"

"They look like it to me," Kordas agreed.

Alberdina's voice came thinly through the pool, as if from a great distance. "I'm no expert on anything but Healing, but this doesn't *feel* like a forest of trees to me," she said. "It feels like one enormous entity."

"There are groves of trees that are exactly that," Ceri said thoughtfully. "They look like a grove of trees, but actually, each tree is a scion of an enormous root system. If something like *that* got caught in a Change-Circle, a really big one, then you wouldn't get each tree looking different from every other tree. You'd get something like this—" He gestured at the pool.

They were all on top of Kordas's personal barge, since the convoy did have to keep moving, and no one wanted to stop on the verge among all the herds, or impede the progress of the horses. Ponu had made the scrying pool by the simple expedient of creating a shallow dish made of magic energies, and pouring river water into it.

"And if that was what has happened," Dole mused, sounding as if he was speaking his thoughts aloud, "then the thing has had five hundred years to proliferate and spread. It could have started out small, and expanded along the water source."

That made sense. That would also explain why the border of it was not a segment of a circle. "But the question is, is it safe to pass it?" Kordas asked.

"I think it is," came Jonaton's voice from the pool. "Briada and I passed it twice, and nothing ever happened. Alberdina says it feels to her like it's dormant."

Dormant doesn't mean dead. Dormant implies it can wake up.

"If we stay on the riverbank, and the herds stay on the riverbank, we should be fine," came Briada's voice. "If it didn't notice a dozen people including four mages and a mage-made construct, I very much doubt it'll be bothered by the convoy."

Ponu sucked on his lower lip and looked at Ceri. Ceri stroked his chin. Koto rubbed his head again. "It is true," Dole said, choosing his words with great care, "that magic-warped things do respond most readily to the presence of mage-made objects and magicians, if they are going to respond at all."

"They're *trees*," Jonaton said in tones of exasperation. "What are they going to do, pull up their roots and come running after us?"

"Don't tempt fate!" all the mages on Kordas's side said at once, at the same time as the sound of a *smack* came from the other side, followed by Jonaton's indignant *"Ow!"*

"What was that for, Sai?" Jonaton whined.

"You're an idiot. And you used to be my apprentice. I reserve the right to continue smacking you when you say something stupid," Sai replied. "How many times have I told you? Words have power for magicians. Say the wrong thing and it *can* come to pass."

"Sai?" Kordas called. "What's your opinion?"

"That no one knows much about things that happen in Change-Circles," Sai said cautiously. "Largely because it's never the same thing twice. This could have been the result of what Dole suggested."

"Look." Jonaton sounded weary. "We've already got the Gates across the rapids set up, with a good strong ley-line to power them. We don't know that we're going to find another. And at least *some* of us are going to have to go back, deactivate the outbound Gate, wait for us to establish a new one *if we can* and power it up. We don't know we're going to find a ley-line this good, and if we can't, we're limited to our own strength. Which means it will take days, instead of marks, to bring the new Gate up, and there is no guarantee that when we do, it will reach the outbound Gate on your side of the rapids. And meanwhile, we *know* there's terror-birds, snake-dogs, and at least one bizarre bear on *your* side. So what do you want to do, Baron? You're our leader."

Yes, I am. Jonaton seemed very sure that those monster-trees weren't going to hurt them as long as they stayed on the bank. But this was going to require a lot of coordination and preparation.

Doesn't everything, right now?

"A compromise?" he suggested. "You all go through that forest and if anything, anything at all, threatens you, retreat. Otherwise go on. If you find another ley-line on the other side of it, move the Gate. If you don't, we'll take all due precautions with the convoy and take our chances with the forest."

He glanced at the mages all standing on the walkway of his home-barge. They all looked concerned, but nodded.

"Good," Jonaton replied. "Now we'll get our string moving again so we *don't* have to stop in the middle of this place. And I suggest that when you get here—"

"—if we have to," interrupted Ponu.

"Fine, *if you have to,* then break up the convoy so that no one has to stop overnight there either. All right? I can tell you that it'll take about a day for you to get to the other side at the pace you're moving. You should be able to figure out how to break the convoy up from that."

"That is a good plan," Kordas agreed.

"All right. And now close this thing down, if you are so certain that you're going to wake a bunch of trees." Then Jonaton laughed.

"What's so funny?" Kordas demanded.

"Well, we were all speculating about where that Change-bear came from," the mage replied. "I don't think we need to speculate anymore."

Sai snorted, but didn't say anything, and Kordas nodded at

Ponu, who motioned to the people standing on the river side of the walkway to move. They did, and he tilted the "dish," sending the water over the side of the boat and back into the river, then dispelled the magical vessel.

Most of the mages left then, taking their mules from where they were walking beside the barge, tethered to it by long leads, and going back to their respective spots in the convoy. But Ceri stayed, staring absently out across the river.

"Your thoughts?" Kordas asked.

"It's almost winter. Normal trees are slipping into winter sleep; probably those are too. That's probably what Jonaton is thinking. He's probably not wrong about that."

"But?" Kordas prompted.

"But we shouldn't let anyone or anything under those branches," Ceri finished. "Which means no foraging, and no taking wood. We'll stock up on the way there. Each section should pause to feed their herds on grain before going in, so they aren't hungry. We tighten up the charms so they all stay as close to the barges as they can get without falling in."

"And?" Kordas sensed that Ceri had more to say.

The old mage sighed. "And we hope that luck is with us and Jonaton and his band find a ley-line on the other side of that *thing* so we don't have to worry about it."

The horses and mules did not like that forest, and neither did Bay. Bay wouldn't even set foot on the bank; he planted himself on the top of the women's barge with his ears and tail down, whining, and refused to move.

Delia did not blame the mastiff in the least. She didn't have anything like a Healer's Empathy, but the nearer she got to those tree-things, the more she felt a sort of . . . dull, distant, background emotion. Like rage, if rage had been smothered and sleeping for centuries until it had dulled down to a sort of ambience, barely there unless you looked for it.

But that ambience of rage did not change when the mages on Kordas's end did their scrying. And it didn't change when they entered the forest boundaries. So after unconsciously holding her breath until she suddenly realized she was running out of air, Delia clambered up onto the roof of the barge with Bay and sat down. The dog immediately put his head in her lap, whimpering just barely loud enough for her to hear.

The horses and mules not being ridden had all been put into harness and attached to the barges. With *all* of them pulling, the pace had gone from an amble to a fast walk, and no one had needed to urge them into a faster pace. Even unflappable Tight Squeeze had his ears back, his tail twitching, and leaned hard into his harness, trying to increase his speed. Clearly, they could not stand to be in this place a moment longer than they were forced to be.

Delia looked at Amethyst, who stood in the prow of her barge with head cocked to one side, as if she was listening.

"What are you sensing, Amethyst?" she called softly, as if too much noise was dangerous.

"Anger, but distant, and sleeping," the Doll replied immediately. "But I do not think it would be wise for you to collect even fallen wood from this place. I feel as if . . . as if . . . as if these trees would know if you did, and if we burned or broke any of it, they would know that, too."

"What *is* it?" she begged.

"It seems vaguely familiar, but vastly changed. Changed so much I cannot recognize what it once was. Something I might have recognized immediately before that change took place." Amethyst shook her head. "That is all I can say for now. We need to be gone from here."

Thank you for the obvious, Delia thought, her own temper irritated by the anger all around her and inescapable. But she didn't snap at Amethyst or let it show. The Doll was doing her best, *had* been doing her best, and it was not fair to get testy with her.

Oh, but she wanted to be on the other side of this thing!

As noon approached, she decided to see if Sai wanted help with getting food to everyone. Obviously they were not going to stop to cook, but if he made up some sort of thing, she could distribute it for him.

She found him in the kitchen in the women's barge contemplating leftover cold goose and cheese. "I wish I'd thought to make up some more flatbreads," he said, as her footsteps told him of her approach.

"They're nasty and tough when they are cold," she reminded him. "What about wrapping up packets of meat and cheese in cabbage leaves? We've got them hanging from the roof of the storage barge."

The storage barge had that same spell on it that they'd used back at the manor, to keep things preserved for far longer than they had any right to be. That was where the precious fat was stored, including some even more precious butter, some few eggs, and a great many vegetables as well as the grains for humans and animals. Everyone knew about winter-sickness, of course, and a very high priority had been placed on keeping things like cabbages sound enough to eat all winter. Sai perked up at that. "That's an excellent idea. Go bring me one."

Under any other circumstances, she would have chided him for lack of politeness, but if *she* was feeling under strain, it was probably worse for a mage.

So she ran off to the storage barge, and came back with a head of cabbage she judged just big enough to supply leaves for wraps and have enough left over to add to tonight's soup.

Oh, how I hope we will actually be out of this place before sundown so we can get that soup!

In mere moments, she found herself running among the barges, passing out cabbage-wrapped packets of minced goose and cheese all held together with mustard and flavored with a touch of salt. Sai had boiled water to blanch the leaves; they were still crispy, but more flexible. No one made any complaints, and it tasted just fine, if a bit out of the ordinary, to Delia, who finally collected her own wrap after delivering them to everyone else.

Then, with nothing more to do, she sat back down with poor Bey, hand-fed him bits of goose and cheese sent by Sai, and stared at the forest.

The dragonfly things were pretty. But—they shouldn't be alive. It was much, much too cold for insects to be alive.

And that was when she realized that she *wasn't* cold. In fact, she felt a little warm. The air seemed stuffy, and smelled musty, like a room that had been closed up in the heat for a long time. Experimenting, she slid down off the roof of the barge to the river side of the walkway, and crouched down. It was definitely colder, much colder. And walking around to the land side, there was no doubt that warmth radiated off of the forest.

Were there shadows under those trees in the distance? *Were they moving?*

She looked sharply away, and then back, saw no change in the shadows, and scolded herself for being too jumpy.

But if the forest is warm, warm enough for dragonflies to live, why is it going into winter sleep? Or have we made a mistake there? What if it isn't winter sleep, just . . . sleep?

Wouldn't that mean it could be a lot easier to wake it up?

"The scouts are on the other side of the forest, with no incident," Rose announced, in late afternoon. Kordas heaved a sigh of relief.

"Have they found a safe place to camp?" he asked the Doll.

"Yes, and they are going to mark it for the rest, because it is particularly defensible." Rose paused. "Would you like me to describe the strange forest for you, as they experienced it?"

There is no such thing as too much information. "Yes, please," he said, and listened as she described in detail the trees, the unnatural warmth beneath them, the presence of the dragonflies, and the sense of simmering rage.

It was the last that tickled some distant memory, but not enough that he recognized it, only that it seemed familiar. But he was not given a chance to probe his own memory, because the next thing that Rose said, in sharper tones than before, was, "Kordas, you are needed ahead. There is a problem."

"How far ahead?" he asked. He was already on Arial with Rose hanging on behind him. He gave Arial a touch of his heel and a loose rein so she would know she needed to make speed and that she could pick her own path through the mingled herd of sheep and goats just in front of him. They didn't like being shouldered aside, voicing their objection quite loudly. But Arial was used to this, and frankly didn't care anymore; those she couldn't move aside, she often leapt over.

"Near to the front of the convoy," Rose replied in his ear as she clung to his waist with her mitten-like hands. "The Old Men are on their way from the front."

"Something magic?" he asked.

"It is a boar." That was all she told him, and he was forced to try to imagine why a wild boar would be a threat that would call for his attention. Was it like that bear the scouts had encountered? But Arial saw a clear path ahead, somehow, and leapt from a standing start into a run worthy of a horseback hunt through the forest, causing sheep to baa in alarm and pigs to bumble out of her way as she powered her way through and over them. Rose hung on for dear life, and he didn't have the concentration or breath to try to talk to her and ride at the same time.

Then she vaulted right into the middle of a herd of churning swine, and he saw what the problem was.

A wild boar.

A wild boar that was roughly the size of a shed. It was *easily* a match in height, weight, and girth for a man mounted on a Tow-Beast. A normal-sized wild boar could easily kill a man on horseback; this thing could probably take him and Arial out without a second thought.

The rational part of his mind knew immediately what had happened. Pigs were social creatures; this one had smelled more of his kind and had come for them, probably attracted by the scent of the sows, though how on earth something that size would be able to mate with a normal-sized pig—

The rest of him knew that there was only one way this could end if he didn't want the thing to turn its wrath on people. He threw up his hand, barked two words, and looked away to save his vision as light exploded from his hand. Looking back up while Arial wisely backed away from the thing, he saw he'd accomplished what he needed to do; he'd blinded and stunned it momentarily. As it stood there blinking its tiny eyes, he caught up his crossbow, slapped a bolt into the slot, cocked it, and shot into its eye, just as he heard the dull *phut* of a Spitter and watched a ring of fire spring up around the thing.

He hadn't expected to do more than annoy it, but either his shot, or whoever had shot the Spitter, got lucky. The enormous monster squealed in rage and pain, reared up on its hind legs, scattering pigs in all directions, and then fell straight down on its side, stone dead.

The ring of fire went out.

The swineherds scattered with their dogs to corral their charges. He coaxed a snorting Arial closer to the thing, as Ponu and Beltran approached it from the other side.

"Is it dead?" the Herald asked, cautiously.

Kordas dismounted, and made sure that there was no sign of life at all. "Dead as the Emperor," he said. Beltran winced, but approached on the other side.

"You mean that was it? Just that and it's dead?" Ponu blurted. "Its skull has to be a foot thick, but the Spitter shot went through the eye into the brain? You're using up all your luck, Beltran."

"Hey, I got it in the other eye," Kordas added. "Maybe my bolt pierced its brain."

"Maybe the shots met in the brain and kissed. I don't know, but the thing's quit the hard work of living all the same. I'm going to take the lucky victory," Ponu declared.

"Change-creature?" the Baron asked Ponu. The mage narrowed his eyes, drew a couple of sigils in the air, and shook his head.

"No, but magic had a hand in making it that big," Ponu replied.

"*Maybe* a touch of a Change-Circle but only enough that it didn't just stop growing when it should have. Nothing else unnatural about it but its size."

Beltran poked at a tusk with his toe. "Well, the important part. Is it safe to eat?"

"I'm not Sai. Ask a butcher?" Ponu said with utter indifference. "All I care about is that we killed it."

"I'm not leaving that much meat to spoil if it's useable." Kordas turned to Rose. "Get me a crew of butchers and hunters here, please? And a squad each of archer and foot to protect them. Beltran, if it *is* safe to eat, see that the bits are distributed equally up and down the line. Tonight, we eat pork!" Everyone nearby made at least a token cheer, because "Tonight, we eat pork!" sounded like a memorable thing for their Lord to say.

"Baron Valdemar's Rallying Cry for Bacon for All," historians will recall it as. My finest hour.

He was already gone by the time the crew descended on the giant carcass, but the good thing about calling a dozen people to render the beast into component parts was that they were able to take it to bits before the convoy stopped for the night. The verdict of the butchers was that it was perfectly safe to eat as long as it was cooked well, and Beltran's solution to "equable distribution" was to call for cooks from the common kitchens to show up with a large washbasin each, nearest first. That was fine with Kordas; he didn't care how the sausage was made as long as it ended up in the larder, so to speak.

And of course, thanks to the edict of "waste nothing," bones were going to get sawn up for soups, innards would be cooked up into dog food, and that hide would almost certainly end up in pieces to be scraped and stretched and eventually tanned.

Surely that hide is going to be tougher than a bull's. They were going to get a lot of shoe soles out of that beast. As he headed toward the middle of the expedition and his own barge, an icy wind sprang up, and he pitied those poor butchers.

There was no further disturbance, and by the time he reached his own barges, the giant boar was nothing more than a swiftly spreading rumor.

"Kordas," Rose told him, as the barge came in sight. "People want to know if there are more of those giant pigs."

"I don't think they need to worry——"

"They are not worrying," Rose corrected him gently. "They want to know if we could send out hunting parties to look for them."

He almost laughed. Except that there really wasn't anything funny about it. He had hunted wild boar before this, and even with a fully mounted party, massive boarhounds and mastiffs, and people who knew what they were doing, there were terrible injuries and fatalities all the time. *We got lucky. More lucky than we deserved.* He reached up to lift Rose down off the pillion, and led Arial to where his horses were being put up for the night. "Tell them no," he said. "Tell them Ponu thinks it was something caught in a Change-Circle, like the bear that the scouts encountered." Because the very last thing he needed right now was parties of the inexperienced ranging through the scrub bushes and stunted trees, trying to find more giant boars. It would slow the convoy down, if they only managed to kick up *normal* wild pigs people could get hurt, and——

"Kordas, your former gamekeeper has an idea," Rose told him, interrupting his worried thoughts.

Grim had already unharnessed and rubbed down the hard-working Tow-Beasts and was waiting——with some impatience——for

Kordas to bring him Arial. The grizzled old fellow held out his hand for her reins, and Kordas meekly put them into it. "Go," he said gruffly. "Ye bain't a green rider what needs to learn to care for his horse. I et already. Off with ye!"

Grim had, as he was wont to do, managed a very good spot for their horses; there was shelter from the wind and plenty of browse. He must have sent people out into the brush as soon as the convoy slowed to a halt, because there were already piles of cut fodder that the horses were greedily helping themselves to. Grim generally let them eat until they were satisfied, then gave them nosebags with precious grain. He collected the nosebags just before he went to bed. That way he made certain no horse stole another horse's rations.

"What does the gamekeeper want to do?" he asked, turning and making his way toward the welcome glow of the lights on the prows and sterns of the barges tied up to the bank.

"He wants to know if you want him to organize beaters and drivers to go out and drive game toward the river," Rose told him.

Oh good gods, no . . . Clearly as the rumor of the giant boar spread, all people could think about was that they were tired of a grain-based diet and that if there was one of these things—

—these *giant killing machines*—

There must be more.

And as sure as he allowed the gamekeeper, who actually knew what he was doing, to create a driving party, every single person in the convoy who fancied themselves a hunter would take that as a license to do the same.

If I wanted to create a cascade of too many injuries for the Healers to treat, that is how I'd go about it.

"No," he said firmly. "We've already had terror-birds attack us once, and we had to drive off snake-dogs from that village back there. And then there was the bear that the scouts saw. We don't know what's out there and we got lucky in killing the boar. We don't have enough men-at-arms to cover hunting groups. I absolutely forbid it."

That isn't going to stop people from doing it anyway, but at least it won't be half the expedition. Just a few idiots.

"And if anyone *does* go out there and gets hurt," he continued, "the Healers are going to be angry enough with the person foolish enough to disobey my direct orders that they are likely to do little more than splint bones and bandage wounds, and tell the offender he can heal up on his own. Tell my gamekeeper that, and while you're at it, spread it to the other Dolls to pass along."

Rose uttered a sound that was very like a wry chuckle. "I have," she said sweetly, and they boarded the family barge.

Isla and the boys were waiting for him; the boys were all perched on his bed, and Isla presided over a covered pot. "No magic boar tonight," she told him. "But the gamekeeper managed to secure the cheeks for us, and they'll be in the morning stew."

"I can wait," he said, and noted how the three little faces fell. "So what do we have tonight?"

"Something lovely," she said. "Boys, you can bring your bowls now."

They jumped off the bed and brought their bowls to the tiny table. Isla opened the pot and a heavenly aroma drifted out that banished all thoughts of pork from his mind. She heaped all five of their bowls with the mashed tuber, studded with lots of grated cheese, bits of bacon, and cooked onion, and put a pat of precious butter into the center of each bowl, scraping the pot so clean he doubted it would need more than to be wiped out.

The boys scampered off to their beds, leaving the two of them "alone" together. He heard Ivy's voice back there, and the boys had shut up, suggesting she was either telling them a story or drilling them on lessons. They weren't getting a *lot* of lessons, but Ivy seemed to have taken it upon herself to act as a temporary teacher.

Is there anything the Dolls aren't willing to do?

"Ivy told me that you forbade people to go off away from the river to drive game," she said.

"Broken ankles, falling into holes or stepping on rocks wrong," he began. "Or broken arms, or broken heads, or gods forbid, broken backs. And of course, not only have we seen mage-made creatures that have not hesitated to attack humans, or at least, attack animals near humans, but we don't know what else is out there. And—"

She held up her hand. "I agree with you, and I can think of other, equally good reasons. There *are* other people out here; they've not approached us, but Ivar has seen signs of settlements in the distance. They'll not take kindly to us stripping the land of its beasts and leaving them with nothing to hunt over the winter."

"We pass, leaving as little mark on the land as we can," he agreed. "We pass, leaving no enemies behind us."

But, he thought, as he slowly ate his supper, *the time will come when we have to stop. And then—*

—we might not have a choice.

14

K ordas and Rose had ridden all the way to the front of the convoy, to be one of the first to see the strange forest when they crossed the Gate to bypass the falls and rapids. Another couple of consultations via scrying pool—far less public this time than the last—had left him with decidedly mixed feelings.

On the one hand, the forest hadn't done anything but unnerve the scouts. Nobody had any reason to go into the Red Forest, and nobody wanted to.

On the other hand, Delia, Alberdina, and Sai had all emphasized aspects of the place that did not fill him with any optimism. The sense that it was a single living entity? He'd never heard of that before, and neither had Sai, who probably knew more about strange things in magic than anyone outside of the long-lost Imperial Palace. The sense of distant rage? Oh, *that* couldn't bode well.

It appeared that the Old Men were of the same mind as he was, because as he approached the Gate, there they were waiting, ready to take their barges through, first in line. Whatever was out there, they wanted to be the first to set eyes on it.

He sent Arial to stand next to their Tow-Beast, one of the False Golds he'd "given" to the Emperor. The Tow-Beast was a beautiful creature, and if his coat didn't shimmer in the thin sunlight as it had when Kordas taken him to the Capital, it was because he, like every other equine in the convoy, had grown a nice, thick coat against the winter.

"Hello, Sunshine," he said affectionately as Arial moved to stand beside the huge beast. Sunshine snorted a greeting, amiably, and nuzzled Kordas's hair. Kordas's hair was easy for the False Gold to reach, because even sitting on Arial's back, Kordas's head was even with Sunshine's nose. Kordas was a little surprised to feel himself choking up, and suddenly he was very, very glad he had taken the time to steal back his horses . . . and gladder still for the intervention of the stable-Dolls who had taken it upon themselves to rescue all the rest, and send them to Crescent Lake. He had since learned that the Dolls had not only saved horses and humans, but every single other living thing in the Palace complex that they could catch up and run with.

There hadn't been a lot of creatures that weren't human and couldn't escape on their own, save for the horses and the chickens. The Emperor had discouraged pets, and even if he hadn't, anyone who truly cared for their animals wouldn't want to risk the chance that the Emperor would order their pet taken, hurt, or destroyed to make a point—or to score one. But somehow, even most of the *chickens* had been saved, at least according to Rose. And he saw no reason to doubt her. Apparently there had been a Portal for food deliveries down in the area of the stables and henhouses.

There were no mews at the Palace. The Emperor knew nothing of falconry, and cared nothing for the sport.

The chickens, however, had not been sent to Crescent Lake, because the Dolls had known they'd have dropped straight into water amid the chaotic rush of hundreds of barges coming through that Portal as fast as the Portal would allow. No, the chickens had been sent to the Emperor's duck and goose farm outside the Capital. Which must have been very confusing for the keepers of that farm. He could just imagine it: suddenly, in the midst of horrific noises from the Capital itself and the violent shaking of the ground, to see an enormous flood of chickens bursting out of their Portal.

Presumably, once they got over their surprise, the keepers had known what to do with the birds. Or surely knew farmers to send them to, even if they weren't equipped to handle that many chickens.

At least they aren't charred chicken, like if they'd stayed. He sighed, with a little regret. He hadn't had fried chicken in a very long time. And although other folks had managed to bring down wild geese and ducks on this journey, so far none of those had made it as far as his kitchen.

"Are you ready, Baron?" asked the stablehand mounted—or rather, perched—on Sunshine's broad back. He was from the more northerly of the Imperial domains, and his skin was lighter than Kordas's own.

"Ready when you are," Kordas assured him. He touched his heel to Arial, and she moved ahead of the Tow-Beast, who strained in his harness, feet planted firmly on the grass of the bank, trying to get his string underway. The barge-towing specialists were called 'hoggees,' though Kordas had no idea why. They were earning their keep and much more, and the Tow-Beasts gained decorations of rope braids, brass, and beads with each passing day, from an appreciative convoy. The hoggees appeared to have earned some treats, too.

Kordas experienced only a brief moment of disorientation in transition, probably because the Gates were so close together. The air that went through a Gate link blew from higher to lower air pressure, so environmental effects from the departure side had been muffled. But he got hit in the face with a blast of damp, chill air and a torrent of intense rumbling noise that startled him *and* Arial, and Arial snorted her dislike of it, though she didn't falter.

The noise was incredible, like thunder that never came to an end. It was pretty clear that, until he got far enough away from the rapids behind him, he wouldn't be able to hear a bloody thing. The air was just a short step above freezing, and so very damp there were tiny droplets collecting on the fleece collar of his sheepskin coat.

Kordas glanced back over his shoulder to make sure Rose was still behind him on the pillion pad—he'd never once lost anyone on a Gate-transit, but it was a habit with him to check—and then took a moment to peer in the direction they'd just come from. Dwarfing the size of the Gate, the sight of rapids and deadly breakers practically terraced upon each other, covering a quarter of the horizon, was awe-inspiring. The sound went into his body strongest through his chest, legs, scalp, and fingertips, then seemed to emerge from the other side of him. The sensation of being a drumskin occurred to him, something spiritual. Being within sound felt like being encompassed by a deific presence who had forever to explain their secrets to him.

Or like the land itself had just taken him by his shoulders and directed his attention. *Here, man. Here. This is what I am. This is my grandeur, my presence, my truth. You are a part of me. With this I remind you, lest you lose sight of it: I am bigger, vaster, and stronger than you can imagine. Tread on me with care, man, for I can crush you on a whim. But respect me, and I might show you wonders like this.*

Kordas didn't blink for nearly a minute.

He returned from his reverie and peered downriver from the waterfalls and rapids. There was no sign of the mysterious forest; there was nothing but scrub brush, stubby trees, and rocks, but ahead of them the river did make a big curve around a hill, so it was probably on the other side of that. He urged Arial forward; he wanted to get well ahead of the Old Men's barges so that he could survey the forest himself, alone, for a few moments.

And once around that deep bend, there it was. It stretched as far as he could see in either direction, enveloping the river completely.

It looked perfectly normal from a distance: a vague, gray haze of bare branches and trunks and a lot of red on the ground that was probably fallen leaves. But . . .

But . . .

Now he understood completely what Alberdina had meant. He felt it, just as she had described, a simmering, deeply buried, distant rage. So distant that he might have attributed it to his own bad temper, had he not been warned about it. Arial felt it too. She tossed her head and stamped one foot, trying to tell him that she didn't want to go on.

But there wasn't a choice, not really. "Rose, I want a Doll stationed on this side of the Gate," he said. "And another on the side where the caravan is. And one right here. The scouts told me it took about four marks to transit the forest, so the Doll standing here will stop the caravan at four marks to sunset. Relay that to the Dolls at the Gates, and end the Gate transit for the night."

"That seems very wise, Kordas," Rose replied. "I do not believe *any* of us should take chances here."

"You sense something too." He made it a statement, not a question.

"It seems almost familiar, as if someone has taken something I know well and twisted and warped it until it is nearly unrecognizable," the Doll said. "I don't understand it. I do know that if I were to put a name on what did this in the first place, it would be the Magic Storms that marked the end of the Great War between human mages five hundred years ago."

He didn't like going under those trees alone, so he waited until the barges transited the Gate and joined him. A plainly garbed Doll he didn't recognize, but who had a thorn pinned through their tunic like a brooch, jumped down from the first barge as they neared him, and took up a station, as if they were perfectly prepared to stand there forever—or at least until the convoy was completely through the Gate.

In the prow of the first barge were Dole, Ceri, and Ponu, their attention completely riveted by that distant haze of trees. Ponu appeared on the side of the barge and waved at him. He thought about riding ahead, but decided that he'd hop aboard for a little bit at least. He wanted to hear their reaction to this place.

He leaned down over Arial's neck, attached the long lead to her bridle, and dismounted, playing the lead out until he could hop onto the barge with the assistance of Ponu and his apprentice. He tied the lead off on a belaying ring on the rail, and could not help but notice that, instead of coming up to walk right at Sunshine's tail, Arial resisted for a brief moment before reluctantly moving along.

The normally placid and unflappable Sunshine didn't like the forest either. He had his ears back, and mouthed his bit nervously, something Kordas had never seen him do before.

"Lovely place you've found for us," Ponu said lightly. "I'm reminded of the traps tunnel-spiders make." Ponu made no outward sign he'd even noticed the hard sidelook Kordas shot at him.

Well, that's comforting. Thank you, old man.

"The scouts are already on the other side. They got through it. Let's hope we can do the same," Kordas replied. "I wish that this river didn't cut right through the place though, curse it. If it wasn't just as bad on the other side of the river, I'd take the time and energy to make a path for the horses and herds to cross the river, no matter the cost."

"We'd lose animals," Ceri said flatly. "Far too many. One or two ridden horses, like with the mages that are ferrying the Gate uprights, that's not a problem, but daft sheep are likely to spook and go off the path, and swine are just as bad. As cold as it is now, and with their fleeces weighing them down, the sheep wouldn't survive a minute. Pigs might be able to swim it, but I wouldn't count on it."

"It's moot." He shrugged as the forest drew nearer and nearer, and he saw with his own eyes what he'd scryed in the mirror. "Those damned tree-things and bugs are on both sides of the river, and so is that . . . anger."

"The anger has a particular subtlety I only just noticed—it doesn't make me angry at anything in particular. It also doesn't give me the impression that someone or something is angry with me. It's just a seething rage without a target in mind. It could well be purely defensive. I'd give a lot if we were just on a leisure trip and I could study this place," Dole mused. "At a distance, of course. I've never seen anything like it. It almost seems . . . Elemental in nature."

"What Elemental has ever taken on the form of a forest?" asked Ceri, scornfully.

"None that I know of," Dole replied, ignoring Ceri's tone. "But that doesn't mean it can't happen." He shrugged. "The cataclysm at the end of the Mage Wars utterly destroyed two of the most powerful mages this world has ever seen, and turned everything we know on its head. The only thing that saved what became the Empire was distance, and the fact that the King put in an extraordinary amount of effort to keep harm from befalling his people. The King knew all about the War—you couldn't *not* know about the War, no matter how distant you were from it—and according to everything I've read, put all of his time, energy, and every bit of magical talent he had into putting a barrier around his Kingdom intended to deflect what he was certain was going to come. He foresaw the War's mutual annihilation at a time when no one else did. That's why he was able to move into the power vacuum left when those two armies destroyed each other, consolidate dozens of little Kingdoms and Principalities that had been left reeling from the Mage Storms, and make himself Emperor. Even so, there were many mages that died, trying to keep those shields up."

This was the most about that ancient war and the aftermath that Kordas had ever heard before. "Where did you learn all this?" he asked.

"From that library that the Dolls brought with them," Dole replied, as the trees grew nearer and nearer. "They organized it for us so all I have to do is figure out what sort of book I need to read and they'll bring it to me. I've been reading as much as I can, trying to anticipate what we might run into as we draw nearer to the lands that were the worst affected."

"Was there anything . . . like this mentioned?" Kordas asked. At this point, they were just passing the outer boundary of the forest, and it actually looked more sinister now than it had in the scrying pool. The horses definitely did not like it here; he didn't think they were going to bolt, but they all had their ears laid back and heads down—and since they were not going to be allowed to go back, it looked as if they had decided to get through this place as fast as they could. They'd picked up their pace to the fastest he had ever seen them pull, and weren't even covertly eyeing the undergrowth for things that might be tasty.

"Nothing this big," Dole replied, not taking his attention off the trees. "But Sai believes that this thing didn't start out this big. He believes it was spawned from something much smaller and has been growing for five centuries. Under normal circumstances, I would have said that it was wildly unlikely for a forest to spread and grow into something this big, but . . . we don't know how fast these trees grow. If they even are trees. They could spring up overnight, like mushrooms."

Kordas began to feel very uncomfortable in his heavy sheepskin coat, and peeled it off. Dole and the others did the same. "Why is it so *hot*?"

"As Jonaton would say, 'magical fuckery is afoot,'" Dole said dryly. "As for why it is almost as warm as a spring day, I can speculate that it has something to do with those dragonflies. The forest may need to keep them alive, for some reason. If it's going to keep them alive during the winter, it will have to keep them warm. The forest may have a life process that generates its own heat. If it used magic for that, it might just ground its magic improperly on purpose."

"To create heat. Any spell or spell-like process would do. Huh. Makes me wonder what's under it."

Kordas peered through the haze that had formed under the trees. Just a thin haze, not enough to impede anything, just enough to keep him from seeing any deeper into the forest than two or three furlongs. "I don't see *anything* else out there. Just trees and dragonflies. No tree-hares, no ground animals, not even birds."

"I would postulate that those things that look like mouths may, in fact, be mouths," Dole replied. Which did nothing for Kordas's unease. "There are marsh plants that eat insects. These things might eat insects too, or larger things. Those 'mouths' could take in a goose, some of them."

"What can you tell me about these Mage Wars that applies to this forest?" he asked, figuring that if he couldn't distract himself, he could at least *learn* something.

"About the wars themselves—not much," the old mage admitted. "Except that the mages of that time were insanely powerful—how they managed that, who knows? Creating Gates was second nature to them, and they routinely created living creatures. One of the mages created gryphons, for instance."

"Wait, they're real?" He cast a sharp glance at Dole to see if the old man was trying to pull a prank on him, but Dole seemed to be entirely serious about this. "Gryphons are real?"

"Seen in scrying, never seen in any lands of the Empire," Dole confirmed. "And *not* seen since the Wars, so they may have all died out by now. But yes, at least five centuries ago, they were very real. But . . . you asked me what, about those mages of old, I have learned that might pertain to *this* place. Regretfully, not much." He shrugged. "You have to remember that the Wars themselves are almost incidental to the Empire's history. The only real interest anyone from the Old Lands had in them was in making sure that when everything went to pieces, the King was able to keep his lands protected—and tightly controlled. Even so, the initial Storms were so bad that about half his mages died keeping that protection up."

"How could anyone protect against an effect bigger than a country?"

"They created protective squads for what they called 'savior-mages,' answerable only to the King. You know. For the people's protection. Heh." He mimed spitting on the ground. "If you think that sounds like a way to get powerful mages and their bodyguards into anybody's domain without opposition, you'd be right. But as shield mages, it is true they were without peer. The plan was simple on the surface. Keep them mobile. Put the strongest shield where it can deflect the most danger, then fall back while the next team positions. That's why the Empire has its roads and canals, and eventually Gates and fast boats." Dole shrugged again. "The plan became entangled in political and territorial pursuits to the point that it was unsustainable. Savior-mages extorted mayors and barons alike. They took bribes to selectively drop shields and let political rivals' estates be overrun. The early Empire was obsessed with expansion, in part because the farther savior-mage teams could reach, the better their 'protection.' In theory. To return to the point, there is very little that is predictable about the kind of magic Storms that resulted in the mutual destruction of the two opponents." He rubbed the skin behind his left ear as he thought. "The reason is not just because two unbelievably powerful annihilation spells went off. It is because—well, you know we can store magical energy in things. Raw energy, usually in crystals. Spells and the energy it takes to make them work can be stored in almost anything."

Of course Kordas knew all this, and Dole *knew* that he knew, but he sensed that Dole was using words as a kind of shield between himself and thinking too hard about this forest. Some people took comfort in explaining and teaching. Really, all either of them wanted was to get past it, but that could only happen as fast as the horses could pull them. So Dole was babbling. Kordas didn't blame him.

By this point they'd both shed not only their coats but their outer knitted tunics. It was as warm as a mild summer day under these trees. *If I knew the magic to make that work . . . yes, but there is always a cost to magic. Always a cost. We might not want to pay that cost.*

"So," Dole continued, "these things that store power are always slightly unstable. Normally that's not a problem; it *does* take a fairly serious impact, magical or physical, to make one of them—well— spontaneously discharge. The kind of impact that probably would have turned the mage that was carrying these objects into a thin red smear on the ground, so the only ones who would be in jeopardy from these things going completely unstable and discharging would be bystanders, or the one who struck the blow in the first place. However . . . we're not talking about a simple firebolt, here. We're talking about a destructive spell intended to level an edifice at least the size of the Imperial Palace."

"I'm following you so far," Kordas said when Dole paused.

"Now, both of those mages had an enormous arsenal of magical weapons, but also an even bigger storehouse of things that were not weapons, but were spell-bound nevertheless, and what they say were banks of raw energy storage. So when those two destructive spells went off . . ." Dole's voice trailed off for a moment. "It wasn't just destructive. It was *messy*. Whatever it was, the bonds that made spells cohesive simply disconnected, like wagon wheels disintegrating at high speed. Spell fragments combined and collided in ways no one has ever seen, before or since. That's why the Change-Circles are completely unpredictable. They contain bits and pieces of everything from a spell on a rock you're meant to use as a campfire, to something intended to liquefy a mountainside, to cures for diseases. And that's why I can't actually tell you enough about the Mage Storms or their effects. It would be like shattering a glass mirror, then reassembling thousands of shards, thinking it would show the last image it reflected."

But Kordas, as always, was distracted by the one piece of information he actually could use. "You can put a spell on a rock to use as a *lasting* campfire?" he repeated as a question.

Dole sighed, and his expression was that of a parent gazing at a child they are trying to educate who has fixated on a double entendre they hadn't intended to make. "Yes, Kordas, we can. And yes, Kordas, among many other things, when we encounter power sources strong enough to give us a surplus, we are storing energy in crystals with the intention of giving each vessel in the convoy at least one of such rocks to use in their barge instead of wood. Just like Sai has been making those marvelous cleansing towels of his, and I have been making mage-lights so we can conserve candles, tallow-dips, and lamp oil. We made a needs list, and the Dolls are keeping track, so you wouldn't have to."

Kordas badly wanted to pursue this, but Dole's expression made him think twice about it. *I put people in charge of things so I can deal with the larger picture. This is no time to ask about spells for keeping me warm.*

Even if it would feel like the gift of the gods to strip down to nothing in a warm boat and have an all-over scrub with good hot water. Cleanliness beyond the basics is not a priority. Especially now. Let's get through these damn trees, figure out what we are going to do about a hard winter, find a new home, and keep everyone and everything fed and healthy.

And there was absolutely no point in wondering how the mages intended to allocate their magic-stove rocks. He already knew. The sick had priority, then the elderly, then very small children. There were, thank the gods, no babies in this convoy. In fact, there were no children under the age of six. Everyone with babies had gone back to Valdemar, joined one of the villages near Crescent Lake, or stayed to build the new village there. Which was a relief; babies were fragile, babies woke the nurturer in nearly everyone, and the death of a baby or a child was a heartbreak that echoed far past the baby's own family. Regardless, there was no way that they could make enough such rocks to heat every one of the barges. And the obvious reason why they hadn't stockpiled these things in the decades *before* they fled the Empire was because no one had ever anticipated that they'd be going on this trek in the first place, and besides, how would they be stored, when even one could heat a farmhouse?

Well, we'd have devised a way. The Plan was always to use the barges as a means to get to a safe spot and stay there. Use them as stationary *living quarters for the year or so it would take to build real shelters on land. We assumed there was going to be sufficient wood for heating and cooking, because we assumed we'd be in a wilderness analogous to Valdemaran terrain, full of deadfall.*

Well, that hadn't happened. Kordas didn't *think* they'd been naïve . . .

Well, how could his father and grandfather have anticipated what had actually happened? It was *never* part of the Plan for someone to murder the Emperor and destroy the Capital! The Plan was that they'd all slip away quietly, after thorough scouting and mapping, during the boat parade that celebrated the Emperor's "greatness" in the fall. Because after that particular celebration, the eyes of the Emperor turned in two directions—wherever the Emperor was currently waging war, and on his own Court. Harvest would be occupying everyone *not* in the Court, and agriculture was dull and uninteresting to the Emperor. After that, despite Gates, winter kept most provincials firmly locked in their own domains. And winter was a *good* time for war, so far as the Emperor was concerned. He didn't have to juggle the needs of the Empire to get the harvests grown and gathered against the need to bring in an ever-flowing source of recruits, and he didn't have to worry about rain and the great enemy of all logistics, mud. Snow mattered not at all to someone with as many mages in his employ as the Emperor had; they could just steer the storms and dump the snow on their enemies, where it would *stay put*, as opposed to rainwater, which flowed where it wanted to flow. And with all the mages in his employ, his troops never needed to worry about the cold.

It was moot now, though. Kordas, to his lasting anger and self-criticism, had acted without sufficient scouting into this new land, and they had no choice but to think fast and work on the run. Even the Plan didn't account for anything as strange as they encountered every day now. He had to be practical about it all; not get caught up in how weird things were, but evaluate whether any given oddity would do harm and how it could be exploited, if at all. There was just the river and the shore now, with all else secondary, and who knew what was ahead. The Plan was now superseded by the Improvisation.

Well, all this goes to prove the old adage that Father used to tell me: no plans survive first contact with the enemy.

In this case, the Plan had started to go to pieces the moment the Emperor ordered Kordas to come to the Capital. Everything after that had been bald, unapologetic opportunism and misdirection.

"I suppose I should be grateful that things haven't completely fallen apart at this point," he said aloud.

Dole snorted. "They won't, as long as you keep doing the things only you can do, and leave the rest of us to manage what we can do."

I do understand that I am less than half Dole's age, he thought with a bit of irritation. *But I do wish he'd stop repeating what everyone else has told me a hundred times by now.*

There wasn't so much as a breath of breeze under those trees. "It's so quiet," he said finally, and realized that all this time both he and Dole had been murmuring their words, as if they were both afraid that if they made too much noise, the forest might . . . notice them.

Nor were they the only ones, apparently. The only sounds were the muffled *clump* of horse hooves on earth, the rattling of metal on harnesses, the creak of leather, and the water lapping against the hull beneath them. There were occasional bumps against the bottom of the hulls, and even when they were shuddering from bow to stern, he told himself it was just snags of debris from upriver. No one seemed to be talking in this entire section of the convoy—or if they were, it was in the same muted tones he and Dole were using, so that their voices didn't carry any further than their boat.

"What on earth are those dragonflies living on, anyway?" Dole mused aloud. "I don't see any other insects—"

"That doesn't mean they aren't there, it just means that they aren't coming to the river to pester us," Kordas pointed out. "Or maybe they are somehow vegetarian and eat those fungi. Fungitarian?"

Dole passed his hand over his brow. "Mycophagy. I want out of here," he growled.

"We're getting there," Kordas soothed. "I'm going to ride back some more. I—I have the feeling I should show myself to everyone in the caravan as they pass through this place. Look confident, look unworried. That might damp down rising panic."

"I'd say you don't need to do that, but I'd be wrong," Dole confessed, as even Sunshine seemed so subdued that when he shook his head, he did so carefully, so as not to jangle his bridle. "That sense of unfocused anger is enough to make some people break and try to bolt back upriver."

"Which would be bad," Kordas observed. "Very bad. Everything we're doing hinges on everyone in the convoy going at a nice, steady pace. Disrupt that cadence, and we could start a cascade of problems that have nothing to do with these cursed woods."

"Go show a brave face," Dole agreed. "I'll see what we mages can find out about this place without the forest . . . knowing we're looking at it."

———

The first section of the convoy managed to get through the forest without anything worse than rattled nerves, though Kordas spent the entire time riding up and down the line, making sure that if anything happened, he would be right there to deal with it. Most of the animals in the herds did not even attempt to forage in the forest. Like the horses, they put their heads down, crowded as close as they could to the river without falling in, and did their best to get past the place as fast as they could. With the cattle, goats, and sheep, that amounted to something just short of a stampede. The ducks and geese kept the barges between them and the forest. The chickens refused to leave their barges. And *most* of the pigs scuttled along as fast as their stubby little trotters could carry them.

That was *most* of the pigs.

There were a few that seemed torn between fear and fascination. There was something in the air that was a definite attraction for them. They put their noses in the air and took enormous, snorting breaths in the direction of the forest. The swineherds' dogs kept them from venturing under the trees, although it was clear that the fascination might have overcome them without that prod.

Even people who were about as sensitive as mud clods were unnerved by this forest. Everyone was relieved when they made it out the other side, and the animals had taken no more hurt than to go hungry for most of the day.

Kordas—and Arial—were exhausted. Too tired to go back to their own barge on the other side of the Gate, Kordas asked Rose to talk to Ivy and have the Doll let Isla know he wasn't coming back. Rose did so, and was silent for a moment. "Ivy says that Isla was fairly certain that would be the case, and that our people come first. And that until everyone is safely beyond this strange place Ivy has described, you must play faithful shepherd."

Well, that was a relief. He took a last look at the forest—which looked no more welcoming in the growing twilight than it had in the full light of the sun—and sent Arial forward. "Rose, can the Old Men lend me a bed for the night?" he asked.

"One's being emptied of books for you," came the prompt reply, which startled a tired laugh out of him.

The next day was the same, and the day after that, and the day after that. He would ride up and down the riverside through the forest, crossbow at the ready—though what on earth he was going to *do* with it against a magic tree, he had no idea—making it clear that the Baron was watching out for them, and would personally stand between his people and danger. He spotted Sydney twice, once atop a supply barge of grain—no doubt there for the mice, and to fight any other cats there for the mice—and once at the stern of the royal boat. Mages had worked out how many barges could pass through the forest between dawn and the cut-off time, and had spaced themselves out along the convoy, arranging for borrowed beds if need be, in order that he always had at least one mage to help him at all times. When Isla and the boys passed through, he did not linger with their barge, though he did wave to them every time he passed them. It was only when they paused for the night that he got to sleep in his own bed for a change, and Sydney slept atop him.

And so it went, for day after day after day. Never once did the forest seem less menacing, although he thanked every god there was every night as he lay in yet another strange bed that it didn't get any *more* menacing. If they had the time to, he'd have brought Gate uprights through the Red Forest and just bypassed the whole thing. A few minutes' figuring showed that shuffling a barge through the hundreds upriver, then getting a Gate set up downriver of the Red Forest, would take three or four more days at minimum than just bringing the flotilla through the place directly. Add in that nobody knew if "crossing through" the Red Forest with more Gate Links would cause trouble, and that was that.

Ceri and Ponu were hunched over pages upon pages of notes on magical interaction on the journey so far when Kordas caught up with them. Them, and a meal, that is. The two Old Men were apparently of the same mind, as pages, markers, and rough maps were held steady by cups and plates. "Passive only," they had recommended, the last time Kordas consulted with them about using their mages' abilities to view their surroundings. "Now that we've met the lizard-dogs, we know creatures here can consume magic as part of their life cycles, and will seek it. It would be unwise to broadcast our location, so, best to carefully analyze what we know, versus actively reconnoitering by spellwork." It was a solid point they brought up again as they chatted with Kordas.

"And speaking of passive observation, we have a friend, a mage name of Angia, wants someone with her on yonder hillock in a couple of marks, and she'd prefer it to be you. Angia wants to watch the Red Forest at night to learn if it behaves differently with the sun down."

"Why me?" Kordas answered between bites. *Strange how the things we dreaded as children become what we want more of when we're older. We hated sitting still and taking naps, but now they're treats.* "I need a nap."

"You and me both," the Old Men answered in unison.

Kordas trudged carefully, using a hiking stick to test the going just a step ahead. His cohort was a well-bundled, stocky middle-aged woman. Angia was said to have a knack with plant magic—and insisted they go no closer than this gentle swell in the field. "Why are we out *here*, specifically?" he asked, huddled in his sheepskin coat and hoping that whatever she thought was going to appear would do so soon, so he could go collect some dinner and fall into another strange bed. Even if this time it wasn't a bed so much as a pad made of sheep fleece on the floor of a kitchen-barge. They closed the shutters on their dark lanterns and let their eyes adjust.

"Because things sometimes show themselves by night that don't by day," Angia replied patiently. "Any plant, or plant-like thing, is part of a system. It seems to me that if there is something *behind* this place, it might come out once the sun is down. I didn't want to sit here alone, and I don't do anything handy like tossing fireballs. And if it comes to it, I think I can run faster than you."

"Good points," he conceded, and finally found a boulder to sit on. It was ice cold, and his rump complained bitterly about the way the rock seemed to suck all the heat out of his body. He *almost* wished he was back among the trees, where at least it was warm.

Almost.

Rather telling that no one has offered to tie up there overnight. Not that I'd let them.

"Huh," Angia said, catching his wandering attention. "Either those dragonflies don't sleep at night, or a whole new bug comes out after the sun sets."

He squinted, and sure enough, he could just make out little lights, like red sparks, flying among the trees. And the haze that always filled the place glowed ever so faintly as well. Not red, but a sort of yellow-green, a little like the color a will'o'wisp had, but much dimmer. So dim that if he hadn't been far enough away from the forest that he could contrast it with the normal countryside, he wouldn't have seen it.

"I need you to know some things," Angia finally said. "Now that I'm certain no one is around, and nobody scrying. There are those of us among the expedition's number who have kept our nature secret, and I know you will come to understand why."

Kordas frowned, a fact hidden by the darkness, but his short exhale from his nostrils betrayed how he felt. *Spies? Is it spies? Did I let myself be lured out alone?*

Angia continued. "For as long as our history is known to us, our kind have been mixed among the regular population. Most of us have kept our secret, but enough has gotten out that we haven't felt safe in generations. We are seldom discovered, because the nature of our abilities warns us of danger. We take precautions to keep it that way."

Kordas heard his neck pop as he unclenched. "All right. Well, you succeeded in picking a dramatic setting. Tell me," he said.

"Tell you your fortune?" she chuckled. "It isn't that simple. But you're close. Funny, I should have seen that coming."

"This is an ominous place for a game of riddles, Angia, if that is who you are," Kordas replied. An edge of anger was in his tone that he hadn't intended.

"Angia is what I am known by, but only I know who I am," she answered as if that was a perfect response, then took on the tone of—a teacher. That is what snapped to mind.

Someone who knows how to get attention, and is there to educate and dominate any setting. Someone who knows how to orchestrate. All right, then. Let's see what she's got.

"Let me ask you, Baron. Have you noticed, in your quietest moments, that you are unreasonably positive about what lies ahead? By strict reasoning, you're constantly gambling with all our lives. You know this. Haven't you thought, if this land supports creatures like we've met so far, how can regular people, not great soldiers and mages, hope to survive even passing by? Why aren't there more of them, and why hasn't the expedition been overrun by disease and misadventure? Have you asked yourself, why am I *sure* this is the right way?"

Kordas exhaled a breath he didn't even realize he was holding. "I admit, I've wondered all of that and more. When I think upon how lucky we've all been, something in me screams, 'We shouldn't be.'"

"And then you stop worrying about it, and you assume you're just being fatalistic. You aren't. You aren't being fatalistic enough, except that you can sense what *we're* doing and it reassures you. This expedition *should* fail miserably at every turn, yet it goes on with very few losses. We have guided this expedition by watching and guiding *you*. When you've faced deadly decisions, we could tell they were coming. When you were anxious, we could look at the most likely results of your many decisions, then make you 'feel better' about the most fortuitous choices."

Kordas turned to face her, though both were still obscured by the night. "And things sometimes show themselves by night that don't by day," he quoted. "You can foresee the future."

"Likely futures, Baron," she corrected. "Some of us can tell likely futures, and others of us can affect how someone feels, or take away their emotions entirely. We cannot tell the future, because, heh, as you put it so well, 'There is no one true way.' The future depends upon factors we *cannot* fathom in full. We can narrow down what *might* happen into what is the *most likely* to happen. Also, we can't choose everything we See. But, I assure you, even that is enough to turn tides, if we can interpret it and nudge small, important moments. Ponds, rocks, ripples and all that."

Kordas *did* feel angry now. "I'm insulted. Not just for the treachery of effectively drugging me, but for secretly acting against the wishes of your Baron. You think I should feel happy with this? You've just told me you lot have mucked with my free will," he growled.

"We have mucked with you getting us all killed," she snapped back. "Your confidence is infectious. Even when you're wrong. People want to believe you. You back that up with a record of success, so they trust you more and more. You use the word 'wish'? I'll tell you about wishes, and what that really means. No, we don't overrule your free will, because by prayer you've asked for guidance many a time. You may have expected glowing figures to speak unto you, but we are who responded to your pleas. We'll continue to do so, unless you go mad. Then you'll just become very calm."

Kordas fumed. "That didn't help your case any," he snapped, then let himself calm down. After a few long breaths, he continued.

"I'm not abdicating my self, or my rule, just because I like the results! Taking away the freedom to fail removes what someone *could* have been. Failures make us stronger and wiser."

"And, bluntly, your failures cost lives. That has to be a consideration," she observed, and Kordas didn't like it, but he had to admit it, she was right. "So think about this. Do you abdicate your free will by accepting help from others? No, because it was your decision to consider help, and it is your choice whether to accept that help. What you're bristling at, Baron, is not being in control. Learning how wrong you could have been, while you were certain you were always choosing right, stings your concept of your *self*. The fact is, we are acting as agents of your free will, because we guide you toward what your declared goal is, and yes, we prosper by it too. You've already freely asked for aid from the unseen." Whether she meant the spirit realm, or her secret society, wasn't clarified at all.

"So I don't like the fact I've been given what I asked for, because it hurts my pride? Is that what you're telling me?"

"I say you dislike the *way* you've been given it. Personally, I think you could always *feel* that fate itself guided you, and you wished it had been in some open way, visible to all that you were Destined." She accentuated "destined" as if it were a call from a stage. "You didn't get the heavens opening up and birds flying and drama you secretly dreamed of. But you did get us. All of us, Baron."

"What do you mean, all of you?"

"All of us there *are*, Baron. Every Gifted sibling, of even the slightest skill, is in this flotilla. You see, Baron, over the years, Valdemar became our secret home. We rescued each other from the danger of the Empire, and when we Saw your Plan, we put our own in motion. None remain in all the Empire. We wanted both security for our kind, and the end of our presence in the Empire, denying them our gifts. What they've done to our ancestors is . . . unforgivable." Angia's voice just stopped for a moment, and she recovered. "If we didn't need to protect ourselves so thoroughly, we'd have openly offered our aid to you. But we just couldn't."

"I'm sorry for what happened to your people. I appreciate your plight, but you are still mucking about in the mind of an entire people's leader. That's not right. Even if I like the results."

"I promise you, Baron. I promise we have respected your sovereignty. We agonized over whether to tell you at all—but the consensus was, you deserve this explanation. Not so you can count on us as if we were known advisors, but so you don't balk against your secret allies when we help you. We feel like you deserve to know and, with your clear head, understand us. To truly think it through, with context." She sniffled, unsurprisingly for the weather, but there may have been more to it than that. "Another thing. All this isn't easy on us, either. We have to decide what possible futures to act upon, to do the least harm. Sometimes, there is no way to avoid tragedy. Danger does not always have a preventable moment. Things will hit us all." She sounded very downbeat about that. "When we help you take a path that will kill sixty people instead of ninety, we've still been part of killing people. It's *never* easy."

"I understand. I've done things that I'm not proud of, and it unbalances and sinks my heart." Kordas let that just rest there a while. Angia didn't interrupt the silence, and eventually, Kordas resumed. "The Red Forest keeps throwing me off. When I think plans through near it, I feel resentment, and I want to kick someone in the throat. It batters my emotions, and I have to work harder every time through just to stay level-headed. Are you all helping with that?"

"Not much," Angia confided. "We give you a mild boost in positivity when we can, without getting you drunk on it. But that's what I'm telling you—even when we nudge you, it's still *you*. Just—my advice?—reconcile the fact that you have positive forces on your side that you can't quite define, and feel good about it. In practice, really, it all adds up to this one thing for you: trust your intuition. When you feel a decision is right, *trust* that. When you have a flash of intuition, here's what it is: you are aware of that sudden feeling, but behind that impulse is more analysis, imagination, and forethought than you're consciously aware of. You *have* thought it through, so quickly it felt like you didn't. You were unaware of the process, but you gave yourself an answer. So listen to yourself."

"So . . . intuition . . . instinct. They aren't divine gifts? They're just—fast thinking?"

"Fast thinking, fast feeling, comprehension. You've worked hard to be like this, so embrace the benefits of the work."

"This is dizzying. But I can see the reason in it. Obviously, you have to protect yourselves, and if I'm being honest, I need the help. Just—don't take anything away from me. I can forgive, and even come to appreciate, your trespass upon me, but don't override me. Don't ever take away who I am."

"I'm not sure anyone could. But I get it. As someone who's spent her life hiding and pretending, the things in my life that I feel are intensely *mine* are vital to my sanity. They form the Angia I know." After twenty heartbeats, she simply said, "I feel good about us talking as soon as we could."

Kordas made ready to get to his feet again. "Answer me this. Why here, in the black and cold?"

"Good question, Baron, which brings up a good point to make."

Presumably, she gestured around, and Kordas nestled back in. "A few marks ago, I realized the opportunity for *everything* we found in our predictions about talking with you would present itself tonight. We knew you and I would talk. All any of us perceived about *when* and *where* was this general timeframe, starlight, darkness, cold wind, and a strange land as the setting. No distinct scents or sounds, and no way to count the marks passing."

Kordas laughed. "So, wait, you're saying that even your *certainty* is a puzzle?"

She laughed too. "The powers must think they're pretty funny, the way only a few bits of knowledge get handed out. What to do with that knowledge, well, we still have to sort that out ourselves." She sniffled and took on a more somber tone. "Kordas. Listen. We'll need to get back soon. Even before the Palace incidents, we knew we were needed. You took on too much, and it would have crushed you and those around you a dozen times over. If we have compromised or diminished you, we apologize deeply." Then, after another pause, "How do you feel about all of this?"

Kordas chewed on his lower lip a while. "I feel like . . . I'm disappointed that I am not everything I thought I was. I never *knew* I was being helped. I thought I led with smart moves and charisma."

"You do. Every star above here as my witness, if you were anyone else, we'd never have left the old land at all. Unless we're stuck with them, believe me, we don't back morons. Morons are only for strong disappointment and weak comedy, and puppets are tedious."

"Thanks for that. Truly. The other way I feel is deeply appreciative. I mean, I prefer to *know* when I'm collaborating with someone, but in this case, the results are good for everybody. I may feel differently later, and resent my manipulation in a hundred ways down the line, but for now, though—I can live with this. Only my pride is hurt, and lives are saved."

"Don't think you're any less brave or clever, Baron. We loaded the dice, but make no mistake, the dice were still thrown. Your success comes from being the *person* you are. The rest follows." Angia rubbed her hands together and Kordas imagined this same discussion, but someplace warm instead. He liked that discussion better.

"Angia, this makes me wobbly inside, and I need to be as sharp as gar teeth. I'll second-guess everything now—I'll wonder if any decision I make is a bad one because maybe you didn't have any visions, and it's just my own decision. I can't believe you're telling me that I am *actually* favored by fate. History has shown that being a Chosen One turns out . . . just awful for everyone except the playwrights."

Angia barked a laugh. "Hah! Nah. Me, I don't see you as the Chosen One type. You know how to back off before you get yourself martyred. Listen, Kordas, we know how people work. You are about to go through a lot, I can't lie. Have faith that even when surprises happen, things will be better," Angia soothed. "Don't worry about everything. Just do what you know is right. Don't feel *bad* that your prayers were answered. You should feel good about it."

She made sense.

"It doesn't lessen you to be helped. It means someone else was willing to put themselves out to uplift *you*."

That sounded true to him. Most of his best memories involved that.

"We *care* about you. We're very close to you."

There was truth in that, too, he was sure. That was a great feeling.

"And don't bother yourself about remembering everything. Over the next few minutes, we'll make sure that all you specifically recall is a cold night, with no results of note, in pleasant company."

The time out, if he thought about it, was a reset for his nerves. Sure, it was cold, but this night was really something he'd needed. He felt like his thoughts had cleared of congestion from being out here, just observing.

They sat there together in the dark as the bitter breeze gleefully stole more of their heat, until he finally sighed. "I don't think there's anything more that's going to come out," he said.

Angia levered herself up off her rock. "I think you're right. Well, it was worth trying."

He was reluctant to open the shutter on his lamp—but he also felt very reluctant to fall over something and break his leg. And he kept glancing back over his shoulder until they were well out of sight of the forest, and the lights of the barges beckoned to them welcomingly.

"One more set of barges tomorrow, and we're through," he said, as much to himself as to her. "It's mostly storage: things no one needs on the journey, but that we *will* need when we find a place to make our land and we've gotten ourselves established." *And the Spitters and Poomers,* he reminded himself. *In the end, I don't think I'd care if we lost those, but after all the work the Dolls did in funneling them to us, I don't have the heart to unload the boats and leave them on the bank somewhere.*

"Don't relax until *everything* has got through," Angia said, a little sharply. "That's when bad things happen—when you let down your guard short of the goal."

But she said that as they got to the cooking barge where he was spending the night, and instead of commenting on her words, he just wished her a sound rest and climbed aboard.

After all, what was the point in commenting? He knew she meant well. He knew the forest had gotten on her nerves. She probably couldn't help herself; it was her fear speaking, not any comment on his capabilities and sensibilities. Angia trusted him.

But he couldn't help thinking, as he found his pad and the couple spare blankets he was being loaned, that she was wasting her breath. *Not likely I am going to let down my guard at* any *time in the near future,* he thought, pulling a corner of the blanket over his head to block out the night lamp. *In fact—I am not likely to let my guard down until I am six feet under the earth.*

And honestly, probably not even then.

15

Don't let your guard down. Don't let your guard down. Don't let your guard down. Those words kept echoing through Kordas's mind as he rode up and down this last segment of the convoy, watching for trouble, watching for problems, watching for anything out of the ordinary. One eye on the forest, one eye on the convoy, and he wished desperately that he had a third eye to employ on the herds. Yes, there were herd dogs and their human masters, but suddenly the riverbank was packed with living beings, and what if the forest could sense that, without any of them setting foot under those unsettling limbs? Thank the gods Arial was what she was, and was as good or better than a dog at keeping track of her human, or he might have disgraced himself by falling out of her saddle, the way his head kept swiveling. All the Valdemar Golds were like that; they'd been bred for endurance, intelligence, and good temper. The glorious metallic gold of their coat was just a happy accident.

He'd have valued them just as much if they'd all been harsh-coated, mud-colored, jug-headed nags.

Rose rode along as usual, and engaged in pleasant conversation after each report. She had a knack for sifting the useful bits from the chaff; when there was a fight among the expedition's complement, she skipped the "why," except if it involved critical resources or discontent with Kordas and his senior advisors. Attrition just from the rigors of travel was considerable. The convoy's barges were taking a beating, and today alone they'd had to transfer cargo from eight of them to several strings at the tail of the convoy, and just let them break up and sink once towed aside. As simple as staging for the passage through the Red Forest sounded, actually accomplishing it was a hurried exercise of expertise. Weights were estimated, Dolls helped carry the loads from one vessel to another, and lining the vessels up side by side, string to string, was backbreaking work. All too literally, in two cases; with motion came injuries, and nobody would heal quickly enough to return to work for days or weeks—leaving even more work upon the shoulders of those who were still able.

Rose reported that the Gate uprights were secured atop a materials barge, third to last, in the last string. That meant the Old Men overseeing that dismantling and loading would join the rest of the flotilla by the time Kordas reached the last string of eight barges. There was no point in waiting any longer. Ten strings remained before the end of the convoy, and the last of the civilians and cage animals had already gone through. Guards, ship hands, Kordas, and Rose would be the last people left to enter the Red Forest, accompanied ashore by the hoggees guiding the Tow-Beasts.

"Rose, relay the order, please. Sail descending, downbound apace." Almost immediately, the sound of Tow-Beasts and their hoggees reached them, and the string was underway.

It wasn't until his third turn-around at the end—the *end at last!*—of the convoy that he saw it. One single young boar, trotting behind the last barge at a distance. Definitely alone. And clearly very interested in the forest. There was an aged shepherd-dog with him that did *not* care for the pig's interest in the forest at all, and kept nipping at him to keep him moving, even interposing itself between the boar and the woods if the boar ventured too close.

The boats back here were full of duplicate, bulky tools, like looms and a disassembled pit-saw for cutting planks. To Kordas's eye, the whole string looked overloaded and sat deeper in their mean drafts than they should, but if the experts had cleared them, it must be acceptable. Kordas spotted someone sitting on the stern of the last of the boats—and directed Arial over there to talk to him. "What—" he began.

"Dog's mine," the old man said, his beard almost the same color as the wool of his coat, his head tucked so far down into the collar that he looked like a turtle disinclined to come out of his shell. "Pig belongs to Cass Pommery, from Coldspring, my village. Damn thing slipped its charm and bolted, didn't like the wilderness after all, but won't let anyone near it to put a new charm in its ear. Cass said to jest let him run along behind, but ever since we got into these damn trees, my old dog decided that there pig ain't got the sense the gods gave a goose, and he's been tryin' to herd him."

Kordas studied the pig. Were teenage pigs like teenage humans? If so, the blasted thing thought itself immortal. "I think your dog has the right of it," Kordas replied. "It looks as if the pig wants to get in under those trees and start rooting."

"Prolly does." The old man shrugged, which looked more like his head was sinking into the wool than like he was raising his shoulders. "Cass says it's a truffle pig, which's why it prolly ran away in the first place. Truffle pigs like to be loose an' huntin' their favorite food. Gray morels, truffles, sagbacks. We find 'em, you eat 'em."

Don't let your guard down.

"I don't think it should go in there, in the forest, I mean," Kordas said carefully. "We've been very lucky so far . . . but if something of ours goes in there and starts messing about, we might not be lucky anymore."

"Aye. That's why I ain't washed my hands of the fool bastard, and why Howler's shepherdin' him." The old man spit over the side of the boat, and made a sign that Kordas recognized as one against evil.

"Don't let your guard down," Kordas said, echoing the words in his own head, and turned Arial to ride back up the convoy.

"Won't," the old man grunted.

Kordas's nerves were stretched just as tightly as they had been in the Capital, and for pretty much the same reason. In his own mind, potential disaster loomed over him and everyone else he was responsible for, and he had no true idea if the disaster was only in his head or was very real, what form it would take, and if it could be avoided. This entire trip had been like that; there had been brief respite at Crescent Lake, but even then he had known in his heart that the respite was only temporary. And now . . . if he was to be honest with himself, he had to admit he had recklessly taken nearly fifteen thousand people off into the unknown without a map or any goal besides "find somewhere we can live," largely on the assumption that whatever happened, he could improvise a response.

The fact that nothing catastrophic hadn't happened yet was minorly due to his leadership, but largely due to good luck, and good luck never lasted.

I wonder if the best idea isn't to shed people and their property wherever we find a spot that can support a village. Wouldn't that be kinder to everyone, rather than dragging people across the face of an increasingly hostile landscape trying to find the kind of choice spot that can support us all?

But . . . I promised them that Valdemar was never the land. It was always the people. And a village isn't large enough to protect itself from a serious threat. Look at that village back at the last Gate we built—and it was an already established one!—that couldn't handle those snake-dogs on their own!

There weren't as many herd-beasts on this last, tail-end piece of the convoy, which made riding up and back along the strings of barges much quicker. The barges back here weren't for individual families, and consisted mostly of cargo they would *want* when they all settled, but would not necessarily *need*. Duplicate tools, for instance: extra lumbering tools, extra farming tools, extra crafting tools. "One to take and one in case it breaks" seemed to have been the rule with most people, and all the "one in case it breaks" things were here at the back. It was a kind of "sacrificial tail" so if anything attacked the convoy from the rear, the barges could be abandoned for the attacker to deal with while the rest of the convoy escaped. There was only one barge tender for each string of about eight barges, and they rode their towing animals. If the worst happened, they could cut the traces, set the barges free, and be off. Each tender had a bed in the lead barge and they all shared a single kitchen, which was manned by a second-rank cook of

Valdemar manor. Kordas was making sure the men—they were all men back here—had no complaints about how they were treated.

And thinking about these mundane—but needful—precautions, and how he had followed the advice of his mages and worked out every disaster he could think of and a plan for dealing with it *did* keep the tension at arm's length.

More or less, anyway.

I certainly didn't anticipate an enraged forest of sinister trees.

On the other hand . . . how could I possibly have anticipated this? Outside of adventure stories, we've always assumed the world was the same as the Empire.

In all the time it had taken to get each section past the woods, nothing had changed in the woods themselves. It was still ridiculously warm. The musty, bitter scent did not change. The dragonflies—if that was what they were—continued to ignore the caravan and flitted among the trees at a distance from the river. And the rage . . . the rage was always there. Never decreasing. Never increasing. It was as if the forest slept here, dreaming, and its dreams were always angry.

And there is no doubt that the last thing we want to do is disturb it.

He was nagged about that wretched boar once the last barge entered the forest proper, but every time he checked, the dog Howler was doing his self-appointed duty, keeping the stupid creature from going off the path. Howler must have herded pigs before this, because he was doing all the right things that worked with a pig, and not doing things that worked with sheep but would not work with a pig. Staring, for instance. A dog could always get a sheep to move by staring aggressively at it. Pigs didn't care. No, Howler interposed himself between the pig and the forest, if need be making short little runs at it. It almost seemed as if the dog could read the pig's mind, although what it was probably doing was reading the pig's body language. Before the boar could make up its mind to go in the wrong direction, Howler made it impossible to go there.

The poor lad was getting tired, though. Belatedly, now Kordas wished he had known about this sooner. A sugar beet dangling from the side of the barge just out of reach would have gotten that wretched pig's attention; a sugar beet was *now*, and truffles in the forest were *maybe*. Such an immediate offer of a reward presented something desirable much better than the forest could. Alas, there was nothing like that in any of these barges.

If I'd known about this earlier, we could have trapped the damned thing.

But most probably the pig's owner hadn't wanted to bother him about it, thinking the problem was trivial, and would solve itself—either the pig would finally decide to rejoin its herd, or something would eat it. It had probably never occurred to the man that the "something" could prove to be a hazard.

And here it is. The unexpected. A thing I didn't anticipate because it never occurred to me that any of these animals would manage to dislodge their charms.

In the case of the pigs and cattle, it should have been impossible, because the charms were circlets of bent metal like earrings, pierced through the thick part of their ears. But . . . somehow this boar had lost his, and not by tearing it out of his ear, either.

Maybe I should ride up to the next part of the convoy and get something a pig would think of as a treat. A nice smelly chunk of cheese . . .

Maybe it was just that the pig, and Howler the dog, represented the very last of the expedition passing through this blasted place. Until they were *all* through safely, it didn't feel like he could lower his vigilance, which irked him. *There always has to be just one more thing, doesn't there?* He sure didn't want to send anyone back to meet him with boar bait, and by the time he rode up to the kitchen and back, they'd be almost out of the forest. To be honest, he didn't want to put more strain on poor Arial. There was a limit to the Golds' endurance, and he had the feeling she was close to it, riding up and down through a stressful place with scarcely a pause all day, every day, and today, most of it being at a trot or canter.

I can't ask her to do more. It isn't fair.

He patted Arial's neck. She hadn't gotten used to that undercurrent of *hate*, either. She wasn't lathered, but her coat was damp from nerves, and he suspected it was only her trust in him that kept her on the now-well-worn path.

Dammit, woods! he thought with irritation. *We are leaving enough lovely manure to keep you thriving for the next decade. The least you can do is show some gratitude!*

The forest was, apparently, indifferent to his wishes. It simply seethed.

By noontime, half this section was finally out in the clear—if freezing—air.

We'll be out of here well before sundown. He concentrated on that. *Can't be soon enough. I'm getting edgier, and I thought I was already too tense about this. Maybe I'm still not sharp enough about it? Being this alert is brutal.*

When three-fourths of the section was out of the forest, he stopped riding up and down the riverbank and stayed with that last barge of the last string. He'd heard the scraping, tapping sounds from every barge that passed, where he'd surmised an underwater tree snag dragged against them. It was then he heard a loud thunk and scraping noise, and he spotted a chunk of broken barge about the size of three men pulled along in the last barge's wake. The barge was taking on water, and with clearly audible cursing, the old man scrambled to reach the bow. Shouts from further up the string took on urgency. Shudders and cracking sounds convulsed the entire string. The old man reached the fore of the last barge, retrieved a hand axe from the fore's toolstand, and half-leapt, half-fell to the second-to-last barge when the slack between them suddenly vanished. The string had stopped, held up by the disintegrating last barge, which was likely seized dead by the underwater snag.

Kordas knew they didn't have much time. Arial gave him a last dash, which brought him waterside to the wreck. "Come on!" he yelled at the old man, who was hacking at the mooring ropes looped to the jammed-up timberheads, stretched taut from the wreck to the barge he was now on. All he got back from the old man was cursing, and more axe strikes.

Behind the barges, three dragonflies landed on the large piece of boat wreckage. Then six.

They left the Forest—

Rose leapt from Arial, and in ten strides, she was on the barge beside the old man. Kordas saw Rose do the only overtly rude thing he'd ever seen her do: she forcefully took the axe from the old man and took over the job of hacking at rope. The man tumbled back and scrambled to get up as the aft of the barge inexplicably heaved up, and its hull cracked amidship. Crates and bundles slid forward and crashed, and this sudden new danger made Rose stop her axe-work and grab at the man. Unfazed, the man yelled to his dog, even while Rose was bodily hoisting him.

The water *frothed* below the broken barges.

In the Red Forest, dragonflies gathered in geometric patterns of two to six, staying at the edge of the trees' shadows. They just—hovered.

The pig was more than worrisome now. It was actively trying to get past Howler, who was running out of strength. And just as the lead barge of this string rebounded from the sudden braking and broke free of the trees, what Kordas had been afraid of all along happened. The pig put on a burst of speed, feinted to the right, then dashed past the dog to the left, running faster than any pig had a right to, especially one that had been fretting and trying to dodge all day. The dog made a dash after the pig, but dropped to the ground at the old man's shout of "Howler! Drop!" swiftly followed by "Howler! Here!" It was probably habit for him, because the disintegrating barge was no place the dog would want to be.

The dog recognized that his master was relieving him of duty, and with a sigh that visibly heaved his flanks, he padded wearily, and warily, toward the barge, its ears back and tail low. More crashes came from the two doomed barges. Loom hardware smashed against the loom's own carefully stacked framework, exploding out in bursts of deadly splinters. On the second barge, waxed canvas tore loudly. Rose and the old man escaped over the split in the sawmill barge's deck to the third-to-last barge—the one with two Gate uprights laid atop it. The uprights hadn't been lashed down. Why bother? A barge was far too stable, and their weight too widely distributed to shift on the placid, slow river.

Below the water, something yellow, striped in ocher and black, punched upward through the barge hulls and flailed like an unbalanced auger, grinding the hull into sections no bigger than a pie pan. It was as if the riverbed was standing up.

The pig, aware that he was no longer being pursued by Howler, bolted into the Red Forest and began snuffling the ground.

Should I shoot the damned thing?

What if the forest reacts poorly to me killing something inside it?

What if the forest reacts poorly to—

But then all those thoughts became completely moot, as the pig found what it was looking for, rooted intensively at one spot, and finally employed its trotters and even teeth on the place. It had found something it wanted to eat.

So had the trees.

In all this time, the air had been hot and still, and not so much as a leaf on the ground had moved. The only activity going on in this place was the ever-flitting dragonflies.

But now . . . the branches all around the oblivious boar moved, slowly uncoiling, untwisting.

And the forest woke up.

A rush of pure anger, like a scream of raw emotion into their minds, ripped through the place, anger so palpable it hit not only Kordas, but the old man, his dog, and Arial. The old man clapped both hands to his temples. The dog dropped to the ground a moment and whimpered. Kordas felt—

—exactly what he had felt on that day, when the mother of the imprisoned baby Earth Elemental had sensed that the protections hiding it from her were gone, and had come roaring up out of the bowels of the earth to free her child and take revenge on its captors. *Hate* and *rage*, like breathing in a deep breath directly from a raging furnace.

Whatever was in the river reacted *violently*. The last half of the barge string was thrown upward, almost free of the water. In midair, Kordas could see the old man grasping for any kind of purchase, and Rose reaching for him.

The uprights flew up into the air, pitching base first toward the river. From the previous barge, sawmill blades, chains, logjacks, and hooks rained down onto them, along with a shower of bolts and pipes from disintegrated crates. Sawblades embedded themselves into the uprights.

Just above the old man and Rose.

Rose caught the man's nearest wrist and hooked the axe into a falling upright, creating a short shower of sparks against the rain of hardware, catching no small part of it herself. The upright provided an instant of cover for the old man.

Then, groaning and snapping, it all fell into the river.

Rose swung the old man toward the shore, where he rebounded off of Arial's ribs and Kordas's right leg. Arial staggered aside, as if newborn. Exhaustion, compounded by the enervation of fear, would likely soon claim her.

In the chaos of the river, Rose was nowhere to be seen. There was hate, knives, water, mud, pieces of hull, horrible sounds of destruction and primal combat, but no valiant Doll.

The old man crumpled up, and Howler closed the distance to his side in his own desperate burst of speed. The dog reached him and, despite its own panting, licked at him as if dog saliva was a healing salve. It could be said that in this case, it truly was. The old man expressed a moment of rapturous joy, clasping the dog's head to himself, then murmured something to him and got to his feet, though not steadily by any means.

Totally stunned for the moment from taking in and processing far too much, Kordas couldn't even move to bring up his crossbow and shoot the damned boar. It was all so fast, it made him feel slow. And he *hated* it. He hated that he couldn't reason this out. He *hated* that he *hated*.

But Arial saved him. She gave an involuntary buck and kick. Not enough to throw him, but enough to break the spell the forest had put on him.

Just as one of the Red Forest's branches steadily reached toward him.

With a squeal, she danced out of the way, getting him out of reach of those branches with a turn and a leap worthy of an expert dancer. The old man and Howler scrambled for distance.

A dozen bizarrely flexible branches lashed out like whips at the oblivious boar, who only realized too late that it was in danger.

The branches whipped around each of the boar's legs, and around its neck.

The tree seized the boar, hauling it up into the air as it squealed in mingled terror and agony. One narrow branch ripped off an ear, and all the branches tightened, splaying the pig out in midair among the branches of the canopy. More branches whipped out to seize the boar, and those round things on the branches seemed to attach themselves to the pig's skin somehow, preventing it from kicking free.

The hideous squeals jolted Kordas into action, and he shot the stupid beast through the heart to end its suffering. Just as well, because the next thing that got ripped off was a leg, in an uncanny echo of one of the Emperor's favorite sentences for a criminal, being pulled to pieces by five horses.

The screams stopped when the boar died, but the trees were just getting started. Kordas watched in horror as the limb that had ripped off the ear stuffed the bloody morsel in one of those "mouths." Two more limbs tore long bloody swaths of muscle and skin off the body, and stuffed them in other "mouths." And more of the trees moved, reaching toward the bloody mess that had been a pig, trying to get a bit for themselves.

Something else made a momentary dome of water in the river. With the explosive sound of storm-driven ocean surf slapping a mountainside, it burst upward. Arcs of deep riverbed mud flew as high as any two barges were long. The air *shook*.

That was more water-weight than all the barges in the string could even displace. What could heave so much water, so quickly? What could do that?

Whatever was in the water lunged forward three—steps?—to the shore, and it was—

Kordas couldn't completely comprehend what he was seeing. Well past a barge-length tall, it was like a water spider—made of water spiders—made of more water spiders—and all made of black and yellow knives. Each leg was striped in ocher and black, and each stripe was a cluster of legs, all too horribly long, with bright yellow stripes, and each of *them* had *more* legs and *more* black knifelike spikes. Mud and river water poured off of its back and legs, no doubt how it had stayed disguised while every vessel of the flotilla had passed over it. The taps and scrapes on the hulls this whole time had been . . . it. Them. The thing, its body easily the size of a barge itself, seemed to split into three narrower versions of itself side by side, each dashing into the Red Forest to attack the trees' branches. Where one leg struck, the smaller clusters—only man-sized—tore off branches.

No, wait—they weren't only branches now. There were also something more. Like boneless limbs.

That's what we were missing. That's how it gets even worse.

The yellow-and-black blurs advanced and retreated. Stabbing attacks by the water-monsters seemed to strobe, so quickly did they dart in and leap back. And when every writhing limb-lash came their way—and before long there were hundreds—the water-monsters slashed the limbs, sectioned them, and devoured them.

And each set of knife-spiders has its own mouth. Right. Or, maybe it's a colony of thousands, and it'll turn into a whole wave of death-knife-spiders next. That'd be just perfect.

Around the perimeter of the sudden spray of muddy water and sap-blood, the dragonflies deployed, now buzzing extremely loudly. Much closer, and the noise would have been disorienting to Kordas and the rest trying to flee. One group of thirty or more dragonflies clustered between one of the spiders' leg clusters, and came away with severed spider bits, only to carry them away into the Red Forest. Dragonflies batted from the air by the spiders were replaced, as more of their kind converged from, presumably, deeper in the Red Forest. At the periphery of the rapidly escalating battle, other dragonflies gathered up, then flew into the Forest with—for some reason—pieces of barge.

The last three barges were now sinking, the fourth was groaning, and all forward motion had stopped. Kordas desperately wanted to fight right now, but rescue was more important. He wasn't going to lose Rose. It didn't feel like she was dead, and he knew she didn't need to breathe, but cargo was still shifting and bucking from the battle raging far too closely to them, and she could certainly be killed by crushing.

From beneath the tangle of the Gate uprights—now planted in the riverbed—and the sawmill hardware, gushes and sprays of muddy water flew in every direction.

Rose!

Amidst a pile of fractured hull strips, belaying bars, and splintered crates, a figure slowly stood up.

Two sawblades protruded from its side. Centering pins pierced it. A riving knife as big as a forearm went through its neck.

Thick mud sluiced off the pale figure, revealing unblemished white canvas and gashes of soggy brown tufts of ripped-out stuffing.

"Rose!" Kordas shouted. He dismounted, much to Arial's relief, and ran toward the river in what was, even for him, an extraordinarily heedless display of terrible judgment.

Rose, her movement impaired by a smithy's worth of hardware through her body, limp-twitched to the shore, to be intercepted by Kordas, while the battle of monsters only escalated behind them.

"I will make a note to speak with the loadmasters about better securing cargo for transit," Rose replied. He didn't know if a Doll could be dazed, but it's how she sounded. "I see you are all healthy. Good." Kordas ducked under Rose's most-damaged shoulder and helped her along. Rose, who could probably have carried both of them, let him, and instead turned her attention to protecting their retreat. Kordas felt a sudden jerk from Rose, and a *whunk* sound, and shrapnel of spar laminate flew past them. No doubt it had threatened them. Despite chunks of stuffing and ironworks sticking out in most every direction, Rose sounded as pleasant as ever. "This is a very good axe," she added.

"Keep it!" Kordas replied, half-running toward the remaining barges while ducking pieces of hull, loom, and sawmill.

Kordas didn't have much time to think. He'd held off from using magic to either defend or rescue the old man, for fear that *both* of the monstrosities would turn their way, but now they had some distance. He did the quickest math he knew, searched his feelings, and determined the truth in an instant.

Now was the correct time to kill everything, in the immediate upriver direction, with fire.

You want me to hate, hells-forest? Oh, I can hate. I've got years of hate to spend on you. He paused in helping Rose as another Doll took her up from him, and another came alongside him to help him escape, too.

Kordas knew well that fire spells were enhanced by hot emotions, so he let it boil up in him. The ground below him began to steam.

You have no idea what I've been through, no idea what kind of daily horror I've been forced into. Hate? I hate being in charge! I hate my future being forced! I hate feeling like everything I do is a salvage! I hate being a hero to people! I hate putting up a false face! I hate picking who lives and dies, defending against fuckery like you! Now you dare come after us? After all this? You want me to hate? I'll sear you with my hate! You can scream in Nightmare Hell that there's more of it for all of you, if you piss me off again!

He paused long enough to yell in rage at the Red Forest and the   Yellow-Black-Hell-River-Spider-Whirling-Knives-Of-Death-Creatures, and flung his hands in their direction so violently his sleeves ripped. A tracking streak flew out an instant before two ragged-edged, jetting spheres of sunlight followed them, to detonate on contact. A percussive sound like sharp, muffled thunder sent a shockwave from the monsters, followed by a shower of small—and wet—debris. The battling creatures may not have started the day as flammable, but they were now. The escape on foot was now backlit by gouts of flame and smoke.

Downriver, the horses hauling the barges were *not* having any of this. The guards pulled the shore escapees onto the first three barges, the two Dolls leapt back to the aft timberheads of the fourth barge, levered, and released the pins that held the sinking barges. The half-string accelerated away. The Tow-Beasts somehow found the strength to lunge against their harness, sweating and foaming, to pull their load at a faster pace, and their panic somehow communicated itself all the way up the line, because *everyone* moved faster, first at a much faster walk, then at a trot, and finally at a near-canter. It was enough speed that, unchecked, would ram one string into another end to end, forty deep. Arial, despite her exhaustion, appeared to be renewed by the company of other horses, and was right with them. As they all broke out of the forest, he looked back over his shoulder to see that the burning trees behind them were a seething mass of writhing limbs, each trying to score a hit on the spider-creatures, or stretching yearningly toward Kordas, the old man, and Howler, while burning black and yellow spikes struck as fast as lightning, advancing into the Red Forest, severing limbs into fiery gobs.

As they got past the last tree, Kordas got hit by such a cold wind that his sweat-soaked clothing froze instantly. His blistered hands crackled inside his gloves, and new burns steamed.

One last surging flail of flaming tree-limb tentacle whipped toward the fourth barge, and was cut off in midair by a yellow-and-black flash of spider leg. It *thunked* atop cases of Poomers, Spitters, and their magazine of ammunition as it sank, drawn deeper by the wreckage it was attached to.

They were free.

Kordas heaved breaths in and out, from amidships on the last barge, and raised both smoking, steaming arms. He made two rude gestures at the fire-and-monster melee behind them.

Don't ever dare me to hate you. I've got plenty built up, ready to hurt you.

"It's a wonder you didn't catch something," Isla said, as he stood in front of the stove, sponging his sweat-stinking body with one of Sai's magical towels.

Kordas's gloves were ruined, having been carefully trimmed off of his burned hands by Isla and a set of thread trimmers. Despite the throbbing pain, Kordas wasn't ready to Heal his hands fully just yet. Sometimes, it was best to let the body carry on with its instinctive processes, so the Healer wasn't fighting them. He just tamped down the pain for now. "It's a wonder I wasn't caught," he replied.

The boys sat on the bed, solemn-eyed, and not at all interested in hearing the story—at least, not at the moment. It wasn't every day they saw Arial using the last of her strength to get him safely "home," to the point where she staggered as she finally arrived at their mooring spot. Odds seemed good that they were more bothered by that than seeing their father's nicks, cuts, and burns—they'd seen that before. They were more sensitive than he had given them credit for, actually. Maybe it was all those years of knowing how careful they had to be about what they said and who they spoke to.

Rose—as Kordas had figured she would—had relayed what was happening to all the other Dolls, even while being carted off to her repair. The entire caravan now knew that the forest had been *just* as dangerous as they had been warned it might be. The consensus, as relayed back from Ivy after the wild ride, was that any animal that lost its charm and wandered off was to be shot if it could not be recaptured and re-tagged within eyeshot of the expedition. No one wanted to lose an animal, but they understood it was foolishness bordering on neglect for them to attract the attention of random monsters with animals that couldn't stay where they belonged—or to let them be used as bait to lure out would-be rescuers. Or, for that matter, to take the animals back; they could return with—hells only knew what. Parasites that gave people extra heads. It could be anything. The entire expedition was learning: count on nothing they encountered to be what it seemed to be.

We're just lucky they were trees, planted in place. And that the—

"Of course," Kordas blurted. He'd have snapped his fingers if he could. "The water-spider-things. I think there were three. Big ones, anyway. Everything passed right over their backs like leaves on the river, but the last string was overloaded, and drafting low because it was taking on water from a hull crack. Every other vessel in the fleet glided right over them, but when the tail actually *hit* the things, they must have reacted to it as an attack." He shuddered. "Oh gods, we had no idea."

Kordas's eldest boy glared at him with a look that read, *Don't you know any happy stories, father? We're children here.*

Kordas bit back saying any more of his thoughts out loud. *Just those three could have shredded every boat in the fleet and all aboard, by the way it looked. Just incomprehensible speed and strength. Oh gods, how many are under us right now? Why did they carve up the hulls, even in mid-battle? Why did the Red Forest only attack the pig once it went in deeper? When it reached out during the battle, it was clear, it could have snatched any of our animals close to the water with its limbs. But the water was where the spiders were, and the spiders weren't interested in easy-to-reach livestock. They went after and ate tree limbs. Gods, were they vegetarian monster spiders? This is what this place can do to you. Once you start questioning and fearing, you're never sure when to stop.*

"I'm very glad that our people decided to deal with stray animals themselves, instead of waiting for you to make an edict," Isla continued, smoothly filling the moment. Then she turned and looked at the bed, where Sydney-You-Asshole was lounging with the boys. "You hear that, Sydney? No losing your collar. There are *some* people around here that wouldn't think twice about shooting you."

"Mama!" little Hakkon objected. "No one is going to shoot Sydney! He's a *good* cat!"

Kordas bit his lip, because while he could be a reckless, bossy bruiser to other cats and most dogs, at least with the children, Sydney actually *was* a good cat. He put up with all manner of mauling from them, including being stuffed into doll clothes. They could tote him like a rag doll. But let an adult touch his Sacred Belly Fur, and said adult would draw back a bloody stump where his hand used to be.

Sydney looked at Isla with an expression that Kordas interpreted as "contempt," but meowed something that sounded *exactly* like, "All right."

So we have talking cats now?

Of course we have talking cats. We're lucky we don't have talking horses, with what we've put them all through. I should just be grateful that they aren't dictating orders.

——

The scouts sat in silence and listened carefully to what Amethyst had to say. "Well," said Sai, as Amethyst finished her calm, almost expressionless recitation of what was happening in the strange forest, "Now we know we can't go back."

"We know we can't go back *that way*," Jonaton corrected him. "What's more important is what's going to happen to any Impies that manage to follow us that far."

Endars's left brow shot up toward his hairline. *"Impies?"*

Jonaton shrugged, and reached for the salt. "Impies. It's scornful and demeaning. They made me wear square-cut woolen trousers with no pockets for years, and I don't forgive things like that. The point isn't what I call our former Lords and Masters. My point is that if there is one thing that Impies *cannot* do, it's keep their hands to themselves. If they lay eyes on that forest, they're going to want to fell some of it, just out of purest curiosity. They're going to want to uproot saplings. They're probably even going to want to catch some of those dragonflies. And that's *before* the trees fight back.

Once they do that, the Impies will want to figure out how they can tame those trees, or use them for weapons. And then the spiders in the river?" He just let that hang there.

It was, in Jonaton's words, "Officially too damn cold to sit around a fire at night," so Sai was using the tiny stove in the equally tiny barge kitchen to make what he could, and he had Delia and Amethyst helping him. Delia was still able to catch geese, ducks, and the odd rabbit and squirrel, and Ivar hunted as he scouted ahead, but now the meals were very different. Cabbage leaves were used to wrap bits of food until the leaves were too hard to pry off the core, at which point the core got chopped very fine and added to a soup kettle that was *always* kept full of all the odds and ends and leftovers. Sai did make a fire on land, right near the barge when they stopped for the day, but no one was sitting around it at night. Instead, the initial flames were used to quickly broil whatever meat they had cut into strips, the bones went into the soup pot, and Sai would make up hand food for the following noonday meal with the meat and pickled onions. Supper was the soup: bones cooked until they were so soft you could actually eat them—Bay got those—chopped root vegetables, chopped squash, cabbage, dried beans. Breakfast was cooked overnight in the coals of the fire, an enormous pot of oat porridge with dried apples in it. Sai tried to vary the herbs and spices he put in. Sometimes he added a precious bit of honey. Bay got the leftovers of that, too, and ate it with a gusto that seemed odd to Delia. After all, there was no meat in it. She wondered why Sai didn't put dried grapes or currants in it, but it seemed such things were bad for dogs. But he did have a sack of dried grapes they could dip into if they wanted something sweet. There was no more flatbread; it got tough and unappetizing when it was cold, and it was too cold to sit there next to the fire and cook it, so instead of that, they had some sort of hard biscuit that the Fairweathers called "field rations" to dip in the soup.

So at the moment, they were all crowded into the women's barge where the kitchen was. Delia had retreated to her bunk with her bowl of soup and one of those biscuits. She had to scrunch into a corner to have enough room to eat, which restricted what she could see, but she could hear everything perfectly well. Ivar and Alberdina sat on Alberdina's bunk, Briada and Bart took up Briada's bunk and Bret part of the floor, and Hakkon and Jonaton were in the bunk reserved for the sick or injured. Everyone else had found a place to sit on the floor. Delia thought about offering someone bunk space, but it was a bit hard to get up here, regardless of the fact that the Fairweathers had somehow popped up into place in the upper bunk like a pair of goats. Amethyst was nearest the prow to keep the kitchen area clear, and her high voice carried very well back to where the bunks were. A soft mage-light enclosed in a cage in the middle of the ceiling cast a pleasantly dim glow over everything.

"You know, I almost wish the Impies would try taking that forest," Hakkon said after a moment, punctuated only by slurping.

"That's assuming that they'd lose; they might not. They might win," Venidel pointed out. "I mean, at some point Imperial mages were powerful enough to kidnap a young Earth Elemental from the deeps of the earth, and not only keep it imprisoned, but hide it from its mother. It doesn't do to underestimate them."

"Particularly not the mages with the army," Briada pointed out. "The ones in the Capital may have been lazy buggers, but the combat mages are sharp *and* ruthless *and* used to improvising."

"They did some terrible things with the power they had," Sai said gravely. "Imagine if they could control those trees. Imagine if they could walk that forest up to people they wanted to intimidate, and surrounded them with it. No getting in, no getting out."

"I didn't think those things could walk!" Bret exclaimed from the floor.

"I don't know that they can," Sai corrected. "But I also don't know that they *can't.*"

"Can we talk about something else?" Delia asked. "We all got past the thing, except for one pig. Don't we need to look forward and not back?"

"They won't like our news back at the fleet," Ivar replied. "The further we go downriver, the stranger things get. Between us, just in the last few days we've seen bright red bare-skinned rodents mimicking the movements of frogs, moving in herds. Bushes that split, and split, so many times they look fuzzy, but they're just masses of tiny blue thorns. Vines that form entire structures like they'd climbed a building, then the building vanished. Conjoined deer. Fish that emit smoke when they surface. Outcrops of crystals as tall as me. Solid rock that looks like flowing waterfalls in the light, with nests of mushrooms for the glowing eels in them. Animal ribcages arranged like a fenced ring and nothing growing inside. It's getting worse."

"Well, I have an idea for looking forward," Briada put in. "Delia, you're our special shooter. Would you also like to learn how to defend yourself at closer hand?" She tucked her now-empty bowl back behind her and leaned over the edge of her bunk so she could see everyone. "Lessons are open for all, actually. I'm thinking combat batons, to begin with. Then move into knives, then staffs, then swords."

Not that long ago, Delia would have laughed at the idea. Now . . . well, as colder weather sent the fish to the bottom of the river where she couldn't see them, the geese and ducks that were showing up were clearly migratory stragglers, and the rest of the animals along the river were spending as much time in their warm dens as they could (or hibernating altogether), there was less that she was useful for during the day. Gathering firewood for the entire day generally took no more than the morning.

And she liked the idea of being able to defend herself, even if it was with nothing more than a stick. "You aren't going to break anything, are you?" she asked Briada, only half joking.

"Well, accidents happen, but I haven't broken any weapons on a student yet." Briada grinned.

"I'd be game for some of that," Jonaton said unexpectedly.

"I would too," Venidel added.

"Anyone else?" Briada asked. "No? Listen, no shame here. I can do some pretty nice woodcarving, and if we end up somewhere unable to move until spring, I'd be willing to teach anyone that, too."

"I'm too lazy." Endars uttered a very dry chuckle.

"I'm too old," said Sai.

"I'd dispute that, Master Sai, but I wouldn't accept you as a student if you wanted me to teach you," Briada replied. "During the day we need you ready to do your finger-wiggling and chanting in case we run into something bad. And at night, well, I'm not teaching anyone at night. Three of you is all I can handle, anyway. Delia's going to be wood-gathering in the morning; Ven, are you willing to take your beatings in the morning?"

Delia finished her soup and the last crumb of her broth-soaked biscuit, licked the bowl clean, and tucked it aside near the window. Then she hung her head over the edge of the bunk so she could see everyone.

The young mage sighed. "It's either that, or clean feathers for his pillow."

"Teaches you patience," Sai said.

"But you said to never use magic for trivial tasks!"

"My pillow is not trivial." Sai snorted. "If I have to explain to you *why* I am telling you to do this, you clearly are not ready for anything more delicate."

Well, after all this time around mages, Delia could certainly think of lots of reasons why Sai would have set that task for his apprentice. Likely it had something to do with learning how to use very, very small amounts of magic energy with fine control. Or it might be it was meant to make Ven figure out an efficient way he could clean lots of feathers at once. But she wasn't going to say anything unless he asked her. Not out of spite! She liked Venidel quite a lot. Sai might seem whimsical, but he never did anything without a very good reason.

Endars snickered just a tiny bit, and Jonaton snorted. "I've been there before. He's tricking you into figuring out how to do it more efficiently. More feathers, more finesse, the same power," Jonaton said. "If you can't figure out your *own* spells, you'll be an apprentice forever."

Venidel hunched his shoulders sheepishly, but said nothing more than, "Thanks, Briada. I'll be fine with morning."

"And Delia is helping me with delivering your midday food, so let's give her late afternoon," Sai ordered. Delia was going to object to his heavy-handed orders, but he was right. She used her borrowed horse to go up and down their abbreviated barge-string to get everyone's food to them, then would chase after Ivar with his and Bay's share. Bay was quite a good dog about feeding himself, but mastiffs didn't have heavy coats, and he needed food to keep himself warm.

I suppose someone could make him a coat. Can mastiffs wear boots? The cold must hurt his feet.

"Well, that's sorted, then," said Hakkon. "Amethyst, is there anything else we should know about from the main caravan?"

"Just that the different sections took it on themselves to pause so that everyone could be one single convoy again," Amethyst said sweetly.

"That was the Dolls' idea, wasn't it?" Sai cackled.

Amethyst bowed her head a little. "Yes, Sai, it was. And we coordinated it. It seemed best, for many reasons, for Baron Kordas to return triumphant to those he defended. We are also discussing what the forest might be, but we have come to no conclusions yet. We are very handicapped by being in these bodies. We are even hampered by physical bodies from speaking to free *vrondi*. It is by no means impossible, but it is difficult."

"Yes, yes, those wretched Impie mages wouldn't have wanted you to be able to warn other *vrondi* about their trap, now, would they?" put in—Bret Fairweather, surprisingly.

"They wouldn't have wanted you to be able to talk to the captive Earth Elemental child, either," Endars speculated. "Hmm. You know, if it isn't all tangled up in the magic that keeps you imprisoned in those shells, if it's just a blocking spell laid on top of everything else, I might be able to fix that. I'm not bad at anything involving communication."

"*Not bad!*" Sai cackled. "False modesty, you old rat. Doesn't look good on you."

Endars made a dismissive motion. "I'm not you or Ceri."

"No, and thank the gods you aren't! If we were all alike, Kordas wouldn't need half of us!" Sai was very pleased with his joke, but Delia was intrigued.

"What can you do, Master Endars?" she asked.

"At the top of my list, I can work out spells that will allow you to talk to anything that has a language," he said. "I already have a lot of spells that will do that—I can summon and speak to wild *vrondi*, for instance—but if I don't have a spell already, I can construct one."

"Can you teach someone how to speak with dogs?" Ivar asked, suddenly very interested.

"The dismissive answer is that dogs don't have a language. The actual answer is that the language consists of body position, movements, scent, and very few words, of which the most important are 'food,' 'water,' 'love,' 'angry,' 'kill,' 'yes,' 'no,' 'good,' 'bad,' 'there,' 'here,' and the most important one of all, *'HEY!'*"

That broke them all up, and Bay, up in the prow on the floor, looked up expectantly, then stood and wagged his rump. Amethyst fished him a soft bone section out of the soup pot and gave it to him. He wolfed it down happily, and lay back down.

"I think I will take a pass on that, then," said Ivar, still chuckling. "Bay knows he's a Good Boy."

Bay wagged again.

"I think everyone speaks enough dog for both parties to understand each other—dogs speak 'honesty,'" Endars mused. "But a lot of what we think of as 'spells' are actually 'language.' Some forms of language can't be fully understood without a matching body shape, too. Bay there expresses a lot with his tail, the angle of his hips, the height of his ears—there is a lot that humans like us just can't express back without an amazing costume. We lack the body parts to 'speak' with." He looked up and around, seeing virtually nobody was following him. "Other than that, I am the second-best scryer after Sai, and I can, with difficulty, set up something between two people that acts like Mindspeech."

"You haven't mentioned the *most* important other than your language spells," Sai chided.

"Well . . . I don't know that it works every time . . ." Endars temporized.

"It's worked every time you tried it," Sai countered. He cocked his head to one side, looking rather like a cat that was excessively pleased with itself. "He can trigger Mindspeech in people who have the potential for it."

Delia's jaw dropped. She didn't know *much* about Mind-magic, but really, nobody did. In the eyes of the Empire, it was a very inferior set of Talents, so the Emperor had not even bothered with collecting people who possessed it. She had never, ever heard that there was any reliable way of triggering it.

"Can you do it with any other kind of Mind-magic?" she stammered.

Endars shrugged. "Never tried," he admitted. "But when Kordas ordered that everyone with Mindspeech be identified, so when the Dolls leave us we'll have a reliable form of talking across distances, I told the Healers that if they found people with the potential, I'd talk to them and find out if they wanted that potential to become a reality."

"You didn't just trigger them and put them on a list?" Briada asked incredulously. "That's how the Emperor would have—" And then she stopped. "But we're not the Empire, are we."

"Exactly," Endars said. "And may we never be. Something like this—something that needs careful training to use, something that they might not *want* in their lives—I'm giving people a choice. And

I don't do it unless we have someone who knows how to handle the Gift available to help them train."

"And Kordas wants it to stay that way," Sai added. "We spoke privately recently, and he spoke from his heart. He said he never wants anyone, as he put it, 'used up, pushed out, or abandoned.'"

Briada glanced over at her cousin. He snickered.

"We're the Fair Baron's men now. Told you we weren't playing by Imperial rules anymore," he said smugly.

She shook her head. "Well, fuck me, we certainly aren't."

16

There were fat snowflakes in the air as Ivar appeared in the distance, coming from between two low hills. Delia's heart sank, because it wasn't even midmorning yet, and it was much too soon for him to be returning to the barges. *What new horrible thing has he found that we need to deal with?* was her first thought, as she signaled to Briada that she wanted to stop the baton drill and shaded her eyes with her hand, trying to see his face.

He doesn't look worried.

In fact, he looks cheerful!

Surely he hadn't found a place for them all to live out here? The landscape had not been promising: no sign of dwellings, or much of anything else. The rocks were twisted, when they came across outcroppings. Some were six barge-lengths tall, and all in layers that either formed skyward spirals, or had peeled off and smashed to bits. Some even stuck out of the river randomly. Furlong after furlong of scrub grass and brush fanned out in unexplained

geometry behind the thin screening of trees lining the riverbank.
Most of those were willows, but even they had odd colorations like
sky-blue trunks or orange-spotted branches and roots. Enormous
stacked fungi were hosts to what she hoped were only ant colonies.
She was no expert, but despite the strangeness, and hopefully with
a lack of toxins and monsters, this could be fine country for goats,
possibly for sheep, and wintering. But without a mage to encourage
grass growing it would not be good for cattle or horses, and at least
to her eyes it didn't look like good farmland, either.

"Amethyst," Ivar said as soon as he was in range for easy talk.
"Please tell Kordas and the rest that we're going to have to consider
whether or not we are going to stop for the winter now, and I think
I have found a good place to do so."

"It is done, Ivar," Amethyst replied, and paused, shaking her
head. Because the Doll was only cloth, stuffing, and fabric, there
was nothing to melt the snowflakes that fell on her, and every so
often she would shake her head vigorously to get them off her
"hair." "Kordas says to proceed to this place you have found,
then report in practical detail. They will catch up. The lead of the
convoy is less than a day behind us, because the convoy sections
went through the forest so quickly."

"I've found a good mooring spot that will hold all of the barges
of the entire flotilla, if we stack them tightly with noses to the bank
and build a heavy jetty just upstream. That many boats will cause
noticeable drag on the current and nothing good will come of that,
so a current-break would be vital or we'd be chasing down boats
every day," he said, and turned Manta around. He didn't urge her
into anything faster than a walk, however, and kept Manta shoulder
to shoulder with Tight Squeeze, Buttercup, and Alberdina's horse,

Dandylion. "Sai!" he called, and Sai popped out of the door in the front of the lead barge.

"Did you find us another man-eating forest?" Sai asked. Delia shivered, and told herself that it was because of the cold. It wasn't. Sai joked about something that could have taken her Kordas away.

"No, but I found a good place for all of us to moor up for the winter if Kordas wants to do that," Ivar replied. "It's the best I've found so far. It's not ideal, but I think we can make it work." Ivar turned his head a little sideways and looked up at the sky, which was gray from horizon to horizon. "In my opinion, we need to pick a spot, and soon."

He wasn't the only one with that opinion. Every morning for the last three, they'd had to break ice away from the barges before they left, and the lead barge—a fore-barge, to be more precise, because it was built to break the way for flatnosed barges with its pointed prow—now had a sharpened iron blade affixed to the prow to break through ice forming on the river. It wasn't very sharp—you'd have had to work hard to cut yourself on it—but winter was definitely here, and it was only going to get colder and travel more difficult. They'd had it very easy, weather-wise, so far. It would not be a good idea to be moving during a blizzard.

"Well, we should make sure to get a good spot," said Sai, and laughed. "Only the *best* spot for the Old Men!"

"The most comfortable place in the land, central to everywhere!" Endars chimed in.

"The Great Old Farts in their Fortress of Comfort!" Ivar added.

Delia surmised that what they would *actually* do was figure out how much of the bank would be taken up by all the barges in the entire convoy nestled side by side, moored to the bank, and stop only when they had passed that point. The barge with the rest of the Old Men would be in the lead of the convoy, so finally the Six Old Men would be reunited.

Well, Ivar will have us stop. He's the one in charge of where and when we stop.

"Actually, I do have a good spot," the scout told him, with half a smile. "There's trees enough to cut the wind—trees as we know them, that is, despite having white bark—and a place that would make a good firepit, and even a spot for an earthen oven."

"You just want something besides soup," the old man chided, waggling a finger at him.

"Don't you?" Ivar countered.

Sai didn't answer, he just popped back into the barge where it was warm.

Wordlessly, Briada jerked her head at the door at the prow, and Delia nodded. She took both batons, and followed Briada inside.

It really was not too bad in here, with the soup filling the air with a pleasant herbal aroma—unfortunately, it smelled better than it tasted, but that was hardly Sai's fault. He was doling out herbs and spices with great care, because once they were gone, there was no way to replace them. No one dared waste any.

Alberdina was in charge today of making sure the soup was stirred at intervals, and that the fire didn't get too hot and burn the soup. Delia had already Fetched enough rabbits to feed everyone for luncheon tomorrow, so after her practice with Briada, it would have been her turn to keep an eye on the soup. Except it sounded as if they were going to moor up soon.

"Kordas wants us to stop at a place Ivar found and let the rest catch up," Briada told the Healer before Delia had a chance to say anything. "I don't suppose you're Landwise?" She sighed. "It would be great if this turned out to be the place we're actually looking for, but only someone Landwise can tell us that."

"I'm not, but Endars is," Alberdina replied. "I won't lie to you, the colder it gets, the more worried I become that Kordas will push us past the point where it would have been wise to stop, and backtracking a fleet upriver feels like more than we can handle." She put the lid back on the pot. "We haven't even had to face rough water, much less a storm."

Delia refrained from saying something like *Kordas wouldn't be that stupid or careless*, because really, determining that involved a very big unknown. How soon would the river ice start seriously impeding progress? That was the real question.

If it hadn't been so bleak out there, Delia would have gone back on deck to see where they were and what the landscape was like. But as sharp as her curiosity was, the wind was sharper, and she was happy enough to climb into her bunk and peer out the little window there instead. It was a limited view, but truly, there wasn't much to look at.

To her pleasure, this side of the river looked more promising than anything she had seen so far since they left Crescent Lake.

I wish we had never had to leave the lake, she thought wistfully. *We could have used all this time we've been traveling to prepare and stockpile for winter.*

But she already knew there wasn't enough farmland for everyone at the lake. It was just a fact, and there was no getting around it.

It appeared that this was a wide valley between two sets of hills. The hills on the far side of the river were closer to the water, and from here, it did look as if there were cave openings here and there. There were actually groves of trees close to the feet of the hills on their side, and instead of unprofitable scrub, weeds, and brush, there was grass, and plenty of it. It looked as if it would be waist high if it wasn't frost-killed and a bit flattened. Well, where grass that tall would grow, grain and other crops could grow.

"There's grass!" she said aloud, and Alberdina came into the rear to look through her window.

"So there is, and that's a blessing," she agreed, and went back to minding the soup. "Even if all we do is winter-over here, the mages can keep the grass growing all winter long, and the stock will do fine."

The practice session had come to an end before Delia even got her muscles warmed up, so for once, she wasn't sweaty and tired. As she lay curled up next to her window, peering out of it and very much liking what she saw, she realized that for the first time in more days than she could count, she was actually on her soft bed, in the warmth, and she didn't have to *do* anything. This was the closest she had come to a lazy, do-nothing, cozy moment since they'd left the Duchy.

The barge didn't seem to be going as fast as it usually did—not that the pace was *fast*, but it was certainly a brisk walk for long-legged horses like Tight Squeeze, Buttercup, and Dandylion. This was more like an amble. With a sigh, she jumped down out of her bunk to see if there was something going on she needed to know about.

Chunks of ice in the water, and ice about a third as thick as her thumb clinging to the bank, told her *exactly* what was going on. The river was slower and much broader here than it had been on the other side of the hills, and while the horses weren't having to pull as hard against the current, the lead barge was definitely having to break through ice.

I think that this is our sign. The ice is just going to get thicker and harder to break through from this point.

Hopefully Kordas will see this, too.

For the first time since they had left Crescent Lake, Kordas, the Old Farts, and his informal Council of the head of his Guard, several mayors, and a couple of Healers were all together in the same place.

One could generously even call that place a "building."

Ivar had commandeered a work crew consisting of a couple of mages who were part of the grass-growing crew, and a motley lot of strong, bored young folks, and had created this place around a dead hardwood tree, which formed the first of many structural columns. He got the mages to thaw and soften the ground, had the labor crew dig it down to about waist deep, then ringed the circumference with upright saplings and slim branches placed so closely together it would have been hard to put a leaf between them. Then he used dead grass with mud made from the earth that had been dug out, and plastered those saplings inside and out until they formed a strong wall as thick as Hakkon's thigh. The mages worked on drying and strengthening that wall until Kordas was quite sure it would stand up to a Poomer attack. Then Ivar built a support structure for a peaked roof out of tree trunks about as thick as a good piece of firewood, working around the center pole of the dead tree. He laid more branches over that structure—some kind of pine, by the looks of it, with thick needles—and plastered over that with more mud and grass, but this time only as thick as Hakkon's bicep. There was a hole in the middle of the roof to let smoke out. And right now, a roaring fire, ringed in stone, fed gray smoke up through that hole. Outside, Briada commanded a crew completing a rudimentary palisade—uneven, but a start. It could become firewood if needed, but as a defensive measure, it would help channel threats through its wider gaps or hold bigger things out.

It certainly wasn't an elegant "building," and it was nothing at all like the manor, but it was a place where a lot of people could gather in relative comfort. With night falling soon, it was a palace for everyone who fit inside.

People had dropped off various things that could be used as chairs here—mostly pieces of sawn tree trunk. Convenient if the fire needed feeding. But the Old Men were not minded to sit on uncomfortable pieces of raw wood, so the Dolls had each brought the sitting pillows they used back at the manor. And Isla had come up with a neat folding wooden chair for Kordas, brought by a clerk who had inherited it with his pen sets.

Probably the closest thing I am going to find to a chair of state right now.

"Well, I've had all the Landwise checking this place to see if it will do for a permanent settlement," Kordas said, when everyone had settled. "And I'll cut straight to it: it's not."

Groans came from those who were not yet privy to that information.

"It floods in the spring, every spring," he continued. "If you've got good eyes you can see the water marks on the bluffs on the other side of the river. The Landwise say it should be all right over winter, but that we'll want to get out before those floods come."

The farmers among them nodded agreement. "Horses and cattle can't take constant wet feet at all, even if it's only standing water," someone spoke up. "We'll lose 'em to thrush. If the current's slow, pigs and goats might manage to walk around in it if it's knee-high to a man, but sheep—their fleeces will just suck up water and they'll drown."

"Well, shear——" began one of the mayors.

"And they'll die of cold," came the flat response. The speaker did not add *don't be daft*, but it was certainly implied in the tone of the response. "Come spring, there's no telling if it'll be warm or drop snow. And night will still get cold."

"On the other hand, this is a good place to winter," offered Ceri. "We have plenty of forage, and we can haul the barges onto the shore *and* put them back in the water with relative ease here."

"Spring flood might put 'em back for you," observed the same speaker, who didn't seem to suffer with awe for Kordas at all.

"I'd hope it wouldn't come to that," he replied. "And we do have a weather-witch or two to keep us apprised of what the weather is about to do. We can take our chances and continue on, but it will be with no guarantee we'll even find a place as good as this, much less an ideal spot, before ice keeps us from going any further. We can also risk putting the barges on runners—"

"I thought that was the plan," interrupted another of the mayors.

Sai snorted. "That was a *contingency* plan, Harkin. If we found ourselves with no prospects as good as this one."

"The wind is going to cut right along the river," Kordas continued. "There is a lot of open space, which is good for grass but bad for keeping warm. We don't have barns for the animals to shelter in."

"But if we go on," Sai continued, "we still won't have barns, we may not have grass, and the wind is still probably going to be wicked."

They pondered this for a moment.

"I say we stay," said the farmer who had spoken up first. *"But!"* He held up a finger. "Send Ivar and the Fairweathers downriver some more with one barge. If they don't run into anything better within a couple days, they come back."

Endars coughed. "I'm Landwise, and I can spirit-ride birds. I could—"

"Nay, lad," said the farmer, who was not that much older than Endars. "I druther you rode that bird a-watchin' for trouble."

Kordas explained to anyone present who needed to know, "Spirit-riding an animal like a bird is delicate, sensitive work. Can't be done while in motion, and takes preparation. If we settle in here, we can build a place to shelter and monitor him, and he can scout for us once in a while."

Well, he's going to be our overhead watchbird for as long as we stay here, I think.

A mayor Kordas recognized, Hale Lorant, cleared his throat and got everyone's attention. "This may not be the best place, but it's a good spot. Now, I'd like some sort of shelter over the barges, and I'd like some sort of shelter for the herds, but other than that, this place looks good, and we've got enough food to see us all the way into high summer without starving. Come spring, this place might have grown on us, or we might find a way to keep back the floodwaters, but it's good enough for now."

Koto cleared *his* throat. "We've got ways of throwing up something that's shelter against rain, snow, and wind in a hurry," he said. "Or *some* of us do. We can have simple barns up in a few days."

Well, that certainly got their attention. *"How?"* blurted about half a dozen people at once.

"The same way the Emperor's mages build Ducal, Baronial, and Princely manors," Kordas said, trying not to feel too smug. "It will be fast because I'll have every mage working on that right now, and the walls won't be but a fraction as thick as manor walls. They'll be like tents, but rigid, and proof against a gale." He didn't bother to explain that the only reason they could do this was because there was a nice, steady ley-line right beneath them. It wasn't as powerful as the one at Crescent Lake, but it could certainly empower his mages to create those shelters.

"There's no fences," argued someone else. "How are we going to keep the herds from wandering without fences?"

"The same way we keep them from wandering now. Are you daft, or just stupid?" Ponu snapped. He'd been one of the people building this earth shelter, and Kordas knew he had to be tired, hungry, and in great need of lying flat in a bed.

"But—"

And they were off. Kordas sighed, and reined in his temper, although Ponu threw up his hands and stormed off to his barge and his bed. This was not the first time he'd brought his "Council" together, and he knew from experience that they just had to argue each and every point to death before they'd finally look to him for answers, usually without another question.

But it was tedious, and he didn't in the least blame Ponu for leaving. As usual, Rose was right at his elbow, and he touched her lightly so that she'd bend down to hear his whisper. "Would you see to it that the evening meal is brought here?" he asked. "And something besides water to drink, if we can spare it."

She nodded without replying. *I'm getting awfully fond of Rose. It's going to be hard when I have to do without her.*

But the arguing carried on for longer than he had anticipated, and *his* nerves were starting to stretch. A glance outside showed snowflakes in the gloaming.

Boom!

He literally jumped. Louder than the loudest thunderclap Kordas had ever heard, the sound shook the walls and sent dirt and dead needles showering down on their heads. *What—?*

Everyone else but the Six Old Men appeared to be frozen in place.

He burst through the entrance—cleverly, it was L-shaped, so there was no way a cold wind could blow directly into the structure—and into the shock of the twilight cold. He could scarcely believe his eyes.

There was a Gate downriver, where the last of the scout-barges were moored. It was the biggest Gate he had ever seen in his life, rivaling even the Emperor's cargo Gates at the former Palace.

A spike of genuine fear held him for a moment. *The Empire. They found us,* he thought. *They've come to kill us.*

The Gate was not framed by uprights. It was not framed by *anything.* It spanned an area of riverbank wide enough to fit six carts side by side, and was correspondingly wide on the river half. Its edges danced, not with the twitch and ebb of uneven magic, but with ribbons of light in diagrams and symbols. One was a series of bright dots: 2, 3, 5, 7, 11, 13, 17. The second ribbon was 1, 1, 2, 3, 5, 8, 13. *Whoever it is, they're educated,* Kordas thought. *It's not like the Empire to announce themselves like this. They go for "We'll pound you into paste" as a first impression, not "Here's how smart we are."*

He gaped at it for one stunned second before belatedly coming to his senses and gathering power from the ley-line beneath him. He wasn't the only one.

Within moments, Hakkon, Ivar, the Old Men—including Ponu—and as many of his personal guards as had come to their senses assembled on either side of him, weapons drawn or hands at their sides, ready to respond.

The air stilled, and snowflakes the size of a silver piece drifted down around them. Nobody made a sound. Even the lapping of water from the river seemed muted and distant.

The Gate was opaque from Kordas's side, and lights on its surface formed into designs. Circles, ovoids, triangles, and a series of patterns that Kordas identified as basic spell construction notation, though much different from what he knew. Fog—genuine fog, not illusory— blew through the edges of the Gate. At the top center, many small lights gradually collected into one bright one, forming beams that swept across, well, everything. They illuminated the entire flotilla, where people by the thousands were popping out to get a look at whatever had made that boom and then lit up the night.

The large light was surrounded by a ring of blue light, which gradually erased itself. When it was gone, another set of bright lights appeared and flooded the shore with crisp, clean white light, and another blue circle appeared, dwindling like the previous one. When it vanished, fog formed everywhere that was lit. It was fog from an area of gradually building warmth, melting frost and snow away.

Another blue circle counted down. When it vanished, easily six hundred mage-lights streamed out from the Gate's edges and took up positions over the flotilla. Another stream of mage-lights took up places six horselengths from the ground around Kordas and the Council, and the temperature was now noticeably warmer. In fact—it was now very lightly raining. Snow alighted on an invisible dome of energy over them, and became warm misting rain. Arcs of rainbow shone in circles around every mage-light, great or small, that was inside the perimeter of warmth and haze. A deep rumbling sound akin to an incredibly large horn came from the Gate. The Gate's background color turned searing red, and the sound's pitch went higher with each color change up to ear-piercing violet, then faded away. Dogs and other animals complained in response, and most of the people witnessing this strange show rubbed at their ears.

At either side of the Gate, colors changed in repeating patterns—rainbow colors, red to deep violet, Kordas numbly noted—while a blue circle counted down, and then there was another flash.

Kiyer! Kiyer! Kiyer! Kiyer!

He heard it the same time as he spotted it—a golden eagle, a *huge* bird, not the size of the terror-birds but surely twice as big as any eagle he had ever seen before, burst out of the Gate, just as it cleared to show what was beyond. Still blinking from the flash, Kordas witnessed more birds flying from the Gate into the night. Hawks, eagles, owls, falcons, ravens, and more. All unusually large, all calling an "I am here! I am here!" call for their species. As if orchestrated by a master, they all went into the sky at increasing heights, circling above the well-lit warm patch in a layered formation. The Gate's opacity shimmered away.

Walking figures were silhouetted on the other side of the Gate by similar lighting on the other side, and as one, they stepped through.

Twenty people. Male, female, some white-haired, some dark, some half-and-half, some with extraordinary headdresses and hats. *White hair from magic use?* He'd heard that had happened to very powerful mages like the Six, but never as young as these people seemed to be. Golden skin, and costumes like nothing he had ever seen before—except maybe on those Dolls whose owners liked to dress them up in fanciful outfits. Or maybe one of Jonaton's more outlandish get-ups. They walked unwary and unhurried, and something itself like a barge glided through behind them. In midair. It was clearly laden, but it was anyone's guess as to what it bore. *In midair,* Kordas marveled. *No horses or mules, and it's in midair.* More birds poured through the Gate, all of them at least twice the size of "normal" birds of their kinds, and they came to rest on the earthen building or the trees around it. It was very clear to Kordas that they had done so to put themselves in a watchful guard over the Valdemarans below them.

Or put themselves into a position to attack . . .

None of the men-at-arms still held their weapons up at this point. What good were arrows and axes against—that? The people strode through the Gate, bringing themselves within ten paces of Kordas.

One of the people at the rear of the group barked a single word and made a gesture in the air, as if he was closing his hand around something.

The Gate's edges broke up into clouds of small lights, which then flickered up like embers from a bonfire to join the stars. When they had gone, the Gate closed.

One man, with silver hair and pale blue eyes, lips and eyelids painted to match his hair, stepped right up to Kordas. His outfit was made entirely of small pieces of brown leather sewn in an intricate pattern of patches and folds. Over his shoulders was a cloak made of bearskin, but it must have come from a bear bigger than anything Kordas had ever seen, judging by how deep the fur was, and how large the skin. The man could have used the skin as mattress *and* blanket, and not ever felt a draft.

Then again, they do grow things big around here, don't they. Good gods. I don't know what to say. He can't know our tongue. I don't dare touch him to learn his. How the hell am I going to keep two dozen insanely powerful mages from vaporizing us all in the next couple of moments?

"Greetings, Kordas, Baron of Valdemar," the man said in a pleasant tenor as if he was a Valdemaran native. "We are the *Tayledras*. We have much to say to you."

Kordas should have found that more chilling than the ice on the river, but instead, relieved, he found himself smiling.

Council and Hawkbrothers alike retired to the shelter. Or rather, Kordas numbly led the way; the Hawkbrothers called down their extraordinary birds to special perching-staffs retrieved from the floating skiff, and followed him into the days-old building. The Councilors, or at least, those who managed to overcome their trepidation at being in the presence of these folk, followed behind them.

And the moment Kordas ushered them inside the rough shelter with its pounded earth floor and ceiling that rained a bit of fine dust down over them all as the birds outside settled on it, he felt acutely ashamed. Whoever, whatever these people were . . . they were powerful, sophisticated, and he felt like a cowherd at an Imperial banquet. He cleared his throat. "I'm terribly sorry, but—"

The leader stopped him with a gesture. "Don't be. This is a proper building for someone who is not going to remain long. It serves the purpose, and when you are gone it will melt into the land again."

Kordas looked around for some place where the newcomers could sit, but before he could say anything, a stream of Dolls poured into the building, carrying skins, small rugs, cushions, stools, chunks of tree trunk, cushions—they must have raided every barge nearby for seating arrangements. And once they had placed their objects at the side of the fire where smoke was least likely to blow into a person's eyes, they streamed out again, as silently as they had arrived. With quiet murmurs of appreciation, the Hawkbrothers arranged themselves on the ground, and the Councilors—rejoined by Ponu—worked out seating on what had become Kordas's side of the fire. And as soon as everyone was in place, the Dolls appeared again, with food and steaming jugs and a motley assortment of mugs and cups.

The leader raised his cup to Kordas. Kordas raised his in return and sipped.

Well. Someone broke out the good *mead. And someone else broke out the spices and mulled it.* Isla. It had to be.

He looked up to gauge his guests' reactions. Nods, slight smiles, and murmurs in a language he could not understand, but which sounded appreciative.

"More light, I think," said the leader. "And perhaps heat."

Each of the Hawkbrothers held out a hand, palm up. A mage-light the size of a child's ball appeared in each of those waiting palms. As one, the lights rose into the air and formed a circle over the heads of the crowd, with the center formed by the roof centerpole. They went high enough that no one was dazzled by the light, which shone down on them all like the light from a clear morning. And as soon as they were in place, something more came from those spheres. Heat. Very, very welcome heat. Soon it was as warm as a fine spring day inside the shelter.

"I trust you realize we have come in peace," said the leader, with a wry lift of his left eyebrow.

"If you hadn't, I suspect you could have done something quite fatal to myself and my Council without ever opening that Gate," Kordas responded, echoing the other's lifted brow.

The leader of the Hawkbrothers chuckled. "Well, we probably could, though to be honest, it would be much easier to let the land itself whittle you away to nothing. You have been lucky so far. The *wyrsa* who followed the fading taste of the charms you put on the beasts you left with Haymouthton are inbred and dying out. The *maka'ar* you drove off your caravan are as well. But you are venturing into territory much more dangerous."

He paused, and Kordas heard his Councilors whispering to one another. His mind buzzed with uneasy thoughts. Were they telling the truth? Were they lying? *But that forest . . . if it had awakened while one of our groups was in it . . . are there more places like that ahead?* What did they want? If they were telling the truth and the territory ahead was going to chew them up and spit out the pieces, then why come to warn the Valdemarans—

"We have been watching you since you . . . drew our attention with your Gate that brought you into the remains of that ancient city destroyed by the armies of the tyrant Ma'ar. It was a rather noisy arrival," the leader added wryly. "And we were concerned. Very. But you engaged in none of the behavior that we feared, and you determined to leave behind you only so many of your folk as the lake and land could comfortably bear. So we were heartened by this, and we set a watch and a few spies on you."

"The *arrows*!" exclaimed Ceri, snapping his fingers. "The arrows that killed the snake-dogs—*wyrsa*, you call them? The ones of unknown origin!"

"Even so," agreed the leader. "You drove off the *maka'ar* rather handily, and we did not need to assist. But the Blood Forest . . ." He shook his head. "You were lucky. Very lucky. Lucky that it had gone into winter sleep. Lucky that when you did awaken it, you were mostly through it. There are many, many more things worse than *that* ahead of you, if you stay on this river."

Kordas's heart sank.

"What's to stop us settling here, then?" said Wymat Rai, not a little belligerently.

One of the strangers' number drew a folding fan and passed it to the leader, who thumbed it open. By some magic, it unfolded itself to form a paper map, upon which the leader traced and tapped positions. "Nothing. But this plain floods every spring, and it is no gradual rising of the waters. There is a place upstream, here, that forms an impressive ice dam. Spring meltwater from the warmer south builds up behind it. When it inevitably breaks the dam, a wall of water taller than a man comes sweeping through this valley." The leader tilted his head to one side. "I can show you, if you require."

"No need," Sai replied before anyone else could answer. "We've seen the marks on the bluffs."

"And how do we know we can trust any of these people? They've enacted espionage upon us already, and revealed themselves in a way clearly meant to impress us with their power," demanded the lone member of the Duchy's highborn on the Council, Lord Ashbern. It was a good question, of course. And even though Kordas winced a little at Ashbern's blunt demand, he was glad someone had asked it.

A Tayledras woman in green and black openly laughed. "That wasn't a show of power."

"Why, because you have the Truthseekers among you, bound into cloth-and-wooden forms," said the leader, gesturing to Rose, who stood patiently at Kordas's elbow. "What say you, Truthseeker? Is not all I have said thus far nothing but naked truth?"

"It is," Rose said in her high, clear voice.

Once again, the Councilors whispered urgently together. But Kordas sensed a change in their attitude. After all this time of having the ever-helpful Dolls among them, the people of Valdemar had come to trust them, and rely on their word when they said that something was true.

"And that is the last reason why we have sought you out, and come to speak with you," the leader continued. "As I said, we have kept a close watch on you, and it is what people do when no one is observing that tells what they really are made of. *You* are not the ones responsible for their imprisonment. *You* have made sure they are treated well, and fairly. *You* have promised their freedom once you learn how to free them. You, Kordas, Baron Valdemar, could have chosen many paths once you arrived at the lake. You did your best to choose the path that did the most good—or at least, the least harm. And so—here we are."

"Well, pardon me for saying this, but . . . where is that, exactly?" Kordas asked carefully. "We don't know anything about *you*, and you certainly seem to know a great deal about us."

"Then let me rectify that. I am Silvermoon k'Vesla, leader of my clan. These are all of the Elders of k'Vesla. This place you have stopped will be safe enough, if uncomfortable, for the winter. But you are looking for a *home*, not merely a stopping place. We may be able to supply you with that home."

Well, that certainly set the ferret loose among the bedsheets.

Silvermoon—and Kordas—waited patiently for the hubbub to die down. Kordas *thought* he even caught Silvermoon giving him a tiny nod as the Baron said nothing. Meanwhile the Hawkbrothers remained quiet, calm, as serene as their leader. Finally all of Kordas's people talked themselves out, or hoarse, and settled again.

"There is always a price for everything," Kordas said into the silence. Of course he knew that. Everyone who had ever been under the Imperial thumb knew that. Favors were contracts in which the expense could be raised later. He caught all of the Six Old Men and eventually the rest of his Councilors nodding.

"And you want to know what the price will be," said Silvermoon, and it appeared, at least to Kordas, that none of these Hawkbrothers took the least offense at his rather blunt statement. "We know all about prices, we Tayledras. You are wise to ask. It will, I think, not be a price that you will find onerous. But—for now, we ask if you are ready for a leap of faith."

"A leap of faith?" Kordas asked cautiously.

"And one into the dark—and we know that this is no small thing we ask of you." He stood up, and all his people stood up with him. He held out his hand. "Come with us, Baron Kordas. Come with us, and bring your chosen experts. If you do not care for what you learn, you are free to continue your journey. At the very least, what we offer you is a more secure place to spend the winter than this valley."

It was not to his Councilors that Kordas turned now. They knew no more than he did, and he was not altogether certain of their emotional state at the moment. They were looking to him to lead them.

But he needed one specific answer.

Rose and the Dolls trusted me, and I think their trust was not misplaced. Now it's time for us to trust them.

"Rose," he said. "Are these people benevolent to our needs?"

"Yes," she said simply. "In this and other matters. Make an ally of them if you can. Cross them never, and let no one mistreat them."

Engage by heart, he thought. *Trust your judgment.*

He stood then, and took the Hawkbrother's hand.

"Open your Gate again," he said, his voice as steady as his own feelings were unsteady. "Without the teeth-rattling noises this time? We will come with you."

17

As it happened, it was too late for travel, and fatigue leaned on everyone. After just having settled in, and with night approaching, Kordas reckoned that people wanted a real meal, some flatbread (if not real bread), and one night when they could sleep securely. He had Rose relay a brief summary to the expedition, so that people could at least try to get some sleep: the Tayledras, or "Hawkbrothers" as their collective name meant, were experts on the area, and came with an offer for a place for the expedition to settle. The Dolls vouched for them, and Kordas and the Council would have news in a few days.

To Kordas's surprise, Silvermoon asked if the Hawkbrothers could spend the night among the Valdemarans.

Maybe they don't want to put an unsupported Gate up so soon after the first one.

"You—what?" he asked. "Surely you—I mean, our hospitality is real, but primitive is too mild a word for what we can offer at this point." Kordas's logistical mind began trying to figure out how he could switch people around to get enough beds in barges, who would cooperate and who would not.

But Silvermoon was not in the least perturbed. "Oh, we are hardier souls than you think we are. If this building of yours is not needed tonight, we will sleep here."

Good gods. Well . . . "Rose," he said aloud, "Can we get enough Dolls to help make this place comfortable?"

"That's easily done, Baron," Rose replied calmly. "Will the birds be inside or outside, Silvermoon?"

"Outside until nightfall, then inside, I think. Even the owl. Thank you, Truthseeker." As the last of the Councilors—except for the Six and Jonaton—left the building to spread their own versions of this unexpected development, Silvermoon looked around with every evidence of satisfaction. "I will consult with you, Truthseeker, as to what we will need."

Well, if he's satisfied with wattle-and-daub walls, an earthen roof, and a dirt floor, we can certainly give him those.

"My name is Rose," the Doll said, with what sounded like pride.

"Very well, then. Rose it is." The arch of Silvermoon's eyebrow suggested that he had never heard of *vrondi* taking personal names before, but he wasn't going to comment on it. At least, not just now. "Now, Baron Kordas, if you would introduce me to your Elders?"

Kordas did so, wondering what his mages were making of these people. Meanwhile, the other Hawkbrothers were using barely a trickle of magic to root those support staffs into the earth at the edge of the building, turning them into sturdy and immovable perches that would be up to their birds' weights. Silvermoon, in his turn, introduced his group to the rest, but before he'd gotten past six names, Kordas was already losing track of who was

"Leafdance," who was "Steelstrike," and all the other names, which seemed to consist of "object-action," except when they were "adjective-object." "There are intricacies in our naming," Silvermoon explained, "and our names can change according to life events. Or, in the case of the highly sensitive, our overwhelming moods. These names are sacred to us, but not so sacred they cannot be laughed at. Sometimes, even though their meaning is usually solemn, they're objectively ridiculous. We had a skygazing poet-scout, Wildwolf, who went through an awkward, dramatic stage of life as Moonmoon." A few Tayledras laughed about that, and half the Six snorted and snickered. "They changed it back after a year."

As the Hawkbrothers and Kordas's mages began talking cautiously to one another—inasmuch as the Six *could* be circumspect when met with incredible artists of the craft—Silvermoon consulted with Rose and Isla, and shortly after *that*, Dolls began arriving with things to make the place less uncomfortable to sleep in.

They started with armfuls of bracken laid around the fire at a distance such that it was unlikely a spark or ember would set the stuff aflame, followed by armfuls of dry, cut grass. Then came the sort of sturdy woolen blankets that were issued to the Imperial Army, and then the tanned sheepskins from the culling at the Lake. Last of all, cushions. Silvermoon seemed to be completely satisfied with this arrangement, and Kordas didn't see any sign of objections from the rest of his party.

By this point Kordas was distinctly torn. He wanted to have a very long, serious discussion with Silvermoon about this "place" the Hawkbrothers intended to take them to, but he also had the feeling he needed to show himself to his people to reassure them that he hadn't been taken control of by the Hawkbrothers, and that this offer the Hawkbrothers were making was exactly what they had been hoping for.

Individual Dolls seemed to have assigned themselves to each of the Hawkbrothers, waiting patiently for "their" Hawkbrother to ask them for something. And meanwhile, the "seven" had each zeroed in on one of the Hawkbrothers as well—or perhaps the Hawkbrothers in question had taken the mages aside—and they were already deep in talk.

Silvermoon watched all this unfold with aplomb, keeping his eyes fixed on Jonaton, who in his turn watched Silvermoon very intently out of the corner of his eye. "I think, Baron Kordas," Silvermoon said, when everyone had settled, sleeping places were being laid out with help from the individual Dolls, and a grate with a pot of water on it had been settled at the fire to heat. "I think you should go reassure your people that we have not taken you over, mind and soul, and are about to lead you and them into one of the three Hells."

"I thought there were seven," Kordas replied, hoping he sounded less anxious than he was feeling.

"And six, and nine, three, and thirteen," Silvermoon said, with genuine amusement. "Apparently, hells are not consistent. That could be why they are hells. Go, and return when you are certain your people's hearts are settled."

———

That turned out to be after nightfall, and once the boys were put in their beds—with orders to *stay* there, much to their bitter disappointment—he and Isla put some more bottles of mead into a couple of baskets and returned to the building. By this point the number of mage-lights had doubled, the temperature was shockingly comfortable, and the Hawkbrothers and Valdemaran mages that Kordas knew personally had been joined by a couple of other mages, Delia, Isla, Alberdina, and Hakkon.

I should have known Hakkon wasn't going to stay away. Not with Jonaton here.

Hakkon was doing a remarkably good job of not glowering dangerously over Jonaton's shoulder, as Kordas had known him to do in the past.

The birds were already on their perches, some asleep, the rest fluffed up and blinking at the fire. They had all positioned themselves facing the fire with their tails to the wall, which was probably a good thing, if Kordas's memory of just how far they could "squirt" was correct. There was a correct falconry term for that particular function, he was pretty sure, but he had never been much of a bird person and the word escaped him. They were magnificent, though, even in their relaxed state.

"Ah, welcome back, Baron," Silvermoon said, his voice just loud enough to carry over the murmurs of conversation—some animated, some subdued, but all sounding quite cordial. "And welcome to our temporary hearth, Baroness Isla."

I'll tell you one thing, diplomacy with these Tayledras is so relaxed, I feel like I'm resting. There are secrets and intimations, but no guile in play. I hadn't realized how stilted and aggressive Empire discussions were until I just found myself getting more done in the same amount of time by just talking with these people.

Isla inclined her head graciously. "We brought drink," she said, holding up her baskets. "Dinner will be arriving shortly—no, Sai, you don't need to get up, we're using our cooks."

Sai settled back onto his cushion. "It will be nice to eat someone else's cooking for a change," he admitted, then plunged back into conversation again.

Isla took it on herself to distribute the pottery bottles as equally as she could, reserving one for herself, Kordas, and Silvermoon.

They all sat down under one of the lights on what presumably would become Silvermoon's bed. Isla pried the cork out of the bottle and poured portions into three ill-assorted vessels, and tilted her head at Kordas, indicating he should open the conversation.

Kordas took a deep breath, and shook his head at Silvermoon while exhaling. "Why?" he asked, simply. "The whole story. We have time."

Silvermoon chuckled, tasted the mead, gave it an approving nod, and licked his lips. "I will give you the shortest story I can," he replied. "I take it that although you are far distant from these lands, you were aware of the great wars among mages five hundred years ago?"

Kordas nodded. "We don't know much about them, except that the last two mages effectively annihilated each other, and the resulting Mage Storms did damage for—well, we don't actually know how much distance. A long way, because there are remnants of what happened even in our former lands. We know about Change-Circles too."

"This close to the original site of conflict, there was far more damage than simple Change-beasts and the wreckage of Change-Circles," Silvermoon said gravely.

Kordas felt someone join them, and recognized the person as Delia. She fastened her eyes on Silvermoon's face with every sign of being utterly fascinated by the man.

Well, he's worth looking at. Kordas judged him to be a little older than himself, with sculpted features that were not handsome so much as *striking*, and a nose that would not have been out of place in his eagle's face. He was one of the ones with pure white hair and pale silver-blue eyes. And he had a low, deep voice that inspired confidence.

"In fact," Silvermoon continued, "the damage done, and the terrible things unleashed, scarcely bear thinking about for long, lest they open the way to despair. Now, what do you think about the gods?"

It seemed an odd segue, but Kordas assumed the Hawkbrother had a reason. "Not much. The Emperor—the all-powerful ruler where we came from—didn't discourage worship of things other than himself, but he didn't encourage it either. I've never seen any signs of the hand of any god in anything in my life, so I suppose I don't really think about them at all," he said, hoping Silvermoon would take that for the honest statement that it was, and not an insult.

Silvermoon was not offended. In fact, he laughed. "Well, our Goddess, whom we call the Star-Eyed, is . . . interventionist. It is not uncommon for someone's god to be described as 'loving,' but in our case, it's very true. She *actively* loves us, if you take my meaning. And after we escaped *our* land just before that final catastrophe, and found a place of sanctuary, she offered our people a bargain: the secrets to using power nearly the equal of those two great Adepts, to protect us from the chaos to come, in return for cleansing the lands of the evils that had befallen when the Storms were unleashed. It was a bargain we were happy to make. And that is what we do. We create a protected home-place that we call a Vale, although it is not always in a valley. We consolidate the power of the ley-lines into a source we call a Heartstone, we protect the place behind shields the like of which you have never seen, and we change, weaken, or eradicate all the twisted things within reach of that Vale. When enough has been cleansed, we move on, and generally entrust the remains of the Vale to beings we trust to use it wisely." He quirked his head to the side like a bird. "And in this case, that would be you and your people. *Why* we chose you, and I swear to you on my Star-Eyed's oath, is because your Gate opened almost five hundred years to the day from when we accepted that burden and responsibility from the Star-Eyed, and that—because we *do* have interaction with gods, and they *do* like portents—struck us as significant. But obviously, just because we saw something we considered auspicious, we were scarcely going to gather in people we knew nothing about. So we watched you, spied on you, listened to your conversations when we could. A great point in your favor was your treatment of the Truthseekers, and the fact that you personally were not only not responsible for their plight, but intend to remedy it as soon as you are able." He spread his hands. "There, in short, is your *why*. Your practice, not pretense, of virtue was enough to tell us that you could be good neighbors, and mindful inheritors of our work's bounty."

"Oh." Kordas was at a loss for words.

But Delia wasn't. "Are the lands we were going through supposed to have been cleansed?" she demanded. "Because you left a few things."

To Kordas's great relief, the Hawkbrother just laughed at her words. "No, they were not. Those were mild things, which fled the dangers of what you would face downriver. The creatures you encountered are not sufficient for us to set up a new Vale there. The *wyrsa* and *maka'ar* are dying out, between inbreeding and a lack of a mage to control them and their well-being. The Red Forest—" He hesitated. "If it happened to be part of a greater swath of hazard, we would have dealt with it already. But it is isolated, it sleeps most of the year, and even when awake, it does not seem aware of anything outside its borders. Fire can kill it, and it is still a kind of plant. Disease or fungus could also kill it. So we have left it alone. Sooner or later it will die. We do not lightly cut short the life of any living thing, even a monster, so long as we believe no harm will come of leaving it alone. You never know what will turn sentient out here."

"What *is* it?" Kordas blurted.

"You know about creatures caught in Change-Circles." Silvermoon made that a statement, so Kordas just nodded. "This was, we think, the case of a small aspen grove and a small Earth Elemental caught together in one. Probably at the height of the Mage Storms. Aspens grow from offshoots of their own roots, so every grove, every aspen forest, is actually a single tree."

Kordas shuddered. The Great Earth Elemental that had rescued its child had been a terrible thing—but at least it had been natural. The Red Forest—wasn't. And every bit of his Landwise sense revolted against it.

"If we stay in your Vale and prosper," he said slowly, "I would like to gather a force and put that thing to the torch one day."

Silvermoon slowly smiled. "And because you actually intend to do these things, you have earned our collective respect. What your people will become, we shall feel honored to have helped. I know it, I can feel it." He had another, deeper slug of mead. "We have a joke, *seeit mut, kes'sia'kut.* 'No gods have yet disagreed.' We are a passionate people. We live our lives with urgency, by a philosophy of *kes'ten'tayul'mae*, which means 'accomplishments in action.' One translation is, 'meant to be in motion.' We don't like to linger, in general, out here. We'd rather not live the same ways all the time, and being idle, even for the best of reasons, feels like a loss." Silvermoon held up his cup for a refill, which was obliged.

Is he—is he getting smashed? This is so very not the Empire.

Silvermoon nearly glowed in his near-inebriation. "Here's why I am not a tradesman. We could have held onto the Vale and squeezed anything we wanted from you before giving in. But—we're done Cleansing here for now. We were leaving anyway, whether the Vale was resettled or not. So we figured, you may as well have it, and the fact that you're pleasant people we look at as divine providence."

Silvermoon had another swig, then toasted his cup high, looking upward.

"All of this, this unprecedented event? Is it meant to be? *Seeit mut, kes'sia'kut!*" he howled, and then fell backward, still laughing.

———

Delia hadn't been invited to the gathering of the strangers—but she hadn't *not* been invited either, and no one had asked her to watch the boys. So at her first chance, once her share of the work in the common kitchen was done, she slipped away before anyone could ask her to do anything else.

When she first entered the makeshift building, what struck her before anything else was the *birds*. They were enormous, fierce, and absolutely beautiful; they sat quietly on their perches now, though she knew that they had been off hunting earlier, and the roof of the building was littered with tufts of fur and bunches of plucked feathers—and, quite possibly, some body bits. She hoped that something would come along and clean those off. She wanted badly to touch the birds, to stroke their heads and their soft breasts. But she knew enough about birds of prey to know that was a very bad idea, and when the biggest owl swiveled its head to look fixedly at her, as if daring her to come too close to it, she decided it was probably a good notion to move away from them before they decided they didn't like her. Every other bird of prey she had ever seen had short leashes that falconers called *jesses* on their legs. In the field, any time a bird was not in the air, the falconer had those jesses firmly in his hand. In the mews, they were attached to a leash that was attached to its perch, to prevent them from striking at their feeders and handlers.

There were no jesses on these birds. There was nothing stopping them from lunging at her or anyone else. And the talons on the big ones were bigger than a man's hand.

Fortunately she spotted Kordas and her sister and joined them, just in time to hear that strange and wonderful story of what, exactly, these people were. As outlandish as Silvermoon's story was, she was inclined to believe it. And the Dolls did vouch for what these people were saying as truth.

Silvermoon in particular was an enchanting man. Not in an "I'm attracted to him" sort of way, the way she felt about Kordas, but in an "I can't take my eyes off him or stop listening to him" sort of way. Like a great work of art and a great bard combined into one, she finally decided. His voice in particular was utterly lovely, and she could listen to him talk about nothing for hours and never tire of it.

". . . *Seeit mut, kes'sia'kut!*" Silvermoon declared and fell harmlessly backward, laughing. Everyone around found it comical too, and conversation picked right back up when Silvermoon was upright again. Suddenly it struck Delia—as if a beam of light had lit up an unseen path in front of her and—just like *that*, their trip was complete! She took a moment of simply feeling. *I was there when Tayledras and Valdemarans first met!*

She told herself not to get her hopes up too much. These people might live in caves or trees or something. But at the least there should be a sheltered place to move all the barges, and it sounded like there would be arable land to support them all. *And we can finally stop moving.*

"I hope I don't sound ungrateful," Kordas was saying, "But are you *sure* where you want us to go is going to be able to support all of us? Most of us are farmers, and—"

"You need arable land for farming, and a great deal of meadowland for your herds," Silvermoon said with a chuckle. "Yes, we understand that. We're quite good at counting," he added, wryly. "And at estimating what resources are required for a given population. You will be on this very river, which we call the Ter'i'le'e—which means 'Singing Water'—and very much reminds me of you, Baroness. Strong, melodious, and capable."

Isla laughed. "You should be called Silver*tongue*, my friend."

He smiled, and continued. "There are no other humans here but us, and we trust you will keep a balance between your tame things and the wild things."

Kordas colored a little. "Well, I hope I didn't offend you—"

"Not in the least. So are you prepared for us to open our Gate to you in the morning?" Delia realized at that moment that Kordas had not yet said "yes" to this proposition.

And suddenly she felt so furious with him she wanted to box his ears. *Kordas Valdemar, what is wrong with you? We're heading into the dead of winter in boats, with ice threatening to stop us at any moment and the gods only know what other kinds of horrors there are out here and someone has offered us a sanctuary and now you—*

"Word is spreading, Baron, that we have been offered sanctuary," put in the Doll Rose in her calm voice. "I fear that if you do not accept it, you will not remain the leader for long."

Kordas laughed, a little nervously. "Well . . . there is certainly that consideration."

"I may kill you myself," Isla said in her sweetest possible voice. "I don't mind living in a boat, but there are limits, Kordas."

Silvermoon laughed aloud at that. "Yes, you are like to be called Ter'i'le'e by my people, Baroness, for you hide peril under your tranquil surface."

Kordas ducked his head. "I appear to have no choice," he said, but in an amused tone. Or at least, it sounded amused to Delia. "Yes, and if this is even half as good a place as you have described, I don't know that we will be able to repay you if our settlement lasts a thousand years."

Silvermoon made a wave of his hand as if to dismiss the need for thanks. "You will repay us by being good stewards of what we leave with you."

"Shall I tell the rest to spread the word to prepare for the journey in the morning?" Rose asked.

Kordas sighed. "Yes, please, Rose. I'd rather not turn my lovely wife into a murderer!"

———

Delia stayed up long past the point when she should have gone to bed—but so did Alberdina. Both of them were fascinated with what the Hawkbrothers had to say, and anxious about what Kordas would say in return. Briada had more sense than either of them, and went to bed earlier. "I'll be just as amazed when I'm well rested, I'm sure," she declared. "And I won't fall over anything." Alberdina eventually followed, but Delia stayed, and stayed some more, so when she finally stumbled to the barge through the excited crowds and into bed, she barely did more than take her boots off and wash down her face and hair with her prized fungal towel.

It was just as well that she *hadn't* undressed, after all. After far too little sleep, she was vaguely aware of the barge moving, and a lot of bumping and sounds on the bank, but it wasn't until she heard Briada shout from the front of the barge that she managed to drag herself out of a very confused slumber.

"Get up, ladies!" she heard Briada call through a muzzy sleep-fog. "We're moving!"

Somehow that managed to penetrate the brain fog, and she would have rolled out of bed if she had not remembered she was in an upper bunk.

Alberdina groaned, but levered herself up and moved to one side of her bunk so Delia could scramble down. "It's so dark," Delia complained. She felt for the cap over the mage-light and slid it aside, wincing at the sudden flood of light.

"And now it's too bright," Alberdina mumbled, sounding cross. "I need my tea. I hope the water on the stove is warm."

Delia squirmed around so she could cling to the edge of her bunk and feel for Alberdina's bunk with her toes. When she was finally down, she got her towel and handed Alberdina hers. Like Delia, it appeared that Alberdina had not gotten out of her clothing before she went to bed.

They politely turned their backs on each other and Delia, at least, pulled her shirt up and her breeches down to give herself a good scrubbing, and felt a little more awake when she had done so. The day-old underthings would have to do.

By the time they clambered out of the barge, there was just a hint of light in the east. But they didn't actually *need* that light, because within moments after they exited, that gigantic Gate sprang into being without any warning, and both the Gate itself and a ring around it added about the same light as a weak, overcast dawn to that of the hundreds of mage-lights overhead. Her eyes adjusted easily. There was good-natured shouting from ship to shore all down the line, horses and mules whinnying and snorting, even some laughter mixed with the noises of dogs running and barking.

They'd barely gotten their feet on land when one of the Dolls pulled up the mooring ropes from the land anchors and tossed them to another Doll who was standing on the stern of the scout barge that was usually second in the string. The Doll then loaded the land anchors into their midships cubby. The first and second barges, rather than being tied one after the other, were being rafted, bound up side by side. The Doll on the second barge hauled theirs along and looped it firmly to the prow and stern of the second, then jumped to their barge just as the first Doll pulled up the mooring line of the third, looped it thrice around the timberheads, and brought it to the Doll on the barges. Their efficiency astonished Delia; they worked so fast, and almost as one! Without a word—but with a friendly wave— the team of Dolls moved on to their next task.

In almost no time, all of their barges were tied together, and the first Doll brought Tight Squeeze, Buttercup, and Alberdina's Dandylion and made them fast to the barges while Ivar took the lead rein. Then the Gate "bloomed" with a wash of silver light, and opened, and Ivar chirruped to them, tugging a little on Tight Squeeze's lead rein.

Delia couldn't help but notice that there was no thunderous *boom* associated with the Gate appearing this time. Evidently the Hawkbrothers had a strong sense of what Isla called "theatrics." *Not that we should complain. That was an incredible show. It felt like there were months of planning for it, but there can't have been more than days at most. Unforgettable.*

Since they were going with the current, it was no problem for the horses to get the barges underway, and on the other side of the Gate, Delia saw a number of people waiting for them on the light-flooded bank with personal mage-lights floating above their heads. Most were Hawkbrothers, but she spotted Jonaton, Sai, and Ceri among them, along with half a dozen Dolls and what appeared to be thickly bundled children that darted around.

Messengers, probably. I haven't seen children in over a month, she realized. *This place must be safe indeed for parents to let their kids run around like that! Energetic kids, too. They jump, run, and then vanish like they're tireless.*

And behind her, the Dolls were turning the next string into a raft, just as they had the scouting barges. Behind her she heard the sound of sheep approaching, baa-ing indignantly, and the yips of the dogs herding them toward the Gate. She could have stepped off the riverbank and into the brush to get out of the way, but instead, she trotted toward, and then through, the Gate.

There was the brief sensation of falling, then she found herself stumbling and caught by someone very short, who hadn't been there a second ago. *Tripping over my own feet! What a way to enter our new home!*

The short person, who was so bundled up in furs they looked like a child's toy, quickly guided her over to the side, and out of the way of the horses coming through the Gate with barge raft in tow.

The short person said something she didn't understand, to which she replied, still a bit sleep-fuzzed, "I'm sorry, but—"

And then the person pulled their furred hood back and looked up. It wasn't a human face that looked at her.

It was a snout. She froze.

But before she could react or pull away, a Hawkbrother in mint green moved purposefully toward her. "Relax," the person said in Valdemaran, with a voice that was either a high-pitched male or a low-pitched female voice—or neither, or both—took her left arm, braced her shoulder, and turned her face to theirs. They were more androgynous than *anybody* she'd ever seen! She couldn't tell, if she spent days on it, which gender they began as, nor which they were now. It was a fascinating look, and she'd never seen the like before. She'd seen actors done up in face paint for a part, but this was their own person, not a role. "Relax. There's no special danger here," they went on. "My name is Calmwaters. Take a deep breath."

Calmwaters gently touched her in the middle of her forehead.

What happened next was like no sensation she had ever felt before. Suddenly she was overcome, tumbled and flailing among a wash of *words*, and images she didn't recognize, and sensations so mingled together she couldn't sort them out.

She staggered for a moment, blinded, deafened, and very disoriented. Calmwaters kept a firm hold, and Delia felt that grip as her center, grounded by it, not her feet. She steadied emotionally and physically at around the same rate, and with a roaring sound that abruptly stopped, she heard shouts and chatter in two different languages, and understood *both* of them!

"Better now?" the Hawkbrother asked politely. Calmwaters touched her again at the elbows and shoulders when she nodded. "Good. You may feel like your head is too full for a while, but it gets no worse than that. Ask anyone for me by name if you feel like something is wrong. I'll be here for the next two marks."

"Y-yes," she stammered. "You're beautiful."

Calmwaters smiled at her blush and just replied, "Or at least new. Life is different when you understand the language. Know the language, know the people. I've given you our tongue, and that will help you understand the *meaning* of things here, not just the names." The mint-green woven straps sewn into Calmwaters' outfit told her that they were a Healer, and the charms in a row down the left breast meant skill in bonesetting, painkilling, mental support, and Cleansing—management and removal of magical symptoms. "This is Jelavan. He'll be your guide. He's a *hertasi*. I need to go give more of you folk our tongue." And with that, the Hawkbrother stepped aside as one of the lizards—

—*hertasi*—

—took her elbow and patiently waited, his big clear eyes friendly and eager.

Delia looked down. "Um. Hello, Jelavan," she said, blinking, as the word *hertasi* conjured up an entire world of information about the lizard-folk, who were—

—-the helpers, partners, and sometimes caretakers of the Tayledras. Craftspeople, houseworkers, cooks, valets, they did all the things that servants would, but were not, themselves, servants. They traded their skills for protection among the Hawkbrothers, a bargain everyone was happy with.

"I'm Delia," she finished, as the information settled itself into the front of her mind and made itself at home.

"Greetings, Delia!" Jelavan said cheerfully. "Very sorry we had to wake you all so early, but we want to get as many of your folk on this side of the Gate as we can before we close it for the night. Our mages have to sleep too, you know!"

"Oh! Of course!" she replied, blushing, although she wasn't sure what she had to blush about. "Am I out of the way now?"

"For now," Jelavan said. "Would you like to have a look around before I escort you to where we'll be stacking your boats? Side by side, not on top of one another," he added with what sounded like a laugh. "I should have said 'arranged.' New language!"

"Yes, please." She took a deep breath to steady herself, and peered through the dim morning light. She murmured, mainly to herself, "Three months ago I was a girl in a manor."

"That must have been exciting! I hope you'll tell me all about it," Jelavan replied. It dawned on her—at dawn, she noted—that her breath was not fogging. It was warm here. The ground she was on was dry, but not two horselengths away, there was a blanket of snow. Jelavan reached up, presenting Delia with a orange-and-purple plum.

Snow here but warm; wintery but a ripe plum? If the sun comes up green I don't think I'll be surprised! It wasn't a plum as she knew them, but one bite told her it was delicious, and surprisingly juicy. It must have showed on her face, because Jelavan beamed the most happy, broad smile she'd ever seen. Especially on a lizard face.

The river was about as wide here as it had been where they'd been camped, and hopefully it would not flood *here* in the spring. There were a *lot* of hertasi around, and about two dozen Tayledras. Most of the Tayledras were on the riverbank, and in a moment she saw why. As the "raft" of barges came through the Gate, one tall Hawkbrother would touch the one nearest the bank—

And she gaped as the barges rose up in the air, to about waist high. The Hawkbrother—Calmwaters—who had touched her confronted the Valdemaran driving the horses, and did to the hoggee what he had done to her. The hoggee swayed and flailed, unbalanced, like she had. Then as soon as the drover shook off his confusion, a hertasi stepped up beside him, said something to him, unhitched his Tow-Beast and plow horse and led him and the horses off, away from the river. Meanwhile, the tall Hawkbrother (he must have been a mage) began walking away inland, the raft of barges obediently following him.

She saw immediately why the Dolls had roped the barges together; by doing so, they were getting these "rafts" through the Gate in a fraction of the time it would have taken to bring them through single-file. At this rate, it might only take a couple of days before everyone was on this side!

The opposite shore seemed to be heavily wooded, and mostly pines. Big ones, too; the sky had slowly turned to a dim blueish gray, and they stood against it like row after row of sentinels, somber and dark, but giving off the very *opposite* feeling of that Red Forest. This forest made her feel peaceful, and there was no sense of any kind of a "presence" here. Actually, it was not unlike Crescent Lake.

This side of the river was more welcoming still. There were plenty of trees, and they were giants of their kind, but there were paths among them, and signs of dwellings that somehow blended into the landscape. Despite the early hour, she spotted a lot of odd-shaped patches of yellow light that were probably windows.

The barges were being taken deeper into that inviting landscape; she glanced down at Jelavan, who nodded with encouragement, and she followed the third set of barges and their mage downriver, past the—were they cottages? Houses? Whatever they were, they didn't correspond to any building style she could think of. There were not many straight lines; mostly the houses were constructed of curved shapes blended with tree trunks and sheltered under enormous vines that covered them like the wings of a protective bird.

She took off her coat, aware she was feeling awfully warm. It felt like a morning in late spring! *How can this be?*

The trees ended in a broad meadow, and in the meadow was— well, it looked for all the world as if someone had laid out a city, except no one had bothered to actually build anything. There were straight paths mowed into the turf, and lanterns placed at intervals along those paths. The paths were broad, too, as big as any city streets she'd known, and they curved around among the largest trees. There was birdsong in the air, along with the birds to go with it. Astonishingly to her, great birds of prey shared the sky with birds that should have been their meals, and bolts of bright colored feathers shot by, flitting in straight lines with purpose. The smell of smoke and cooking mixed in.

The area they walked in was longer, running along the riverbank, than it was deep. The tall Hawkbrother steered his "charges" to the rear of the meadow, where hertasi awaited. One jumped up onto the barge nearest to them and began untying all the ropes that had held them together. Taking the mooring ropes, more hertasi pulled and pushed the barges into what must have been a pleasing configuration in their eyes, then dropped the ropes, as if they were "ground-tying" a horse. The Hawkbrother mage lowered his hand, palm down, and all the barges softly settled into the grass. The barge hulls creaked, and the barges that weren't flat-bottomed tilted. The tall mage leveled them with minor gestures, and hertasi streamed in with timber to provide temporary support.

Satisfied with the work, the Hawkbrother ran back to the river, and as she turned, Delia spotted another mage with a raft of barges swiftly approaching. She didn't need Jelavan's urging to get out of the way.

"Where are the herds being taken?" she asked the little lizard.

"I'm not sure," the hertasi said. "But it will be somewhere safe and nearby, with plenty to eat."

I really am getting awfully warm. I want lighter clothing now! The recollection of how warm it had been in the Red Forest provoked a sudden rush of unease.

The hertasi was unwinding himself from a tangle of scarves and coats. "You might want to take your warmer things off. We're behind the Veil here, and we have a spell that is keeping the earth nice and cozy so the grass can grow, and none of you will need fires except for cooking. Fire is all very well, but *I* wouldn't want it in one of those barges with me, especially not when I was asleep. You could so easily be trapped in there if something took flame!"

He has a point. They were *terribly* careful with fire, but all it took was a spark or an ember in the wrong place . . .

"Anyway, would you like to go back to your barge and sleep?" Jelavan continued. "It's down and in place now. You look tired." Jelavan hissed with his mouth open, which she had learned by this point was the hertasi equivalent of giggling one's head off.

As she shifted her sheepskin coat in her arms, she had to admit that the gentle warmth, like a particularly nice spring day, was making her drowsy all over again. She wanted to look around, but the light was still dim, she was afraid she would get in the way of the Hawkbrothers and their helpers that were moving all the barges in to form an orderly arrangement, and she was feeling just a bit stupid with lack of sleep.

"I probably should," she admitted reluctantly. Not even the sight of barges floating through the air, water still draining off from their time in the river, was able to compete with the thought of her bed—and how comfortable and cozy it was going to be, without the need to tend the fire in the stove.

"Your barges are right there at the start of that row," Jelavan said, pointing with a claw at the rearmost rank. "I'm assigned to all of you in your group as your guide, so when you wake up again and have something to eat, just ask for me." Somehow, Delia knew that the hertasi didn't mean to ask *someone*; he meant, ask the air. If Jelavan was in earshot he'd hear, and appear.

"*Gesten,* Jelavan. Thank you very much," she told the lizard with great sincerity, and stumbled through the knee-high grass to where the barges were, with Buttercup, Tight Squeeze, Dandylion, Manta, and the other horses from their string happily tearing up giant mouthfuls of the fresh, tender stuff. There were more towing animals tethered here as well. Evidently these Hawkbrothers were keeping the towing beasts with the barges they towed until someone told them what they wanted to do with the beasts.

The covers over the mage-lights in the ceiling of the barge had been slid back, except in the rear compartment where the bunks were. This time as she readied herself to go to sleep, she peeled off her clothing, wrapped up her smalls in the towel, and threw on her sleeping things before she climbed into her bunk. She fell asleep to the sound of one of the horses tearing up and chewing grass outside her window. Her *open* window, so she could get a fresh, warm, grass-scented breeze in her face.

She didn't sleep for long—by the sun it was probably not quite mid-morning—but it had been one of the most refreshing passages of sleep she'd ever had. She'd forgotten what it was like to *not* feel the motion of the barge, and although there were people who liked the way the barges swayed, she didn't. Especially not when she was just falling asleep, and someone in the barge would move and interrupt the rhythmic rocking.

Based on the balmy air caressing her, when she slid out of her bunk again (being very careful not to wake Alberdina) she put on much lighter clothing and left her coat behind. When she walked out onto the foredeck, there were barges as far as she could see. It was an astonishing sight. They had worked *much* faster than she had ever dreamed they could.

The barges had been neatly arranged in groups, with room for an outdoor kitchen in each group. Sai was already well into getting *his* kitchen set up—most especially the oven for his baking. She jumped down and hurried to help him.

"Ah, bless you, Delia," he said, as she handed him a flat brick before he could reach for it. "Our mages are mostly helping the Hawkbrother mages moving barges. It's going very well! I want my kitchen, though. I never feel quite right without my kitchen."

"Where did you get the bricks?" she asked him, because these were *not* the kind of fire-bricks that had been loaded into the supply barges. These were a different color, and clearly had been used to make ovens before, by the scorch marks.

"Those little lizards brought them to me," he said, and chortled. "Seems they've heard of my bread!"

"You see? I told you your bread was legendary," Hakkon called out as he approached; it looked as if he must have been helping place barges himself, or doing some other manual work, because he was shirtless and there was a sheen of sweat over his muscles. He handed Sai a little woven grass bag, and Delia another. "I brought you two breakfasts. Your first breakfast, Delia. This will be Sai's second."

"I've been working hard, I deserve a second breakfast!" Sai replied. "I took my turn with the barges—glories! The amount of power that Heartstone feeds to a mage is enough to set your hair on fire! But now I want to get us properly settled so we can attend to the business of building a city with houses and gardens. The sooner that happens, the sooner we can start having lives again!"

Did we ever really have lives of our own with the threat of the Emperor looming over us all the time?

"I'm pretty certain everyone here agrees with you, Sai," Hakkon replied. He opened his grass bag, and Delia and Sai opened theirs. Inside was what looked like a large bun, except it hadn't been baked, and was a creamy white in color, with a shiny skin.

Sai sniffed at it approvingly. "Steamed buns! I've heard of those, never got the chance to try them!"

"Talk to the hertasi. They do all the cooking around here, and they'll probably teach you. I'm told they live in tunnels under this place. The Hawkbrothers call it a 'Vale,' even though it isn't in a valley. There's a kind of shield over this entire area that keeps it nice; it keeps the winter out, at any rate. What falls as snow outside falls as rain in here when it passes the shield." Hakkon bit into his bun and Delia saw there was some sort of reddish-brown filling inside it. She took a bite herself. It was a paste, a little sweet, very pleasant. "I'm going to miss that Veil when they go," Hakkon continued.

"Hello, friends! And the Veil will remain for a while." Jelavan trotted up to them, looking very dapper in an outfit of linen and leather that somehow suited him completely rather than making him look like a scaly pet that some child had stuffed into clothing. *Good heavens, it's designed for a hertasi and nothing else.* "We want to make sure you have all the advantages you can while you settle here. Now, I've been sent to bring you to a meeting, Master Sai, and you two if you want to come as well. Otherwise, feel free to look around—"

"Oh, I'm here to move our horses," Hakkon replied. "But Delia, you should go. Tell me everything you can when you get back! See you, Jelavan!"

The hertasi beamed his irresistibly cute grin and heartily waved to Hakkon, sighed happily, then made a welcoming gesture to the ground beside him. "Come, Lady Delia," Jelavan said politely. "We don't want to keep your elders waiting!"

So, although she hadn't had any intention of being involved with this "meeting," Delia found herself following the little lizard as he trotted toward a path among the trees. Every once in a while, soft thap-thap-thapping of hertasi feet would build up behind her and a hertasi would sprint by in a dead run. *These hertasi are hilarious! They have three speeds—slow stroll, steady march, or sprint, and nothing in between!*

I'm going to wake up at any moment and find myself back on the freezing river, while Kordas and his Council argue about whether we should push on or stay where we are. But while I'm dreaming—I'm going to enjoy this.

18

Never in a hundred thousand years would I have thought that I would be best friends with a lizard, Delia thought with bemusement, as she looked down at the top of Jelavan's head. It was amazing and kind of funny how they had fallen into friendship, as if they had known each other all their lives. She'd never had a friend like this; Sai was a surrogate father, Briada was a mentor, Jonaton was an eccentric big brother, but none of them were just friends. Her sister? Well, Isla was old enough they hadn't really had anything in common before she married Kordas, and afterward, that just put more distance between them. Jelavan was a friend who always seemed to know what was going on, and how to explain it to her. She'd been accustomed to servants of all sorts back in the Duchy, but Jelavan was too *fun* to think of as a servant; he didn't come across as a dreary, duty-first type, he was a cheery, everything-gets-done type. Like her scouting team, come to think of it.

It was only two days until the Midwinter Festival. The Valdemarans had been overjoyed to discover the Hawkbrothers of k'Vesla celebrated Midwinter too, and both peoples were determined to celebrate it together. Kordas was in complete agreement. After all they had been through, they needed a celebration!

Delia and Jelavan had been assigned to work on decorations. So now they were busy putting up strings of inedible red berries, pine cones that had been bleached and somehow gilded, and beautiful stars, *tervardi* (beautiful creatures that were humanoid birds) and *dyheli* woven out of gilded grass. As mages moved along the paths and the tunnels underground, they left tiny mage-lights no bigger than a fireflies behind them. All of this was in their spare time, of course, but now that they were no longer on the move, there was more of that than there had been before.

Nearly every day, Delia saw or learned of something new, wonderful, or just odd. The first had been the *dyheli*, graceful creatures that looked like a more refined and much larger version of goats, with a pair of branchless, twisting horns. *They* had taken over the management of the equine, cow, and sheep herds, without even being asked. Somehow they managed to get all of these creatures to drop their dung in corner "latrine" areas so it was easier to collect and drop into compost pits. To Delia's wonderment, some of the dyheli could speak mind to mind with people who didn't even have the power of Mindspeech. She was particularly enamored of the King Stag, Akayla. He was endlessly patient and never seemed to lose his temper. When she'd asked him why the dyheli had taken on the management of everything but the pigs, he had snorted. :*No one sane wants someone's dung on their dinner, no?*: he'd replied. Which, of course, made perfect sense. As for the herds of swine, for the most part they were all living in spacious sties, which was where they liked to be. At least, according to the swineherds she'd talked to. The dyheli had simply "told" them that from now on, they were to relieve themselves only in special "latrine trenches" along the wall at the lowest part of the sty. They were, evidently, perfectly happy to comply. The trenches led to more compost pits. In all cases, a touch of magic sped up the usual process of decay, turning the dung into usable compost over the course of a single day, and keeping the smell to a minimum.

Kordas had been over the moon about this. *I suppose,* she thought, as she hung up a lovely straw star, *that this is not only part of his responsibility to his people, to keep them healthy, it's also in his own self-interest, because he is Landwise, and anything that hurts the land hurts him.*

Meanwhile, the thing that had *her* excited was taking place uphill, at the northern end of the Tayledras compound, near the Heartstone.

They were growing a manor house.

At least, that was what Delia was calling it in her mind, because a manor house was, more or less, what it was going to be in function. Kordas wanted to be able to crowd all fifteen thousand people into it if they were attacked by something they couldn't immediately drive off, and he'd sketched out his basic idea to the Hawkbrothers, who had nodded and said it could be done. *"They won't be* comfortable," Kordas had said. *"But they'll be alive."*

She'd assumed it would be "built," because obviously—but no. The Hawkbrothers had some sort of *thing* already in the ground, a thing that grew buildings, and right now, the roof and most of the top floor were sticking up out of the dirt. She still could not wrap her mind around that concept. A "thing" that *grew buildings*! If the evidence hadn't been up there right in front of her, she never would have believed it. That was why it was near the Heartstone, so the "thing" could take energy from the Heartstone to help it build.

Still . . . as they got to the vicinity of where this building was growing, she paused in her decorating to admire it. It was enchanting. It looked for all the world as if it was a normal building, but one somehow being built upward, rather than from the skeleton of the framework outward and inward. It was going to be quite impressive, with granite walls and a slate roof. Then she frowned as the true size of this building became apparent to her.

"What's wrong?" asked Jelavan.

"This would have to be twenty stories tall to fit fifteen thousand people in it," she pointed out. "Kordas is going to be upset." *Huh. Either I am getting very good at estimating how many people you can pack inside a building, or—maybe I overheard someone saying the same thing and don't remember it?*

"Oh, that's not a problem." Jelavan waved away her concerns with a claw that still held a straw tervardi. "All your people don't have to fit in the building."

She sighed. Jelavan had a habit of wanting to tease things out into conversations that could have taken place in a third of the time. Still . . . it amused the little hertasi, and he deserved some amusement for all his hard work. She had thought the Dolls worked hard, but the hertasi worked harder.

"And why is that, exactly?" she asked patiently.

"Oh, you would learn eventually, so I might as well show you now. It's not as if we've kept it a secret from under you."

Evidently she was getting better at taking hints, because the answer practically leapt out of her mind. "The tunnels! You're going to show me the hertasi tunnels!"

"I am, in fact." Now Jelavan's mouth was halfway open and he was making the little panting sounds that meant laughter. "You are more clever than you look!"

"You're lucky there's no snow here," she retorted. "I'd put a snowball down your back!" And that was when she had an idea.

She pictured a big snowdrift that she knew was just outside the Veil, firmed that picture in her mind, and "reached" for a handful—and stuffed it down the back of Jelavan's tunic.

The sight of Jelavan trying to get the cold stuff out of his back, yipping and dancing, completely made up for the way he "innocently" jostled her so that a leaf full of water spilled over her head.

———

Kordas examined his growing "manor." The building itself was unexpectedly handsome. But—

"This building is only supposed to have four stories and a basement," he pointed out, beginning to feel anxious. "There—"

"Is no way that fifteen thousand people will fit in it, even if we stacked them like cordwood," Silvermoon said, smoothly interrupting him. "Our tools and magic are good, but they are not going to grow you a building that large. Leaving aside the fact that even if we *could*, the people on the uppermost floors would curse you every day they had to go up and down all those stairs. As we have learned with our *ekele*, four stories are quite tall enough unless you have safe platforms to haul things up by, pulleys, and counterweights as they do in mines, and as we do in other Vales."

That would mostly be the servants going up and down all those stairs, poor things. No, he's right—

"So what's the solution?" he asked bluntly. "Because I know you are hiding a solution up one of your sleeves."

"Ah, you have come to know me so well." Silvermoon smirked. "The hertasi tunnels, of course. This entire area is riddled with them. We decided that instead of collapsing them as we usually do when we leave a place, we'll leave them open for your use. The tunnels are a lot easier to defend than a building."

Kordas looked at him with alarm. "Isn't that—the foundations would be undermined—sinkholes—"

"Please, give us more credit than that. Never mind, I'll show you. Come along." He beckoned, and Kordas followed him into what he had *thought* was an ornamental planting, but in the center of the planting was a round door in the ground. Lifting the doorhandles revealed a set of well-lit circular stairs. He couldn't identify what they were made of. Too warm to the touch for metal, but the color of wrought iron, and apparently just as tough and quite thoroughly anchored to the wall, because they didn't even tremble as the two of them made their way down. Kordas marveled as they wound their way to the bottom. This descent into the underground could have been alarming, but there was *nothing* that was in the least disturbing about this staircase. There was plenty of light on the stairs, thanks to mage-lights, and plenty of light at the bottom. It was only about one story down, and they found themselves at a crossroads of four tunnels.

The lighting was considerably dimmer down here than the sunlight of the surface, but that was probably because the eyes of the hertasi were more sensitive than those of humans. It was definitely humid, though not uncomfortably so. Much like a wine cellar, actually.

And now Kordas saw why Silvermoon had assured him that these tunnels weren't undermining the surface above. The walls of the tunnel looked like glazed brick, and they were properly reinforced at intervals by heavy arches of more glazed brick.

"You see?" said Silvermoon. "Nothing is going to collapse. Not even if there was a fire down here. It would only make the tunnels stronger. The only thing that can collapse them is explosive magic, and you'd have to know exactly what to do and where the tunnels were to make that collapse happen. At any rate, come along, I'll show you a little. The hertasi have already prepared the area next to where the basement to your building will be, and once the basement is completed, they will be putting in concealed entrances to these tunnels."

"Because we might need to escape fast, and we don't want whoever or whatever has invaded our building—"

"Palace," interrupted Silvermoon. "You're going to be a King, you should have a palace."

Kordas felt himself blushing. "Oh, it's very high class to be a king," he replied, with mockery in his voice, though he was mocking only himself. "But it's very *crass* to *call* yourself a 'king' and even crasser when you are 'king' of a place no bigger than a small duchy."

Silvermoon snorted. "Just wait," was all he said. "But yes. We'll be completing the building with hidden entrances to these tunnels where you can hide, or escape, as you choose. And if you are attacked in force, you can put every single person you brought down here, as well as some of your animal stock. They won't be comfortable, but they won't be miserable either, and they *will* be safe."

Silvermoon stopped talking and held up a hand. Kordas listened, and heard a voice he recognized, echoing from the tunnel to their left. Delia!

". . . and it's no fair that you haven't offered Sai some of those mushrooms yet," she was saying. "Oh, what he can do with mushrooms is—"

Delia and a hertasi stepped through the doorway and stopped. Kordas recognized the little lizard as Jelavan by his blue tunic with bronze feathers picked out along one shoulder.

They both stopped stock still. Jelavan recovered first, and nodded his head respectfully. "Oh! Welcome, Baron! I take it that Silvermoon is showing you our own little kingdom."

"I hope we're not trespassing," Kordas replied.

"No, no, nothing of the sort! Most people just don't like coming down here because it's *very* disorienting until you learn the code!" He pointed to the keystones in each arch. "Blue is east, green is west, red is south and yellow is north. Then you pay attention to the patterns in the brickwork—" He began rattling off a long series of things Kordas was supposed to be looking for, then stopped, probably because Kordas couldn't keep the dismay off his face. "Or, of course, you can just keep going in one direction until you come to a staircase or sky-blue ramp. They will always bring you to the surface."

"That's probably my best plan, should I have to come down here," Kordas agreed.

"We have everything a creature could need here," Jelavan said proudly. "We have storehouses, we grow mushrooms, there are workshops of all sorts, we make pottery and metalwork and cook and weave and sew and make jewelry and embroider, and work leather. We always make more room than we will actually need, just in case we have to take in another clan. We have a system for disposing of waste, as I believe you had in your manor back in the Duchy. We have lots of private quarters—oh! You need to avoid anything with a door with a hertasi sigil carved into it. That's someone's home. Or at least, you need to avoid those places until we're all gone."

"I'm not looking forward to that day," Kordas told him candidly. "I find I am really enjoying the company of your people. And the Hawkbrothers too, of course!"

Silvermoon struck a subtle pose. "How could you not? We are vastly good company at even the worst of times, and at the best of times, we are a delight. But let's continue our tours. Delia, Jelavan, would you like to join us?"

Kordas refrained from objecting. It wouldn't do to hurt Delia's feelings, though being down here in very close proximity to her was not something he was particularly comfortable with.

But to his surprise, after a moment of thought, Delia shook her head. "Silvermoon is going to show you boring, important things. I want to see the fun things." And she giggled.

He smiled at that. *Now that's what I want to hear.* He still felt a lot of guilt for dragging her out into the wilderness, when at her age, instead of being one of the linchpins of a scouting expedition into dangerous lands, learning how to fight, learning survival techniques, she *should* have been teaching her foal, being courted, maybe. Certainly she would be introduced to suitable potential partners at parties and celebrations. And of course, at this time of year, there would have been a fortnight of celebration and feasting, she might have been making herself a new gown—or sitting beside the fire and reading, maybe with Sydney-You-Asshole purring at her feet—

No, not that last. Unlikely to say the least. Another cat, or a dog, but never Sydney.

Still, this mad plan of his had stolen experiences from her that she would never have. Were the ones she'd had instead worth it?

Well, it looks like this one is.

"Come see the workshops, then!" Jelavan scampered off down the west tunnel, with Delia at his heels.

Delia is—running. To keep up with the hertasi, not telling them to slow down for her. Would you look at that.

"And what would *you* like to see?" Silvermoon asked.

Kordas sighed. "What I want to see is those workshops. What I *need* to see is the forge and anything else connected with tools, defensive weapons, and their making; I assume there is one down here?"

"More than one," Silvermoon assured him, and led him eastward. "And we will be able to speak freely. The route I have in mind is proofed against spying, and will remain so for many years to come. Not forever, though. Sometimes it is wiser for us to leave a spell or enchantment going, to fade on its own. If no known magic-eater is in the territory, we might even attract some if we leave it loud." He shrugged. "It's a kind of dance, and we are obliged to negotiate with the land as well as cleanse it."

Kordas understood about half of the terms Silvermoon used when speaking about magic. Kordas was not bad, not bad at all, when it came to his magic, and had very good control atop that. The concepts that Silvermoon spoke casually of—the ones in practice! and not theoretical—would have changed the Empire forever, if they were known. "Like the *wyrsa*? Why would anyone want to attract them?"

"A few good reasons. They may not have been nature-born, but they are a fact of the ecology now, and if they go, so does something else. Additionally, our task is to put order to magic in the Pelagirs, wherever we find what we can call by that term. Not all forest in this region is considered Pelagirs. "Clean" forest appears here and there and isn't encroached upon, for reasons we don't even know yet. Like little islands of cleanliness in a sea of corruption. Ideally, that is what we'll turn this region into, and what it becomes then, well, my new friend, only fortune-tellers and story-tellers know. But until then, magic-eaters like the *wyrsa* are like mowers to grass, for us. They home in on aberrant magical creatures and effects, and trim them down. They maintain a level of stability that makes our work last, and prevents the Pelagirs from encroaching right on back."

It was an intentionally convoluted answer, but Kordas understood why. *When one makes the story convoluted, it portrays that the speaker thinks in a convoluted way. It expresses that they think everything mentioned is connected. Silvermoon explains like that to also give me an empathic personal expression of the subject, and its meaning to him. It creates sympathy for the strangeness. He's masterful.*

"It makes sense that out here, you would want to use every resource you could for your holy cause—whether you control them or not. But isn't just leaving them alone a way of controlling their future, too?" Kordas was taking a risk in being so direct in what had the appearance, so far, of just pleasant conversation, but had been diplomatic dueling since "We are obliged to negotiate" was said.

That is a Tayledras declaration of verbal dueling. Everything spoken after that moment has been aimed for dominance and respect.

Silvermoon stopped walking. Without turning around, he answered. "You have more on your mind than forges. It's understandable." He then led Kordas only three more turns before entering what could only be termed an open-air cafe with a guard post built into it. Or—a cafe garrisoned by armed chefs. Everyone was friendly and before Silvermoon even got to the rear entry, smiling and waving a bit, he'd been handed three baskets of fresh food, which he brought along. *As if he had already planned for us to be here now.* Silvermoon knew how to create a frame of reference for negotiation: *We know all, we can lead you where we want to, we see all, you are surrounded, we run this show, and I'm the one who asks the questions here. You are at an utter disadvantage.*

This is fascinating, and gives me a few advantages.

They crossed a threshold declared in paint on the floor and a stack of mage-lights on each side. In the four steps it took to cross it, Kordas felt his magical senses caving in on themselves, as if they were being dammed up, but all of his nonmagical senses were unaffected. Then his magical senses were silent. Very silent, not just quiet. Just—gone, with an absence that felt like an ache. It was—belittling. *Demeaning, for anyone to just take away someone's senses without even a mention. This is a power move and he's not afraid at all to declare it.*

"Oh, it's good to get that noise out of my head," Kordas said after a few moments. *You want to fence, let's fence.*

"Oh, that," Silvermoon replied. *Dismissive, downplaying.* "I'm sure you have one, too. Ours are all over, for convenience for all sorts of things." *Hint that they're used strategically.* "We could surveill you and you wouldn't find a trace of us magically." *Crafty.*

"Well, it is pretty amazing what good loaders can fit on a barge. We're lucky to have so many strong men and women with the best tools. It feels like we could handle anything we might need to." *Loaders, in this case, obviously standing in for troops. Slight emphasis on need; imply we don't want conflict but can outperform them in sheer manpower, and that we have superior "tools" of warfare.*

"Our greatest strength is always in our people. May they always be our art." *Oh, nice. Okay, I have to admit, that was good. Imply that a majority of approval is needed or we'd collapse while also reinforcing that, as individuals, his people are far more powerful per capita. All right. 'The people as our art' means our societies become what we make them—we, specifically, who are in a position of senior power. 'Our art' means specifically us, without*

any Council. That's all about declaring who is in control here, and it's us two.
He recognizes that we have something in common in workable diplomacy—
   All negotiation eventually comes down to two people.

They gave each other a side-eyed look, and stalked, entirely alone, through ever-branching hallways of mixed stone, wood, and sculpture, waterfalls and flowerflows, and ramps, even using their walking as a declaration of attitude. *Competitive walking? This is childish. So I'll do it better.* They came to rest in a curve-walled lounge, complete with washroom, filled with maps and instruments as well as comfortable hanging chairs, narrow beds, and mage-lights, adjoining a wide, open-lofted chamber within a dome. *For meetings that go very, very long,* he surmised. The chamber it opened onto was ringed in benches, tables of all sorts, and odd instruments, and was smooth-paved in gridwalk, which his Tayledras language infusion told him was a markable surface treated to take chalk diagrams and timing notes precisely. Boards of the same stuff were placed around the chamber, as well as one in the lounge. The view was beautifully and artistically lit, giving an effect that Kordas hadn't even realized was possible until now. Angling and directing light for emotional effect was simply not a thing that would have occurred to him, Kordas realized. He tried to avoid looking at the chamber's center directly, but even with his discipline, it wanted all of his attention. He found himself actually holding his breath looking at it—

In the center of the chamber, radiating its own version of sunlight sprinkled with flares of light and a nimbus of rotating particles, was a Heartstone.

It glowed from deep within, a sculpture of crystals, glass, purified silver, and steel, scintillating from arcane energy, tapping out rhythms in synchrony to the types of magic going through it/

through him/through everything. A slow swell and drop of *deep earth world-life-birth* magic, a prime beat faster of *life-energy-sustainment-intent*, backbeat of *I-love-you, it-will-be-all-right, you-are-loved-Kordas*—

Kordas exhaled quickly, blinking from the lights. Even without mage-sight, he could sense all of that. That weirdly specific emotional impact. He had to admit, he had trouble reconciling that.

"You have been expected. I take it that this needs no introduction." Silvermoon raised his arm to present the scene. "This is where we do work that affects and influences the world. The number of Vales, outposts, ward-cities, and defense-holds varies, but they are all part of our network of active control points and Heartstones. Each one different, each one especially fine-tuned for its place and constellation. Adjustable, even mobile, in some cases. The number varies, but a fully operational Heartstone can pull ley-lines to itself, link them with other Heartstones, and skim their power for our use."

By all the gods, that is enough power to obliterate any foe, if it was even casually applied to warfare. And this is what they work with every day? It isn't even an event for them to move a ley-line around? I had no idea at all that could even be done. I thought too small. And they do it right . . . there.

Silvermoon murmured, in utter honesty, "It will always be a kind of home to me, this place. It's almost powered down completely now, and I'll never see it like this again. You know how that feels," he said with some sadness in his voice. There was genuine affection here. Kordas stayed politely silent. *Do the Heartstones have personalities? Are they elemental themselves? Is he going to miss—a friend?* The wistfulness in the statement was disarming, but it hinted at much more to be explored. It also signaled *personal feeling. Duel suspended.* It was a show of honor and respect to let any personal talk be *only* personal, without applying it to the subtextual maneuvering. As such, it was also a test of empathy and consideration.

"And now, with a lovely view, we will have a discussion with no witnesses," Silvermoon said, without even attempting to make it sound less ominous than it most certainly did.

———

Kordas was actively sweating, in the second mark of his occasionally tense leader-to-leader talk with Silvermoon. Boundaries were defined, expansion principles agreed upon, and baseline laws for nature, reserves, wildlife, and stock management were set. Exploration phases were agreed upon. Trade standards were agreed to in theory, dependent upon what yields would be. Expertise was agreed upon, to lead to an estrangement break with the Tayledras more or less completely in a set number of years, and updated according to need. Mutual-aid pacts and non-aggression pacts alike were reasoned out. Kordas bargained up defenses, pointing out that the Tayledras could—and were honestly expected to—build in any bypasses they would need to reassure them in case of armed conflict. Since the Tayledras weren't threatened in any way by Valdemaran defenses, Kordas argued, then their boosting of essential defenses would only aid the Valdemarans' survival versus regional dangers, and would ensure they lasted longer as a Tayledras eastern defensive partner. Silvermoon did mention, without explaining, that a fair amount of the region's northeast was protected by a fellow nation's 'hard border,' but didn't elaborate. Silvermoon established early on, and bluntly, what Kordas knew, but dreaded: he outright stated that at the moment, the expedition were also hostages for the Tayledras. They were all bunched up—or split up—exactly as the Tayledras placed them, and even their methods of escape were inland and rested on foundations. Kordas had little to bargain with that the Tayledras did not have hundreds of already, and the Hawkbrothers could demand nearly any price of them if they wanted to. Fortunately, the Tayledras had some much different practices concerning goods and properties, and Silvermoon was, in a word, reasonable. Cultural and population exchange, intermarriage, and meeting events were agreed upon, freedoms of passage worked out, and a token set of tributes from Valdemar to their benefactors was worked out based around booze, beer, and bread as starting points. They even made agreements about the city-seeds, as Kordas named them—the utterly alien creatures that the Tayledras cooperated with to create actual buildings like the growing manor and the water-and-waste infrastructure for settlements.

Kordas was brow-furrowed, mentally compacting and splitting blocks of resources for the next round of their brutally honest state-to-state battle of wits, when his attention was split by a polite knock on a side panel. A pair of hertasi in what Kordas thought of as livery uniforms stood side by side at the lounge's entry, on the far side of its threshold. That is, they seemed to be perfectly respectable hertasi in matching outfits, with knives and short spears sheathed on their persons, bringing picnic baskets. Silvermoon gestured and the pair entered, silently in that way hertasi had. Kordas was learning—when a hertasi didn't want to be noticed, it just wouldn't be. It could be unnerving, because even though a hertasi might be silent, it still displaced air when it dashed by or sprang up, and *that* felt like a spider on the skin. These two, though, made a point of being seen, then went about their work efficiently. They swapped out every glass and tankard for fresh, replaced the fruit plates and mint dip, swapped in a new coal for the chafer, and then, to his surprise, handed him and Silvermoon a sheaf of notes. In quick but legible script was a summary of what had been happening on the surface while they were down here—in Kordas's case, it bore Herald Beltran's ink-stamp. There was a list of resources and changes in their amounts, notes on health and manpower, and ten good bits of gossip. *Yes, in the annals of history, it shall be forever recorded in Official Documents that ten beets are owed to Mrs. Gully by Goosecatcher Phobro in exchange for a midsized pie pan, and Hoggee Ferbrow has swollen ankles.*

The hertasi duo suddenly lined up side by side, bowed in unison, and darted out.

"It's a dilemma for them. They want to be unobtrusive by nature, but they also do not want to undermine trust during negotiations by slinking around unseen. So they overcompensate, and make sure they're intrusive," Silvermoon commented. "In a lot of ways, they are more Tayledras than the Tayledras. They are true friends. They remind us who we are when we forget."

"That is one of the best things a friend can do. No matter who we are, we can go too far. There's just no substitute for someone who cares enough to save you from yourself," Kordas replied.

Silvermoon leaned forward, reaching for some sliced-up orange fruit, which he speared on an eating knife. "In that exact spirit, new friend, I'm going to warn you of some important things, with no pretense otherwise. Both warnings and threats. I speak for the Clan and the Tayledras in general when I tell you—don't interfere with us. Keep to yourselves, because I assure you, we can keep you out of anywhere you think you want to go, and we prefer not to murder. We try to be kind, but when we work, we face horror and misery, and we will die for our mission. To understand that, you need to understand the Pelagirs more—and you will, in time, from a safe enough distance. For now, I will tell you directly—the Pelagirs is a system of evolving, self-optimizing entities that advance in sophistication every year. If we did not oppose it, it would become sentient, exceed us, and cover the world."

Silvermoon was not joking in the least. He just let that statement lie between them like a corpse on a buffet that neither wanted to comment upon first.

Finally, Kordas broke the uneasy silence. "If you lose, we all lose," he replied.

"Yes. It's much more than romantic-quest material for a hero story. We have been dedicated, at great cost, to the same task for *centuries*. To interfere with our work is to interfere with our very identity. Take this into your consideration about the enormity of the Pelagirs threat: we were tasked with this because an actual Goddess didn't think she could do it alone." Silvermoon dunked crisp-edged venison into the mint dip, and after a few bites, continued. "I'd prefer that you be a strong ruler, for a very long life. What your settlers will become is not only *your* interest. I'd prefer you were like us in our outlook, but all we can realistically hope for is tolerance and distance. We are the best allies anyone could want—or dare—but we aren't easy to stay friends with. We wish to be seen as more impressive, and frightening, than the monsters we oppose, because that stops the naive and exploitive alike from venturing into Uncleansed lands. Make us myth, Kordas."

"I can understand wanting to control a narrative in official history," Kordas replied, intrigued by the venison and dip. "Maybe more so than anyone," he murmured. He took his first bite. Savory, with a tiny amount of bitterness from the charred edges, then cooling mint with a hint of something sharp. "I can direct storytellers to create a mystique around the Tayledras. You can be characterized as enigmatic benefactors of our earliest days, fiercely territorial and inscrutable." He pointed at the rapidly emptying platter with his pinkie finger. "This is very good. I'll barter for the recipe."

Silvermoon laughed merrily. "If we surrender our recipes to you, what will we have left to bargain with?"

"We officially prostrate ourselves at your feet for your culinary guidance." He paused to dab at his face with the same sort of leaf Silvermoon did. "It irks me to prevent *any* history being known, but some things are better left as mysteries. We can leave out details of just how *much* you've helped us."

That seemed to satisfy Silvermoon. "I feel it's best if the Tayledras welcome, help, and then just leave. It will strengthen your nation if you stress your own identity as robust, adaptable explorers, over being weakened chicks scooped into a warm nest by us. We like the feeling of being respected and honored for our good work, but in the past we have interfered too much with new tribes and nations, and suffering followed. The ones who opposed us, or went in dark directions, are *all* gone now. Their leaders were too short-sighted, and because they did not curate their own freedoms, they rotted and fell, to be absorbed into other, wiser nations. Now snakes live in their ruins."

"What do you mean about curating their freedoms?" Kordas was not so sure he liked every implication of the phrase. It could definitely be taken in some pretty dark ways.

"Imagine a nation as a living creature, with an actual personality collectively made up of what every inhabitant feels. Courage, strength, history, happiness, and wonder, and the fulfilling pleasure of mattering. Curating your freedoms means taking care of what matters so it is not taken away by others. It's looking after what you have control of in your lives. Live wisely, live well, be smart and honest with each other. Watch for the signs of rot, and heal what is sick. You are talented, Kordas, but you will not lead this expedition for millennia. Build a country that wants to *be* you, as the people think of you. Think of being that personality, as the ideal of every citizen. Living by certain virtues is powerful at that scale, and that generates more Goddess-aligned power than even praying. The country, barony, outpost, or tribe that can do that becomes an incredible force for primary magic. When that happens, believe me, it makes our work easier."

"Ah, all right. So you mean, staying mindful of the signs that things are going badly, then taking care of them compassionately, IS like prayers on a national scale?"

"Those flavors of magic are pure in a way no other tones or flavors match. It's a quirk of the universe—like what water can do."

Kordas had to admit, Silvermoon lost him completely sometimes. It was as if Silvermoon had begun talking about the intricacies of making hawk-equipment, a subject Kordas knew nothing about. So he listened and watched how Silvermoon acted as well as what he said, and inferred an 'equivalent' meaning, based upon what of Silvermoon's emotions he understood. It made him perceive conversation as a flow, which in itself was an expression of broader meaning. *That's why I like Silvermoon so much, so quickly. The man absolutely wants to engage, and once you've matched velocity with him, the conversation takes on artistry and rhythm.* This was communication of complex, important ideas in ways that would never be guessed at in the Empire. *It's both sophisticated and personal. I can't get enough of this. I know Silvermoon is probably dumbing it down for me, but it's like the conversation* itself *is encouraging creativity and expression in how I respond.*

"I approve of water—simply amazing stuff. What can't it do?"

Oh, that blew it for the sophisticated conversation, Kordas. He'll be so *impressed by that big insight from your deepest soul.* He caught himself nodding too much. *He completely thinks I'm a dolt now. Save this, change the subject, now now now.* "And then you use it?" *Tactical failure.*

"Well, something would be worked out then, of course, and incentives would be involved. Power is as appealing to the benevolent heart as it is to the villain. Placing that power with those most experienced in its uses simply makes sense. More of the work done in fewer years is appealing to us."

Steady this crash. Call back.

"And you were telling me about the loving care of freedoms? Curated?"

"Yes. Curated, because one wants to present the very best, significant, and understandable examples, in ways that give them meaning in context as well as now. We have a ceremonial tradition, born with the Tayledras ourselves, of expressing our feelings about important things as messages for our descendants. It gives us the longest of views, the arc of our history in our ancestors' own words, since our inception as a people. As years passed, our ways of recording information got better, leading to images lifelike in their appearance, synchronized to a copy of the sounds and voices depicted. It was as if we could talk to them, and a resurgence of interest in our origins made us more aware of who we were as a people. We leave messages for our descendants a few times a year now. I like to think I'll be heard by Tayledras for whom the work is done, someday in the far future." Silvermoon poured himself another cup of wine, and added some to Kordas's own. "This talk with you will feature well in my next message."

Kordas blushed.

"I will tell you of a warlord. No records exist of anything that he loved or cared about, except acquisition of power, from his apprenticeship on. He was brilliant, and he was, we suspect, incapable in the blood of being compassionate. He became a 'Kiyamvir,' the symbolic embodiment of a nation, and what you might call an 'Emperor of many tribes,' before he even lay with his slaves. He became known as Ma'ar. Just the single name. Ma'ar ruled by division, over scores of city-states, in a constant state of conflict with each other for reasons that changed with the breeze. His cunning, coupled with his indifference to others' suffering, led him to become a conqueror by disruption as much as by arms. Within ten years, he had three dozen city-states loyal to him, with more absorbed every year.

"Ma'ar had a particular method that *always* worked. In each tribe he wanted, his agents would find a minority—around ten percent of a population. That ten percent would be relentlessly portrayed by Ma'ar's agents as horrors, perversions, or outright enemies, until the remaining ninety percent felt like they were facing implacable, relentless foes out to 'get them.' In truth, the persecuted were never more than one finger of both hands, else they could have been effective at fighting back.

"When Ma'ar got the people of a tribe riled up enough, they would 'cleanse' their population of that ten percent—which by then the citizens and slaves alike thought of as an overwhelmingly powerful, evil, hateful, and unknowable force. That made the persecutors *feel* as if they'd struck a great blow, even though their beatdown was at nine-to-one odds, and few of them had done anything at all but passively agree. They felt like glorious, rebellious heroes of their people, taking down a vast network of evil that outnumbered them. Now that Ma'ar had made the population easier to direct, congratulating their obedience and bravery, Ma'ar would recruit, and place provocateurs in the next targeted city-states. They'd pick another enemy—almost always at nine to one—and repeat it, until every small group that might have opposed them was systematically 'cleansed' from what was now a large, united civilization. Doubters within that civilization had seen from the inside what happened to dissenters. Nine to one. A certain size of mob will always win, and that is hard for idealists or artists to comprehend. Ma'ar thrived by it.

"They regressed, that civilization. They lost momentum, joy, and the openness that causes a people to feel the discovery of new things as a pleasure, not an unwelcome incursion. Even their food became homogeneous.

"The survivors of Ma'ar's purges fled, driven south mainly, and in defiance, they made beauty even from their persecution. Songs of salvation and hope, stories of love overpowering mobs. With their creations, they could confront despair by weaponizing sophistication and hope. You see, the people most likely to fight a tyrant are those who give a people their vibrancy. The ones who escaped had their revenge by bringing their emotional artistry with them, and they created more every year.

"One of our proverbs is, 'Do not interrupt an enemy while they're destroying themselves.'

"The refugees gathered around an inherently kind soul, an Archmage called Urtho. Urtho didn't want to lead anyone but his hundreds of apprentices. He simply wanted to be a creator of wonderful things, but he answered their pleas and brought the strategies of a genius to oppose Ma'ar's cunning. 'Let there be love' was the simplest summation of Urtho's philosophy. That simple. That magnificent. Under him, they innovated. Ma'ar's side just poorly copied, and fanatically pushed their violence.

"And in the end, it could stand no more. The mobs overwhelmed the refugees, and they fled again. Only this time, what was left of both their lands was two wide craters." Silvermoon traced his fingers around a huge lake that Kordas now knew they called Lake Evendim on the map, and far south, a wider, shallower crater.

"The Mage Wars," Kordas whispered.

"The Mage Wars, yes. The wound we're healing," Silvermoon answered. "And now you know why I warn you. You are refugees. A rock to the skull is not a sophisticated attack, but it does kill every time. Hate and fear are crude and cruel, and unenlightened, widely ignorant people are puppetted by appealing to their aching anxieties. It can come from within a people, too—and compared to armies, it's even inexpensive. Rage, hate, and fear can smash through any defense made of rock and wood, and can cause a people to unknowingly give themselves freely to the very ones who have secretly terrorized them. The only times it fails in all of known history is when people have more understanding of each other than the hatemongers can defeat, and the education to recognize deceit. It can be stopped when it's small, and it's detected by listening closely to people's problems. There are few things in life, Kordas, as deeply saddening as a lost possibility for something wondrous to have happened. In a few notorious examples, pre-Tantara, even when nations knew to watch for it in principle, sadly, the ones that fell were those who were too slow to act upon it."

"And our new settlement is a haven for a new nation, and you see it as just as vulnerable."

"Maybe more so, because your people's loyalty is built around you. They're no dedicated wildland explorers who would have come here anyway—they wouldn't be here at all, ever, if it wasn't for your leadership. They are here because they trust you. If you fail them, they'll fail to become what you could make them. They would plummet in esteem from 'chosen-by-a-visionary' to 'idiots-abandoned-in-the-woods.' They would struggle, their numbers would drop, and if they survived that, little would be left among the survivors of the ideals you brought along." He paused and shook his head. "I apologize for the blunt analysis, Kordas, but you all are what you are. A purely strategic, economic, and wisdom analysis has to be factual. And history shows that with every doubling of population comes a doubling of would-be Ma'ars.

"Don't box them in by regulating freedom. Just make sure they know what truly counts, and help them have it. Ten people with good intentions and healthy minds can accomplish what ten thousand with torches cannot. You need to create standards of behavior and be certain they work in practice. Don't be so sophisticated or detached a leader that you lose track of your people staying happy, because Ma'ar's strategy I speak of always works. Don't use behavioral laws as a means of diminishing your people, however odd they may seem. From oddity comes comparison, from comparison comes perspective, from perspective comes compassion, from compassion comes prosperity." Silvermoon leaned in again to Kordas, to meet his eyes and make a direct, solid eye contact to deliver his vital ultimatum.

"I like you. I've seen deeper into your soul than you think, and so has the Star-Eyed, and so have others whose best futures depend upon what you do. I believe you can outmaneuver the dangers all tribes face, within and without, and you can make a lasting nation of quality. A year ago, we didn't know you existed, and yet we Tayledras were here for a decade before, in the right place at the right time, to give you a place to begin. Only when your expedition Gated in did we realize it." He gestured as if presenting the whole world as a prize in a tourney. "And we weren't even shocked by it. Provident luck, amazing coincidences, unexpected solutions to thorny troubles, mistakes that secretly aren't, and the discovery of or the placement of aid that might not matter for another fifty years. This is what life here is like. We know we are subject to the will of others, and we don't do this work alone. Unseen powers connect everything. Accepting that as a reality may take you a while to embrace fully, but I know you already accept it as a concept."

"Well, there's no denying the unlikelihood of us being here, 'us' meaning the expedition's flotilla and population. Yet here we are. One thing I am in awe of is the casual, almost indifferent way you Tayledras talk about and handle power that would incinerate us even in our best attempts."

"Ah. That came up in our discussions about you all, you know. More than one of us wanted to make no contact with you at all, figuring that you would experiment with what was in this abandoned Vale and we'd come back and sweep up your ashes afterward."

"Yes, pragmatic. You're very relaxed with the concept of killing, if I may say so."

"We kill a lot. Selectively ending lives is a part of the work, and once we get used to it enough, it's always there in our minds as an option. With what we face, we have to be that way for our sanity. Being able to kill isn't a fantasy for us, like it may be for some. We will kill, and we will be killed. It's only the minority of us that

die peacefully. But this—talks like this—this is what we crave."
Silvermoon paused, most likely going through memories of his
own lethality. "A thing about people, Kordas, is that everyone
loves to think of themselves as the hero of the story they're in. We
Tayledras, though, we live by it. We're *all* raised to be heroes. Life
is easy to come by—meat makes meat—so generating population
is not an issue for us. We could triple our number easily enough.
It's the *quality* of that person that we care about, as a reality for the
children that are already born. Fewer people consuming resources,
highly educated, skilled in physical, mental, and emotional
excellence, and the most fully themselves that they can be. The
magical power, the spellwork, the Heartstones—we have them
all, because we don't permit poverty. There are never more of us
than we can handily provide for. We *like* to be intellectual. Early
education establishes the baseline for an entire society. Keep them
smart, Kordas. Train everyone to read, cipher, and have general
knowledge of worldly things, both adults and children."

"I've been curious about that. Where are all the children, anyway?"

"I'll tell you about ward-cities soon. This was productive,
Kordas. Unless you'd like to do more than build treaties a while,
we should get back to directing our charges. We must think
improvements through well enough that they aren't just built
for now, they can be upgraded too. Plan for contingencies, with
generations ahead in mind. A monarch's sweetest crop is the
quality of his people, so tend to it well. Don't neglect the future,
or it might just leave without you.

"How about a look at some forges," Silvermoon suggested then,
with a smile, "and we'll address some of your other concerns."

By the time they emerged, up another staircase that let out near the vegetable gardens and was concealed by a false boulder, he had seen everything that his people would need in the case of a siege. And he was confident that yes, all of them *could* fit down there, and fit comfortably, and so could enough of the herds that even if everything was lost, they could rebuild. He was also quite sure that for living quarters, given a choice between the tunnels and their barges, most people would be sticking to their barges. It was dim down there by human standards, and claustrophobic, because the tunnels were intended for the *hertasi*, after all, and humid. Of course, the "dim" part could be solved with mage-lights, but claustrophobia could not. The ceilings were *just* high enough for humans to walk down here. People as tall as Hakkon and Ivar would probably be touching the ceiling.

"Something I need to point out," Silvermoon said, as they stood there blinking, waiting for their eyes to adjust. "When we move the Heartstone, we won't actually *move* it. We'll transfer most of the power from it to our new Heartstone. When we do that, we'll leave just enough for the Veil to stay up for about three years. Presumably all of your people will have built themselves some kind of homes and won't be living on their barges then."

"Or they'll have built something *around* their barges," Kordas amended. "And if they haven't, those things are supposed to last a hundred years, and it's no worse in them than living in a very small cottage."

"Well, when we do that, the above-ground portion of the Heartstone will crumble, leaving the root, somewhere about the level of the hertasi tunnels. I plan to have the hertasi create a room around it."

Kordas tilted his head curiously. "The Heartstone is not all that far from the end of the building you are 'growing' for me . . ."

Silvermoon grinned and tossed his long hair. "Yes. Once the Heartstone is down, I'm going to start an annex growing that will hold the root in its basement. Not all my fellows are going to be . . . amenable to that. So I'm doing it this way, without bothering to tell the Council, and waiting until the last moment to give you access to it. As they say, it is easier to get forgiveness than permission."

"You surprise me—" Kordas said. "That you'd leave us with an object *that* powerful when you really don't know us."

"Ah, but I do. Your actions coming here speak far more loudly than any entreaties could." He smiled slightly. "I think you will be good stewards of this place, and I want to make sure you have all the help you need to succeed. I'm not entirely certain what you can actually *do* with the root, but it's a powerful artifact on its own, and it does record everything that happens around it, and will continue to do so long after we are gone. So you may be able to use it to learn some of what we can do."

Kordas took a moment to think about that. So far, as individuals, the Hawkbrother mages were the most powerful he had ever seen. Certainly Silvermoon would, by Imperial standards, be counted as an Adept. Being able to learn how they wove some of their magic? It would be priceless.

"This gift—" he stammered. "I just don't know what to say, except *thank you*."

"Oh!" Silvermoon suddenly said. "Oh, there *is* one thing more, but it has nothing to do with your buildings, the Heartstone, or the hertasi tunnels. Our mage Cloudcaller and your mage Wis have not yet worked out how to free the Truthseekers from their Doll shells, but as of this morning, they discovered how to allow them to communicate with their free siblings again."

"They have?" Kordas felt his mouth stretching in a happy grin. "Silvermoon, that's *wonderful*!"

"Well, yes, it is, because Elementals can talk to other kinds of Elementals, and once your Truthseekers can speak to their brethren, perhaps there is one of another Element that has the key to freeing your friends." Silvermoon tucked his thumbs in the wide belt of his soft green robe.

"I truly hope so," Kordas replied sincerely, as they left the vegetable garden and headed for a kind of airy, outdoor structure that the Valdemaran mages had taken for their own. What the original purpose had been, Kordas had no clue, but no one had objected to his mages making it more or less their headquarters. It had a roof to keep the rain off, but the walls were open panels full of vines, and the floor was a very soft and pleasant moss that apparently thrived on being trodden on. That wasn't where they all actually lived—the Hawkbrother mages had their own houses, dwellings that they called *ekeles*, and the Valdemaran mages lived in their barges as almost everyone else did, but it was where they could gather and consult with each other. The fact that there was also one of those outdoor hot soaking pools that the Hawkbrothers liked so much very near the place was certainly part of the attraction.

The Hawkbrother Vale was so artfully constructed with carefully managed, lush growth that you could be within a few arm-lengths of someone and never know they were there unless they spoke. And even then, you would just make out a distant murmuring. So Kordas didn't know how many of "his" mages would be in their pavilion until he and Silvermoon turned the corner into the short path that led to it.

Wis spotted him before he spotted Wis. "Kordas!" the mage called out happily. "Has Silvermoon told you the good news?"

"If it's about making it possible for the Dolls to talk to the free *vrondi*, yes, he has," Kordas replied. As a courtesy—as he had quickly learned to do here in the Vale—he and Silvermoon stayed on the "threshold" of the pavilion until they were invited inside.

"Come in!" The invitation came not from Wis, but from a Hawkbrother in light leathers with the texture of bark. This, presumably, was Cloudcaller. Like Silvermoon, his short hair was completely white, and his eyes were gray, the marks of a quite powerful mage. Kordas and Silvermoon crossed onto the moss, which looked so soft Kordas longed to take off his boots and walk barefooted on it.

"We've already set the spells in motion, using the messenger birds." Wis whistled, and one of the brightly colored birds dropped down out of the rafters of the canopy to land on his outstretched finger. Kordas felt a silly surge of envy—as a boy he'd longed for birds to come to him spontaneously like that, but he'd never managed to make it happen.

Huh, but maybe it does, here. He whistled and held out his hand and a little bird with a curved, red beak the color of a ripe pear flitted to his finger and looked at him expectantly. Kordas lit up with delight.

"If you aren't going to give it a message, pet it," Silvermoon said, holding out his own hand, so that a red-and-yellow bird did the same for him. Silvermoon put his index finger up to the bird, which enthusiastically rubbed its face and neck against his fingernail, scratching itself. Kordas offered his finger to his bird, which did the same, and he felt elation as his childhood dream came true.

"So we used the birds as carriers for the spell completion," said Cloudcaller. "More efficient, since they can go faster than humans can, and the Dolls don't have to come off of their work for it. At this point, I think all the Dolls can talk to their *vrondi* kin. And any other Elemental they come into contact with."

"Did you break something that was on them, or add something to the old spell?" he asked.

"Added something," Wis told him. "We tried teasing out just the strand that kept them from talking to their kin and kind, but it was just too tangled up. By accident or design, those Impie mages created something that's such an intricate knot that it'll all have to come off at once. The frangible vessels the vrondi are held in are glass."

Kordas frowned. That was not what he wanted to hear. This meant that it was going to take a lot of power to free each Doll, and doing so was going to release a lot of heat. And that meant he'd have to free them slowly and painstakingly, one at a time.

But we promised. And we'll do it.

He quickly smoothed his expression into one of approval. "Wis, Cloudcaller, excellent work. Keep working on how we can free them altogether, but meanwhile, at least they aren't limited to communicating only with their fellow Dolls."

"I absolutely agree. Well done," Silvermoon said warmly, and lifted his hand to assist his little messenger bird into the air. Kordas did the same. Off they flew with a whir of wings, chasing through the air out of sight.

"Now," Silvermoon continued, "shall we discuss Midwinter festivities?"

———

Delia was alive with anticipation. Midwinter back in Valdemar generally meant that Kordas would fling open the manor, invite all the nobles in his Duchy to come and stay (some did, some didn't, because he also threw open his festivities to people like the Squire), and there would be two weeks of celebration—one leading up to Midwinter, and one following Midwinter. During the daytime there would be a Midwinter Fair on the manor grounds, minstrels in the Duchess's solar, the (generally unused, and closed up) Dowager Duchess's solar, and the library, and more rambunctious sorts of entertainers in the Great Hall. All during the day, sideboards in the Great Hall had cold food laid out. Then every night there would be a festive dinner for all the guests (not a feast, not yet) and dancing and music afterward. On Midwinter Eve itself was the *big* feast, with full entertainments and a "vigil" till midnight. "Vigil" was not quite the right word, since it mostly meant staying up, being entertained, and then cheering at the stroke of midnight. Perhaps at one point it had been something more religious, or mystical, but the Emperor preferred all attention to be on himself rather than gods, and that had been the case for at least the last three Emperors, so Midwinter had gradually become almost entirely secular in nature.

The second week was devoted to more outdoor entertainment. By day there were hunts, skating, and entertainments at the Fair— and a lot of contests. Archery, knife and axe throwing, livestock competitions, races both on foot and skating, and the most exciting of all, horse racing. But not just any sort of horse racing. The competitors didn't ride. They wore long, flat boards on their feet and were pulled by draft horses. Obviously you didn't dare go fast enough to endanger the horses in any way, and there was a lot of hilarity when people lost their balance, or they fell into a drift, and the traces that attached them to the horse's harness broke free of their belts. And it took a lot of skill, because you had to manage both the traces and the reins.

Now, these festivities were rather rural in nature, and shifting to them was designed to encourage the departure of those whose interests did not extend to the same sorts of entertainments enjoyed by the farmers and laborers. Food was presented at actual mealtimes, and they were served at "country" hours. Breakfast (far too early for those who were not "country" people) was the real feast of the day, and the last meal of the day (though most people would not realize it) was composed of artful presentations of what were, essentially, the previous week's leftovers. There was quiet music after supper instead of raucous music and dancing. Drinking was not encouraged, and early bedtimes were. Things didn't *quite* go back to "normal" until the end of the week, but the second week definitely had more of a tone of "relaxing with friends," and those who were there to see and be seen generally found this sort of provincial entertainment . . . provincial.

Obviously a Hawkbrother Midwinter was going to be nothing like this. There were the decorations, for one thing, but she wondered what the heart of the celebration was going to be like. Delia was looking forward to seeing and experiencing it all.

Somewhat to her disappointment, Jelavan told her that there really wasn't anything but decorations and perhaps some individual gift-giving until Midwinter's Eve.

That was not to say that there *wasn't* a lot of Midwinter frolicking going on among the Valdemarans, because there certainly was. But constraints being what they were, from the need to be careful about supplies to the lack of a Great Hall or any other places where there could be gatherings, even among the nobles who had followed Kordas here, the celebration was a lot more restrained and a lot more "provincial" than it had been at home. There were no big feasts, but with the help of the really good cooks, and some careful culling of wildlife, there were quite a few "small" feasts, things that took all day to cook and were served a bit later than supper usually was. The Hawkbrothers were not behind in offering good things as well, but there were a lot more Valdemarans than there were Hawkbrothers, so quite a bit of the Tayledras offerings were things like herbs and mushrooms and fresh vegetables and fruits from their gardens. Still it was winter, and fresh vegetables and fruits were prime luxuries at this time of year. And since there wasn't much for the farming folk to *do* in the middle of winter, other than tend their stock, those winter games had been resurrected.

Thankfully, it didn't appear that the Hawkbrother culture practiced intensive gift-giving at Midwinter, so she didn't feel pressured to produce anything more than little tokens. She wasn't any good at needlework, but she had hit on the idea of cleaning the fleeces still stored in the barges from when the culled sheep had been sheared. Virtually everyone was happy with cleaned and carded wool—if you couldn't spin, you could trade it to someone who did for yarn, and if you didn't need yarn, you could always find *someone* willing to take it in trade for something else. Cleaning the wool was very labor intensive and repetitive, but strangely soothing. And the lanolin from the wool made her hands the softest they had ever been. In return, she'd gotten a few little gifts, like new stockings and a couple of books—small things in comparison to past times, yet where would she put anything substantial? The storage-barge?

Finally the day arrived. The Hawkbrothers had kept their plans very much a secret, and Jelavan had been impossible to tease anything out of. "Sleep late," was all they were told. "And don't eat much. You'll be eating all day, and staying up very late."

So it was with growing impatience that Delia waited with the rest of the Valdemarans until the sound of a horn summoned them all into the Hawkbrother groves.

Groves which sparkled with tiny mage-lights and had decorations and food and drink laid out *everywhere.*

And that was just the beginning. As Delia explored the Vale, she discovered that in nearly every place you looked, there was something simple yet delightful to do, see, or listen to. Tervardi and Hawkbrother musicians in trios and quartets provided music the likes of which she had never heard before. Dyheli offered rides to children, on special saddles padded so one didn't get bisected by their very sharp backbones. Other Hawkbrothers taught and played games, everything from simple things children could do, like ring-tossing, to a very complicated board game that used miniatures, stacks of books, and strange dice, which Delia didn't even begin to understand.

"Try this!" Jelavan would say, thrusting something that smelled wonderful into her hand. "Let's go play this game!" he would say as soon as she had finished wolfing the tasty treat down. And off they would go to a guessing game, or a quoit battle. There were no prizes for winning these games, but both children and adults were enjoying them anyway.

But it was what the Hawkbrother mages were doing—with the assistance of some of the Valdemaran mages—that was special. One had flocks of the little, brightly colored messenger birds doing tricks, singly and together. They fascinated Valdemarans and their cats alike, but fortunately, the little birds had enchantments to bodily defend against predators. Several junior mages accompanied storytelling with illusions playing out the scenes before the wondering eyes of the audience. Some created miniature fireworks. One made the flames of a fire itself dance to music.

Jelavan made sure she saw everything—at least as far as she could tell, anyway. With him scampering in the lead, she was pretty sure they explored every nook and cranny of the Vale in search of delights.

They stopped just long enough for a lunch, a sort of browse along a table crowded with vegetables and noodles in sauce, vegetables grilled and stuffed and roasted, vegetables mashed and served in their own skins, and an assortment of raw vegetables with sauces to dip them in. That was when Delia asked him a question that had been lurking in the back of her mind for some time. It had seemed odd to her that the hertasi wore anything at all. The dyheli and tervardi didn't. And Jelavan had, multiple times, urged her to ask him anything, even if it seemed rude. So she did.

"Why do hertasi wear clothing?" she asked. "You don't need to, do you?"

Jelavan hiss-laughed. "Of course we don't need to, at least in the Vale. But we like to! We love clothing, we love jewelry, we love all things ornamental as much as our partners do! Maybe more! When we are working in the fields and gardens or anything else where we might get clothing dirty, we don't bother, but the rest of the time?" He flung up his claws and turned, inviting her to admire a verdigris-green tunic and trews covered with tiny copper beads and leaves. "Who *doesn't* like to look fabulous!"

Delia snorted. "Jonaton?" she suggested. And since Jelavan had been distressed earlier by one of Jonaton's "fancy bags" and had rushed to the mage to offer hertasi expertise, he immediately erupted into laughter.

The entertainment continued after dark. Gradually some of the

Valdemarans got up the courage to perform for their hosts, who seemed far more appreciative of what was played for them than Delia would have thought.

The grand conclusion to all this was just before midnight. The Heartstone, she was told, had been raised up from its usual home in the center of a domed building, and its stand held it a barge-length high now. It was awe-inspiring to think that around her was a society that felt so comfortable wielding so much power that it would use a Heartstone as a holiday decoration. Everyone gathered at the Heartstone for a grand display of much larger magical "fireworks," which was capped by three of the Hawkbrothers in androgynous garb hanging from impossibly silky scarves suspended from nearby trees, who "danced" in midair, spinning, climbing, falling, twirling to the sounds of a chorus of tervardi singing and Hawkbrothers playing—it was all so beautiful it took her breath away. And just at midnight, the Hearthstone lit up like a fountain of colored lights, with streams of sparkling motes rising from its tip, shooting skyward, and cascading down its sides.

Delia could not bear to tear herself away, and she was not alone. But eventually, once that great finale ended, and the various entertainers began closing down and going to their own rest— usually in pairs or more, she noted—she did find herself stumbling to bed, hands full of sweet grapes, and eyes full of stars.

19

The day after Midwinter, the first heavy snow fell.

Inside the Veil, it was a continuous rain, a real downpour, as the Veil melted the falling snow and turned it into a rainstorm, but without the lightning or thunder. At least inside the Veil it was a warm rain. It went on for a full day, and this was when the first problems began.

At the intersection of the Veil and the outside world, snow piled up in a crusty frozen ridge that had to be broken down with a pickax so people could get to the herds that were outside the Veil. Hauling green hay to them had been a chore before the snow; now it was complicated four times over, at least until the stock tenders beat down a path—which was, of course, covered over when the next heavy snow happened a few days later. Meanwhile, inside the Veil, you had to be sure your footgear was waterproof and your hems hiked up above your ankles, because the ground was soggy, and if you went outside the Veil with soggy clothing, it immediately froze to ice, which was both uncomfortable and potentially dangerous.

The Tayledras "move" from this new Vale had always been planned as a piecemeal operation, with the last few to remain being the ones who would feed the power to the new Heartstone along a ley-line, and shut down the old one. It had been going on since before the Valdemarans had been recruited to take possession of the Vale—there were a lot of creatures that depended on the Hawkbrothers, like the little messenger birds, that couldn't take cold and weather. A new Vale, with a new Veil, had to be established first before those delicate beings were moved.

The Hawkbrothers had all known they were going to be moving in winter; strategically speaking, winter was the best time for it. A lot of hazards went into hibernation, and the rest would have trouble moving around in the snow.

It was actually a variation on what the Valdemarans had done, but without the part of "living in your barges." The Hawkbrothers made use of their powers to create sledges and barges that floated just above the ground for their belongings and everything else that they were taking with them.

They moved as the Valdemarans had moved—with the assistance of Gates. Long before Silvermoon had come to bring the Valdemarans to this Vale, their initial party had found a suitable spot for a new Vale, cleared out immediate threats, created a Veil, and set up a Gate. All the time that the Valdemarans had been here, floating barges had been going through the Gate here full, and coming back empty.

Singles and couples had left first; most of them hadn't had dwellings bigger than one or two rooms. But now larger groups of Tayledras were moving. So as ekeles emptied, some of the more adventurous of Kordas's people moved into them and out of their barges. Not everyone found the light, woven screens that the Hawkbrothers used as walls to be comfortable to live with. "Not enough privacy," was the general consensus, and Delia—as charmed as she was by the Tayledras—couldn't help but think that lack of privacy was a standard of life for them. Hertasi watched from everywhere, messenger birds and bond birds watched from above, the walls were thin, every noise made by humans and others carried, and anybody could—and apparently did—just walk through lovers' assignations in the more public areas. She would ask Jelavan about it soon.

Even so, Delia took to one of the ekeles immediately. With the Vale always at a pleasant temperature, even at night, she enjoyed having fresh air moving through her living space at all times. Her storage in the barges was emptied, and slowly she was finding spaces for all the things in her boxes and trunks—and Jelavan was extremely helpful in either finding her furniture, or having it made for her.

After discovering that he'd not only managed a boxed bedframe for her, but arranged for sliding drawers to go under it, she felt terribly guilty about how she had unthinkingly assumed he'd manage just that. So after thanking him, she'd apologized. "You're not my servant, after all," she said. "You're under absolutely no obligation to do any of this for me."

"Oh, of course not." He laughed at her. "We hertasi are so numerous that no one ever *has* to do anything. We help because we like to—and because in return, we have someone protecting our homes, and all the skills of the Tayledras to draw on and to learn for ourselves. We wouldn't last long on our own in the wild, you see. It's a mutually beneficial arrangement."

"But I—"

"I help you because I like you. It's fun to show you things and see your reactions, and it's a pleasant challenge to help you create the kind of environment you're used to. So hush." He stamped his foot, and nodded decisively. "Now, what, exactly, is a bookcase?"

"The open cabinets that my loose books were secured in. Jelavan, I think our people are kind of like yours in some ways. Hertasi prefer to—to not be seen doing what all they do. We're used to privacy, but it feels like *everything* is watched by a dozen eyes in here."

"Oh. Yes. The Tayledras are great believers in the sanctity of secrets. In a Vale, though, it's turned on its head. The Pelagirs has all kinds of threats: infiltrators, diseases, parasites, and even more exotic things. Tayledras are *this* open to observation in a Vale for a very practical reason: it's quicker to notice an infiltrator, or aberrant behavior from disease or influence, if everybody is watching, and that protects everyone." Jelavan speed-sorted Delia's things. "To have one thing, it costs another. We all give up most of our privacy, because out here in the Vales, there is an existential reality of danger if we didn't. Secrecy is strategic, and privacy is available if it's desired, but that's an event, not a standard. It works," Jelavan cheerfully summed up. "They know about it coming in, and all of us in a Vale aren't bothered by it. Over time, as a people, most shyness went its way. We all see each other during bathing and a few special occasions, but as you know, we all love our clothes for their practicality and aesthetics. And expression! Like the masks you see, they are for moods, or declarations, not for hiding identities. Silvermoon and the Elders have everybody fully clothed to help your people adjust to us."

Which implies . . .

"Now, what we hertasi love about it all is, we learn so much about everyone in a Vale that we can anticipate what they'll want. We're also well-known matchmakers. Someone on the far side of a Vale might never find a compatible mate or two if we didn't see to it that they met!" Jelavan hissed his happy little laugh, then darted out again.

Kordas and Isla tried an ekele for their family, and immediately regretted it, as the boys awoke as soon as there was any light and immediately went looking for adventure. After pulling them out of the hertasi tunnels, out of trees, and out of hot soaking ponds, all before breakfast, the couple gave up and moved back to the barge, where they could at least keep their offspring out of trouble until *they* were awake.

There were, of course, not nearly enough vacant ekeles for people to take over—the Valdemarans outnumbered the Hawkbrothers by many times—but it was enough to allow the adaptable and adventurous to get out of barges where they were packed in like salted fish. And that permitted those who had been crowded to spread into newly vacated barges. Unsurprisingly, all the mages took to ekeles. The Six Old Men even found one big enough to share, as they had shared their tower, and went back to enjoying their bickering from their big, overstuffed pouf pillows.

But as Hawkbrothers grew fewer, the snowstorms grew more frequent, and it became harder to get out to the stock to feed them. Then the debates began: should the rest of the herds be moved inside the Veil, and take the chance they would pass sickness because they were overcrowded? There were debates about it every day—at least it seemed that way to Delia. And while she didn't particularly mind all the scattered flocks of fowl inside the Veil—the chickens were very useful, weeding and de-bugging the gardens—some people were complaining that they didn't like having to dodge goats and chase ducks out of soaking pools. But to move the stock outside meant exposing them to danger, not to mention that it was infinitely easier to keep them fed within the Veil. There didn't seem to be any good answer for the problem, and the debates went on and on until she just stopped paying any attention to them.

Finally the day came when Silvermoon took down the Heartstone. Delia just missed seeing him do so, but Kordas assured her she hadn't missed anything. There was something in his tone that meant he was sad about it.

Isla was not entirely happy that Delia had her own little home to herself. Delia was fairly certain that her sister's main problem with it was that Delia was "unsupervised." But really, she was no more "unsupervised" in the Vale than she had been in Valdemar Manor. It wasn't as if she was ever alone . . . and with those thin screens in place of walls, if she'd been getting up to mischief with a young man, half the Vale would have known about it.

So matters stood, when the last of the Hawkbrothers left.

———

The four *Tayledras* stood beside the Gate that would take them to the new Vale. They were leaving the physical Gate still charged and still in place, in case the Valdemarans wanted it, although Silvermoon warned Kordas that they were severing the connection to their new Vale out of caution.

"We never leave an open Gate behind us," Silvermoon reminded the Baron, as a rather small party gathered to see them off. "Not even I can persuade my fellows to break this rule; they are irritated enough with me that I did not completely destroy the Heartstone as we usually do. We are trusting you to take good care of this place,

Valdemarans," Silvermoon added gravely, as he and Kordas shared a quick, back-pounding embrace of the sort that the Hawkbrothers preferred to shaking hands.

"We'll do our best," Kordas replied, sounding quite sure of himself. *But then again,* Delia reflected, *we've been here a couple of moons, and so far, we* have *taken good care of it.*

"Then good luck, and may your gods watch over you, as the Star-Eyed cares for us." Silvermoon waved at his three fellows, and the dyheli towed the last of the floating barges through the Gate, followed by the Tayledras—

—and the Gate silvered over, flared too bright to look at for a moment, and then shut down. Jonaton sighed. Delia folded her arms, deep in thought. Sydney-You-Asshole sat down next to her and thoughtfully licked his balls.

"We're on our own," Delia said aloud, and although she had not intended it to come out that way, the words sounded melancholy.

"We have been since we left Valdemar," Isla reminded her. "We are in a much, much better position for winter than I would have thought. Look at what they left us with!" And she gestured at the in-process manor, and Silvermoon's last gift, the maze wall.

The growing manor had finished the second floor now, and was working on the third. It had become a favorite place for the builders and apprentices to take meals, intuitively knowing that if they watched this, they'd learn astonishing insights into structural support and rigidity. But that was not nearly as important as Silvermoon's Winter Solstice gift to the newcomers: the wall. Silvermoon had paused the construction of the manor and coaxed the thing that made the building into putting up a defensive wall—which had gone *much* more quickly. It was a very impressive wall, all round the edge of the Veil itself, two full stories tall, two towered gatehouses—more accurately, towers with the space for gates to be installed later, but still defensible now—and wide enough that men could walk around on the top, shielded by a parapet. Its cityward surface was textured in interweaving branches of some fantastic tree or hedge fit enough to climb, yet nearly as smooth as slate on the outer side. The "maze" of the structure's insides was meant only to harmlessly waste the time of interlopers; its paths and tunnels wove over and under each other, to ultimately exit at a door next to its entry. Spyholes, trap doors, and murder boxes could be installed later. Despite the apparent thickness of the maze wall, its purpose was not to stand forever against all attacks, but rather to split up and channel ground troops, and frustrate wildlife. And, just in case, it could be occupied as an emergency refuge and closed off.

Delia had no idea *how* the Tayledras had managed to get the thing below—*I just accept thoughts like, "The thing below, sure, there's a thinking creature that filters water and grows buildings under us all" as a daily thing, now*—to "grow" something like that, or the access staircases to the top inside, but Silvermoon had promised her that the manor would absolutely surprise her, and she was impatient for it to finish growing so she could see just what he meant.

The wall had only taken about a fortnight to grow, and the Valdemarans had just finished installing massive wooden gates on the two openings into it. Eventually those would be replaced by metal bars backed by the wooden gates, but that would have to wait until the Valdemarans found the source of iron ore that the Hawkbrothers had handily marked out on the maps that

Silvermoon had left with them, mined it, refined, and poured it . . .

In fact, there was a great deal marked out on those maps, things that the Valdemarans were going to need. Back home, whatever they needed could be traded for and it would arrive by cart or boat. Here—well, if they didn't already have something, they were going to have to find or extract the raw materials for it. Things like iron, copper, and other useful metals. And minerals, too. They would have to be much more careful about extracting those resources than anyone in the Empire had ever been. Silvermoon had been quite clear about that. "Clean up after yourselves. Do not poison land, air, or water. Do not be greedy. We may have eliminated the worst of the hazards here, but there are still strange things that will not take kindly to finding their world threatened."

Delia believed him. She had gone up onto the wall several times since it had been erected to gaze out into the lands around the former Vale. Most times, she saw things she recognized. But sometimes . . . she got glimpses of things that she didn't.

Kordas gave himself a shake, as if to jar himself out of a reverie. "Back to work for all of us," he said aloud. "I have an idea."

"And I have grass-mowing duty." Delia sighed. She had hoped, now that they had finally settled in their permanent home, that she'd have some leisure time again.

But no. In the mornings, she was on the crew that supplied fodder to the herds out in the snow. While she didn't have to actually *cut* the fast-growing grass—that was being done by farmers' children, who had a lot of experience in harvesting—she was tasked with moving it. Well, she and Venidel. Venidel spun the cut grass into balls just at the limit of how much she could move a short distance. She moved the green balls of the mowed grass to one of the few floating sledges that the Hawkbrothers had left them. When a sledge was weighed down with as much as it could carry, a pair of Tow-Beasts moved it out to the outside herds and the herders spread it over the snow with pitchforks and rakes for the herds to eat.

I liked things better when I was with the scouts.

But at least she didn't have to work in the snow. And while she didn't exactly have the afternoons *free*, she wasn't doing the boring job of hauling grass balls out and spreading them with a rake.

She worked diligently all morning, which brought an end to the grass cutting; at this point the horses and cattle within the walls were moved to the mowed meadow to graze, because they could be depended on not to eat what was left down to the roots, unlike the goats and sheep. In the afternoon, the green mages would take over in the field that the herds had been moved out of, and grow the grass to mowing-high, fueled by the dung that the herds had left behind.

But for now, everyone went to luncheon.

Being on mowing duty was the first that Delia had spent any amount of time among actual farm folk. The Squire didn't really count; he didn't work the land or tend the pigs himself, his farm workers did. These were the people who actually grew the food, and to be honest, they were all pretty relieved that the convoy had landed in such a good place. They were happy. Ecstatic, really. They were taking the quality of the soil in the meadows and gardens here as a token of what it was like outside the walls, under the snow, and were thrilled.

Since everyone was generally so tired at morning's end that they just wanted to sit, the mowing crew all ate lunch together: pickles and sometimes something from the gardens, cheese from the stores, bread baked fresh that morning. And every other day, butter, also from stores.

And—oh treasure—brandy and cider. Cider was brought out to them in clean milk pails—there was no need for milk pails right now, since it wasn't calf season—by Dolls who had mugs festooned around their middles like a strange garland. Down in the hertasi tunnels was a vast store of barrels of slightly alcoholic cider, as well as the brandy. The cider was about as strong as good beer. The brandy could lift the hair on your head and leave it standing on its own.

"Hey, Delia," said one of the mowing lads, as a Doll handed him a mug of cider. "Y'know why them Hawkbrothers left behind this sweet gold?" He gulped down a mouthful and smacked his lips.

"Well, Jelavan showed me on the map where there's an apple orchard out there," she replied, waving her hands vaguely westward. "He reckons it's easily over five hundred years old. Anyway, the Hawkbrothers didn't like the apples to go to waste; they always stored everything they could, in case they might get besieged into the Vale, so they gathered them up every year. Cider and brandy's a good way to keep apple-stuff for a long, long time. They've been making and storing far more than they could ever use since they got here. They didn't want to take it with them, and thought we might like it, so—" She shrugged.

"And we can make more!" The lad's eyes sparkled with glee. "Me Da is going to be right happy to hear that. Anything else good down in them tunnels?"

"Not that I saw. The hertasi cleaned out almost everything except the forges and a few things built in or too heavy to move. Don't go down there without a map or a guide, though," she warned. "We might have to send dogs to find you."

The Dolls came around to gather up the mugs—there was *never* so much as a crumb left of the food—and the crew dispersed off to their afternoon jobs. Everyone had one, or at least, something like a job.

What Delia had was time to practice. Target practice, and following that, fighting practice with Briada. She wasn't the only one taking fighting lessons now. Briada held four lessons every day for anyone who wanted to sign up and potentially become one of the Guard. Delia shared her lesson now with six lads and three lasses, as young as fourteen but no older than nineteen. Some of these "new recruits" were farmers, one was a blacksmith's son, four were children of some of Kordas's nobles, and the rest were a mix of craftspeople and merchants.

She wasn't nearly as good at this as some of the others were, but she was quite pleased she was at least competent enough to avoid getting hurt and do pretty well at defending herself and others. Briada and her cousins seemed reasonably satisfied with their progress. Today's target practice went *really* well. When she went to join the others at hand-to-hand drill, she was wondering if she ought to switch to another weapon, like a longbow instead of a crossbow, because she could not miss now unless she planned to.

"Sword and shield today, my lovelies," Briada greeted them when they arrived at the little stretch of grass next to the manor that was too small to use for grazing. Some of them groaned, and Delia didn't blame them. The wooden practice shields were ridiculously heavy, but that was entirely on purpose, to get them used to the weight, so the actual fighting shields would seem light and easy to move in comparison. She was not looking forward to this, either. She wasn't at all good at it, and Briada had told her not to use her preferred form of defense, which was to trip her opponent with her Gift, or Fetch his sword right out of his hands and out of reach.

And, in fact, Briada looked her right in the face and added, "And no magic shenanigans, girl. We know you can defend yourself with them already, you need to practice how to defend yourself with—"

The rest of her speech was drowned out by the sound of a horn blowing at the main gate in the wall. It wasn't the alarm call, though the sound certainly sent a shock entirely through Delia's body, and she struggled to remember which call it was.

Visitors? No . . .

But they were all interrupted again by the Dolls streaming past them, heading for the gate. And they weren't armed. That settled her; practice could wait. She abandoned the group and followed the Dolls.

———

Kordas *felt* the change in magic energy in the ley-lines centered on the former Heartstone before the alarm sounded.

He had been on the threshold of the pavilion that the Six used as the spot where they were accessible to anyone. And then, out of nowhere, a surge of power flashed through the line nearest him, and away again. Then another. And another. As if something large and very magical was sending power down the line with every heartbeat.

He froze—and inside the pavilion, all six of the elder mages froze as well. Even Sydney-You-Asshole, sitting in a shallow box, turned into an inky statue.

The gate guards trumpeted the call that meant: *strange thing at the gate, not yet hostile.*

Then the Dolls, which had been passing by in the course of errands, or puttering around the Old Men tidying up, stopped everything they were doing for the briefest of moments, then straightened, turned, and began trotting for the main gate. Instinctively, Kordas followed them, pausing just long enough to snatch up a random coat left in the pile at the pavilion entrance. Whatever it was that had alerted the Guard was obviously on the other side of the gate. Beyond the Veil.

In the snow.

So he was going to need a coat. Because whatever it was, he was not letting it inside the Veil until he knew it was harmless.

The Dolls were moving faster than he was, so by the time he got to the gate, there were about a hundred of them waiting, impatience written in their body language, while the Guard stared down at them with a puzzled frown.

"Open it!" he called up to the Guard.

The Guard snapped to attention, but didn't move. "But Baron, there's—something uncanny out there!"

"Has it attacked the herds? The herdsmen?" he countered.

"No—"

"Then open the gate!"

Reluctantly, two of the men on the wall itself came down the stairs, unbarred the gate, and began to pull it open. But the Dolls were too impatient to wait. Six of them took each side, whisking the massive thing open as if they were opening a bedroom door, and the rest began pouring out into the snow.

Kordas followed, as more Dolls streamed out of the gate, passing him in their eagerness to get to—well, whatever it was. He couldn't see *what* it was through the crowds of Dolls. In fact, even when they stopped hurrying past him, he couldn't see what it was they were now crowded around.

He could certainly feel it, though. Power, raw power: power that was to the power of the ley-lines that the power of a wild river is to a millstream, the kind that he knew would scorch his mage-sight if he wasn't careful. Power he had only felt once before, and that had been—

—at the Imperial Palace—

—in the Chamber of the Beast.

Surely not . . .

Slowly, cautiously, he made his way toward the creature, getting glimpses of what looked like rock between the Dolls that were crowded around it in a massive group embrace. Finally he spotted Rose, her cheek pressed up against the thing, as heat radiated off of it, melting the snow down to the bare ground. "Rose!" he exclaimed. "Rose! It's Kordas!"

It took her a moment to respond. It was as if she was lost in some kind of reverie.

"Yes, Baron?" she asked.

"Is this the young Earth Elemental from the Imperial Palace?" he asked, hesitantly putting his hand out to touch the surface. After all, if the Dolls were embracing it, it was probably safe to touch.

Beneath his hand it was smooth, polished. Not a mirror-polish like you could get on marble; more like water-polished granite. And it was *very* warm; almost, but not quite, too hot to touch.

How do you talk to an Earth Elemental? he wondered. This was not something that had ever come up in his magic lessons. Magicians were wise to steer clear of Elementals, even the small and relatively harmless ones like *vrondi*. There was too much potential for harm—usually harm to the magician injudicious enough to try interfering with them.

Harm on both sides, actually, now that I think about it. Look what happened to our poor vrondi.

"Yes, Baron," Rose confirmed. "It is."

The Earth Elemental began to vibrate. Then a sound came from it. At first it sounded like millstones grinding together, but gradually the sound changed, first to something like the earth groaning beneath intolerable stress, then increasing in pitch until he began to make out—words?

"Uhhherrr," it said. *"Aahherrr. Saaa. Saaaveerr. Saver."*

"Saver?" he replied, confounded.

"Yesssssss." It paused. *"Mamaaa saaaaaay. Thaaaank. Thank Saver."*

And he was almost overwhelmed for a moment as magical power surged into him—not like getting hold of a ley-line that was too strong, but more like something being poured carefully into him until his reserves were completely topped up, and then a little more, somehow expanding his reserves to hold more. He hadn't even known that was possible!

"Thank Saver. Good Saver. Thank vrondi. *Good* vrondi.*"*

Now instead of power, the Elemental radiated emotion, and one he certainly recognized.

Gratitude. Gratitude so sweet, simple, and heartfelt that he found himself sobbing, pressing up against the "little" Elemental, cheek to the warm stone, as the Dolls were doing.

"Good. Good. Good," it crooned. *"Mama say thank. Me say thank. Thank good Saver. Thank good* vrondi.*"*

Something deep inside him broke like a dam, and all the regret, the guilt, the fear, the anguish over all the things he had not done, or *had* done but had not done *well*, came flooding out to be engulfed in that sea of gratitude. He sobbed, not brokenly, but in response to that gratitude. As if he was being given forgiveness for every one of his blunders, for lives lost that he had not saved, for so many things he had left undone.

He was not at all sure how long he stood there among the Dolls, arms spread wide, pressed against the surface of the Elemental, lost in a wordless haze of gratitude and forgiveness and salvation, sobbing and being comforted. It was a while, though, maybe as much as half a mark, before he finally dropped his arms, resting only his right hand on the surface of the Elemental, feeling healed again, healed of wounds he had not even realized had been suppurating away inside of him.

He blinked, and looked back over his shoulder, over the heads of the Dolls who surrounded him. It appeared that they all had an audience. He spotted Sai and Jonaton and waved at them over the heads of the Dolls. They made their way to him, as the Dolls shifted to let them through.

"Futtering felines," Sai said mildly, though his eyes were very wide. "Is this a Deep Earth Elemental? The same one that the Yellow Toad was torturing for power?"

"Yessssss," said the Elemental, before Kordas could answer. *"Mama say, go thank Saver. Go help Saver. So I go. Hard to find.* Vrondi *help."*

Kordas had often heard the saying "and his jaw dropped," but he had never seen it happen. Until now, that is, as both Sai and Jonaton stared, first at him, then at the Elemental, then back again, their mouths agape.

Sai recovered first. "This . . . is unprecedented."

"Well," Kordas managed, "what happened back at the Imperial Palace was unprecedented. Uh . . . can we invite it inside the Veil?"

Jonaton's jaw worked. "Uhm. I don't know. I don't know if it's safe to do so."

"I be good." All three of them started at the words. But Kordas acted first. Because those words, and that tone, sounded so like his youngest, Jon, that he simply could not deny the creature.

"Please enter the Veil, my young friend," he said, and a little tiny voice inside whispered *and hope you don't regret this.*

The thing moved under his hand, heaved itself up on what became six stubby granite legs, and began moving—slowly, one weighty, careful step at a time—toward the gate. The Dolls parted to let it move, and so did the crowd of Valdemarans bundled up in their coats and cloaks. No one said a word, but they certainly were watching, some with curiosity, some with concern, and a few with wonder. He remained with it, walking slowly beside it, and then had a moment of panic when he realized it was not going to fit through the gate—

But as the Elemental approached the gate, it began to—stretch. A little like a slug, in fact—it elongated itself, spreading the bulk out behind it on new legs that appeared at the end of it, until it was as long as three barges and supported on twelve legs, six on either side.

It paced deliberately through the gate, Dolls following, people following the Dolls. Once inside the Veil, it paused for a moment, then moved toward a patch of grass next to the slowly growing manor, and settled there.

"Help," it said simply. *"I help."*

And at that, the manor lurched a little, and visibly grew by another hand's-breadth, while the Valdemarans gasped aloud.

A new sound came from the Elemental then, a sound that Kordas could only compare to the sound of tinkling pebbles tumbling over one another in a barrel. After a moment, he recognized the sound for what it was.

Giggling.

He pulled off his coat and used it to sit on, settling himself down at the creature's "head." "So far away from—there—and here you are," Kordas replied, wiping his forehead and hair back. "How did you find us? How did you get here?"

"*Follow mama's wise knows. She say, 'Saver is where you feel* true *he is.' I dive into world-home, come back up here.*"

"I'm impressed. We are all very fragile compared to you. Thank you for being careful," Kordas quite honestly spoke. An Elemental was immensely strong, physically, and this was a youth who might be somewhat clumsy, if it was anything like humans, horses, and hares. "And I think we should get to know one another."

"*Yesssssss,*" it agreed. "*Mama say, no give true name. Saver give me name.*"

Well, that was easy enough to understand. Elementals that had a sense of self seldom revealed their actual names to humans. Names had power, and knowing the name of something often gave a mage power over that thing. Knowing that, choosing a name for an Elemental, might affect them in ways he didn't know, so no Doomchip Boulderdeath name for the child. Something innocuous. "Well then, let's call you Pebble, shall we?" he suggested, thinking the creature might be amused at being compared to a tiny stone.

He was right. It giggled again, and radiated delight.

"And I am Kordas," he continued.

"*Kor-dasssss. Saver,*" Pebble confirmed. "*I help Kor-dassss.*"

The creature spoke very slowly, which—so far as Kordas's limited knowledge told him—was normal for an Earth Elemental. Its sibilants sounded like escaping steam. The Six, Jonaton, and every other mage who wasn't terrified to get near Pebble soon gathered around it to hear what it had to say. Kordas was obscurely relieved when Sydney appeared, tail high, sniffed the front of the thing, leapt to the top of it, explored for a few minutes, then settled in for a nap on the warmth. Meanwhile, every Doll that wasn't in the initial welcoming party came by and patted the side of the creature.

It was slow going, and needed patience, but Pebble was quite clear, if slow, and eventually they got the whole story. After the fall of the Capital, Pebble's mother had taken it away and healed it, and listened while Pebble recounted what had happened from the time it had been stolen from her in the midst of a romp on the surface to the moment when she had sensed Pebble at last, and erupted into the Palace to free and avenge her child. And it very soon became obvious that while Pebble might be a child, it certainly was bright, observant, and, even in slavery, and despite its pain and confinement, able to "see" things quite clearly. Pebble was friends with the *vrondi* in the Dolls, and they commiserated on their captivity. It had immediately understood when it saw Kordas that he was very different from the mages whose job it was to torment it. It had asked the Dolls about him, and heard from them that Kordas was going to send the Dolls to free it.

And it knew exactly who to thank for freeing it.

And once its mother had it back again, and her raging temper had cooled, it had told her about the human who was different. The "Saver." Kordas.

Once all the lingering wounds had healed, she and Pebble had set out to find the Saver.

That had proven to be beyond even *their* formidable powers. So Mama had turned to the other Elementals for help—at least, the ones she could contact.

That, too, had proven fruitless—until, suddenly—it wasn't. And the *vrondi* had flocked to the two Elementals to tell them what they wanted to know.

"Oho!" exclaimed Ceri. "That would be when we cast the spells that let the Dolls talk to their kin!"

"Was that what the *vrondi* told you, Pebble?" Kordas asked.

Kordas sensed Pebble emote something like a shrug. *"Day, day, day, many many day, no. Then day yes. Vrondi say here,* true. *Mama say go. Pebble come. Pebble thank. Pebble help Saver."*

"The Hawkbrothers would be gobsmacked if they could see this," Jonaton muttered to Kordas.

"Pebble, every bit of help you can give us will be wonderful," Kordas said carefully. "But you must be careful. You must not hurt yourself, or make yourself sick or weak. And tell us if you need something. Do you understand?"

"Pebble understand." There was the sense of a yawn. *"Pebble go far. Pebble tired. Pebble sleep. Sun, dark, wake with sun."*

"Yes, please do that, Pebble," Kordas told it, and stood up. "We will speak more when you are awake."

"Yessssssss," Pebble agreed.

And then, silence.

20

The next morning saw Pebble awake, and charmingly eager to help. So eager, in fact, that it humped up on its stubby legs, trundled itself down to the gate, and waited politely for the guards to let it out, like an eight-legged stone puppy. The guards sent for Kordas, of course, who told them to open the gate for it. He assumed that now that Pebble had politely said its thanks, it was going to go back to its mother. He'd brought a coat just so he could see Pebble off.

I don't want Pebble to go, he realized, as the gate opened, and he followed the "young" Elemental out into the snow. *The connection . . . it's a lot more powerful than I thought. We both suffered at the hands of the Empire. And we both are responsible for the Emperor's downfall.*

But no, Pebble apparently had no such ideas. No, it proceeded to push and melt its way down to the fields where the rest of the stock was being kept, as if it knew it was making a nice, clear road for them, while Kordas followed it, bemused.

The stock were kept in their fields by virtue of those same charms that kept them close to the barges of their owners. Each charm had been firmly attached to a rock in the center of each field, so the animals would stay within the confines of their designated area.

Pebble stopped at the edge of the field furthest from the Vale, as if it sensed where the invisible boundary was. *"Pebble go in?"* it asked politely. It was already much better at human speech than it had been last night.

Kordas had a moment of alarm. Did it want to eat the stock?

"Pebble melt snow." As if it had read his mind, the Earth Elemental supplied the answer to his unspoken question.

That's—not a bad idea. There's still plenty of edible grass and weeds under that snow. "Yes, please, Pebble. Go in and melt the snow. The animals in there will be very happy if you do."

A quick wave of warmth flushed over him from the Elemental; it felt awfully good out here in the freezing air. *"Good! Good! Make animals happy!"* And having been given permission, it trundled into the first field.

There were no fences or actual boundaries yet, because as long as the animals were all being held in their respective groups by the charms they were still wearing and the ones in the center of each field, there really was no need. There was a little mingling of creatures at the edges of each field, but cattle, horses, sheep, and goats generally had no problem sharing a field with each other.

Pebble seemed to sense exactly where the boundaries of the charms were, however. It started right at the edge, and simply walked back and forth, like a plow, leaving matted-down, brown-green grass in its wake. It must have increased the heat it was giving off, because the snow melted very rapidly. And the horses in this first field, while shying off away from the moving rock at first, were quickly tempted by the uncovered grass, and when Pebble made no aggressive movements toward them, slowly edged their way over to the cleared sections. They still kept their eyes on Pebble, but when all the Elemental did was continue to melt snow, they gradually began to eat.

Within a mark, Pebble had cleared the first field and moved on to the next one, this one with cattle in it. The cattle could not possibly have cared less, perhaps because they had already watched Pebble clear the horse field, and had seen nothing to alarm them. The herdsmen drifted over to watch along with Kordas, clearly bemused at their new helper.

Then Grim frowned, shaded his eyes with his hand for a better view, then stepped gingerly into the field. He looked around for some time, as Kordas wondered what on earth he was looking for. He returned to Kordas's side, now wearing a puzzled expression on his weathered, bearded face.

"M'lord Baron," the Horsemaster said. "Would that thing be eatin' the dung?"

Kordas blinked. "I don't know," he replied. "Maybe? Is that a problem?"

Grim snorted. "The opposite. Means no dung for the mages to dry up and us to collect, and nothin' to burn the grass. Until we get these beasts spread out into their owners' fields, I druther yon rock eats it than the boys shovel it."

One of the junior mages had just come down from the Vale in time to overhear this, and his whole face lit up. "Does this mean we aren't on drying duty now?"

Kordas could only shrug. "I suppose it does, at least down here. We'll have to see if Pebble wants to clean up in the Vale as well."

Pebble was still at work—if, indeed, this constituted "work" for an Earth Elemental—when Kordas left to get his breakfast. Maybe it wasn't work. Maybe it was the equivalent of grazing.

When it came close to the watchers, Kordas called to it. "Pebble?" he said. "Are you eating?"

"Yessssssss," the Elemental said, with what sounded like great satisfaction. *"Eating. Very good. Is more?"*

"In every field with animals, and you should eat as much as you want," he told it. There was that sound like tumbling pebbles again.

"Thank Saver! Is good!" it said with great glee, and proceeded on its slow and careful way.

I guess I can leave it to work unsupervised, he decided at last. *Though how on earth I would stop it, I have no idea.*

When word got around that there was a helpful Elemental here, though, Pebble had no lack of requests. Kordas finally made a ruling: no jobs for Pebble that could easily be done by hand. That cut back on the requests, but there was one that Kordas particularly supported. It turned out that Pebble understood what scale was. After some quick sculpting of a model and some coaching, Pebble walked into the river. Not half a mark passed until the first of many bridgetowers to come erupted from the icy span, with a giggling Pebble atop it. Steam roiled off of the stone as it moved and blended into layers, each stretching laterally a little more than the last until a surface wide enough for three wagons ramped up from the riverbank. Then Pebble rolled sideways into the river with a tremendous splash, and the next one came up the same way. The "little" Elemental was apparently having the time of its life, casually making bridgetowers that would have taken Kordas's people years to even attempt. The Tayledras didn't use bridges—they probably had Gates if they needed to get across the river—so Kordas had been resigned to his people only having access to the other side of the waterway via boat, and only at certain times of year. If need be, the Gate-arches could be employed for the "short hop" across the river, but they'd decay away eventually. Now, Valdemarans could reach the far shore via bridges that looked like they'd last a thousand years, and reach the beautiful Grove there that he'd seen on brighter days.

It turned out that Pebble had helped the livestock just in time. That afternoon, a blizzard moved in, and if Pebble had not cleared the fields, the animals would have been in real danger. As it was, Pebble and the mages together were able to make three-sided snow shelters, roofed with branches hastily cut from anywhere that they could be spared without killing the bushes or trees, that all the various herds could huddle together in. Pebble extinguished most of its warmth in order to plow snow rather than melting it, the mages packed it down, and Pebble then warmed up just enough to melt the surface of the wall and let it freeze hard again, so the walls would hold up almost as well as walls made of stone.

Pebble did not like the cold, however, and came back up to the Vale. Inside the Vale, the mages had figured out a way to manipulate the Veil to shed the snow instead of melting it into rain. Whether this was a good idea or not—Kordas wasn't entirely sure. It could mean they'd end up with a wall of snow overtopping the rock wall, or worse, ice. But for now, this seemed to be the best temporary answer, because otherwise they'd all be ankle-deep in water with nowhere for it to go.

Kordas had another "meal" set out for Pebble in that strip of meadow it seemed to like, and as soon as the Elemental got there, it fell on the dried dung as if it was starving. Literally fell on the dried dung—its legs disappeared into its body and the dung vanished underneath it.

"Good. Good," it sighed when it was done. *"Good eat."*

"We've got thousands of people, and plenty of livestock. We'll make sure you're not hungry," Grim told it, patting its side with caution.

Kordas got a sense that it had turned its attention on the Horsemaster. *"Who?"* Pebble asked.

"Grim. This is Grim, and he is a friend," Kordas replied immediately, just as Sydney appeared, scrambled up onto the Elemental, kneaded with his paws for a moment, and settled down, purring loud enough to make everyone smile. Sydney was followed to Pebble by Jonaton, dressed at last in one of his fancy, embroidered robes. Jonaton's ability to grasp almost any task meant he was always in demand, but he had finally come to have a look at the creature. Jonaton strolled around it, fascinated.

"It makes legs?" the mage asked Kordas, eyes wide. "Can you get it to do that now?"

"Not make legs," Pebble said, startling Jonaton so much the mage jumped. *"Not wake rumble friend."*

Rumble friend? Oh! The cat!

"That's a cat," said Kordas. "One of the things we call him is 'Sydney.'"

"Like cat," replied Pebble. *"Sydney is good boy."* And as they said that, Kordas noticed that Pebble had dished its back a very little bit, the better to cradle the now-dozing Sydney.

"You wouldn't like it very much if you weren't made of rock," Jonaton muttered, looking at his scratched hands ruefully. "Kordas, why is it that damned cat lets your boys toss it around like a rag ball, but when I try to pet him, he lacerates me?"

Kordas tried not to laugh. "He's your cat, Jonaton. Why ask me?"

"Good cat," rumbled Pebble. *"Who?"*

"My name is Jonaton, Pebble," Jonaton replied. "A friend." He was already grinning; Pebble, Kordas had noticed, tended to have that effect on people.

Well . . . it's a very sweet creature. And resilient. It seems to have recovered very well from being a tortured captive for so long. Perhaps that was the nature of Elementals. They were so long-lived, practically immortal, that "a long time" by human standards might just have been the equivalent of a short while to Pebble.

By this point, most people seemed to have gotten over their fear of Pebble, and had come to the strip of grass to have a look at the heat-emitting, talking rock. And more cats than just Sydney had decided that Pebble's back was the best place to sleep, ever. In no time at all, Pebble was playing host to almost twenty cats, and the Elemental was surrounded by the curious. Kordas left Jonaton and Pebble to answer their questions, and returned to his family barge, only to meet a barrage of questions from his boys. The youths had all been kept away from Pebble until it had been determined that the Earth Elemental was safe. And they wanted to know everything he knew about it.

As long as it wasn't raining, people still living in the barges preferred to spend as much time *on* their barge as in it. So Kordas gathered the lads up and took them to sit on the roof. Moments of rest, or even just calm, had been rare in his life for too long. He wasn't prepared to settle down too much, but at a time like right now, it was appropriate. *Taking a moment is all right. I let the Plan and this expedition steal too much away from me. I resent it, and I damned well* will *have time with my family now. We made it here. I don't have to feel guilty over doing anything even for a minute that isn't for the people of Valdemar. I can ease up.*

But he hadn't even begun to answer their questions when Rose came sprinting up the path to their barge. "Baron! Baron!" she called, and for the first time he could remember she had fear in her voice. "Pebble is calling for you!"

She stopped below him before he could reply. "It thinks something bad is coming. And—we feel it too!"

———

Delia was fascinated by Pebble, and she wished with all her heart that Jelavan was with her to see the "little" Elemental. *Jelavan would have been beside himself, and asking all sorts of questions.* Pebble's vocabulary wasn't large—at first—but the more people asked it questions, the more it seemed to learn, and learn quickly. It made an odd little interrogative *"Uh-errr?"* when it didn't understand something, which was strangely charming, and always elicited the response of the questioner carefully rephrasing their question in simpler terms.

It was impossible to tell Pebble's "head" from the "tail"—if, indeed, there was any meaningful difference—but most people were clustered around the end where the voice seemed to come from. There wasn't anything like features to read, and yet, Delia was absolutely certain that Pebble was curious about the people around it, delighted with the purring cats lined up on its back, contented with its surroundings, and—even though the poor thing had been held captive and tortured by *other* humans—trusting of the people around it. Did it have some sort of Empathic sense, as Healers did? Was that why the Dolls all loved it?

She had the irresistible urge to *pet* the thing, even though it was taller than she was, and about as long as two horses and carts, and looked like nothing more than a big, water-smoothed boulder.

Finally, she gave up trying to resist the impulse. Gingerly, she reached out to put her hand on it, and found that it was about the temperature of sun-warmed rock. *Just* comfortable, although if you leaned against Pebble for too long, or sat on it, she reckoned you'd probably be sweating and overheated before too long.

The cats *loved* the heat, though. And even some of the encampment dogs were coming to Pebble, putting their backs to it, and curling up for naps—with one wary eye on the cats.

And in the space of a breath, all that changed.

Beneath her hand, Pebble—stiffened. That was the only way she could describe the feeling. Pebble's surface texture changed from smooth to undulating waves of stubby points. The dogs immediately alerted, jumped to their feet, and fled—perhaps back to their masters. The cats woke up, all at once, and scrambled en masse.

A throng of Dolls appeared from nowhere.

"Kordasss!" Pebble wailed. *"Need Kordasss! Need Kordassss!"*

What? she thought, with a sudden feeling of dread. This was not helped when Kordas came running as fast as he could, accompanied by Rose, as the once-attentive crowd backed away from Pebble in alarm.

Pebble emitted a high whine, as if it was struggling with speech; Kordas placed both hands on its "head" end, but he couldn't seem to calm the Elemental enough to get it to speak properly. And now the entire creature trembled, as if with its own internal earthquake.

Finally, words came out of it again. *"Bad thing!"* it cried. *"Bad, bad thing coming! Big bad thing!"*

Kordas did not hesitate a second. "Rose, get all the herders to bring their stock in from the fields and get them behind the wall. Tell my

Guard and all the mages to man the wall—" He paused. "Pebble, where? Where is the bad thing coming from?"

"*Riverrrrrrr!*" Pebble whined. "*Riverrrrrrrr!*"

River? Where Pebble made the bridges earlier?

"Lift me up high, Pebble! Show me the direction!"

Pebble grew legs again, and an extra two at its "face" end. Kordas stepped in toward Pebble, and those two legs formed into stony platforms backed by broad, crude "thumbs." Pebble "sat up" and raised Kordas above its head. It was noticeably calmer with Kordas there, physically touching it. Kordas braced himself against Pebble's thumbs and covered his eyes. He knew there was a risk of being scorched by his own mage-sight, but he hoped he'd get lucky by invoking it while he was being lifted, looking downward and opening his eyes slowly. Easing into it, he couldn't see much of anything except the blizzard, but mage-sight showed him some strange things. Strangely *vague* things. Normally, when Kordas focused his attention on something, using mage-sight, it enhanced its detail. Mage-sight itself was something like a hyperfocus: seeing something so well you see past its physical form and into its energy traits. This time, though, gazing in the direction Pebble turned him, a "glow" marking a large life sign was an uneven, but moving, cloud, many furlongs away but closing. It matched the contours of the land, and flares and spits of energy discharges were in its wake, occasionally exploding as far as he could See. When he refined his mage-sight back onto the nearing cloud, though, it didn't appear to be a cloud at all. Its collective aura broke into thousands of moving vertical 'sticks,' like toothpicks, whose energy peaked at either end, flowing over the landscape like a—

Like a swarm. The mage-sight is right—it isn't a cloud, it's thousands of individuals traveling like one, alongside the water.

Water—swarm—the—the knife-water-spiders? He pushed *that* thought aside. *Right now, I do not need that in my life. From spending time with my boys directly into a swarm of giant death-spiders?* Just the thought of it angered him.

"Man the wall on the river side!" he shouted from his impromptu command tower. "Incoming danger! Guards and Auxiliaries, all hands, all muster! Report to wall stations! Gunners, to revetments! Dolls, support the Guard! But get everyone *inside* the wall, now! If stock has to be left behind, so be it, but I want every *person* inside this wall now!"

Delia didn't wait for instructions; her Fetching Gift could well be useful, so she ran for the wall on the river side and sped up the steps to peer through the thick curtain of snow toward the largely invisible river. If she was needed somewhere else, well, they had plenty of ways of contacting her.

More and more people, most of them inadequately armored, but armed to the teeth, came running up to join her on the wall. She moved as much out of the way as she could while still being able to look toward the river, but the jostling of the Guard made her want to hit back at them. It irked her maybe more than it should, but—and then she felt it.

Hate. Waves of *rage* and *hate*, coming from where the riverside should be. And just for a moment, the skeins of snow parted, and she got a glimpse of a red blur. A disheartening ululation, like momentary shrieks spreading outward through a crowd, made everyone stop what they were doing. Most arrayed on station just stopped their preparations and stared unhappily into the blizzard. Two Guard auxiliaries stumbled against each other, and the first of them smacked the second right across the mouth.

Her heart plummeted, her mouth dried, and her throat closed. *No . . . no, it can't be.*

The snow swirled as if a curtain had descended. But the *feelings* didn't go away; and as she glanced around her at the Guards and mages clustered up here on the wall, with the Veil streaming water a scant arm's-length away, she saw from the looks on their faces that they felt it too. And they recognized it. The damnable ululation sounded again, only much, *much* closer.

Then the snow parted again, and what had been a red blur became something she had never expected to see again. A red glow, disturbingly wide, diffused through the snow. The ground rumbled, and Delia noted that the rumble made wave patterns, and significant softening, in the mud below. She heard people yelling and livestock leaning toward panic—and possibly, stampede. Dogs barked at the previous ululation, but this time, they stopped barking entirely.

The red glow pulsed, from one center point, outward from horizon to horizon from Delia's viewpoint. It pulsed again, brighter, but from two points of origin outward. Then three. Brighter each time. Closer.

Blizzard snow billowed as if pushed against the Veil by breath, backlit by a steadily pulsing red glow, and the third breath later, it appeared.

The Red Forest. Only *now* it was moving, and moving uncomfortably quickly, one gigantic living thing that filled the river valley. Even from this distance, all of the trees visibly seethed and writhed, and the thing was moving at a terrifying speed, like a flash flood, coming down the riverbank and heading straight for them, thousands of voices shrieking.

Now all that preparation, using Mindspeakers as well as the Dolls, paid off. Rose kept pace with Kordas as he raced for the nearest barge containing the Poomers and the Poomer ammunition. Six Dolls fell in behind them, keeping pace, while Rose kept a running update on what was happening elsewhere.

And just what it was that they were about to face.

That made him slow and then stop in his tracks. The Red Forest. *The 'Blood Forest.' Hate and rage will hunt you forever,* he thought, for no apparent reason. When he caught his breath back, his thoughts tasted of despair. *Is it here because of the Empire? Is it their revenge against us? Would Poomers be of any use against that thing? Ball, maybe, if they gather up close . . . bolt bundle—useless, caltrop lines—useless, stinging gas—double useless. We'd only flavor them. Assuming attrition as a primary principle, reducing their numbers is most likely to succeed—because of course, they could have dead-switch reflexes or Final Strikes, the sort of end-game that ends the game for both sides. Chainshot could slow the thing down, but they'd have to aim very low to strike below the canopy. And chainshot's heavy, so increased load times would impact the rate of fire, and the only deployed Poomers are all on the perimeter of the Vale. So the one thing we've got that's sure to cause damage is too far away to use. Of course it is, because I wasn't smart enough for this. I took time for myself, and my boys, and Isla, and now we're all going to die, because I didn't spend that time making better emergency plans. I could have spent that time saving them! I hate myself for that. I just assumed everything would be all right. Just because we reached the milestone of a settlement. I let my guard down at the last moment. The last moment of the expedition. Oh gods, can it really be that? I slowed down, I wasted time on myself, and I could have done without that time if I'd known it meant I was going to get people killed. People who trusted me.*

"I do not believe that standard projectiles will be of much use, Baron," Rose said, echoing his earlier thoughts. "But . . . perhaps the things that *send* the projectiles might be? The cartridges?"

"Yes, maybe we could make them explode, but how, without it being a suicide mission? Every one is locked against enchantment and force, and breaking that would take too much time—also, worth mentioning, they might explode. We didn't steal any clockwork strikers or tread-on webs, or we could just throw them. Firing crossbow bolts at the cartridges is more likely to waste arrows than—"

People who trusted me. People who still trust me. People trust me. And if I can't *make everything all right like they trust me to, I can at least feel hope for longer. I can act like things are all right, and they won't have as much fear. I know how to act. I'll make the fiction create the reality. I can do that. If I know* anything, *it's how to fake looking competent.*

And then it occurred to him. "Delia! Where's Delia?"

"On the wall facing the river, Kordas," Rose replied.

Perfect. "Get me a floating barge and a fast heavy horse to pull it, and have them meet me at the storage barges." *Nobody believes a heavy horse can be fast until they've been shoulder-checked into the next county by one.* He tried to pick up his pace, but now his path was blocked by herds of frantic sheep mingled with frightened horses, chased into dubious safety from outside the wall, to interfere now. *I should have thought of that,* he cursed, and tried to shove his way through—

And found himself picked up bodily by Rose, who threw him over her shoulder and somehow managed to shove her way through the livestock. He twisted around to something approximating sitting up like he meant to be there. *What in all the Hells. I've learned to depend more and more of my rule upon others, and now I'm literally being carried by them? If it wasn't so funny for its absurdity, I'd be offended at the thought.* By then, he was only in a seated position as far as regally wrapping one arm entirely around Rose's head while flailing the other. More terrified animals filled the spaces around all the storage barges, but the Doll leapt twice between wildlife-islands and closed ground that much more quickly. There were three more Dolls, and a Tow-Beast with an empty hay wagon, waiting for them when Rose put him down, twisting Kordas to face him the right way. Without needing to be told what to do, Rose calmed the Tow-Beast, who was taking his cues from the milling horses around him, and the three Dolls formed a chain, passing the Poomer cartridge loads out of the barge and into the wagon at an alarming rate.

Thank the gods that those things are meant to take rough handling. They had to be; after all, the Empire only had heavy wagons or canal barges to move their stores, and once out of the Empire and onto the battlefield, there were no canals, and probably no roads, either. So transit would not be kind to lesser builds. Unlike the Spitters, which used stone balls or stubby "bolts," the ammunition for a Poomer was whatever the Poomer loaders fancied, from glass fragments and pottery shards to chains to solid projectiles. Those were all inert enough until fired to be handled roughly, but the explosive cartridges—if those went off prematurely, you could lose half a supply column. So they had to be triggered, very precisely, by a spring-loaded mechanism on the Poomer itself that snapped into a special divot on the back of the cartridge.

They loaded the barge with all it could carry, and without being directed, one of the Dolls took the Tow-Beast's head and led it toward the river wall as fast as the Doll's legs could go—which was a *lot* faster than a human, and just about matched the Tow-Beast's trot. Mud roared up as high as the Dolls' heads with every beat of the heavy horse's hoofbeat. Ten more Dolls formed a flying vee and pushed—and in a few cases, threw—the livestock out of the way, for the speeding barge to get through the maze wall's nearest gate. Out of the crowd of milling animals and herdsfolk came a floating barge, another Tow-Beast, and another Doll leading it. And three more Dolls on top of it, to add to the work crew.

"I need—" he said to Rose.

Before he could finish the sentence, she had picked him up in her arms again and was running for the wall.

Thankfully, she put him down at the foot of the stairs, although at this point, the last thing he was worried about was his dignity. His heart racing, he ran up the steps two at a time, and with Rose close behind, impatiently shoved his way past the guards until he reached Delia, whom he found in the middle of the pack of mages.

"It's the Red Forest," Sai told him, expressionlessly. Jonaton was cursing, fluently and fervidly, under his breath. "I thought those damned Tayledras said it would be no problem!"

"I guess we just found out they're fallible," he replied, peering through the curtain of snow at the huge red blur charging up to the wall. "Careful with your mage-sight, but it's left a trail of magical damage behind it. What the hell is there in magic that we can use against that thing?"

"The green mages seem to be able to sap it, a little, but they tell me it's like handling poisonous thorn-branches with thorns as long as your hand. They're having to be careful or it can turn against them and infect them. They've slowed it down, at least, but they can't do more than that." Sai shaded his eyes with his hand, and finally spat in disgust. "I didn't want to do this, but—" He cleared his throat. "Schwande! Logan! Sera! Moklas! Clear this damned snow away!"

Those were their only weather mages, who normally confined themselves to predicting weather, and occasionally steering it gently.

Back in the old land, they'd limited their powers to keeping actual disasters at bay: slowing a downpour so it didn't become a flood, carefully coaxing rain into being when things were too dry, steering rain away from fields that still needed harvesting so that if you happened to be there, you would see the unharvested field dry and ready, and the harvested one next to it getting dumped on. They had never, in all the time *he* had been the Duke, used their powers to directly *disperse* weather. Such large-scale interference in weather was the provenance of Imperial weather mages with the Army. Generals did not care what collateral damage occurred, as long as they got the result they desired, so the four had been especially secretive for years.

As a mage himself, he sensed energies moving high above him, but that was the limit of what he could understand. The price to be paid for it, it seemed, was the sudden headache everyone got from the intense change in air pressure. Guard and mage alike winced, popping their ears. Loose snow lifted from the ground before turning to raindrops, which immediately fell back down. The snow in the air vanished from the Vale and the river valley, as if cleared away by an invisible hand. Sun broke through the clouds, which cleared away from above the Vale, as an ever-expanding, rainbow-lined hole in the overcast.

A low moan—involuntary—escaped from virtually everyone on the wall, as the enemy lay fully revealed below them.

Acre after acre of the thing, seething with hate and anger, every "tree"—though only the gods knew what those *things* actually were—thrashing in seemingly coordinated waves. *Is it going to come over the wall? Can it come over the wall?*

"Magic might backfire on us, if we try anything like a spell to control it or attack it with pure power," Ceri cautioned. "It might absorb the magic and become even stronger."

"Hey! Before we try any more magic on it than we already are, try shooting something at it?" Jonaton suggested, although his worried face and his tone suggested that he didn't expect anything they threw at it physically to work.

The thing had stopped just short of the Veil; Kordas didn't know if the Veil had stopped it, or if it wasn't sure what the Veil *was*—or even if it had any thoughts at all. The tops of the "trees" were just below the top of the wall, and lower than the parapet—but he had the feeling that if the thing wanted to, or realized that it *could*, it would climb right over the wall. He raised his voice. *"Guards! Fire at will! Any target!"*

A veritable rain of bolts arced down at the nearest "trees." And as he had expected, there was no reaction. The arrows might as well have been dewdrops.

"Someone bring me up one of the Poomer charges," he shouted, somehow keeping his voice steady. "Delia, come over to me."

Delia made her way through the mages to his right until she was at his side, crossbow in hand pointed downward. She looked as white as the snow had been, but her voice was steady when she answered him. "What can I do?"

"You know how the Spitters work, right?" he asked, as he took the cask-sized cartridge from Rose, who had gotten it from another Doll mid-staircase who had brought it up from the barge. It was a gray cylinder, flat on both ends, with a spot in the middle of the "back end" where the snap trigger of the Poomer was meant to strike. "This is just like the cartridges for the Spitters, but on a much larger scale."

She nodded.

"Plant this thing somewhere down there in the Red Forest, and then hit *this* spot as hard as you can with a bolt," he said, pointing to the recessed, red-painted spike pit. Kordas held it with the pit facing directly upward.

She looked away from him and stared at a spot just below them, among the thrashing trees. The rippling edges of the Forest advanced, then retreated as they touched the Veil, then advanced again . . . but each time, they stayed in contact with the Veil a little longer. And Delia just stared, as if mesmerized by the movement, while she mechanically cocked her crossbow. He restrained the urge to shout at her. *Why is she taking so long?*

Suddenly his hands were empty, and the trees just below them winced out of the way of the gray cylinder that appeared to have spontaneously appeared among them, driven halfway into the ground.

Before he—or they—could react, Delia had her crossbow in her hands, aimed, and fired.

POOM!

The cartridge went off spectacularly, blowing a hole in the forest that showed the ground and snow beneath it, sending bits of oozing tree, dripping substrate, and snow in every direction, as the people on the wall ducked behind the parapet. A few of the dragonflies buzzed drunkenly around the mess before seeming to get their bearings and ducking back inside one of the "mouths." The hole was easily the size of three houses, and at the sight of it everyone cheered.

Until the hole closed right back up again before their very eyes.

"Bring up another," Delia said steadily. "And if any of the rest of you have some magic way to drop a cartridge trigger-side-up in that mess so I don't have to—"

"Guards! Loading line for Delia!" Kordas shouted behind her, and four guards formed into a close circle behind Delia, with her as the fifth spot of the circle. They all readied crossbows, and as Delia fired one bolt, the guard on her left took the fired bow and safely pointed it downward, then handed it to the second guard, who pulled it, handed it to the third who loaded it, who then handed it to the Guard on her right, who then placed the ready-to-aim loaded crossbow in Delia's hands while her previous crossbow began the loading circuit.

Half a dozen of the mages, including Jonaton, made a grab for the cartridge another of the Dolls was bringing up, and within moments, there were more Dolls forming another chain on the parapets to put Poomer cartridges in the mages' hands.

Some levitated the cartridges gently into place. Some apported them—apportation worked a lot like the Fetching Gift, except that any mage who had learned the spell could do it. As a rule, it was meant for short distances, but in this case the spell had enough range. It didn't take long for the mages to start dropping cartridges in choice places; what did take some care was placing the cartridges far enough away from each other for maximum damage. While they were placing the cartridges, Kordas kept an eye on the Forest; it may have appeared to have "healed" almost instantly from the damage it had taken— but from the uncoordinated way in which the trees in the spot were thrashing, it hadn't actually recovered. Meanwhile, Delia's face was completely expressionless, her eyes narrowed in concentration.

"We're hurting them!" Kordas yelled, and a few guards cheered at that, while one audibly asked, "Them? Just how many forests are here?" Kordas shot him a baleful eye, then turned back to business. He knew his levitation skills were not all that good, but—*maybe my aim is good enough*. And although he didn't have a bow on him, he *did* have his Spitter and a pouch full of projectiles and cartridges. *If it can take down one source of rage and hate, it can take down another.* He grinned to himself for a moment, kissed his Spitter, loaded it, sighted on the trigger point of the planted canister nearest him, and carefully squeezed the trigger, at the same time that Delia aimed and fired her crossbow.

POOM-POOM!

Two canisters going off side by side made a *much* bigger hole in the thing than he would have expected, and the trees went wild. Delia was triply faster at reloading than he was, but once he'd reloaded, another two cartridges went up with an equally satisfying result.

Three more, and the Forest abruptly pulled back from the wall, and he dared to hope.

But then it did something he hadn't expected. Staying at a distance from the wall, the thing split into two, and began to encircle them. *It's smart enough to know not to cluster up when an explosive is in play. And to keep a part of itself out of our apparent range.*

"Fuck!" Jonaton swore. He grabbed the knife off his belt and cut off his fancy gown at the knee, tossed the bottom aside, and made a sprint to the right.

"Some of you follow Jonaton!" Kordas barked. "Sai, you, you, and you—" He pointed at three of the guards. "Support Delia! The rest with me!"

He sprinted to his left, followed by guards and mages, and the ever-present Rose. He left a trio of one mage and two guards at intervals along the wall until he ended up at the back of the Vale and met with Jonaton.

The Forest had already beaten them there. The Vale was completely encircled too.

The *POOM*s of cartridges going off echoed back and forth around the Vale, as the Valdemarans who were not part of the guard either sought shelter or came to the foot of the wall to offer any help they could. Someone brought up casks of the Tayledras's hard brandy to the foot of the wall, and before Kordas could shout at him not to be daft, he called up "Lad! This'll *burn!*"

Dear gods, it will! The Tayledras had introduced them all at the Midwinter celebration to a game that consisted of snatching nuts with your bare hand out of a bowl of burning brandy, and he knew from that, as well as drinking it, that the stuff was potent— and flammable! He gestured to the people below to bring casks up—and this time, there was no finessing about. The trees had closed in to direct contact with the maze wall, and beat upon it. Footing on the parapets became slippery while the trees beat upon the structure, and it was increasingly unnerving when they began their disorienting screams again, and the pounding upon the walls took on rhythms. *Can't say I like that,* Kordas thought. *This thing hasn't even breached the wall and it's beating us up. Out of mood, off balance, distracting noises, frightened, and we aren't even sure what kind of fight we can ultimately put up.* After a prompt, Rose smashed in the top of a cask, and splashed the contents over every part of the Forest she could reach.

"Baron Kordas, I believe they should be on fire," Rose said, with a hint of humor.

"Right you are, Rose," Kordas replied. "You read my mind." He grounded his magic, thrust out his hand, gathered power from the ley-line below, and lit off a fireball.

The result was gratifying; with a *whoompf,* the brandy ignited, and the trees caught fire, thrashing in agony.

But once again, the feeling of triumph was short-lived, because the damned things began lobbing chunks of snow and mud at the flames, putting them out.

If they're fighting fire, they aren't fighting us. "More brandy! Bring torches!" he ordered. "They can't keep putting it out!"

Then the sky split open; a jagged lance of lightning arced down out of the clouds to a point outside the wall to his right and a peal of thunder that shook him to his core left him half blind and breathless. The weather mages were at work, somehow managing to generate lightning out of the blizzard clouds pushed back by their snow-clearing. Within seconds he saw smoke roiling up from the other side of the wall. *Try being resistant against* that, *Forest. Nothing comes away unharmed from lightning!*

But would all of this be *enough*?

They were merely humans, and every time a human did anything, but especially magic, there was a cost in energy and endurance. Battling the sound, shaking, emotional assaults, and simple fear tired people out even faster. This thing seemingly had no such limits—or at least, it was so huge that its limits were far past those of simple human beings. *They* were also depending on a finite supply of Poomer cartridges, brandy, and other weapons that were going to run out. Their enemy, the Forest, *was* a weapon, and now it split into six equidistant sections against the maze wall's perimeter and shuffled side to side.

Someone apported a cartridge into a nest of trees right below him. He detonated it, but this time the hole filled in faster than it had before. He saw then that the trees were grouped more closely together than they had been, forming tight clumps that joined their canopy together, resisting the blast. They were hurt, but now it was mainly upper-level leaves that blew apart.

Another pair of lightning bolts arced down, and thunder rattled even the "stone" of the wall.

We're not winning. We're barely holding our own. And if this thing starts to think . . .

"Kordas, we are losing people on top of the wall," Rose said, shouting into his thunder-deafened ears. "Where there are no mages, the trees are snatching people right from the top."

The sounds of anguished screams came from the right and left.

"Get that brandy to everyone!" he ordered. "Let's burn this damned thing to the ground!"

He *said* that . . . but behind his façade was pure despair. Because out on the edges of the clumps he saw new trees—growing.

And something horrific occurred to him.

What if the thing underground here, the thing that had made the wall he was standing on and was growing a manor for him, was *akin* to the Forest?

What if the Forest could feed off it?

Bleak despair delivered a punch to his gut, and he clung to the wall for a moment as his knees grew weak. For a moment, blackness closed in around him, and he could not see a way out of it.

A steadying hand on his shoulder recalled him to himself, and he looked up into Isla's eyes.

Like her sister, she was pale and trembling, but her voice was steady. "Tell me what you need, my love."

Maybe I can't save us all . . . but maybe I can save the future. "Gather up everyone who doesn't actually *want* to be fighting, all of the children, and as much of the livestock as you can. Get them down the ramps, and get them all underground," he said hoarsely. "Then seal all the entrances. With luck, if the wall fails, you'll be safe there, and all our spare food will be down there with you. I need *you* down there with them. One, you're a mage, and two, if I'm lost, those that survive will need a leader."

She didn't protest, she didn't argue, and she didn't complain. Instead, she took his head in both her hands, kissed him fiercely, and flew down the stairs, trailed by Ivy and Daisy, shouting at the people huddled in confusion away from the wall. Whatever she said, they started following her.

He turned his attention back to the enemy. He had put his people in the best hands he knew.

It was his job now to give them as much time as he could. The rest was up to chance and fate.

That damned pig

2I

Next to Kordas, Jonaton apported canister after canister into the thrashing trees, his mouth set in a grim line, his hair plastered to his head with sweat. Dragonfly wings no longer attached to an insect fluttered wildly in clouds. A little farther down on the wall, someone had gotten hold of a small catapult—the gods only knew where and how he had—and was sending cracked casks of brandy into the trees, while Hakkon put fire arrows into them as soon as they hit. On his other side, a Healer tended a lucky bastard who'd only gotten lashed by a tree and not pulled down into the monster to be torn to pieces. "Only" meant that his arm had been flayed in a wide line down to the bone from his shoulder to his wrist, and the Healer sewed him up with careful stitches. He wasn't screaming, because he had passed out.

Kordas was in a state of deliberate *not thinking*, because if he thought about any of this, he knew he would fall to pieces. Strategy was useless, plans impossible. No help was coming. All that he—all that any of them—could do was hold the line and buy more time. Not for themselves, but for their future, hiding underground. He hadn't said this, of course. What was the point? He didn't want to shame anyone who couldn't bear this any longer and deserted the walls for that hoped-for safety in the hertasi warrens. He didn't want to put anyone in the unbearable position of disobeying orders or dying—probably horribly.

Don't think about it. Just aim, and fire. Aim, and fire.

"Kordas," Rose said calmly into his ear, as he aimed for one of the canisters and exploded it.

"Rose, if you Dolls can get out, or get down into the underground with Isla, you should," he replied, sending another Spitter bolt into a canister, and shouting to be heard over the din—although to his abused ears, his own voice sounded muffled. "You didn't come with us to get slaughtered by a monster."

"Irrelevant," said Rose, over the explosions, the thunder, the screams. "Pebble wants you. It's just below us."

He wanted to curse. He wanted to weep. He did *not* want to be pulled away from this completely doomed fight on the wall, because every moment they held back the Red Forest was another moment when more people could escape into the underground and maybe live another day.

"Please, Kordas. This is important."

He repressed the urge to do—or say—something unforgivable. Instead he looked down, behind him. Sure enough, there was the Earth Elemental, pressed up against the wall like an anxious puppy. Kordas looked back at the Red Forest; he'd blown a big enough hole in it that it was struggling to grow back. He thrust the Spitter into Rose's hands. "You know what to do," he told her, not wondering whether she could even use the damned thing. "Aim for the dot. Try not to miss." So what if she wasted bolts? It wasn't as if they had a reason to hoard ammunition right now.

"Kordas—we Dolls can't participate in warfare. We're restricted."

Kordas stepped back, and touched his forehead to Rose's. "Rose . . . this isn't warfare now. It's a rescue." He pressed his pistol pouches to Rose's hands and left.

He sprinted down the stairs, and he hadn't even gotten halfway down before he saw that Pebble was vibrating. With fear? Anger? *It's just a child,* he reminded himself, bit his tongue before he snapped at it, and put his hand on the warm rock of its side. *It's probably terrified. It probably wants to run, but it's afraid that I'll be angry if it does.*

"Pebble, if you can escape, you need to escape, now," he said, as calmly as he could, although his voice broke a little. "Don't worry about us. I know you can go underground. Go somewhere safe. Go back to your Mama—"

"Noooooooooo!" the Elemental wailed. *"Not go! Help! I help! Say how! Mama come!"*

Kordas did not comment on the absurdity of that last statement. Even if Pebble's mother was inclined to help humans, who had done very little for her but kidnap and torture her child, she must be hundreds of leagues away. How was a notoriously slow, gargantuan Deep Earth Elemental going to get here before they were all dead? Impossible, of course.

But Pebble could do one thing . . .

"Can you give us power?" he asked. Not that he expected that Pebble would be able to produce enough magical energy to save them—but maybe Pebble could buy them a little more time. More time for all the noncombatants to get underground.

"*Feed stone, feed you?*" Pebble asked anxiously. "*Like bad bads took?*"

"Yes," he replied, assuming that Pebble meant the Heartstone. "Can you do that?"

Pebble said nothing . . .

But in the next heartbeat, he felt power surging into him through the ley-lines and from the Heartstone. He jolted against the wall. This was power of a sort he had never experienced in his entire life. It was the sweetest of tastes, the most refreshing of waters, the contentment of a still lake. It was the high and low pitches of the same instrument, factoring their frequencies, and simply passing through him, cleansing along the way.

This was *like* the power he'd felt in the Chamber of the Beast, where a wounded Pebble had been lying, healing itself, and emitting vast amounts of magical energy doing so. But it wasn't the same, any more than water from a cesspool was like water from a pure, clear spring. And it wasn't the same, because Pebble was giving this to him and all the other mages, rather than being drained of it by Imperial spells, through what was left of the Heartstone. Freely given, tuned to their abilities as Masters, literally rock-steady power. He practically felt his hair stand on end, and up on the wall, he heard Jonaton's wordless exclamation of shock and surprise.

"Hey! Hey—nice! Yeah, let's have more of *that*! *More of that!*"

And up beyond the wall—the Veil began to glow, a pale blue light that rippled like the surface of a Gate coming into lock.

He ran back up the stairs to see Jonaton standing as still as a statue, arms spread above his head, also haloed in a faint blue light. *What—*

"Kordas!" Jonaton shouted, not turning his head. "Get back to the front gate. I've got the Veil! We can hold the thing off back here!"

As if to affirm that claim, a whipping branch soared up into view, hit the Veil, and—disintegrated.

He can't hold alone! Not for long—

But it appeared that he could. Or at least, he would die trying.

"Saver!" shouted Pebble. *"Gate! Gate! Gate!"*

He didn't stop to think. He just moved.

At least by this point, the animals still remaining above ground were all in hiding, probably huddled together in the center of the Vale, not running about in a panic. He should be able to sprint—

Just as he thought that, a Doll came running up to him, pulling a panicking horse along by main strength—the horse wasn't bridled or saddled, in fact, all it had was a hackamore, but that was all *he* had ever needed. He tapped into his levitation abilities, vaulted onto the gelding's back from the lower stairs, grabbed the reins, and gave it a smack on its heavily sweating rump. It took off at a barely controlled gallop, carrying him around a tightly packed mob of mixed animals, cutting directly across picturesque, winding paths, veering around little groves and homes among the trees, and ending him up at the front gate.

He leapt off the back of the poor beast and it immediately ran away. He didn't blame it. The cacophony was worse here than it was at the rear; he sprinted up the stairs, taking them two at a time, past stationed Dolls to where Delia, Sai, and the loading team stood. The Veil glowed here, too; Sai stood in a pose nearly identical to Jonaton's, as the tree branches thrashed just out of touching range of the Veil.

Delia was still hard at work, mouth set in a grim line, exploding canisters as fast as she could Fetch them into the Forest. Sai glanced at Kordas, then turned his attention back to the trees.

"Pebble?" he asked brusquely.

"Pebble," Kordas confirmed. "How long can you hold?"

"Until I drop," Sai confirmed. "And then—it won't matter how much power Pebble feeds us, because we won't have the strength to use it. But this has bought us some time."

"Ye—" Kordas began.

He stopped speaking as a high-pitched whistling sound—like *nothing* he had ever heard before—made him whip his head around to the left.

Just in time to see a ball of fire a hundred times bigger than anything *he* could produce hurtling out of the sky to land in the midst of the trees.

The sound it made when it hit wasn't as loud as the thunder accompanying the weather mages' lightning, nor as loud as the canisters exploding, but it was more than enough to make everyone on the wall wince and instinctively drop behind the parapet.

The Veil flickered a moment, but Sai and the rest popped back up and went back to work reinforcing it. "What in the *hell* was that?" Sai shouted.

"Damn if I know!" Kordas shouted back, taking over from Delia in shooting the canisters so she could concentrate on Fetching them. "Whatever it is, it's on our si—"

And another fireball came arcing into the Forest on his right, with similar results.

It was difficult to tell for sure, between the *POOM*s of the canisters and the crash of thunder, but he thought he heard more of those fireballs hitting somewhere out of sight, to the left, the right, and the rear. But were they making a difference?

He felt a tiny, tiny bit of hope creep into his heart. Where that fireball had hit in front of them, there were trees actually *engulfed* in fire, there was a hole among them showing the bare earth and rocks, and nothing was throwing snow on the fires. Of course, that could be because by this time the ground had been branched free of snow. But—wait! The trees nearest the ones engulfed were trying to beat the flames out. And getting set on fire themselves for their trouble.

It was a good thing those fireballs were taking long, leisurely arcs to get where they were going, because he heard another one coming in that sounded—well, too close—and he had just enough time to scream *"Duck!"* at the top of his lungs and grab Delia's shoulder and throw her beneath the parapet when the incoming fireball landed right in front of the closed gate.

The wall shook under them, and even though he managed to clap his hands over his ears at the last minute, once again, he was deafened.

Fortunately the reinforced Veil deflected most of the flames away, but when he cautiously looked back up again, the ends of Sai's eyebrows had little wisps of smoke coming up from them, and his face was distinctly redder. He hadn't ducked. He hadn't fallen, either. *They are my heroes, I swear,* Kordas thought.

He had grown so accustomed to the waves of rage coming from the forest that at first he didn't notice when they intensified. But when Delia abruptly put both fists to her temples and dropped to her knees, and the exhausted Healer that stumbled over to her did the same, a moment later he got hit in the face by the brutal anger, and nearly went to his knees, himself. He fought the alien emotion back, clinging to the parapet, and surveyed the battlefield, his eyes burning and watering with the effort—and from the smoke that billowed over the wall from the burning trees.

That gave him a little more hope—until a gust of wind blew the smoke away, and he saw that the trees had closed in all the holes that had been blown in the forest, and the smoke was because they had stopped burning and were only smoldering.

Wait—

"Kordas," Rose said in his ear. Well, actually shouted it in his ear, because mostly all he could hear was a ringing sound. *If we live through this, the Healers are going to be treating us all so we don't go permanently deaf.*

Speaking of Healers—the one he'd last seen crouched next to Delia was supporting the girl as she sagged with exhaustion, sobbing silently, the tears pouring down her face leaving tracks in the soot. It was clear Delia had wrung herself dry of energy. *Nothing I can do to help there—*

Sai still stood defiantly, valiantly, pouring magic into the Veil. Kordas tried not to look for signs of exhaustion on the old man's face.

"Kordas!" Rose shouted again. "The Forest has pulled back from the rest of the wall and is regrouping. Everyone but a couple of mages is on their way here."

Wait, what? Hope rose again. Were they actually holding their own? Could they possibly win?

Before that thought had done more than merely flash through his mind, out of the corner of his eye, he saw Sai sway slightly. He moved to help, but Rose was faster than he was, and caught the old man before he fell.

He didn't even think about it; he invoked full mage-sight, connected himself fully to the ley-lines feeding from what was left of the Heartstone, and took Sai's place in reinforcing the Veil.

This moment is all there is, he said in his mind, and "heard" it replied to by the other mages holding the Veil up. *"This moment is all there is."* He felt himself drop into the kind of half-trance that really *big* mage-work required, the sort of thing that needed a dozen mages if not more. This was something he'd done maybe three times in his life. He ceased to be *Kordas*, and became one strand of the greater web. All emotions repressed, to prevent rattling the others, he became one with the whole. Not *absent* emotions, not as such, but they were cast into the background and made invisible, so he could concentrate on what needed to be done, this moment. And this moment was all there was.

He closed his eyes. He didn't need outer sight, he needed inner sight right now. He called it up, established his strongest shields, and opened his vision to the world around him.

And . . . this was, in every way possible, *nothing* like the land he had come from. There, back in the Duchy, everything magical was orderly, tamed. The ley-lines pulsed with their many-colored energies in regulated waves. Elementals were few—and now he knew why, given the terrible use that the Emperor had made of the *vrondi* and little Pebble. There were concentrations of magic, like spires of power, in places where Imperial mages lived and worked. Like Heartstones, but turned inward, denying their power to the greater world instead of sharing it with the world. In that lost world, he and the mages he sheltered had to slink around in the shadows, and do their work as undetectably as they could, between the lines of the web that others could read from. The magic of the Empire was so regulated that he and his had spent as much time hiding their tracks as they did actually working.

Not here . . .

Out here there were ley-lines, of course, but they did not pulse with the measured regularity of a heartbeat. They *flowed* like wild, unfettered rivers, intoxicating and dangerous, the colors of their magic braiding and unbraiding as they flowed. Tributaries flowed in and out of them, mainly with the surface levels of the land, but also deep into the ground and even into the sky. The tributaries had their own flares and prominences, flinging out power with a rhythm of their own. But the ley-lines were the least of the things he saw.

Because the land was full to bursting with chaotic life. Not just material life; immaterial as well. The water, the air, the earth, were full of things he had never seen before; there were magical beings everywhere, some material, most not. Some he recognized as Elementals he had studied, even if he had never personally seen them. Some were—well, there just was nothing in his experience to compare them to. Some he couldn't even "look" at directly: it was as if they twisted in and out of the reality he knew. Some were so incomprehensible he felt his mind trying to grasp them and failing utterly. Some were clouds of infinitesimally small motes that radiated power all out of proportion to their tiny size. And high in the sky above were creatures like skeins of light, undulating across the heavens with little to no regard for the clumsy creatures of earth.

His "view" encompassed all the degrees of the compass as well as up and down, since he was not limited to his physical eyes. He sensed Pebble behind him, valiantly radiating power as hard as it ever could. And in front of him, the Forest, and Sai had been right: this ravening thing had once been an Earth Elemental itself; not one of the Deep Earth Elementals, like Pebble and Pebble's mother, but one of the sort that slumbered amid the landscape until awakened, in the guise of a rock outcropping, or a hill, or a gigantic boulder. And it had, indeed, been caught in a Change-Circle in the aftermath of that long-ago war. Once, it might have been at least as intelligent as Pebble, but when its body was mingled with the tree-grove it had slept near, between the pain and the scrambling effect of the pure chaos of the Circle, what intelligence it had was lost. Now what was left was agony and instinct, and not much else. It hated, fiercely, but intellectually dimly—some part of it *knew* that it had once been greater than it was now. It was full of rage for the same reason. It lived to destroy, because destruction permitted feeding, and the pleasure of feeding was what eased its pain for a little while.

And—to his surprise, he realized that they had hurt it, back when they first encountered it.

They were nowhere near killing it, then or now, but they had *hurt* it, and that angered it more than anything it had ever encountered in all the centuries since its creation.

And it was very, very hungry. They were the teasers of the best food source it had ever encountered since its violent and agonizing birth, when it had been torn apart and mingled with insensate wood. And they had dared to fight it, to hurt it, and then to escape from its clutches, and presumably take that good food with them.

So driven by rage, hate, and hunger, it had roused from its winter hibernation and come looking for them.

But the Forest was by no means the most powerful thing within the sphere of his comprehension now. There was something greater.

Much greater.

At first, She—for it was a female entity—was merely a light-filled shadow in his mind nearly as vast as the sky. The great Air creatures flowed and danced around Her, in tribute to Her beauty and power. But as he became more aware of Her, She became more aware of him, and for one brief moment, showed Herself to him in all Her strength.

Vast as the night, and as full of incandescence as the night is full of stars, She regarded him with eyes without whites or pupils, only an infinite starfield. He could not tell what She thought of him, but a tiny, still-thinking part of him recognized from Silvermoon's tales what She might be.

This was the Star-Eyed. And She had taken notice of him.

So when the wall began to shake under his boots, for a few heartbeats, he didn't even sense it, so frozen was he in the deep regard of Her gaze.

:: *Have hope, Kordas. You are beloved. All will be well.* ::

But then the shaking increased, and the enchantment on him—if it was such a thing—snapped, as he was nearly knocked to his knees.

Maybe it was because some deep part of him, a part of him seared with pain and memories, *knew* this shaking, and recognized the shaking for what it meant. He shook himself free of mage-sight, and looked out over the thrashing trees of the Forest, the arcing fireballs, the lightning strikes, and the occasional exploding canister, and saw—

The raw, red, fiery surface of the Great Deep Elemental that was Pebble's "Mama," thrusting her way out of the earth. As she shoved her way to the surface, the forest around her caught fire, circling her in a halo of flames. He remembered this creature all too well; unlike Pebble, she was not featureless rock. And she was anything but *small*.

Two sets of glowing, yellow-white claws splayed out on the surface of the earth on either side of her. He could not begin to measure the size of those knife-like talons, but they were at least three times the height of the enormous trees now aflame on either side of the erupted earth through which she had thrust her body. Chest, neck, and head rose above them, to a dizzying height. The pointed head was mostly jaws. Weirdly, it looked like a bird's head and stabbing beak—or perhaps the narrow head of a lizard. Her head, neck, chest, and forelegs glowed red mottled with black, and molten rock jetted back and forth underneath, as if he was seeing fast-pumping arterial flow in translucent blood vessels. White-hot eyes glared from the glowing red of that head, throwing beams of light—but they were not glaring at Kordas, nor at the Vale.

The creature stared at the Red Forest. But not with the same malevolence he had felt from her when she had come to rescue Pebble. Fierce, yes. Malevolent, no. No, the way she stared at the Forest looked more like revulsion.

And he heard her voice in his mind for the first time, a mental impression of white-hot bronze, dignity, and immense age. But with that voice in his mind, came a real, physical voice, like an enormous brass gong or bell.

"This is abomination."

She contemplated the Red Forest for several heart-stopping moments more.

"THIS SHALL BE CLEANSED."

But she didn't move. Why didn't she move?

Wait, if she moves—she might wreck this entire area, the way she destroyed the Capital. And she doesn't want to do that.

As if she understood what he was thinking, she raised her head skyward and let out a challenging roar. It sounded like an avalanche. Molten rock spattered from the roar, falling as lava bombs over the Red Forest, igniting trees.

Kordas was out of the Veil trance, but was still tuned to ambience enough to sense the Forest wavering. Half of it wanted to keep on attacking the humans in their cursed protections, and get to the food. Half of it wanted to go after this new—likely delicious— challenger. He felt the Forest's hunger . . . and Pebble's mother was a *giant*, radiating source of magical energy. They were both

Earth Elementals; the Forest knew instinctively that if it fought and vanquished her, it could absorb all of her. Then it could turn back and obliterate the ants that were resisting it now.

"Help Mama!" Pebble cried from behind him, still fiercely radiating magic. *"Push! Push!"*

Wait, what?

"Push! Push!" Pebble insisted. All Pebble could do was supply power; it didn't know how to *apply* power. And Kordas didn't know what it wanted.

"For fuck's sake, Kordas!" An exhausted Jonaton stumbled up the stairs behind him. "Are you dazed or stupid? The cute rock means *push the Veil!*"

Bloody hells . . . Hitting himself in the head could wait until later. He was the freshest, most rested mage on the wall, since he hadn't been using his powers nearly as much as the rest. He'd been shooting canisters while they'd been reinforcing the Veil or igniting the apple brandy.

But how?

Chances are Pebble understands magic instinctively, though it is limited in what it knows how to do. But I have those skills that it doesn't. So he did what Pebble wanted. He *pushed.*

He felt Jonaton, exhausted but grimly determined, join him in the moment. Then Ceri. Then Venidel. Then, from underground, to his delight, was Isla, her power joining his power like hand joining hand, and with the power came belief in himself that he sorely lacked at the moment. Then, in a ragged chorus of *there is only this moment,* all of the rest of the mages still standing were united.

As obedient to their will as if they had erected it themselves, the Veil began to expand.

Almost immediately, it contacted the Forest.

The Forest made no sound, but it certainly reacted immediately. It pulled away from the Veil, bunching itself up more. Kordas was looked to within the trance as their leader, regardless of rank, and he gladly assumed control of them all. He shoved harder, Pebble feeding him so much power that he became lost in it, lost to everything except the inexorable advance of the Veil and the slow retreat of the Forest and the sweet song of magic in his veins. It felt good. Even though on the outside, everyone was scorched, bloodied, soaked, and unsteady, in the trance, they were *winning*.

The Forest resisted for a dozen furlongs. Then, abruptly, it stopped retreating. It held for a dozen breaths. Kordas and the others scraped up a little more strength, and *pushed*.

Then, suddenly, the "head" of the Forest that had been facing them became the "tail." In a reversal that almost put Kordas on his face, the Forest threw itself in the opposite direction from the Veil and the puny humans inside it.

Toward Pebble's mother.

She screamed another challenge at the Forest. Still silent, it charged her. It was actually undulating up off of the ground, and looked for all the world like it meant to whipcrack her with its collective body.

"Help Mama!" Pebble cried, and Kordas allowed the Veil to snap back in place where it began, and became the conduit for Pebble's power, since poor Pebble didn't seem to know how to actually *direct* power, only how to make it.

He had to feed the mother now. *This is going to hurt . . .* He already skirted ruin by even tasting a Heartstone, and now he dared to channel it to—a major Elemental? How could connecting with something that massive, that strong, *not* hurt? To her, the mages were scarcely worth thinking about, surely. And she was an Elemental. They were not known for subtlety.

Comes down to it, Kordas thought, *nobody's going to remember me for my subtlety, either. So let's do it. Clean, open-ended, and direct, please accept our handshake.*

He braced himself for the fire, and reached out to her.

He found himself embraced by the gentlest of touches. A touch so gentle, it was child's play to make a solid magical connection with her—and trivial to open himself up, to become a kind of human ley-line, and feed her not only Pebble's magic but all of the magic of the ley-lines that fed the remnant Heartstone.

The Elemental sang a paean of triumph, and braced herself for the impact of the Forest.

On the walls, those who had been fending off lashing branches, launching kegs of brandy, and doing their best to add to the fiery mayhem slumped against the stone parapet, minds gone dull with exhaustion. Those mages who could do no more joined them, watching the battle with awe, dread, and a touch of hope. Only the weather mages were still in play, continuing to lash at the Forest with lightning conjured out of the clouds.

Mother was giving off enough heat that what came from the sky now—at least directly overhead—was actual rain. Superheated steam rose from her in clouds, and the mages got the bright idea to send it straight down the Forest's throat, with a wind.

The Forest definitely did not like that. And it fought back, the rearmost trees moving in coordinated waves now, to create a counter-wind.

Despite the fact that the branches burst into flames as soon as they touched Mother's surface, the trees kept thrashing at her, tearing bits away from her body. Kordas felt her pain as if it was his own.

And fear closed his throat as he realized that they *could still lose*.

Then the fireballs started again; they rained down on the rear of the Forest, disrupting the trees back there, and then began stitching a line of destruction right up the middle. The weather mages saw what was happening and directed their lightning strikes to follow up the same pathway.

Kordas felt Mother's eruption of pure glee. Then he saw it for himself.

They had cut the Forest in half. And the fireballs began falling on the right-hand half, while the lightning kept the division open, and Mother reached upward with all her appendages and *fell* on the left half. For an instant her entire body liquefied and splashed yellow-hot stone and metals a furlong wide on each side of her. Heedless of the rocks still being torn out of her, Mother reformed and slashed and burned with her titanic, white-hot talons, while fireball after fireball punched more holes in the other half of the rage-quickened Forest.

He sensed, rather than saw, the moment of victory. When the Forest ceased to be able to protect itself, to *think*, if that word really applied to the monstrosity, and all the trees thrashed in uncoordinated chaos and the pain of approaching death.

"*Open door!*" cried Pebble, and the guards didn't even pause to question Kordas; they unbarred gates slashed deeply and scorched black, and Pebble elongated and sprouted what must have been a hundred stubby little legs, and flowed down to its mother like a millipede.

"*You may rest,*" he heard in his mind, and he did not question the order, or the source. Apparently they *all* heard Mother give the word, because Jonaton slid down the inside of the parapet to slump bonelessly onto the top of the wall, and Kordas did the same. A little away from him, Sai pulled his knees up to his chest and rested his face on them for a moment.

Within the wall, all was quiet. Outside the wall, there was nothing but the sound of splintering wood.

Finally Sai turned his head toward Kordas, in clear exhaustion and pain.

"Am I missing—an eyebrow?" he groaned.

"Not—entirely," Kordas replied. "Trim the burned bits off and no one will notice."

"Good," Sai said, and put his face back between his knees.

Someone came and put hands over both of Kordas's ears, and after a while he realized he was hearing normally again. Which was a relief; he had not entirely been certain that a Healer *could* do anything about the damage. Some time after that, he sensed Isla approaching up the stairs—he was acutely sensitive to *all* the mages in the Vale right now, and probably would be for a little while longer, until the connections faded. He raised his head and blinked blearily at her.

She was carrying a pail and a cup. She dipped the latter in the former and shoved it toward him; he took it, and noted absently that it was sticky. She didn't have to order him to drink; he was parched, probably had been for some time, and had shoved that aside along with every other nagging physical problem.

He gulped the contents down. It was some sort of herbal concoction, with a touch of salt, but at least half honey. Under most circumstances he would have gagged; now he wanted a second cup, and got it.

A little more revived, he saw that other people and Dolls were moving along the wall with pails or pitchers and cups, making sure everyone up here drank their fill.

He wanted to know—and dreaded to hear—how many people, how much they had lost. But he had to know.

"Not as many as you're afraid to hear," Isla said, anticipating him. "Not more than two hundred; probably closer to one hundred than two. No one we actually know."

But they are still my people. They trusted me, and I led them here to die.

"There are a couple of the weaker or older mages who are going to be touch-and-go for a little, but the Healers seem confident they'll pull through," Isla continued. "We lost very little stock. There is no damage inside the Veil, and the only property damage is the spare barges down by the river. That monster ate them."

He nodded wearily, too tired to speak.

"The Hawkbrothers came down out of the woods; they want to talk to you," she continued.

Well, I want to talk to them, he thought with a ghost of anger. *I thought they said we didn't need to worry about the Forest.*

Rose and Isla helped him to his feet and steadied him down the stairs to the still-open gate. He glanced at the spot where he'd last seen Mother savaging the Forest. She and Pebble were both down there; the raw, burning spots where great chunks had been torn out of her hide were healing, and the two of them seemed to be—grazing.

Good. I hope they devour every speck of that thing so it can't regrow.

But he didn't waste much time on that, because the Hawkbrothers, led by Silvermoon, were waiting for him. And "sheepish" did not even begin to describe the looks on their faces. Also "chagrin," "regret," and "how-could-we-have-been-that-stupid."

That cooled his anger a little.

Sheer weariness kept the rest of it in check.

Silvermoon spread his arms wide. "There are no words for our regret," he said. "When last we surveyed the Red Forest, it was mostly asleep. We reckoned it would stay that way. We are—" He shook his head. "*Sorry* is inadequate."

Anger made him want to lash out, but diplomacy won. Besides, if that damned thing had been tracking them all this time, if they had remained in that wintering spot, they'd all be dead. "I . . . assume you were watching us to see if we were as good as our word." The words came out flat, but Silvermoon did not seem to take offense.

"Wouldn't you?" the Hawkbrother asked, wryly.

He couldn't argue with that.

"I would like to say that we *were* making sure that you would not encounter anything you couldn't handle," Silvermoon continued, "but I would be lying, because we didn't even consider that would be the case. And after all, we left you with everything you could need. And when that infant Earth Elemental turned up and began helping you, well . . ." He shrugged. "You had more than you'd need, and we watched you to see how you would treat it."

"Its name is Pebble, and it's the one I freed when I fled our Capital." He'd given the brief version of the story to Silvermoon during one of their evenings of talking and sharing information.

Silvermoon nodded. "So this would be its mother." He glanced at the wall, where the top curve of Mother's neck was just visible. "I have never, ever, ever, in all my studies, encountered someone who earned the loyalty of a Great Elemental. Not *any* of them." Now Silvermoon fixed him with a penetrating gaze, as if he would like very much to read Kordas's mind.

"Right now, I am a weary man, but I have another duty to do. Two, actually," as an idea somehow escaped from the depths of his consciousness and presented itself eagerly to him. "You're welcome to come with me while I speak with Mother."

"Ah. No, thank you," Silvermoon temporized. "I think it's best if she only sees people she knows. Ah . . . good luck. I'll see you at dusk in the negotiation room."

And he backed up a little, clearing Kordas's way to go down to Pebble and Mother.

Somehow, that was the funniest thing Kordas had seen in a long time, and he choked back laughter as he made his way down to the blasted plain.

Well, when you're dealing with the likes of us, you do want to be careful about the impressions you make.

Silvermoon called after him, clearly meant to be heard by everyone around, "Well fought, King Valdemar."

22

As ever, Rose was at Kordas's elbow as he trudged down to where Mother and Pebble were still grazing lazily. Rose returned his Spitter and pouches—all conspicuously empty—and she resumed her duties of briefing him until they were past the gate. *I didn't even think how she was going to fire this thing, when I gave her my Spitter. I guess she used her thumbs?*

Kordas was pretty sure that the Elementals were taking great pains to gobble down even the tiniest bits of the Red Forest. Of course, that wasn't entirely altruistic on their part; it looked like all the wounds that the Forest had torn in Mother's sides were completely healed, and he didn't need mage-sight to tell that both of them had completely replenished any magical energy they had lost—as well as taken the Forest's.

He had to stop a good distance away from Mother; the heat coming off of her was still quite enough to set fire to anything flammable near her, even though she had dimmed that heat until her surface was a very similar texture to pumice stone, only darker. She and Pebble did not appear to pay any attention to him as he lingered on the edge of the field of ashes and churned up soil around them.

"I came to thank you, Mother," he called hoarsely.

Slowly, she raised her head. Her eyes had been closed as she "grazed" methodically. Now she opened them, and they were still white-hot. He could feel their blast when she looked at him, and his lips were cracking.

"The thing was Abomination, and needed to be set to rest," she said, her actual voice sounding like brass gongs. *"We owed you debt. Our debt is paid."*

"Seems to me that it was overpaid," he replied candidly. And he spoke those words knowing he was opening himself up to demands from someone who might ask more of him than he could give.

But she—laughed. *"The feast repays all,"* she replied. *"We shall eat and cleanse this soil, and then go. You will need to make the soil here rich again, or it will grow nothing when we are done with it."*

She must be sterilizing the soil as she sifts through it for bits of the Forest.

"Thank you again," he managed. And then asked the important question. "Do you see my companion?"

"My child knows your companion," said Mother. *"He knows that your companion and her fellows with you are the Truthseekers, trapped within those bodies."*

"Do you know a way to free them?" he asked.

Rose actually made a sound like a muffled gasp.

"We've tried to find a way, but all our studies say that if the glass that contains them is broken, they die. That is woven in the spells that confine them to the glass. But they cannot be freed from the glass without breaking—"

"You did not have me," Mother interrupted, with the natural arrogance of something as powerful as she was. *"No human like you can ever muster the power, or the fire, to melt the enchanted glass they are trapped in. But I can. And I will. For we owe debt to the Truthseekers as well, who did what they could for my child."* Mother didn't shift her posture, but her eyes redirected to Rose. *"Do you want this, Truthseeker?"*

"More than *anything*!" Rose cried, and clasped her mitten-like hands just under her chin—an unconscious, or deliberate, imitation of Delia, he thought. Then she composed herself, and glanced at Kordas. "But—"

Kordas licked his lips. They stung. "Rose, this is your chance. I told you that we would find a way to free you, and when we did, we'd do it immediately," he interrupted.

"But I—we said we would stay with you as long as you needed us."

Kordas was struck by the forceful impression that Mother was listening carefully to every word he said, so he chose them deliberately. "Yes, you did. And, yes—you did. But if we do not free you soon, we will never learn *not* to need you Dolls. And you will never see freedom. Just because you have chosen to stay with us . . . that doesn't make you any less prisoners in those bodies, and we damned well *never* will own slaves."

He had an audience now, an audience of the hundreds of Dolls who were coming down to where he and Rose stood with Mother and Pebble. What one Doll knew, they all knew, after all. How could they have kept away?

"It's time for you to be free, in your proper forms," he said, raising his voice. "It's time for us to learn how to do without you." He held out his hand, and Rose put one of hers in it. "It's not as if you can't stay hereabouts if you choose to," he pointed out. "You just won't be giving us *physical* help. But we'll know you're there." He laughed a little. "I'm sure that if we can talk to Mother and Pebble, we can learn how to talk to Ivy and Amethyst and Rose. And meanwhile, you'll be what you were *meant* to be."

He could tell that Rose was reluctant, but the rest of the Dolls certainly were *not*. They crowded up against him and Rose, practically vibrating with eagerness to be gone.

Rose bowed her head in acquiescence.

"Back up, Kordas, Kamaje-*friend,"* Mother intoned. *"I do not wish to cook you where you stand."*

The Dolls spontaneously parted to give him room to get out of range, as Mother cupped her talons before her, with an opening between them, and they began to glow as white-hot as her eyes. He kept backing up until he was nearly halfway to the gate, and only then, as the Dolls flowed around him, rushing—and yet moving in an orderly fashion, no jostling, and no competition—did he notice that Rose was still with him. As they ran, the Dolls tore off, untied, or otherwise removed the items they'd been marked with, dropping them into the mud behind them.

Mother's talons were so hot now that it was hard to look at them. The wave of Dolls began to race—and he understood, somehow, that they were going to have to pass between those deadly hands as fast as they could move, or they ran the very real risk of losing the ability to move before they reached the place where the heat was enough to melt, rather than break, the glass containing their "selves."

Even so, they were entirely *on fire* as they passed into the space between Mother's hands. It was surreal, and not a little terrifying, to see all these human-like figures rushing to their apparent doom, to see human-like figures burning, burning, burning and still moving into the fire instead of away.

And it was there between Mother's talons that the Doll bodies actually vaporized.

He not only *saw* the *vrondi* then, he heard them—he saw them spiraling up and around Mother, singing her a wordless song that held thanks and praise, gratitude and boundless good will. The Dolls formed a river, a river that ended in annihilation and freedom, and he wasn't entirely sure of his own feelings at this point. Gratitude mingled with regret, happiness with sorrow, it was all one tangled mess. He realized he was holding Rose's hand, and she was holding his.

Finally the flood became a flow, the flow became a stream, the stream became a trickle, and the trickle ended. "Your turn, Rose," he said.

She turned toward him, picked up his hand, kissed it in her own way, and let it go.

"You are the kindest, best, and bravest human I have ever known," she said, voice shaking with emotion he had not known she could feel. "You are not always wise, or intelligent—but you are unfailingly compassionate and determined to make bad things right."

He started, hearing those words, and sought for something to say and could not find it. She patted his face with her hand, and spoke again. "We cannot always have love in the way that we want," she said tenderly. "But we can have love in the ways that we dare. And I will always love you."

She stepped backward. "Watch for me, Kordas Valdemar. If fate will have it, we will be together again."

And with that, she turned and flung herself toward Mother, running faster than his fastest horse ever could. He held his hand out behind her but jerked it back as if he'd touched a griddle. The heat had burned his fingertips and he clutched it to his heart.

And then—in a flicker of light—she was gone.

———

The Hawkbrothers were back, and with them, a cadre of the *hertasi*. Delia only learned this after she had been helped to her bed, given something for what could only be described as a skull-splitting headache, and left to recover. She'd fallen asleep as soon as she was certain the attack was over, although she didn't find out what had actually happened until she woke up two days later.

She'd actually awakened a few times during that period, but it had only been to eat and drink what was left for her, attend to the necessary, and go back to sleep. When she finally woke without a headache, and without feeling as if the inside of her head was bruised, it appeared to be about noon, and she could tell from the sounds outside her little home that the place was, once again, full of hertasi and Hawkbrothers. The noise of the birds was back—she hadn't realized how quiet it had been without it—and the high-pitched voices of hertasi were not to be confused with even human children.

She grimaced a little, hoping she hadn't kept anyone out of their old home, and searched for some clean clothing. Dressed and more or less ready to face what was going on, she almost ran straight into Jelavan, who had a pitcher in one hand and a bowl of hot oatmeal mixed with dried fruits. "Oh good, you're really awake. The Healers thought you would be."

"I'm also starving," she admitted, but she was polite enough to hug Jelavan with one arm while grabbing for the bowl with the other.

He didn't bother her while she gobbled down the food without the least shame for her manners. He just stiffened his tail and used it as a prop—or maybe a sort of stool—for his rump as he waited, and told her what had happened after the pain in her skull had made her pass out despite how hard she had fought to stay conscious.

"So all the Dolls have been set free, and I completely missed everything from just before Pebble's Mother turned up." She sighed, and combed her unruly hair out of her face with her fingers. "I *always* miss *everything*. I suppose all of you Tayledras were actually in the forest spying on us to make sure we weren't going to turn out to be like the Impies."

Jelavan sheepishly scratched the side of his snout with a claw. "Well," he admitted. "Yes. To all of it. But to be fair, we were not expecting the Red Forest to rip itself up and come follow you. We didn't know it could move, actually. We also watch you because you're *hilarious.*"

"And don't you ever forget it. We're gods-blessed delights you better keep safe. Well, it's nice to know you lot aren't omnipotent and omniscient," she replied mockingly, licking her spoon. "And you were the ones sending those fireballs."

"Sometimes, explosives are the best way to show you care."

"I sure didn't care for that Forest. Why didn't you all destroy it before we got here? Or was this some kind of test, to you?"

Jelavan pretended to ignore that last comment. "It had been mostly quiet for so long we made the mistake of thinking it had gone dormant. Well, again, to be fair, it wasn't emitting much in the way of magic, but I suppose that was because it was eating magic, not putting magic out."

"That's short-sighted of you." She couldn't resist digging the knife in a little deeper.

"Oh, pray, do not remind me. I assure you, inquiries about that are coming in from many directions." Jelavan made a rude noise. "*Oh!*

What has happened to my memory? One of the Dolls left something for you." He bounced up on his feet and went to one of the woven vine shelves that had been cleverly bound into the wall. "Here it is."

Delia recognized it immediately. It was the bead embroidery piece centered by an amethyst that had adorned Doll Amethyst's forehead. It had been neatly cut out of the canvas of her face, leaving just enough fabric to sew it to something else.

She took it in her hand, marveling again at the delicacy of the work. "I am going to miss Amethyst," she said wistfully. "But not as much as Kordas will miss Rose, I think."

"She told me it was too pretty to burn up, and she wanted you to have it to remember her fondly by. And she said to make sure to tell you that it didn't hurt at all to cut it off." That last made the last of Delia's worries vanish.

"So how long are you staying *this* time?" she asked, hoping it was going to be a while. "And how many of you are there?"

"At least two moons to help with the damage, and two dozen moons with attendant hertasi." Then he sighed. "You all have so much to learn that we didn't even think to teach you. We have tools you haven't even seen yet. And there is going to be so much cleaning up the underground before it's fit to sleep in again, we may just incinerate. How did you manage to cram that much livestock down there?"

She had to laugh. "I have no idea. I was too busy punting Poomer canisters into the Forest to blow them up. Like you said, 'Sometimes, explosives are the best way to show you care.' But don't worry." She put the bit of beadwork away carefully in the box she kept her comb and mirror in. "You don't need to hurry to clean it all up. You and anyone else who can fit in here can stay with me, as long as I'm not usurping someone's home."

"You're not! You are welcome to it!" Jelavan exclaimed happily. "You won't regret having us in here. We can fit thirty in here! We stack! Oh, should I ask Kordas first? After all, I am a strange being, and you are inviting me to come live with you a while——"

"Strange, yes, but in the best ways. Kordas has no say in the matter," she said firmly. "I can make my own decisions. To be honest, I hope you or some of the Tayledras can give me an idea how I can increase my endurance when using this Gift of mine. No one here seems to know much about it." The very idea made her quietly excited. She'd gotten used to being an effective part of a team as a scout. *And if I'm honest, getting praised for something only I can do was awfully nice.*

"I'm sure we can!" Jelavan said gleefully. "Steelrain knows a very great deal about Gifts, when you can get her out of the armory. Oh, this will be fun! I will enjoy sharing living space with you, Delia, and think of all the things we will have to talk about! I will do all I can to prolong our stay here! I shall run and get my things!"

"And I can tell you all about how Kordas turned to me for help!" she blurted back. "Now shoo!" And off he scrambled, leaving Delia to wait for him, smiling to herself.

It was good to have her friend back, even if it was only for a little while.

And I—I have things to do. Things to learn. Things to become.

———

"*Some* people are never going to forgive you for letting the Dolls go," Sai said, a fortnight later, after the two of them watched a group of sheepish, even contrite Hawkbrothers help some of the other mages strengthen the Veil so that it would last longer before it began to fade, by way of reparation for leaving them to face the Blood Forest. By the time the Veil became ineffective, he hoped they'd have built enough proper buildings that the Veil wouldn't be needed. And by then they'd have mastered creating smaller versions that could serve as greenhouses in the winter. Most of the mages and Tayledras spellmasters had adjourned to here, a sort of open lecture hall in the Vale, where Sai and Kordas watched from a close-by pavilion. With beverages.

"*Some* people can learn how to pick up after themselves, and mind their own lives. We didn't depend on the Dolls so much that we can't relearn how to do without them again," Kordas replied, as he waited for the Tayledras to call upon him for aid. Or not. Most of the time he was just left to supervise in absentia. They seemed to think that it was more important that Kordas save his strength and tend to the complaints and needs of his people than contribute to the building and rebuilding going on. Or maybe it was about pride. Either worked.

More snow had fallen, covering the place where Mother had killed the Red Forest, but not before Pebble had gone over it all, evening and flattening it out.

They'd used the spot for the colony's cemetery, to bury the two hundred-odd people that had been killed in the fight. The ground was soft and well-worked by Pebble, it was in a good spot for such a thing, and it seemed an appropriate use for the area.

Those deaths were probably why the Hawkbrothers were helping now, because if they had even bothered to check on the Red Forest before they "left," no one would have died. And while Silvermoon had said that death was just another daily thing for them, they sure did take the burials seriously. *If there is one thing Valdemarans can do, it's wring feelings out of people. The Tayledras act like they're devastated about it, but none of them are talking about it.* They and the Valdemarans could have set up an ambush for the Forest, in a place prepared well in advance. *Prepare the battlefield, win the battle. We need to work on that. The Forest literally just ran up to our wall. I have some ideas for architecture as channelling traps and time wasters.* It would have been a hard fight, but it was one that could have been won without any deaths.

Kordas had felt guilty that he really hadn't known those who had died that well—but at least they had all been within his Guard. They had all known they were going to be fighting against danger. But still, the sight of each wrecked body as it was put into the ground had devastated him.

But—

Sai unexpectedly whacked the back of his head with an open hand.

"Hey!" he said indignantly, putting his hand up to his abused skull. "What was that about?"

"You're brooding again," Sai replied. "You're going down that same old path of 'but what if I hadn't,' and frankly, it's getting old. Get out of your rut. Anything could have happened. You followed your grandfather's Plan. You did the best you could. Most of us are alive and well. Those who aren't, aren't. The rest of us *go on*."

"That seems—harsh," he remonstrated.

"Life is harsh. Life is hard. We're doing well, extraordinarily well, really. Unexpected allies, a secure place to start, and the farmers are raving about the soil." Sai shrugged. "I won't say things will be easy in our lifetimes, but we'll manage for a while, then we'll do pretty well for a while, and then we'll thrive. Or a giant rock will fall out of the sky and we'll all die, but I don't see that happening. Where's Delia?"

The abrupt change of subject caught him off guard. "I have no idea," he admitted.

This time Sai slapped him on the back. "Good! Good!" he enthused. "Then your plan when you sent her out with the scouts worked. She has her own life and she's not moping around trying to become part of yours. She's a good girl, by the way. She'll find her own way."

He realized after a moment that he actually had not caught sight of Delia in days, and then only in passing. Mostly with one of the hertasi. He hoped that she would pick up some of their skills. *Then again, this is Delia. Will I be usurped? How could anything stand against Delia armed with vast skills and experience?*

Briada joined them at that moment. In the wake of the attack of the Red Forest, he had learned that she and her cousins had held almost a quarter of the wall against the Forest with a handful of the Guard, using a fire-and-retreat tactic atop the parapets, at a less-demanding tempo. In the wake of that, he'd appointed her the head of the Guard, and somewhat to his bemusement, no one had argued with him. "Baron," she said, and threw him a modified salute.

"Captain," he replied. "Something I need to know?"

"Inventory is done," she told him. "As I'm sure you guessed, we haven't got many Poomer canisters left. Fifty-nine, to be precise. Nice stock of other equipment, though, and on my own initiative I've got ballistas and ammunition positioned every three lengths along the wall." She paused, waiting for his approval or disapproval.

WW"They were all kits in crates, and came with waterproofed coverings," she told him. "They'll be fine. Whoever packed them up and sent them on to us knew what they were doing."

That would have been the Dolls, when they were looting the Imperial supplies for us, he thought, with a twinge of sadness. He missed Rose. And Ivy. And—he realized he missed every one he'd known by a name. *Be wise in the ways of names* was one of magic's most basic and purest of rules. When anything is made distinctive, it is made more than simply mortal.

"Carry on, Captain," he told her. "You have a hundred times the military experience that I have—probably fifty times the actual military experience of anyone here. I depend on your judgment. If you don't, I'll use my spooky magical powers on you. They get more powerful every time I hear about them."

She snorted. "Put me on the spot, why don't you? All right, I'll do my best to get us readied for anything I can think of. But I'm not a trained strategist—"

Sai barked a humorless laugh. "Imperial strategy seems to consist of throwing bodies at the enemy until they are either defeated or so buried in piles of bodies that they can't move. Don't do that. You'll do fine."

Briada sketched an entirely mocking salute at Sai. "Whatever you say, crazy old man."

He shook his fist at her. She laughed. "Are those new eyebrows?" she said, and went on her way.

"There were times in the past year when it's felt like I was inventing new hells, Sai," Kordas admitted. "Felt like I was being batted around between every power that could get a grab on me for a moment. Mostly, though, we did all right. Better than I would have expected. We're at our best when we're cooperative."

"Or in your case, not cooperative so much as 'Oh! Is it time for me to do more than any fifty of you, then fall over in wearying self-doubt? I'll be right there!' Hah, I know you, Kordas!" Sai was giving him a hard time, sure, but the tone of the last part was leaning heavily toward affection. "We've been with you a long time, and I can't speak for the others, but if it was up to me, and you'd been a lout, I'd have replaced you with a puppet regime centered on my comforts. So never forget, you've got that to be thankful for."

Kordas had to laugh at that. "Funny you'd say that. Feeling like a puppet has been in the back of my head a long time now. It's a weird kind of doubt that comes with—" He paused to pick the right phrase. "—being in charge, but not being a tyrant? People don't think I'm a tyrant. I don't think I'm a tyrant. But with that comes *doubt*. Tyrants don't have doubts. But oh, do I. When the Plan went into motion, I thought for about the first few weeks I could run it all, but the doubt got to be too much. I reached out, and was given help. I found myself connected to things I hadn't fully grasped, and all of the time it was getting more complex. To cope with that I suppressed a lot, I borrowed from other priorities, I—admit, I neglected so many things. But I didn't *want* to. I *had* to. And I can't get that time back. I need to meet my kids," he laughed, but unenthusiastically. "I owe them at least a year."

"Oh, at least a year. And a pony for each of them. Take them on patrols," Ponu added, joining them to slowly, carefully sit down on an open chair.

"Hah! Not a bad idea. I can include them in duties I once thought were mine alone," Kordas answered, trying to stay serious.

"'Alone, alooone.' Well, you needed the solitude for truly good brooding," Jonaton chimed in, picking up a chair to join them. "I've seen it. *Top*-quality, *romance*-poetry brooding." Kordas faked an illusory fireball at him while overacting his affrontery, and Jonaton mocked diving away in fear.

"It felt essential to give these people my *all*. So I thought, if I saved everyone, I saved my family too. And if I didn't try to save everyone, I wouldn't be who my family believed me to be. They believed in me, so I believed I could be what they wanted. Which turned out pretty well. You can't imagine how lucky I feel in this moment."

"Imagine how lucky we feel that we aren't family," Wis cackled, before sitting with them in his own folding chair.

"It's worth more thought, though, you think? I think the really amazing part is that, even when my world fell out from under me so many times this year, I got the feeling that every one of you would try to catch me if you could, and that is something I never thought I'd feel so intensely as I have the past few months." Kordas looked to each of them, and out to the magic lecture where the rest of the Six, or Seven, or maybe Eight, were. His expression was joyful.

"Oh! Oh, hey, got to go!" Ponu said after four heartbeats, and got up.

"Look, I was having a *perfect* wistful moment there and you're just going to *spoil* it?" Kordas gasped.

"Bah! *They're* doing something different," Sai said, perking up. "I need to see this." And with that, he trotted off to the group of mixed mages and parked himself where he had a good view of the magical proceedings without getting in anyone's way. Everyone left, as part of the gag, but Kordas did wind up watching them on his own.

Well, I'm not getting anything accomplished here. Time to move on. He felt a little jealous of Sai. But perhaps he could get lessons from Sai later. Slow ones. The Tayledras mages knew these spells in their bones, and they moved a bit too fast for him to follow.

Being a mage is not your primary job, he reminded himself. *This is no different than riding a circuit of the Duchy to see how things are going. The only difference is that everyone is crammed together in one place, and I don't have to ride.*

Well, next on his list should be checking with Isla, who was in charge of all the common supplies. He'd have liked to appoint someone else, because he felt unsure about asking her to continue the role she'd taken in the convoy, but she was good at it, she didn't seem to mind doing it, and he knew he could trust her. Of all the things that needed doing, keeping accurate accounts of the supplies was probably the most important.

He found her, as he had expected, down in the hertasi tunnels, checking food out with the cooks. His old Seneschal was in charge of the same task at the gardens, since the poor fellow had such fierce claustrophobia that as soon as he'd been coaxed down there during the Forest attack, he'd fainted dead away.

". . . and when are we a-going to get a proper watermill?" one woman was asking querulously, her arms around a basket containing a share of wheat. Kordas's analytical side immediately recognized it as enough for bread for ten people. "I'm mortal weary of grinding grain."

"You and everyone else, good dame," Isla replied, her even tone betraying none of the irritation she was surely feeling, given her phrasing. "It won't be until spring at the earliest. Just be glad we saved one barge of millstones, or it would be years before we could build one."

The woman went away, grumbling under her breath. Isla closed her eyes; he knew that look. She was counting to twenty to cool her temper.

"We managed to save all those dubious bags of oats," she said, opening her eyes. "The Healers say there's nothing harmful in them, not even to animals."

He took a deep breath. "That's good news."

"And I've got better. It's all cleaned up down here again. Don't mind the smoky smell. I've got people moving everything from the barges that people aren't actually living in to storage down here. We should be done by suppertime. Anything that needs a preservation spell on it is being tended to by Venidel."

They had a pleasant little conversation about who was doing what that came under Isla's supervision, and as always, he was impressed by her management skills. Clearly she hadn't ever actually *needed* the Seneschal's help back in the Duchy; she had probably just accepted it to be polite.

"The boys asked permission to overnight with four friends in one of the tree-ekeles," she finished. "They've been uncommonly good and helpful, so I said yes."

She finished the sentence with an arched eyebrow, and lowered eyelids.

"Where are they eating supper?" he asked, responding to her signals with an appreciative smile.

"With their friends." She returned his smile. "I've got a little treat I put away just for an evening like this."

Her look was as good as a caress.

"Yes," he answered. "But what will we do for supper?"

"Oh, you!" She laughed and made a shooing motion. "Go away and let me work. I'll see you then."

He had only just emerged from the tunnels when Jonaton ambushed him. Although it really could not have been called an *ambush* as such; there was nothing subtle about his outfit.

At least it's not searing my eyeballs. "What is it, Jonaton?" he sighed. Because it was clear from Jonaton's body language that he wanted something.

"Hakkon and I want to take over part of the tunnels," he replied. "Isla won't let us without your permission."

"How much of the tunnels and why?" he asked. Because it was

always a good idea to ask Jonaton exactly what he intended to do—
and hedge him around with conditions.

"That spot in the far south with the dead end and three chambers
off it," Jonaton supplied, fiddling with fringe on his sleeves as long
as Kordas's forearm.

He's up to something.

"I'm not up to something, I swear!" Jonaton added, which
cemented Kordas's impression that, in fact, he *was* up to something.
"And it's empty now. Isla wants to put smelly old fleeces in it. I've
got a better idea."

Kordas suddenly knew exactly what Jonaton had planned.
"You're going to make a window-Gate down there, aren't you?"

"Well . . . yes." More fiddling with fringe. "The chamber I want
to use has a really good door that locks from the outside."

"So if something goes wrong you can lock the door on what you
let in," Kordas responded flatly.

"Well . . . yes."

Kordas sighed. Bad idea. But better to let him do it and hedge
him around with conditions than forbid him and watch him do
what he wanted to anyway. The proverb about apologies and
permission cut both ways, sometimes. "One," he said, holding up
a finger. "You will *not* be spying on the Hawkbrothers' new Vale."

Jonaton sighed. It was clear that was exactly what he had intended
to do. "All right," he said sorrowfully. "I don't know why you don't
trust me, Kordas."

"I'm not done. Two. You will *not* be looking back at the Empire."

"What?" That startled the mage. "Why not?"

"Because *spy-holes* work both ways. You've got to have four layers
of countermeasures behind six misdirections before I'll let you.

Three: you will have Ceri or Sai with you at all times when you open your little window. *All times.* And if they don't have time, then you don't play with your toy. Is that clear?"

Jonaton frowned, but he behaved like he was sixteen sometimes. "It isn't like I'm asking for Heartstone access!"

"Only because you won't ask, you'll do it and we'll have to rescue you."

Jonaton ground his teeth together.

"And one more thing. Keep cats out of the window room. I mean it."

"You are such a tyrant," Jonaton groused. "All right. I agree."

"Then go find some hertasi to help you carry your things from your barge to your new cave," Kordas told him. "I expect you to have everything moved by this time tomorrow."

Jonaton picked up his skirts in both hands and raced to find Hakkon. Kordas looked after him, vaguely certain that he had left something vital out of his admonitions, but not sure what it was.

No matter. I'll find out, and probably sooner rather than later.

He looked up at the winter sky past the branches of the trees and the shimmer of the Veil. *Well, it could be worse. It could be raining.*

And at exactly that moment, a fat drop of water hit him in the eye.

Shaking his head and laughing to himself, Kordas set off for his inspection of the defenses on the top of the wall. He was accompanied along the way by a satisfied-looking Sydney, who had the look of a cat that had *definitely* been up to something.

AUTHOR'S NOTE

Special thanks to Arath Darastrix and Joshua Murcray for their research, to Ben Dobyns, Hudson Stryker, Scotter, Connor, and Mike Grodeman for their support, and in memoriam, Marc Curlee.

ABOUT THE AUTHOR

Mercedes Lackey is the *New York Times* bestselling American fantasy author behind the *Heralds of Valdemar* series, *The Elemental Masters* series, the *100 Kingdoms* series, and many more. She has published over 100 novels in under 25 years.